The Journey

JAN HAHN

A *Pride & Prejudice* ALTERNATE PATH

Oysterville, WA

Also by Jan Hahn

AN ARRANGED MARRIAGE

THE JOURNEY

For information: P.O. Box 34, Oysterville WA 98641

ISBN: 978-1-936009-15-2

Graphic design by Ellen Pickels

Front cover: "A Study," Edmund Blair Leighton, 1895.
Back cover: "The New London Royal Mail," Charles Hunt Engraving, 1851.

Acknowledgments

Writing a story is a solitary exercise, but transforming it into a book requires assistance. I am deeply indebted to the following people for giving this tale of mine a life of its own.

To my dear family for indulging me with the time to write and loving encouragement to follow my muse;

To Beth Miller and Jennifer Padgett who provided edits, suggestions, and generous support in the preliminary stages of writing;

To Debbie Styne whose sharp eye, keen insight, and editing skills made the story so much better;

To Michele Reed and Ellen Pickels of Meryton Press for Michele's patient guidance and Ellen's talented sense of style and form;

To Janis Blackburn and Janet Taylor for their confidence in me, their excitement in the project, and their loyal friendship;

To Patricia West, an extraordinarily generous reader I met online, who was the first person to truly urge me to publish this book;

And to Jane Austen, who created Mr. Darcy, Elizabeth Bennet, and all the other fascinating characters in her books. Her genius has delighted countless readers for two hundred years, and I am blessed to be numbered among them.

In memory of my beloved Mr. Darcy

Chapter One

My back ached with a sharp, persistent pain by the time he slowed the horse to a walk. We had galloped hard and fast for more than an hour at least, much faster than I imagined one could ride a horse through woods thick and tangled as a briar patch.

There was no definite trail to follow, no easy path; rather, we pushed our way through brambles and thickets, sharp branches scratching at my cheeks and neck. I must admit that he attempted to avoid them, pulling me in the opposite direction if he spied the tree limbs before they hit us, but two people on a horse could lean only so far without falling off, and this man had no intention of falling or allowing me to slip from his grasp. No, he had locked his arms around me, one hand secured upon my waist, holding me against his body in the most intimate embrace I had ever known.

I felt the heat of his hands upon me through his black leather gloves. He was dressed entirely in black, from boots to cape to the jaunty hat on his head with a fluffy dark feather stuck in the band. Blonde curls escaped from beneath his hat and provided the only contrast to his dark appearance. He possessed the bluest eyes I had ever seen, a blue I had witnessed in neither man nor woman—almost crystalline—eyes I would have considered striking if encountered in a ballroom or parlour. Staring straight ahead through cut-outs in the black mask covering his face, however, they appeared deadly.

"Make haste," he said, motioning to the four horsemen behind us. "From here on until we know the cottage is vacant, be silent as a corpse."

We began to climb a slight hill. I grew even more conscious of my precarious position when he leaned forward with the incline and in doing so thrust his head against mine. We rode almost cheek to cheek, his breath warm against my face.

How had I come to be in such danger? I was amazed at how quickly my life had changed, how one decision altered its entire direction, and how, unknowingly, I embarked upon a journey that was to have such a profound effect upon my future.

Two hours earlier, Mr. Bingley's carriage had rocked back and forth in a rhythmic, singsong cadence, monotonous enough to lull a person to sleep. That is, if a person felt at ease with her fellow travellers. Neither Mrs. Hurst nor Miss Bingley had ever put me at ease, and Mr. Darcy was the last man in the world who would inspire tranquillity.

I strove to keep my eyes from the gentleman's person, a daunting task since he sat directly across from me. Miss Bingley had fluttered about him for the first hour of the trip, remarking upon the weather, the tedium of travel and her gratitude to have his company to brighten the journey. She spoke of various people of society they both knew and denigrated the ladies in the most casual of terms unless they were titled, married, and particularly fond of her. And then she went on and on about how she could not wait to reach Town and leave the boredom of country society behind.

Mrs. Hurst agreed with each of her sister's comments, adding her own encouragement when given the opportunity, but I noticed that Mr. Darcy said little, responding only when pressed to do so. Conversation was rarely directed at me, and thus I was relieved of making but few remarks.

Yet, even though I was not required to enter into the general conversation, escape into slumber was all but impossible under Mr. Darcy's continuous, disapproving scrutiny. I did my utmost to avoid meeting his eyes, watching the passing landscape with more than usual interest or turning to observe Mrs. Hurst, sitting beside me, when she was allowed to speak.

I also found it amusing to watch Miss Bingley edge closer and closer to Mr. Darcy on the seat they shared. She could not have chosen a more pleasing position for herself, I thought, unless she could rid the carriage of her sister and me. Alas, we would plague her efforts for the duration of the journey to London.

"I trust your relations in Town are in good health, Miss Bennet," Mr.

Darcy said suddenly.

I startled, shocked at his address. "They are, sir, thank you."

"And so I understand this trip is not one of necessity, but pleasure?"

I nodded, but before I could respond, Caroline jumped in. "Well, from what I have heard, it is perhaps both, is it not, Miss Eliza? Are you not in need of escaping an uncomfortable situation at home?"

"I do not have the pleasure of understanding you, Miss Bingley. I do not escape anything. I join my aunt and uncle at their invitation."

"You speak of your mother's brother who resides in Cheapside, do you not?" Caroline purred.

"Yes, Mr. Edward Gardiner." My first thought had been to correct her by saying that my relatives lived *near* Cheapside, but I did not think she deserved the compliment of that particular information.

"And pray tell us, Miss Eliza, what is your uncle's occupation?"

"He is a merchant."

"Ah, in trade." Caroline arched her eyebrows with a knowing look at her sister. "I see."

I bit my tongue to refrain from making a sharp retort, but I was truly surprised when Mr. Darcy said, "Was not your grandfather also in trade in London, Miss Bingley? Perhaps he knew Mr. Gardiner's father or grandfather."

Her eyes widened as she beseeched Mrs. Hurst with a desperate look. Her sister quickly answered for her. "That was many, many, many years ago, Mr. Darcy. None of our family has been in trade since then, I can assure you."

"Yes, well, many of us profit from the endeavours of our ancestors."

His remarks put an end to the topic, causing a strained silence in the carriage until Caroline returned to the question of why I was making the trip to Town.

"I heard that you wished to leave Longbourn because of a proposal of marriage. My sister and I were both shocked to learn that you refused Mr. Collins's generous offer."

"Yes," Mrs. Hurst joined in. "I would think the gentleman might have made an excellent match for you. Is he not to inherit your father's estate in the future?"

Feeling condescension dripping about me, I wanted to snap at them, but I steeled myself to answer graciously. "I did not deem his inheritance a sufficient inducement for matrimony."

"Well," Miss Bingley said, "for your sake, I hope you do not live to regret it. I sensed a shortage of eligible prospects in Hertfordshire."

"Aye, might I suggest you look elsewhere for a possible husband, Miss Bingley, for although Hertfordshire contains excellent men, I doubt that any one of them would be a suitable match for you."

"Me? I was not speaking of myself, Miss Bennet! I most certainly do not seek a husband from anyone residing in the country. When I marry, it shall be to a man of breeding, a man who possesses a certain air, a definite manner of carrying himself, a cosmopolitan at home in London or Vienna, not someone who buries himself in country society."

"'Tis a pity," Mr. Darcy said, "for that excludes the eligible gentlemen from Derbyshire."

Caroline gasped, realizing she had placed her foot squarely in her mouth, and began to stammer and sputter as to what she truly meant, but Mr. Darcy said nothing further. Indeed, the entire conversation ceased, and we rode no little way in complete silence.

He turned to look out the window, and I happened to catch a glimpse of his face, detecting a slight smirk about his mouth. Despite Miss Bingley's enchantment with him, obviously he was not similarly inclined. I took a deep breath and sighed, marvelling once again that I was in that carriage and making that trip with the last three people alive who wished for my company.

Although I had evaded giving Miss Bingley an answer for the reasons behind my excursion, in truth I *was* making somewhat of an escape to Town in order to avoid my mother's wrath. Since I had refused Mr. Collins's proposal, disappointment had rendered her distraught. She had directed her livid anger at me for over two weeks. Even though my father had taken my side in the matter, it did little to change her opinion, and life at Longbourn had become excessively unpleasant.

When Papá had returned from Meryton earlier in the week and called me into his library, I was surprised and yet relieved to hear his news.

"Lizzy, how would you like to visit the Gardiners for a while, at least until they join us for Christmastide?"

"Very much, sir, but must I go alone? May Jane go with me?"

"No, no, your sister is needed here for my sanity if nothing else. I cannot part with both of you when your mother is in such a state, but you shall not go unattended. I have procured a means of travel for you that shall be quite safe. I met with Mr. Bingley at Sir William Lucas's house this morning, and he informed me that his entire party is returning to Town at the end of the week. When I said that I was thinking of sending you to visit your aunt and uncle, he invited you to make the trip in his carriage with his sisters. Now, what do you think of this fine arrangement?"

"Mr. Bingley is leaving Netherfield Park? For how long?"

"He did not say, my dear, but what is that to you? What is this down at the mouth expression I behold? Are you in love with the young man? I thought your sister was the one so affected."

I blushed. "Of course not, but I should hate to see him leave just now. It will render Jane quite desolate."

"Well, so it may, but they have enjoyed three months in each other's company, as well as dancing together over and over at the ball he recently hosted, have they not? Surely, they can bear to be apart for a few weeks."

"If it is only for a few weeks, sir, I agree, but if he is not to return, then what will become of Jane's chances with Mr. Bingley?"

"Would you have me send Jane to London in your place then?"

"I would, Father."

"That would defeat the purpose. I proposed this trip to remove you from your mother's sight until she has made peace with your refusal of Mr. Collins. Surely, you can see the wisdom of my plan, can you not?"

I nodded but sighed. "Very well, Father. Of course, I will enjoy a trip to Town, but I dread making the journey in the presence of Mr. Bingley's sisters. I am certain they regard me with little felicity and would much prefer Jane's companionship."

"It is not all that far to Town. Hopefully, they can bear your wretched company that long." He patted my shoulder, and I kissed his cheek. It was my strong desire that his prediction proved correct and that the horses would run freely on the day of our trip.

As it came about, however, all was altered. At the last minute, Mr. Bingley changed his plans, deciding to remain at Netherfield for another week because of estate problems requiring his attention.

His sisters were distressed at delaying their journey because they had previously accepted invitations from friends in Town for two days hence.

And so, it was settled that Mr. Hurst would remain at Netherfield with Mr. Bingley, preferring seven extra days of shooting to the parties awaiting him in London, and Mr. Darcy would accompany the ladies, since his sister awaited him in Town, and he did not want to disappoint her. Thus, this strange mixture of travellers now proceeded down the road.

I had felt a recurring sense of disquiet whenever I had been in Mr. Darcy's presence, and I wondered if he shared such tension or simply enjoyed provoking it. I would have preferred Mr. Bingley's company, for he was all ease and amiability, his face breaking into smiles when in conversation. I had yet to see a smile grace Mr. Darcy's countenance. At times, I wondered if the man's mouth was capable of turning in an upward direction.

It was not just his lack of good humour that caused my unease, however, but a feeling that, in his eyes, I was found lacking. He appeared to hold me in haughty contempt along with everyone else he had met during his brief stay in Hertfordshire. With every breath he took, he seemed to express disapproval of all he surveyed.

I wondered at the cause of his discontent. Was our local society that deficient? Mr. Bingley seemed to suffer no like disability, but rather joined in our assembly dances, teas, and suppers with great cordiality. His sisters, however, obviously did not share his opinion and held themselves apart, making the required conversations and responses when pressed upon in a manner that alerted all in their presence that they esteemed themselves far superior to others. Their feelings were plain.

Mr. Darcy, however, was enigmatic. He had flatly refused to dance with me at the assembly ball when we first met, and yet upon the very next occasion of our meeting, he had offered to dance with me when Sir William Lucas suggested it. I assumed that he was pressured to offer the invitation, and by that time, of course, I had resolved never to dance with him and thus refused.

Subsequently, Jane fell ill during a visit with Mr. Bingley's sisters, and she was forced to stay abed at Netherfield for several days. When I received a note confirming her illness, I called on her, and Mr. Bingley prevailed upon me to remain and look after her. Naturally, I was thrown into encounters with Mr. Darcy during that visit, and he baffled me with his behaviour. At first, he was all concern and politeness, inquiring as to my sister's health, and next, he was almost insulting in his obvious disapproval. When Jane recovered and we left there to return to Longbourn, I truly hoped never to be thrown into his presence again.

Shortly thereafter, the Netherfield ball was held. My four sisters and I, as well as Mamá, eagerly anticipated it, each for her own reasons. Mamá and I hoped it would further Jane and Mr. Bingley's attachment, with my mother almost certain that a proposal would be forthcoming.

The militia was quartered in Meryton for the winter, and my younger sisters looked forward to dancing with the soldiers. In truth, I also anticipated dancing with one of the young officers, a Mr. Wickham, whom I had met recently. Tall and handsome, he was most pleasing in appearance and demeanour, and I thought I detected a preference toward me on his part. Unfortunately, he did not appear at the ball, and I suspected the reason why.

He had told me a shocking tale of how Mr. Darcy deprived him of his inheritance. Mr. Wickham was the son of old Mr. Darcy's steward and a favourite of the master. He had educated Mr. Wickham and provided a living for him in his will, but after the elder Mr. Darcy's death, his son flatly refused to honour his father's wishes. I was shocked when I heard that revelation! Thus, one could not fault me for holding Mr. Darcy in poor regard.

When he singled me out to be his partner at the ball, I was so flustered that I could not think of a plausible excuse, and I was compelled to suffer his company through two dances that surely lasted twice as long as any other set that night. His behaviour throughout the exercise was clearly uncivil. He barely conversed with me until I shamed him into doing so. Oh, I hoped never to be in Mr. Darcy's company again!

Unfortunately, there I was—forced to search about the enclosed carriage for any object upon which to look rather than his face.

After an hour on the road, I knew the interior of Mr. Bingley's carriage in detail. If asked, I could even tell you how many brass nails outlined the crimson upholstery above the heads of Mr. Darcy and Miss Bingley.

Repeatedly, I watched as the black feathers protruding from her green turban bent to and fro, flicking against the roof of the carriage. If they had been a scant half-inch longer, she could not have worn that hat in the equipage, for she was a tall woman with a long neck, and carrying herself as she did with that certain air she prized so much, she appeared even taller. Why, when I thought of her, did the image of a well-dressed stork always appear?

"Tell me, Miss Bennet," Mr. Darcy said, "was your cousin overwrought with disappointment at your refusal?"

I was dismayed that we had returned to a discussion of *that* subject. He looked at me without the slightest hint of a smile when he spoke, and I could not determine whether he actually wished to know the answer to his question or he was baiting me.

Before I could respond, Miss Bingley did so for me.

"Obviously, the poor man was not too distressed, for I hear that he has now attached himself to Sir William Lucas's oldest daughter. Are they not to be married right away?"

I nodded, and Mrs. Hurst asked, "Where exactly does Mr. Collins live?"

"At Kent. He is vicar in Hunsford Village."

"Does not your dear aunt reside near there, Mr. Darcy?" Caroline turned to him and, in doing so, took the opportunity to move even closer.

"She does."

"Oh, how I would enjoy a visit with dear Lady Catherine! I have heard her speak of Rosings Park when visiting in Town, and from her description, it sounds like paradise."

"The park is well maintained."

"And shall you be visiting there any time soon, sir?"

"I generally go during the spring."

Oh dear, I thought, I hoped he did not go at Easter, for I promised Charlotte I would visit her then.

"You and Miss Lucas are good friends, are you not, Miss Bennet?" Mrs. Hurst asked. When I confirmed that we were, she went on, "The two of you will regret your parting, I am sure."

"We will."

"It is but fifty miles to Kent," Mr. Darcy said. "I would think you might visit with great convenience."

"Fifty miles? That is some distance, sir."

"What is fifty miles of good road? An easy journey when a good friend awaits you."

"Perhaps for you, but I am not at liberty to travel as freely, although I do plan to visit Charlotte when Sir William and her sister attend upon her."

"Indeed?" A sudden light seemed to appear in his eyes, or perhaps it was but a reflection from the window. "And when might you go?"

"At Easter."

"Ah, a beautiful time to visit Kent. Perchance we shall see each other, as that is the time my visit is also planned."

Miss Bingley began to flutter. "It always rains at Easter. I would not think you would care to travel then, Mr. Darcy. I had hoped we all might remain at Pemberley until after that time. I know that Charles is pleased that you have invited us to spend the winter months in Derbyshire."

He looked out the window, a bored expression descending upon his face. "My plans are not yet fixed. I prefer to wait and see how things develop."

With his last words, he turned and looked directly into my eyes. Once again, I was perturbed, wondering what lay behind this strange man's unreadable demeanour.

"Miss Bennet, your family has made friends with many of the officers quartered at Meryton, have they not?" Mrs. Hurst asked, quite decidedly changing the subject. She seemed particularly cognizant of her sister's wishes in that regard.

"My father has made Colonel Forster's acquaintance, and he and some of the officers have been good enough to call upon us."

Miss Bingley arched one eyebrow and literally looked down her nose at me. "Your younger sisters seem quite fond of the soldiers. And do you not favour one of them yourself?"

"I . . . I do not know of whom you speak. As I said, several of the officers are friends of my parents."

"But is not Mr. Wickham a particular favourite of yours?"

Mr. Darcy made a sudden movement, sitting up straighter and returning his face to the window. No one could mistake his discomfort with the subject.

"My family considers Mr. Wickham a very congenial and pleasing acquaintance, even though I understand that certain other people do not," I said.

Miss Bingley turned to Mr. Darcy and placed her hand upon his arm, causing him to face her. "I did endeavour most heartily to warn Miss Bennet of Mr. Wickham's unsuitability, but she would not have it."

I bit my tongue to keep a civil tone. "If I did not accept your warning, Miss Bingley, it is because I heard you accuse Mr. Wickham of nothing worse than being the son of Mr. Darcy's steward, and as I told you previously, he informed me himself of that fact. I have found the gentleman to be in good humour and agreeable in spite of suffering grievous misfortunes at the hands of one he considered a friend."

"You take an eager interest in that gentleman's concerns," said Mr. Darcy in a more animated tone and with heightened colour.

"Who that knows what his misfortunes have been, can help feeling an interest in him?"

"His misfortunes! Yes, his misfortunes have been great indeed." He made not the slightest effort to conceal his contempt.

"And of your infliction," I cried, suddenly unable to control myself. Mrs. Hurst and Miss Bingley both inhaled audibly, a hissing sound reverberating around the carriage.

Mr. Darcy's face darkened as his frown deepened. "And this is your opinion of me? This is the estimation…"

Suddenly, the carriage lurched and swayed, and our argument was halted by the violent sounds of men's voices yelling from without, followed by a gunshot! Miss Bingley screamed and grabbed Mr. Darcy's arm. Mrs. Hurst grabbed her bosom.

Someone yanked open the door to the carriage, and both ladies began to scream in earnest at the sight of a masked man brandishing a pistol in their faces. Mr. Darcy immediately tried to move between them and the highwayman, but another man stuck the barrel of a gun in his back from the window on our side.

"Get out!" the first man yelled. "Now! Out here, all of you."

Miss Bingley began to whimper as she and her sister climbed out of the carriage, clinging to each other. I followed them down the steps with Mr. Darcy behind me. Besides the two men on the ground, two more masked men remained on horseback, waving their guns around as well.

"Hands up! Stand and deliver!"

The order came from one of the men on horseback. Clad in black, even down to the mask on his face, he appeared to be the leader. Both footmen had descended from the rear of the carriage, and at the highwayman's demand, the driver threw down our luggage from the top.

Caroline squealed, "Those are my clothes! Remove your hands from them at once!"

One of the masked men only laughed as he began to rummage through her valise, throwing gowns and undergarments here and there.

"There's not much here," he said, after doing the same to the other suitcases. "Only a bit of trinkets."

"Off with your jewels!" the leader shouted. "Drop them in the bag."

Caroline and Mrs. Hurst began to slip off their bracelets and rings. When Mrs. Hurst's hands shook too much to undo her necklace, the highwayman grabbed the chain from around her neck and broke it, and then he jerked the eardrops from her ears. Both she and Caroline cried aloud at such treatment, and Mr. Darcy stepped forward to protest.

"Aha, we got us a hero in our midst," one of the men yelled, as he placed his pistol beneath Mr. Darcy's chin. "All right, mate, let's see how brave you be!"

Mr. Darcy, of course, was forced to back down, and I could see his fury at being rendered helpless. I had dropped my garnet cross in the robber's open bag by that time, and he then forced Mr. Darcy to remove his signet ring and pocket watch.

"Let's see what we've got," the leader said, motioning to the man with the bag. "Puny pickings from the likes of this bunch. Those two in the feathers and silks are bound to have more than this. Go through their luggage again. And that gent, there—did you search his pockets?"

His orders resulted in more rough treatment of Mrs. Hurst's and Miss Bingley's belongings, and a thorough search of Mr. Darcy's coat pockets. Eventually, one of the men discovered his money clip.

"This be more like it." He handed the prize to the leader who added it to the bag of loot. "Now, what do we do, shoot the lot of them?"

Caroline screamed again until one of the men raised his hand, threatening to strike her.

"We'll not hold the screechin' one for ransom, will we?" he asked the man on horseback.

"What's your name?" the man in black asked Caroline.

"Miss Ca . . . Ca . . . Caroline Bingley."

He motioned toward her sister, and she answered, "Mrs. Ambrose Hurst," her voice quavering.

"Never heard of them," the leader said.

"Yeah, but what with the fine clothes, they must come from money," the man on the ground said.

"Of course, we have money," Caroline blurted out. "You just wait until— "

"In truth, they do not." Mr. Darcy raised his voice.

"What do you know about it? You married to the screecher?" asked the man holding the gun on him.

"No, but I know them and their family. They have no money. The little they have is spent on such fripperies as you see before you. Their father is deceased, and their brother is in trade in a small town up north."

Caroline gasped aloud, but Mrs. Hurst stepped on her foot, causing her to cry out in pain and thus say nothing to refute Mr. Darcy's fabrication.

"He barely makes a living. In fact, I am on my way to London to withdraw funds for a loan he has requested."

Mr. Bingley's sisters gaped at that statement, their eyes huge with wonder at Mr. Darcy's mendacity. The leader of the highwaymen said nothing. He looked them up and down and then surveyed Mr. Darcy, as though weighing whether he spoke the truth or not.

"Allow the women to go free. If you hold anyone for ransom, let it be me. I am Fitzwilliam Darcy of Pemberley Estates in Derbyshire. My uncle is the Earl of Matlock who will pay you what you will for my release. These women are worthless. They will bring nothing but trouble on you."

"He's probably right about this 'un," said the man on the ground, grunting his displeasure at Caroline.

The man in black rode over to the other horseman, and they spoke in low, indistinguishable tones. He then directed the footmen to unharness the two horses from the carriage.

"Now, you women," he said, motioning to Mr. Bingley's sisters, "get in the carriage. And, Merle, tie the rich man's hands together."

The man moved to carry out his instructions, while the other man on the ground began to herd Mr. Bingley's sisters toward the carriage. I walked behind them, but just as I reached the bottom step, the man grabbed my arm and pulled me back. Out of the corner of my eye, I saw Mr. Darcy start toward me, only to be jerked back by the other highwayman.

"Hey, Morgan, this one's bonny. She's no fine lady—she's dressed in muslin—but I fancy her eyes. Cain't we take her?"

The other man on horseback began to snicker. "She is a bonny wench."

"Take your hands off her!" Mr. Darcy shouted, taking steps toward me.

The man who had tied his hands grabbed him, and with one swift upswing, knocked him to the ground.

"If she's not rich, there's no reason to take her. She'll slow us down," Merle said.

"Wait," the leader said, "money's not the only thing to gain from this little jaunt. I think old Sneyd's right. This one pleasures me just to look at her."

I was suddenly conscious that I had been holding my breath, and when my lungs insisted on taking in air, I began to pant. My palms turned icy cold, and yet my face burned with shame at the thought of what those horrid men suggested.

"Come on, let's put her on a horse," Sneyd said, his ugly face so close to mine I could smell his foul breath and see his rotten, yellow teeth. "She can ride with me, Morgan. What do you say?"

"If she rides with anyone, it'll be with me," he replied. "Bring her here."

Sneyd frowned and cursed, but he pushed me toward the man in black, and with one swift move, lifted me up onto the horse. The rider pushed my bonnet back and peered closely at me, his rough hands gripping my waist. I could feel the cold steel of the pistol rub against my side. Fear petrified me! I tried to hold myself away from him, but he persisted in pulling me close.

"You're right, Sneyd. This lass *is* worth the trouble."

"I can tell you right now," Mr. Darcy said, his voice strong even though he struggled to stand after having the air punched out of him, "that if you harm her in any way, you will not receive a farthing from my uncle."

Each of the robbers stopped, Sneyd jerking around as he turned to face Mr. Darcy.

"And why is that?" the ruffian holding me asked. "What possible difference would it make to his lordship what happens to this little country miss?"

"Because she is not some little country miss. She... she is my wife."

My eyes widened, and once again, I forgot to breathe. I heard audible gasps from both of Mr. Bingley's sisters from inside the carriage, but I prayed the highwaymen would pay them no mind.

"Your wife?" the leader said in disbelief. "You would have us believe your wife dresses in plain garb, and yet you say you're rich?"

I saw Mr. Darcy swallow and wet his lips as if he needed time to think of an answer.

"I... I dress simply when I travel," I said quickly, "precisely because of creatures like you." My voice shook, and my hands trembled, but I held my chin up and looked him directly in the eye. "That is why I do not wear jewels on the road. I—that is, *we* have been robbed before."

The men looked at each other, and it was evident that they doubted what we said. Mr. Darcy spoke once again. "I can assure you that my wife is a favourite of the Earl of Matlock and my entire family. They might conceivably consider foregoing my ransom, but they would pay any amount you ask for my wife's freedom if—and only if—she is unharmed."

The three masked men looked to the man called Morgan, who turned his eyes first upon me and then Mr. Darcy.

"Put him on one of the carriage horses, but you keep the reins in your hands, Sneyd. And you, *Mister* Darcy, don't even think of trying anything, or I'll cut her throat—ransom or no ransom."

Chapter Two

I wondered how the highwaymen would abscond with us in daylight, knowing that the road to London was well travelled. I never dreamed they would lead us through thickets, hedgerows, woods, and forests deep enough that no one could find us.

As we fled, my mind darted frantically from thought to thought, wondering how Mr. Darcy and I might ever escape this predicament. Surely, when our carriage did not reach Town, someone would come looking for us. My aunt and uncle were expecting me, and Mr. Darcy's sister awaited his arrival.

We had ridden for some time by then, and I wondered whether Miss Bingley and Mrs. Hurst had been rescued yet. The robbers had pushed the carriage minus its horses into a wooded area. They gagged and bound the hands and feet of the ladies, the driver and footmen, forced all of them into the carriage, and tied the doors shut.

I could not imagine the indignity Mr. Bingley's sisters felt, trapped in such close quarters with common servants, but that thought shamed me. I should not have mocked them, for were we not all in desperate straits and Mr. Darcy and I in the worst of them?

Just then, I felt the leader remove his hand from my waist. He signalled for all the horsemen to stop while he motioned to the man called Merle to go on ahead. No one said a word. Shifting slightly, I attempted to adjust my seating, as pain from the prolonged ride radiated down my back and into my legs.

I took the opportunity to glance back at Mr. Darcy and saw his eyes upon me, a fierce scowl across his face. He had been forced to ride bareback on one of the carriage horses, his hands tied behind him the entire journey. I thought him an excellent horseman to keep his balance in such a position.

I opened my mouth, wanting to say something, anything to him, but winced, instead, when the highwayman grabbed my face with one hand, jerking my head back to face forward.

"Not one word," he hissed in my ear, his lips against my hair.

A few moments later, Merle returned, crashing through the underbrush on his great horse. "Come on. Didn't spy nobody at the cottage but Gert. We can go 'round back."

Within minutes, we had rounded the knoll and come upon a clearing in the woods. A small, rustic cottage sat a few hundred yards back from a stream of swiftly running water. My mouth was dry, and I longed to taste the coolness of that brook. Two of the men dismounted and entered the cottage through a rear door, their pistols drawn.

Not long thereafter, the man called Merle appeared in the doorway. "Bring 'em in."

Inside, a slattern of a woman lounged against a long, rough table. She looked to be middle-aged and well used by life, her hair in need of a good wash, her skirt soiled and patched.

"Nate," she called, as the leader pulled me through the door and into the room. "What's this? Ain't I told you not to bring your fancy pieces back here?"

"Shut your mouth," he growled, pushing past her down a dingy hall. He kicked a door open and shoved me into the room. "Bring the *gentleman* back here," he called to the others.

Immediately, Mr. Darcy was thrust into the room. Sneyd, Merle, and the leader closed the door behind them.

"Now," he said, "heed my words, 'cause I'm saying this but once. There's no way out of this room. The window's nailed shut with iron bars on the outside, and this door stays locked, so don't even think about escape. You got that, *Mister* Darcy? And you, Miss or *Missus* if you're really that, do you understand? 'Cause if you don't, I've got a real nasty way of teaching you."

He stood very close to me, less than a foot between his face and mine. I swallowed and nodded.

"Mrs. Darcy will not go anywhere," Mr. Darcy said, moving to stand between us. "You have my word. Can you not untie my hands? If escape is impossible, why should I remain bound?"

The man let out a short laugh. "Your word? Hah! I wouldn't give a fadge for no gentleman's word. Leave him tied!" With a sneer, he turned and walked out the door, the others following close behind. My heart sank when I heard the key click the lock shut.

Mr. Darcy strode to the door, and leaning against it, placed his ear next to the rough wood. "I cannot distinguish their conversation. The door and walls are too thick, which may be in our favour."

"How?"

"They, in turn, cannot hear us if we speak softly." He walked around the room, searching every corner, examining the single window, turning his gaze up to the ceiling. The only other possible exit was through a narrow door at the back of the room.

"Try to open it, but step back in case there is someone there."

I did as he instructed, hoping it led to the outside, but I was dismayed to find nothing more than a tiny room containing assorted rubbish: old rags, broken, discoloured crockery, portions of a saddle and bridle, a chamber pot, and a cracked ewer and basin. Mr. Darcy searched the tiny room with me, motioning with his head when he wanted me to pull things back or move trash around, but it was all to no avail. There was no window, no trap door, no hole in the old stone wall, no provision for our escape.

"It is useless," I said, returning to the larger room.

The late afternoon sun streamed through the high window. Disturbed dust particles danced in its illumination. A small wooden table, one of its legs broken and propped up with a brick, sat on a threadbare rug. Two small, hard chairs were the only other furnishings in the room. Against the far wall lay what appeared to be an assortment of more rubbish partially covered with a tarp. The room contained neither bed nor quilt.

I suddenly shivered, cold and fearful of the night to come. How would we manage? What would we do to stay warm? The room did not have a fireplace, and it was early December. I turned and faced Mr. Darcy, my apprehension evident.

"Miss Bennet, I know our circumstances appear formidable, but we can survive this." He walked across the room and stood before me. "Do you think you can untie these knots?"

"Of course. I should have done so immediately."

He turned his back, and I struggled with the rope tied in multiple knots around his wrists. When I could not loosen it, I reached for a hairpin. My bonnet had been lost long ago, and I became conscious that most of my curls streamed down my back, but I did find two or three pins still remaining and, with one, pried open the tight binding.

"Resourceful." Mr. Darcy rubbed his wrists. "Now, we must make something of a plan."

"A plan? What kind of plan? We can see there is but one way out of this room, and it is locked. We are at the mercy of desperate men, sir! There is nothing we can do."

"We can stay alive, and that is of the utmost importance. The first thing we must do is consider how to represent ourselves as a married couple."

"How... how do we accomplish that?"

"For one thing, we must address each other by our Christian names. Would not husband and wife speak thus?"

I barely nodded. I had been astounded at how imaginative he had been during the entire situation. I recalled how Mr. Darcy had teased Mr. Bingley at Netherfield concerning his air of humility, going so far as to call it deceitful. Yet now his careful attention to truth seemed to have vanished, for he had conjured up one tale after another at lightning speed and all in order to prevent harm to Mr. Bingley's sisters and to me. I could not imagine portraying his wife and yet, within a heartbeat, he had declared me to be just that. Now he proposed that we enact those roles.

"And perhaps you should stand closer to me when the highwaymen are present, as though you wished to cling to me."

"I am not the clinging type, Mr. Darcy, and I have observed few married people engage in such manner while in public."

"Of course not in the society we are accustomed to, but these are extreme circumstances, and they call for unusual measures. Would not a frightened wife cling to her husband in the company of ruffians such as those in the other room?"

Again I nodded slightly, somewhat put off that he had placed himself in control of both of us and yet grateful for his earlier intervention. Still, I felt uncomfortable at the thought of his suggestion. I sank down heavily on one of the chairs and immediately regretted it, for a slight moan slipped out unbidden.

"Are you unwell?"

"No, no, it is nothing," I felt my cheeks grow warm.

"What is it, Miss Ben—Elizabeth?"

"Truly, it is of no significance. I am not used to riding a horse for such a lengthy time."

He smiled slightly and turned his head aside. I rolled my eyes, wondering how I had come to this point in my life where I must confess to the last man in all of England I wished to converse with that I had a bruised derriere! I decided to speak of another matter.

"Will the earl truly provide the ransom funds?"

"My uncle would not hesitate to secure my freedom with whatever monies are requested. The only problem may be whether he believes this gang actually has me in their possession."

"Why should he doubt that?"

"It depends upon how the ransom is requested. If they demand it for the release of myself and my *wife,* he may suspect it is counterfeit."

"Oh." Dismay filled my heart.

"Do not be disheartened," he said, pulling out the remaining chair and sitting across from me. "My signature on any written note may be enough to win my uncle's approval, and surely the remainder of our party will soon be found, and they can testify to our situation."

"If you had not named me as your wife, your chances would be much greater."

"Perhaps, but you would have had no chance at all."

The tone of his voice was oddly tender, and I turned aside, unwilling to meet his gaze. Could it be that this man, whom I had considered devoid of kindness or obligation toward Mr. Wickham, had another facet to his character?

He rose and once more crossed the room to the window. "From the position of the sun, it appears we have travelled east, although I cannot be certain, for with all those twists and turns in the woods it was impossible to ascertain our direction."

"We did not travel towards London, then?"

He shook his head. "I doubt it; however, we may not be that far away. Hopefully, a rider can reach the earl's estate in less than a day. We must insist that they contact him immediately."

Just then, the door opened. Sneyd stood upon the threshold. "Darcy, you ain't one what insists on nothin.' We do the insistin' here."

Mr. Darcy whirled around and strode to my side.

"I see you got the ropes untied. No matter. It don't mean you be goin' anywheres." He entered the room and stood before me. "You, Missus, are to come with me."

"Where are you taking her?" Mr. Darcy demanded.

"Morgan wants her."

"I insist on accompanying my wife!"

Sneyd pulled his gun from his waistband. "I told you a'fore. You ain't the one what does the insistin.' Now, get out of my way."

"If you harm her— "

Sneyd just snickered and pushed Mr. Darcy back with the tip of his pistol, seeming to take great pleasure in robbing him of any power whatsoever. Grabbing hold of my arm, he pushed me through the doorway, slammed the door, and turned the key in the lock.

His hold on my arm was rough and bruising as he propelled me down the hallway and into the main room of the cottage. There I saw one of the outlaws cleaning his pistol while Gert stirred a foul smelling mixture, cooking in a great black pot that hung in the fireplace.

Morgan sat at one end of the table. He raised his head when I appeared, raking his glittering blue eyes up and down the length of me. For the first time in my life, I felt undressed by a man's stare, as though he could see right through my gown and undergarments.

He no longer wore a mask—none of the men did. I was shocked to see a long, jagged scar slashed across his cheek. I was also astonished at how handsome he was and how little the scar diminished his appearance. In another setting, another time, his fair looks would have attracted every woman in attendance. Dressed in black, however, a rough, blonde stubble covering his chin and the chilling expression about his eyes, I could deem him handsome but not in any manner attractive.

"*Mrs.* Darcy," he said, motioning with his hand. "Do come and sit down."

Sneyd prodded me slightly, and I took a few steps, pulled out the chair farthest from the leader of the highwaymen, and started to sit down.

"Not way down there," Morgan commanded. "Come and place yourself beside me where I can behold your comely face."

"I prefer to sit here."

"And I prefer that you sit beside me!" He slammed his fist upon the table. "You'd do well to remember that *my* preferences are obeyed here."

Sneyd pulled me from the chair and pushed me toward him, forcing me to sit at the table next to the man in black.

"Bring that slop you're cooking, Gert—a plate for me and one for our guest."

The woman shot Morgan a dark look, but she did as he ordered. She placed bowls before us containing a type of soup with a few chunks of unidentifiable meat swimming in greasy broth.

"Where's the bread?" he demanded.

"Keep a civil tongue. I'm gettin' it!" she spat at him.

Setting a board of bread before us, she sliced it while the other men filled their bowls from the pot over the fire. They all soon sat at the table and slurped the distasteful food into their mouths with disgusting noises. When I turned away from the bowl, Morgan stopped eating and leaned back in his chair.

"Not good enough for the likes of you, right, Missus?"

"I have little appetite." I reached for the glass of water set before me.

"I don't blame you. Gert's not much of a cook."

"Gert's not much of anythin,'" Merle said, causing Sneyd to break out in raucous laughter.

"Shut your filthy gobs," the woman said, raising an iron skillet she held in her hand.

"Whether you like the food or not, *Mrs.* Darcy," Morgan said, "eat it. Since your husband says you're the prize filly, I won't have you wasting away before your uptown relations pay up."

I reached for a slice of bread, and slowly tearing off small bites, I forced myself to eat, washing it down with a swallow of water. Suddenly I realized the depth of my thirst and drained the glass.

"Pour her some ale," he directed the woman.

"I have had enough, but may I take it to Mr. Darcy?"

"*Mr.* Darcy? I thought the man be your husband."

"He is, but I—I refer to him in that manner when . . . in company."

"And what do you call him when you're all alone?" Sneyd asked, inclining his dirty face near mine and laughing.

"Leave her alone," Morgan commanded, slamming his fist on the table once more. I jumped at the noise and sat up straighter in the chair. "All of you, get out. You, too, Gert. Either outside or to bed. Merle, you relieve Rufus and take first watch tonight. Fetch him a plate, and tell him to sleep out back in the stable."

"But Nate, I want some more of this soup," Sneyd whined.

"I said, get out! Now!"

Each of them obeyed his command, and the room soon emptied. I sat alone with the man in black, trembling as gooseflesh crawled up my spine. What did he intend to do with me?

Rising, he strode to the fireplace, and while doing so, I took the opportunity to snatch another piece of bread, which I hid in my skirt for Mr. Darcy. It appeared the highwaymen had no intention of feeding him that night. I barely had time to fold a portion of my skirt over the crust before he whirled around and narrowed his crystal eyes at me.

"I want the truth," he said, his voice menacing. "Are you that gent's wife?"

I took a deep breath but did not turn or break his gaze. I looked him dead on and lied. "I am."

He waited a few moments, his gaze boring through mine as though he would stare the truth out of me. "And just why would your husband's people be more troubled about your well-being than they would for his?"

I bit my lip, took a bite of bread, and chewed slowly before answering, my mind frantic to concoct a reason. "Because... because I am with child."

"With child?"

"Yes. I carry the heir to Pemberley, and the babe's welfare is of utmost importance to my husband's family."

Dear God, what had I done now? In less than a day, I had gone from an unmarried maiden to not only a wife but an expectant mother.

"Your figure's not that of a woman with child."

"It is very early."

"And do you have other brats?"

I shook my head. "That is why this one is of such consequence. We... we have waited a long time."

"You don't bear the looks of a woman old enough to have waited long."

"I—I have always possessed an unusually youthful complexion. And

I... I married quite young."

"Is that so? How young?"

"I was but sixteen." I had not yet seen my twenty-first birthday, but I desperately hoped he would think me older.

The man continued to stare at me, striding around the room while doing so. I sensed that he was contemplating whether anything I had said was plausible, and I prayed that he would believe me. At length, he stopped and retrieved a wrinkled sheet of paper from his pocket. He fetched a quill and pot of ink from the mantel above the fireplace and placed them before me.

"Write what I say: To the Earl of Matlock—My husband and I are held by Nathanael Morgan, leader of the most notorious band of highwaymen in all England. He wants—no, he demands five thousand pounds in gold by—"

I wrote nothing, and when he ceased pacing to look over my shoulder, a scowl furrowed his brow. "Why don't you write?"

"It would be better for my husband to write to his uncle."

"Why? Why should he write and not you? I thought you're the favourite."

"I am... but I am not in the habit of corresponding with the earl. In truth, I have never written to him before. He would not recognize my script, whereas he would be well acquainted with that of his nephew. If it came from me, he might consider the note false, written by any fortune hunter seeking extortion."

Once again, he began pacing, rubbing his beard as he walked, and obviously thinking about what I had just proposed. Then, striding to the hallway, he hollered for Sneyd. "Go get the other one! Bring him in here."

How could I alert Mr. Darcy to the new fabrications I had invented so that he would not appear surprised or make some slip when they were mentioned? My pulse raced as I worried. Surely, there must be some way I could signal him. Before I could think of a solution, however, Sneyd shoved him into the room.

He immediately strode to my side, looking at me intently. "Are you unharmed?"

I had barely answered with a nod, when Morgan interrupted. "Your *wife* is fine, only she refuses to write to your uncle. Says he won't know her hand. So here." He moved the paper in front of Mr. Darcy, who sat down beside me. "You write what I say and not one word more."

"Why do you not write the note yourself?" Mr. Darcy asked. Sneyd snorted with laughter until Morgan silenced him with a glare.

"Because I give the orders!" He slammed his fist on the table once again. "And because it will mean more coming from you. But don't fancy I can't read or write. You write my message only. Understand?"

"Yes," was the only reply he made before taking up the pen and dipping it in the pot of ink.

Once again, Morgan began to dictate the same message he had recited earlier. He named a time and place for deposit of the ransom and added, "It's essential that you do exactly as this note says, or never again will you see either me, or my wife, or the heir to Pemberley."

Mr. Darcy had written quickly, but with that last statement, he startled so that he caused a large ink blob on the page. Glancing at me with a look of utter astonishment, he raised his brows in question.

"Do not be alarmed, sir," I said with haste, "that I have shared news of our expectant child with Mr. Morgan."

"Very well," Mr. Darcy mumbled. He recovered, completed the ransom note, and handed it to Morgan, who peered at it closely. At last, he appeared satisfied.

"All right. Take them back to their room, Sneyd."

As we rose from our chairs, Mr. Darcy asked, "May we have bedding for the night—there is neither mattress nor fireplace in the room—and a candle as well?"

"And some water, I pray you, sir," I added.

Morgan ordered Sneyd to fetch his blanket, which provoked another round of snivelling and complaining from the man, but he did as he was told. He indicated that I could carry the pitcher of water from the table, but he refused our request for a candle. Soon we found ourselves once again alone behind a locked door, this time in total darkness except for the moon's faint light glimmering through the window.

"I brought you some bread," I said, offering Mr. Darcy the hidden slice.

"Thank you." He began to tear off small pieces. "My thirst is greater than my hunger."

"Aye," I agreed.

He handed the pitcher to me, and I drank from it before giving it back so that he could do the same. Suddenly the intimacy of that simple gesture, drinking from the same vessel, unnerved me. How could it be that I was sharing the necessities of life with *that* man, the last man I could imagine?

Unbidden, my eyes turned toward the lone quilt. Who would have thought Mr. Darcy and I would ever spend the night alone in the same room? I began to tremble, grateful for the cover of darkness.

"You can imagine my surprise to discover we are having a child, Miss Bennet. Do you care to enlighten me as to why?"

I felt my face flame, and once again, I was thankful there was little revealing moonlight. "The highwayman doubted that I was your wife, much less that your uncle would care more for me than for his own nephew. An heir was the only reason I could think of at the moment. I had little time to devise an answer."

"Very clever. And is this our only child?"

"Yes. That is the reason this child is so important. We have attempted to have a babe for years, but to no avail."

"Oh? And why is that?"

Although I could not see his face clearly, I could hear the amusement in his voice. "I do not know, sir, perhaps because we married when I was quite young."

"Indeed? How young?"

"Sixteen."

"Sixteen! Am I a robber of cradles?"

"Forgive me, but I was desperate to convince Morgan. Surely, you care little for your reputation in the eyes of these criminals."

"You are correct, Miss Bennet. I care nothing for their regard other than they believe who I am and contact the earl. Forgive me for the strength of my reaction. I have a sister who is that very age, and I cannot abide the thought of any man preying upon her youth."

"I have known several girls who married that young."

"Perhaps in your sphere, but rarely in mine."

Oh, there we were, back to his unbridled superiority!

"Is that so? I understand that in years past members of the royal family have entered marriage even younger, but then perhaps they, too, do not reside in your sphere."

"I meant no disparagement, madam, but I have observed that your younger sisters frequent society at a much earlier age than most of my acquaintances."

I blanched at the remembrance of Lydia and Kitty's forward behaviour at the Netherfield ball and of the way Mary had embarrassed us all by putting herself in the forefront at the pianoforte. Nevertheless, I bristled at his condescension and shot him a look that would have withered any other young man in my society.

The moonlight provided just enough radiance for me to see his eyes narrow, and he opened his mouth to speak, but I rose quickly, signifying that I did not wish to discuss the matter further. In truth, I had not the energy or strength for any further altercation that night.

Picking up the blanket, I looked around the room, wondering which corner would prove warmest. I knew that the stone floor would not only be hard but cold. If I lay down against the far wall away from the window, perhaps with my coat and the cover, the night would afford me some rest.

Then the thought struck me that I might be in a somewhat vulnerable situation. Only one blanket existed! I certainly did not want Mr. Darcy to think I offered him an invitation by opening it as though I were making up a bed. He was a gentleman and I a gentleman's daughter, but I knew nothing of his private life—or his morals for that matter. Quickly, I sat back down and placed the quilt upon the table, not bothering to fold it.

He picked it up and held it out to me. "Take the wrap. My coat is much heavier than yours."

When I did not move, he rose and carried it to the far wall. "'Twill be a hard bed, but this should be the most sheltered spot in which you might sleep."

"Where will you—" I could not bring myself to finish the question.

"A chair will do for me. I can rest my head on the table. Besides, I shall probably sleep but little."

"I should think you exhausted, sir, after that dreadful ride. I know that I am."

"Then let us say good night, Miss Bennet."

I spread the quilt on the floor and, lying down, wrapped myself up in it. Since I had nothing for a pillow, I raised my arm and reclined my head upon it. I did not sleep for some time, though. The events of the day tormented my thoughts, and no matter how tired, I could not quell my fear.

Over and over, I relived the nightmare of our abduction. What would we do, and how should we escape? When I did not arrive at the Gardiner's at the expected time, my uncle would most likely contact my father on the morrow, possibly by express even tonight, and my entire family would be worried for my welfare. I worried for my welfare!

I began to turn back and forth, unable to find a comfortable position. At last I gave up, and rising, I tiptoed across the room to look out the window.

"Are you unwell, Elizabeth?" Mr. Darcy's voice startled me.

"No. Forgive me, I did not mean to awaken you."

"I was not asleep. Are you having difficulty resting on that hard floor?"

"Very much so." I heard him rise and soon felt his presence at the window. "A greater hindrance is that I cannot remove the events of this day from my mind."

"Nor can I," he replied, "but have faith. I shall do everything possible to get us out of this predicament. We are both intelligent people. In truth, I have been attracted to that part of your character. Together we will survive this."

Attracted? I felt a slight catch in my chest. That was the closest thing to a compliment Mr. Darcy had ever bestowed upon me. Suddenly I was aware of how closely we stood.

"Thank you, sir," I murmured. "I shall attempt to dwell on that thought."

"Shall we try to sleep once more?"

I agreed and returned to my pallet while he made his way back to the table and chairs. I found that I could breathe easier when he was safely across the room, but I still had difficulty sleeping, for I could feel his eyes upon me, and I wondered if it was but an invention of my fanciful imagination.

Chapter Three

His rough hands encircled my waist once more, but this time I faced him. As he placed his cheek next to mine, the stubble on his jaw scratched my skin, and when I pushed away from him, I saw the coldness in his glittering blue eyes.

"Do not resist me," he commanded, and with one hand, he pulled me toward him. His eyes devoured my lips as I soon imagined his mouth doing the same. "I will have you, my pretty, no matter the consequence."

Nearer and nearer his mouth approached mine, and I knew that I was helpless, unable to break free. Just as his lips brushed mine, I turned my head with every ounce of effort I had left and began to scream. Over and over, I screamed and screamed and screamed!

"Elizabeth!"

I heard a man crying out my name, and I screamed anew. I felt myself gathered into his arms, as he shook me slightly. At the same time, I heard other voices and the violent sounds of a door thrust open. Slowly, I opened my eyes to see that it was Mr. Darcy who held me while Morgan stood in the doorway. Sneyd followed behind, lifting a candle up high.

"Elizabeth, wake up!"

"What's going on in here?" Morgan demanded. "What's all the screeching about?"

Mr. Darcy released me and stood up to face the highwaymen. "Obviously, she suffered a nightmare—hardly unusual under the circumstances."

"Is that true?" Morgan took the candle and held it close to my face. "Are you unharmed?"

"Yes," I murmured, "I am well."

"Look at this, Nate." Sneyd motioned towards the table. The chair in which Mr. Darcy had slept lay on its side. "He what kicked over this chair be in a mighty hurry."

Morgan turned his sight from the chair to Mr. Darcy to me, once again holding the candle aloft for closer inspection. "Why do you not sleep with your pretty wife, sir, if she is your wife?"

Mr. Darcy made no reply

"Hmm? What's wrong? Is your brain too foggy to make up another lie?"

"I have no idea what you mean." Mr. Darcy lifted his chin.

"The game's finished, Darcy. We heard you kick over the chair when the girl started screaming. She slept alone, didn't she? I don't think you two are married at all. I think you're playing us for fools."

My heart turned over. *What had I done?*

"You, sir, are mistaken." Mr. Darcy drew himself up even straighter than usual. He was a tall man. With an erect and imposing stature, he appeared to be one few would dare question.

"There is a simple explanation. Of course, she is my wife. She has been for several years, and she now carries my child. Because of her condition, which if you doubt, you may fetch a doctor to confirm, and because of the torturous journey you forced upon her, I allowed her the scant comfort of this poor excuse of a quilt. By any gentlewoman's standards, it can hardly be deemed large enough for one, much less two people. I assure you it was only for her ease that I elected to spend the night in a chair, and the fact, of course, that I wished to keep watch."

"Keep watch!" Sneyd sneered. "We're the ones what keeps watch!"

"Shut your mouth!" Morgan demanded.

Once again, he stared hard at me and then moved the candle toward Mr. Darcy's face, as though its dim light might reveal whether he spoke the truth. He paced up and down the length of the room several times. I held my breath, wondering what he would do next. He stopped abruptly and narrowed his eyes.

"Lie down with her."

"What?"

"I said, lie beside your wife!"

Mr. Darcy looked at me and opened his mouth to protest. "We . . . we are hardly in the habit of displaying such intimacy in the company of others."

Morgan drew his pistol, and stepping even closer, he placed it beneath Mr. Darcy's chin. "This is the last time I'll say it. Sleep with the girl!"

Immediately, Mr. Darcy dropped to the floor and sat beside me.

"Now, keep your *wife* quiet. One more peep out of her and she sleeps with me. Do you understand, *Mister* Darcy?"

He nodded. Without another word, as though we had practiced it, we both reclined at the same time, lying side by side under the blanket. Sneyd began to snicker until Morgan silenced him with a curt nod of his head. They departed the room without uttering another word. The only sound to be heard was the slam of the door and click of the lock.

We lay there motionless. In truth, I held my breath. I strained to hear departing footsteps, but it was impossible through the thick slab of a door. After a silence of some moments, I began to breathe easier.

"Shall you not get up now, Mr. Darcy?" I whispered.

"No."

No! What did he mean by that? In all my life I had never lain beside a man, and I found it most unsettling. Certainly, I was grateful that it was Mr. Darcy beside me and not Morgan, but I could not sleep beside a man, even if he was a gentleman!

"Why ever not, sir?"

"For two reasons—our captors may return at any moment to see that we obeyed their commands, and because I do not intend to have your outcries summon them again."

"I did not cry out on purpose. One can hardly be blamed for one's dreams."

"I do not blame you, Miss Bennet. I simply state the facts. You are in a position to suffer a recurrence, and I shall not hazard Morgan making good on his threat. If I remain here beside you, I can awaken you before you resort to the earth-shattering noise you uttered before."

"Mr. Darcy, I protest. I shall not spend the night under the same quilt with you." I sat up, intending to rise. Immediately, I felt his hands upon my shoulders.

"Lie down!" With one movement, he pulled me down beside him. This time he kept one arm under my neck so that I lay on his shoulder with his other arm across my waist.

"Mr. Darcy!" I cried with force and volume.

"S-h-h! Have no fear that I am attempting to take advantage of you or the situation in which we find ourselves. I do this for your safekeeping, certainly not for any disreputable reason you may imagine. Believe me, I wish to be as free of this position as you do."

Now, the man not only held me against my will but also insulted me!

"Let me go," I said evenly.

"Will you remain beside me if I do?"

"Yes," I spat out, "but only because of necessity."

"What other reason could there be?"

He removed his arm from behind my neck. I attempted to move over slightly, but when I did, he followed me. "Thank you, Elizabeth. I appreciate your cooperation."

"Could we please refrain from conversing any further?"

"As you wish. Good night."

I turned on my side away from him, scooting as far away as I could, which was not far, given the scant dimensions of that quilt. Still extremely conscious of his presence, I could smell the scent of his skin, hear the gentle hum of his breathing, and feel the warmth of his body next to mine. I knew with certainty that I would never go back to sleep.

How had I ever come to be in such a dilemma? And if we did survive, as Mr. Darcy put it, what would happen to my reputation? When it became known that I had shared not only a room with this man, but slept beside him, how could I ever again hold up my head? Would anyone believe it was innocently done? I could imagine the gossip, how tarnished my good name would be, and what it would do to my family. How could Jane or any of my sisters ever hope to obtain marriage to honourable men after this? My entire family would partake of my shame.

Repeatedly, I wrestled with my worries, and when they began to diminish, instead of succumbing to sleep, my poor brain returned to the danger in which Mr. Darcy and I found ourselves. It did little good to worry about my name when my life was in jeopardy.

By morning light, I had slept less than two hours. I had remained in the same position the entire night, fearful that I might turn over and unknowingly touch Mr. Darcy. Thus, I was stiff and sore when I sat up and rubbed my eyes. I intended to move quietly in order not to awaken him, but when I turned, I was shocked to see him sitting at the table, watching me.

"Good morning, Miss Bennet."

For some reason, my hand immediately flew to my hair. My curls were all in disarray, and I was acutely conscious of how wrinkled my gown appeared. I pulled my pelisse closer, feeling exposed.

"Good morning," I mumbled, as I walked across the room to the small storeroom that served as a poor excuse for a water closet. I doubt that I had ever been as embarrassed in my life at having to share such a necessity.

Behind the closed door, I took my time, using the advantage to smooth my skirt by hand as much as possible. Oh, how I longed for the simple pleasure of soap and water with which to wash! Water alone would have been welcomed, but we had drunk all that was given to us the night before.

I raked my fingers through my hair, discovered the hairpins that were still intact, and attempted to pin up as much as possible. I did not need a mirror's reflection to tell me that my entire appearance remained unkempt. Well, naturally Mr. Darcy would not look perfect, either, I mused.

Sure enough, when I returned, I observed that his breeches appeared creased with wrinkles, and his redingote was less than impeccable. A razor and comb would have benefited him as well, but I had to admit, he probably looked much better than I did.

In truth, the dark shadow on his face and tangle of curls falling across his forehead did little to disparage his good looks. If only he had a pleasing manner, he would be a most attractive man. But then I remembered how horridly he had treated Mr. Wickham, and I knew that no matter how fine his visage, I could never be attracted to Mr. Darcy.

As I advanced into the room, he rose and walked to the window without acknowledging my return, for which I was grateful. If he were only half as bothered by this forced intimacy as I was, he would wish to afford me some semblance of privacy.

I sat down at the table and peered into the empty water pitcher, hoping it had somehow been magically refilled. We remained in silence for no little time, and I wondered what scene outside provoked his interest. As he did not remark upon it, apparently, there was nothing there. I assumed he was simply avoiding my presence. At last he turned and walked back to the table.

"Were you able to sleep?"

I shook my head. "Very little."

"So I suspected."

"I apologize if I kept you awake."

"You did not. My own thoughts were impetus enough."

I glanced at him then, meeting his eyes for the first time that morning. "Do you wish to share them?" I doubted that he had entertained the same fears of the future that I did.

"I thought of ways we might escape our captors, and if we do, in what direction we should strike out."

"Escape? Do you still entertain the thought? How?"

"We must be on our guard, Miss Bennet, and take advantage of whatever opportunity arises."

"What do you mean?"

Before he could answer, we heard the key turn in the lock. Sneyd and the woman called Gert entered. She carried a tray containing bowls of gruel, two cups of strongly brewed tea, glasses, and another small pitcher of water. Sneyd remained at the door, while Gert slammed the tray down on the table, sloshing some of the precious tea out of the cups.

She then proceeded to the storeroom and returned with the embarrassing chamber pot. I turned away, unable to face Mr. Darcy, while Sneyd began to snicker. Mr. Darcy, however, acted as though it were the most natural action in the world. Of course, he was accustomed to servants carrying and fetching for him. For that matter, I lived in a house containing servants, although I assumed not anywhere near the vast number he employed. Still, I could not help but feel uneasy. This should be a deed carried out in the privacy of one's bedchamber, not in front of a snickering highwayman or in the presence of the most arrogant man whom I had ever encountered.

I suddenly remembered that I was to act as though I was married to that arrogant man, and so I raised my head and gave Sneyd the coldest of stares. "I require water and towels with which to wash. Will you see to it?"

"Oh, you *require*, do you, Missus?" He ran his eyes up and down my body, lingering about my bosom. "Well, we'll see 'bout that."

"See that you do it immediately!" Mr. Darcy barked.

"I'll do it when and if Morgan says so, and not because the likes of you orders me to!" Sneyd drew his gun and waved it in our direction.

I saw Mr. Darcy straighten his spine and the angry expression about his eyes. Before there could be any further altercation, I spoke in a much more placating voice. "Tell Mr. Morgan that I would be grateful."

With an answering scowl, he departed the room, and Mr. Darcy and I sat down to break our fast. Without sugar or milk, the tea was only tolerable, but we both were thirsty and I, at least, relished it. The gruel was another matter. Our hunger prevailed, however, and we both ate the distasteful dish. I had just finished the last spoonful when the door opened again. Gert returned with the emptied utensil for the water closet. She then literally gathered the dishes out from under our noses, placing them on the tray with a harsh clatter. It was obvious that she resented having to serve us. I attempted to soften her attitude by thanking her, but a sullen glare was all I received for my effort.

My request for bathing materials was never acknowledged, and eventually, the day grew long with such enforced imprisonment. In time, Mr. Darcy and I tired of straining to hear footsteps or voices. He still crossed the room to the window at the faintest sound from without, but after no attention from our captors other than a noon meal of the previous evening's leftover, greasy broth, we soon grew less anxious and settled into the monotony of existing in a room without diversion. Devoid of books, newspapers, callers, even the interruption of servants, and lacking the freedom to come and go as we pleased, we were forced to rely upon each other for company.

Once more, we discussed the possibilities of escape. I was not clever enough to think of any, but Mr. Darcy envisioned several ideas. He reassured me repeatedly that his uncle and his cousin, a Colonel Fitzwilliam, would move heaven and earth to rescue us once they learned of our whereabouts.

"My cousin possesses the resources of his regiment, so you see there is little to fear. If we do not escape, we shall be found."

When at last we had exhausted that subject, there remained only the topics of polite conversation. Since Mr. Darcy and I had never done well with each other in that realm, I doubted we could discover a theme on which we both agreed enough to converse. I was mistaken, however.

He surprised me by asking my opinion on several concerns that were currently of interest throughout the country. Not only had my father introduced me to the London newspapers at an early age, but also he had taught me how to weigh the facts and arrive at my own conclusions. I think I surprised Mr. Darcy by competently rendering my views. He appeared pleasantly diverted by the fact that I knew of what I spoke.

"Miss Bennet, you obviously are an extensive reader, no matter your demurring remarks upon the matter when teased by Miss Bingley at Netherfield."

"I would not employ the term extensive, sir, but if the subject holds my interest, I do my best to explore it."

"And what, besides the events we have just discussed, holds your interest?"

"Oh, I would say an assortment of things—I enjoy certain novels, many of the current poets, and lately, I have been much taken with a book by James Sowerby."

"Sowerby? So you consider yourself a student of nature?"

"Hardly, but I do love learning the names of trees, flowers, wild shrubs, and herbs. I find it fascinating to discover various uses for these old plants I have known all my life."

"My sister, Georgiana, enjoys her stillroom and whiles away many afternoons drying flowers and concocting aromatic mixtures. You will have more than music to discuss with her once you meet."

Once we meet? Unsure of how to respond, I fumbled about for another subject. "And do you have other siblings, sir?"

He shook his head. "No, I am not as blessed as you are with all of your sisters."

That caused me to smile slightly, for we were both well aware of his disdain for certain of my sisters. "At times I feel my blessings are somewhat excessive. My home overflows with them."

"And so you would not want always to live near Longbourn?"

Had I spoken of leaving Longbourn?

"Well, I have always wished to travel. I have seen little of the world, and yes, I long to visit new places. Tell me about your part of England."

"Ah, Derbyshire. You will find that I am somewhat prejudiced, as I consider it the ideal place to live."

"It is in the north country, is it not?"

He nodded. "Yes, it is filled with mountain peaks and rounded hills, forests, rivers, and the greenest of meadows to create what I consider perfection. You must see it for yourself. I cannot do justice to its beauty with words."

"Perchance I shall. My aunt and uncle have invited me to tour the lakes with them this summer."

"Your aunt and uncle?"

"The Gardiners from Gracechurch Street—near Cheapside."

He frowned and looked away.

Our conversation lagged then, and I knew the reason why. Mr. Darcy did not care to be reminded of my unfortunate connections—that my uncle was in trade—even though I thought him one of the finest men in our family.

I rose from the table and took a turn about the small room. How I longed to go outside if only for a moment. I now understood how caged animals must fret at their captivity. I had just made the length of the room and turned back to retrace my steps, when he joined me.

"Shall I walk with you? I fear this prolonged sitting provides little advantage to our dispositions."

"As you like." I continued on my way. At length, I decided to change the subject and once again return to Mr. Darcy's family. He had made it plain that he disapproved of mine. I would question him of his. "And does your mother reside at Pemberley?"

"No, my mother died when Georgiana was quite young, and I lost my own excellent father five years ago."

That shamed me. There I was hoping to discover some disparagement regarding his relations, and he had few of which to speak. "I am sorry, sir. And so your uncle is your closest connection?"

"And, of course, my aunt in Kent, my mother's sister, Lady Catherine de Bourgh."

I recalled Mr. Wickham's information. "Yes, my cousin Mr. Collins has great admiration for her. Does she not have a daughter, and have I not heard that you are engaged to marry?"

Mr. Darcy stopped abruptly. "Who told you that?"

"I am not certain; it seemed to be much talked of in Hertfordshire society."

"Did Mr. Collins spread that story?"

"No, sir, I do not believe it was Mr. Collins."

"Then who?"

He *would* ask, so what could I do but answer? "It was Mr. Wickham. He said you had been engaged to your cousin since childhood."

A darkness descended about his face. "Do not believe everything Mr. Wickham says, Miss Bennet."

"But why should he say such a thing if it is untrue?"

"I cannot account for Mr. Wickham's motives. I can only warn you to take care with any information he imparts."

"That is a dastardly accusation! Do you call the man a liar?"

"I could call him much worse."

He turned on his heel and strode to the storeroom, slamming the door behind him. I know not whether he had true need of its facilities or whether it was the only place where he could escape my presence. Frankly, I did not care. I hoped he stayed there!

That evening, I was once again summoned to dine with Morgan while Mr. Darcy was left to eat alone from the meagre dish Gert had served him. It may have been just as well, for we had little to say to each other since our disagreement over Mr. Wickham. He remained a sore point between us, for no matter what Mr. Darcy said, I preferred to believe Mr. Wickham until he was proven wrong. What possible reason would he have to lie?

Mr. Darcy had injured him severely, and Mr. Wickham, in my opinion, had borne it exceedingly well. He was making the most of his life with his new position in the militia. He was always amiable and never rude or arrogant. Although he had the greatest possible reason to hate Mr. Darcy, he had displayed no such emotion in my presence. In fact, he had gone out of his way to speak somewhat favourably of the man, saying that he was well thought of in the society in which he moved, while on the other hand, Mr. Darcy could not mention Mr. Wickham's name without anger. No, it would take some doing before I believed evil of the handsome young soldier.

At the table with Morgan, however, I soon forgot about Mr. Wickham, for that night all the men except for the one called Rufus joined us. They were rough and crude in their manners, again slurping from their greasy bowls and insulting in their remarks toward Gert. The way they looked me up and down made my stomach turn. I almost desired that Morgan would send them away as he had done the night before, but it did not happen. His only response was to call them down when they became abusive toward the serving woman. I wondered what his connection with her could be.

After they were chastened, they talked little until the man called Merle asked Morgan when they were to make their move. I listened closely, hoping they might give away some clue as to what had happened since the ransom note had been sent to the Earl of Matlock. Nothing was said that alerted me to any further knowledge, however, and they soon began to talk among themselves, raucous laughter erupting from time to time. As Morgan did not join in, I quietly broached the subject of bathing supplies with him.

"Mr. Morgan, did your man relate to you my request for towels and water with which to bathe?"

The highwayman looked up from his plate but continued to chew. Unfortunately, at that moment, a lull occurred in the conversation between the others, and the ugly man called Sneyd overheard me. He spoke up, laughing openly, his mouth full of food.

"Oh yeah, Nate, the fine missus here wants a bath."

"I be glad to wash her back," Merle said, which resulted in even more coarse, guttural laughter. I felt the blood rush to my face, flushing scarlet.

"Shut your mouth," Morgan snarled and then addressed me. "We're not much on bathing here and especially not in December."

I leaned back in my chair and kept my eyes on my lap. Why had I even asked? It was pointless and only provided fuel for these animals' crudeness.

Suddenly, I felt a finger lift up my chin. Morgan stared into my eyes. "Don't mind the boys. They're scamps, all of them, and they're not used to the presence of a lady. I'll see what I can do about your request on the morrow."

I said nothing, hoping that he would let me return to my room without delay. His hand lingered upon my chin, however, and I felt his fingers caress my jaw line.

Oh, dear Lord, I prayed silently, rescue me from this place!

At last, he motioned Sneyd to escort me down the hall. I was never so glad to reach the sanctuary found behind that locked door. Perhaps cages had their merits after all. I shuddered slightly as I advanced into the room, and holding my arms, I ran my hands briskly up and down them as though I might restore heat to my blood, for it had turned bitterly cold.

Mr. Darcy hurriedly rose and crossed the room to my side. "Elizabeth, are you unharmed?"

I nodded.

"What has happened?"

I shook my head. "Pray, do not ask me any more questions. I am not hurt. I learned nothing that will help us tonight. There, I have said all I care to say. Please let me be."

I sank down on the pallet and drew the quilt over me, turning my face to the wall. Would we ever be delivered?

Not long after that, Mr. Darcy picked up the blanket and lay down. It startled me, but I moved slightly so that he might share the cover. This was to be the second night we were to lie beside each other, and it continued to unnerve me. What must he think of me, allowing such intimacy? Should I protest again? Surely, he knew that I would never enter into this arrangement except for necessity.

Shadows of tree branches from outside the window jerked back and forth in a macabre sort of dance up and down the wall that I faced. The skittering sounds of a mouse could be heard from within the storeroom, and I shuddered again, hoping it would not find its way along the floor on which we lay.

We were in a situation fraught with danger and at the hands of cruel, heartless men. All of my earlier bravado had evaporated with nightfall, and now fear took hold of my heart and pulled me down into its clutches.

"Elizabeth?"

I inhaled sharply at the sound of Mr. Darcy's voice, but I made no audible response. I held my breath and hoped he would think me asleep. Could he not honour my request and leave me alone? I was very near to tears, and I did not wish to break down before him.

He said my name again softly, but when I said nothing, I heard him sigh and turn his face away.

Chapter Four

On the morning of the third day, after Gert served Mr. Darcy and me our usual fare for breakfast, Sneyd stood in the doorway while she cleared the table. I shuddered as his eyes swept over me. He grinned and bared his yellow teeth.

"Come with me, Missus."

I turned to Mr. Darcy, who immediately rose and stood by my side. "Where are you taking my wife?" he demanded.

"Wherever Morgan says to." Sneyd advanced into the room.

"She will not go anywhere until you give me the truth!"

"Still the big man, are we?" Sneyd pulled his pistol from his waistband. "Be you big enough to match this?"

Once again, Mr. Darcy was forced to allow me to depart. I glanced back at him over my shoulder and saw the alarm in his eyes and the frustration of his helplessness. There was nothing he could do short of taking a bullet for me. Sneyd locked the door with one hand while holding the pistol levelled at me.

"There is no need to point that thing at me. I have little recourse but to follow you."

He snickered—I had long since learned to hate the sound—placed the gun back in his waistband, and grabbed my arm roughly. Instead of ushering me into the main room where I had eaten the night before, he took me down a hallway and out a side door.

The brightness of the morning sun almost blinded me, but I welcomed its warmth and the smell of fresh air. At the same time, I began to fear my destination.

Although short and stocky in stature, Sneyd took long steps, and I had to tread quickly to match his gait. We walked around to the front of the cottage where I saw the highwayman named Merle stationed as guard. Across the creek I could see the man called Rufus up on a slight hill, walking back and forth like a sentry. Morgan was nowhere to be seen.

"Where are we going?"

"You wanted to wash, Missus. Here's your tub." He spread his arm wide, pointing toward the creek.

"Surely you do not expect me to bathe without privacy!"

"Your privacy ain't my concern. Morgan says let you wash, so wash." He snickered even more than before, and I could hear the man just outside the cottage join him with his own ugly chuckle.

I drew myself up, livid with anger and indignation, and narrowed my eyes, staring at him with all the vehemence I could muster.

"I require a bucket!"

He actually seemed taken aback somewhat by my tone, but not enough to release me. Merle, however, must have had some pity in his soul, for he picked up an old wooden bucket sitting beside the door and handed it to me.

"Thank you!" I said and directed my next remark at Sneyd. "I can hardly wash unless you release me."

"All right, but don't try nothin.' Remember, I hold the gun."

I glared at him. "How could I forget?"

I marched down the slightest of inclines to the water's edge and observed with dismay that it had evidently rained sometime during the night, for mud two feet wide lined the bank. I glanced around, searching for a drier spot, but the only choices I could see were either to plod through the mud or attempt to hop over it onto a huge flat rock that protruded out into the stream. I elected to try my luck with the rock and was pleased when my efforts were successful.

I walked out to the edge and knelt down on one foot, but the water was too far below to reach easily. I surveyed the creek from the entire surface of the stone, but all the way around, the depth remained the same. At last, I dropped to both knees, reached way over and scooped up a handful of water. It was icy cold, but how delightful it was to wash my hands. As I lifted it to my face, I was thrilled to see it was clear, nigh to pristine.

I could hear the sound of falls somewhere up ahead and realized that we must be right below a small dam of some sort. I would remember to relate that piece of news to Mr. Darcy. Perhaps it might aid him in discovering our whereabouts.

"Is that all what you wash?" Sneyd's voice was an irritating reminder of his presence. I glanced over my shoulder to see that he had followed me onto the rock and stood directly behind me.

"I prefer to finish inside."

I bent over once again to fill the bucket. I rinsed it a couple of times and had just dipped it into the stream the third time, when I felt his hand cup my bottom. Instinctively, I straightened and hurled the bucket of water at him!

"Devil take you!" He staggered backward, shaking the water from his doused stringy hair. "Why, you little— "

Knocking the bucket aside, he grabbed both my wrists and angrily began to force his face close to mine. I squirmed and screamed, trying desperately to push him away. He was far the victor in strength, however, and before I knew it, he had twisted both my arms behind me and held me against him in a tight grip, his vile mouth about to bear down upon mine.

From out of nowhere, two arms wrenched Sneyd away and threw him down on the rock, perilously close to the water! To my amazement, I saw Morgan tower over him, both fists clenched, a furious scowl upon his face.

"I told you she was not to be trifled with!" he yelled. Sneyd cowered before the leader of the gang. "Get in the water!"

"What? Nate— " Sneyd muttered incredulously.

"You heard me. Dive in and snatch that pail. It's the only one we've got."

"But, Nate, I'll catch me death! The water's freezin' cold."

"I'll not say it again, Sneyd. Get that bucket!"

Morgan's tone was deep and ominous, and I watched the shorter man discard his jacket and gun, and then pull off his boots before he gingerly stepped down into the creek. He cursed with every step and began to shake uncontrollably when the water reached his waist.

Morgan picked up Sneyd's gun and tucked it into his waistband, next to his own weapon. He then turned to me. "Come on. I'll help you off this rock."

"I can manage on my own."

"Oh, can you now? And here I'm thinking you needed my help. If you can manage so well, why did I disturb my rest to rush down here and rescue you from the likes of Sneyd?"

I said nothing, for it was fruitless to argue. I knew full well that if he had not appeared, I would now be fighting a battle I could not have won.

"Very well, Mr. Morgan, I accept your offer."

I held out my hand, thinking he would take it and assist me across the mud. Instead, I inhaled sharply when, in less than an instant, he scooped me up in his arms and carried me from the rock to the dry part of the riverbank. Once there, I expected him to release me, but he simply turned and observed Sneyd's progress in the creek while I remained in his arms.

"Will you put me down?" I spoke with as much dignity as I could find in the situation.

He turned his eyes from the stream to me, and I watched them begin to glint in amusement. "In good time, Mrs. Darcy, in good time."

That infuriated me, but I refused to blanch and stared back at him, a difficult task since our faces were so close. At last and just before I feared my eyes would cross from the strain, he laughed softly and deposited me on the ground. I straightened my clothes and did my utmost to show my disdain, but in truth I was grateful for his rescue.

"Keep going, Sneyd," he yelled to the swimmer. "You've almost got it."

We watched as the man managed to snare the bobbing bucket and turned around for the shore. He had almost crossed the entire stream, which was no small feat, as it appeared quite deep in the middle.

When he crawled up on the rock, Morgan added, "Now, fill it up and fetch it to the cottage for Mrs. Darcy."

Sneyd gave us both a dirty look, but once he shook the water from his long hair, he did as he had been told, all the while muttering something about that being a fit task for Gert.

Morgan took my arm and led me up the incline and back toward the cottage. He did not apologize for Sneyd's actions, but his grasp was gentle, and I could not be anything other than grateful for his presence. I decided to use his goodwill to my advantage.

"This is a lovely setting, Mr. Morgan. Does the land belong to your family?"

He looked at me with a curious eye. "And why would you be wanting to know that, Missus?"

"Because it appears to be rich in timber. I wonder that you do not make your fortune by its harvest."

He stopped and cast his eyes upon the woods, densely tangled with all kinds of trees and bushes. "It is a good forest and one my grandfathers lived by—but not I."

"And why is that?" I prodded gently.

He turned and stared at me, and when he spoke, his voice came out harsh and angry. "Because my grandfather was robbed of the land by the likes of you and your husband!"

"I do not know what you mean. Neither my husband nor I have ever robbed anyone."

"Aye, perhaps not you, but those like you. Land grabbers, all of them. And when my poor grandfather couldn't pay the taxes, they were all too glad to jump in and take what belonged to my family for centuries!"

"Then you no longer own this land?"

"Not with money, Missus." He chuckled slightly. "With what I've got resting in my waistband, though, I own it. My name's known up and down this part of the country, and that rich bugger who stole this land hasn't shown his face at this cottage in many a year now."

"And does that make you the better man, sir? Or just the better thief?"

He scowled. An angry mask once again descended upon his face. "Come on, get back in the house."

His touch was no longer gentle as he pushed me toward the door. It seemed I had hit a nerve. Before we reached our destination, I surveyed as much of our surroundings as possible. A small outbuilding on the side of the cottage evidently served as stables for the horses, for I could hear their soft whinnying sounds. Also in that direction I observed the beginnings of a well-worn path or narrow roadway lining the woods. Perhaps it led toward some village or town.

I thought of asking more questions as to our whereabouts but decided against it because of Morgan's change in mood. I doubted that he would reveal anything more, and I had learned enough for now.

Inside Morgan grabbed a towel from the table, thrust it into my hands, and prodded me toward the back room. Sneyd had arrived at the door by that time, whereupon Morgan grabbed the bucket of water and followed me. Mr. Darcy stood just inside the doorway and immediately took my hands when I walked into the room.

"Elizabeth, are you unharmed?"

I nodded, but he pulled me close nevertheless. To say that I was surprised by his embrace would be an understatement, but I recovered quickly and clung to him to continue the artifice he so obviously initiated. Surely, Morgan would now believe we were a loving couple displaying affection.

He said nothing, however. Dropping the bucket on the floor with little concern for spilling its precious contents, he slammed the door behind him.

Somewhat clumsily, Mr. Darcy and I disentangled ourselves, each of us avoiding the other's eyes. I wondered if he found this charade as uncomfortable as I. Hurriedly, I gathered up the towel and started toward the bucket of water, but he picked it up before me and carried it to the storeroom.

"I waited at the window, and I heard you scream. You must tell me what happened."

"It—it was nothing."

"That cannot be, for you do not frighten easily, Elizabeth. Tell me the truth. I insist upon it."

I placed the towel beside the bucket of water and then closed the storeroom door, hesitating as long as possible before answering. I looked everywhere other than face him, but finally meeting his gaze, I knew I must give an answer.

"I shall tell you on one condition, sir."

"And what is that?"

"That you promise to keep your wits about you, that what I say will not harrow up your wrath."

"When has my behaviour ever failed to be ruled by reason?"

"Whenever you fear that I am in danger."

"Oh? And would you have me not react, Miss Bennet? Shall I leave you to the reprehensible desires of these criminals?"

"No, of course not. That is not what I meant. I am grateful for your interference— that is—for your protection. It is just that I did not come to any harm, and I would not have you injured by proposing to defend my honour. Besides, Mr. Morgan came to my rescue before any genuine damage occurred."

Mr. Darcy's eyes narrowed at the mention of the highwayman's name, and I saw the line appear between his brows.

"*Mister* Morgan? What *has* he done to elevate himself in your esteem? Tell me the incident in its entirety, Miss Bennet. Now!"

I bristled at his demanding tone, speaking as though he were my master. I considered with distaste that whoever eventually consented to be his wife would most probably have to endure such overbearing dominance on a daily basis. Well, I was not his wife, and I would not tolerate being treated in such a manner.

"Do not order me about, sir. It is not your right."

A few moments earlier, he had begun to pace back and forth. He now stood directly in front of me, and I could see the fire in his eyes.

"If you do not tell me what happened, Elizabeth, I shall call out Morgan post-haste."

"Would that not be foolhardy, sir? You do not even possess a gun!"

"And is not your refusal to cooperate just as foolish, madam?"

My colour was high, and I knew it, for I could feel the heat burn my cheeks. The man was the most infuriating individual I had ever known! We stared at each other no small amount of time, each of us refusing to budge, but finally I relented. I would not have him killed simply because I refused to obey his commands.

"Very well, Mr. Darcy. You shall hear this silly tale, and then you shall wonder why you insisted upon bullying me into relating it. I was allowed to fill the bucket from the stream. That dreadful Sneyd accompanied me to the water's edge and there he—well, he attempted to put his hand upon my person."

I could see Mr. Darcy's chest move, his breath coming short and hard. "Sneyd put his hand upon you? Where?"

I could not believe he asked me that!

"In a place he should not have! And do not ask any further details, for that is all I shall say about the matter."

"I will kill him," he fumed. "I will call him out immediately!"

"Are you mad? My dignity was all that was injured. Is that sufficient reason to kill the man or risk losing your life? Besides, I defended myself. I am capable of doing so, whether you realize it or not."

"You? How? What could you do?"

"I emptied the bucket of water over his head!"

For the first time, I caught a glimpse of a smile on Mr. Darcy's face and admiration in his eyes as well.

"Excellent! Well done, Miss Bennet. But there is more, is there not? I heard you scream more than once. What transpired after that?"

"Naturally, my actions made him furious. He grabbed my hands and tried to force himself upon me."

I looked up to see the nerve on the side of his face begin to quiver. He pressed his lips together and said not a word, but his eyes darted here and there as though he were making an extraordinary attempt to control his fury.

"But Morgan saved me," I said quickly. "He threw Sneyd down and ordered him into the creek."

"Into the creek?"

"Yes, to retrieve the bucket. It had fallen in the stream after I tossed it at him. And that is all there was to it," I said with a tone of finality.

For some reason I omitted how the highwayman had carried me to the cabin and held me longer than needed—why I do not know. An intuitive feeling warned me against it, and I was relieved that he did not question me further.

At that moment, we were interrupted by Morgan's presence. Thrusting the door open, he marched into the room. Standing with hands on hips, he surveyed the area as though he were king and our quarters a part of his domain.

"Mrs. Darcy," he said, his tone imperious, "I shall require the pleasure of your company at my table again tonight. And Darcy, I have serious doubts that your wife's truly with child, for she was light as eiderdown when I carried her from the water's edge. Just exactly how far along is she in her confinement?"

Mr. Darcy's mouth gaped open, and I quickly answered. "I am not yet three months, sir, and if you question my condition, my husband has already suggested that you fetch a physician to confirm it."

His only response was a narrowing of those cold, azure eyes before he whirled around and departed the room as quickly as he had appeared.

I suddenly had a new fear, and as soon as the door closed, I voiced it. "What if he does send for someone, perhaps a midwife?"

Mr. Darcy's answer was brusque and dismissive. "There is little chance of that. He is bluffing. He would not suffer an outsider knowing our whereabouts."

Then he caught my hand and turned me around to face him. "Why did you not tell me that Morgan *carried* you to the cabin? Did he, too, attempt liberties with you?" I avoided his eyes and tried to loosen my hand, but he persisted. "Miss Bennet? What have you refrained from telling me? What did he do?"

"There is nothing to tell. As I said before, Morgan rescued me. I am much obliged to him."

"Obliged! To that criminal? I fear that your admiration of the highwayman's appearance may have robbed you of your good sense! Or perhaps you relished the close embrace necessary for such transport."

"Mr. Darcy, your suspicions are beyond annoyance. I pray you remember that you play the role of my husband, but in truth, I am not your wife. There is a difference, and you would do well to remember it!"

He blanched at my words as though I had struck him, and releasing my hand, he strode to the window. I took advantage of the respite and vanished into the water closet, slamming the door behind me.

The third night of our imprisonment found me seated once again at the highwayman's table. I was relieved that it was Merle instead of Sneyd who accompanied Gert when she brought Mr. Darcy's plate, and he, in turn, escorted me to the main room. Evidently, Sneyd had been banished to the sentry's post without, for I saw no sign of him.

Once the woman had placed the meal on the table, she and the others quickly quitted the room. Morgan and I were to dine alone.

Our intimate dinner scene unnerved me somewhat, but I put on a brave face and refused to allow him to witness my trepidation. The contents upon my plate appeared somewhat finer that night, for I detected the aroma of venison among the chunks of potatoes, and I could not believe my eyes when I saw him pour me a glass of wine. Where had that come from?

He had said not a word since I entered the room. We ate the meal in eerie silence, and it endured until he cleaned his plate and emptied his glass. Leaning back in his chair, Morgan struck a match to light his pipe and turned his gaze upon me. I lay my spoon upon the table and sat back, waiting. He still said nothing, but sat there watching me.

I began to wonder if he had taken instruction from Mr. Darcy, for both men had the gift of provoking my unease with their prolonged stares. With Morgan, however, I would not give in.

Why should I speak first? I was there at his pleasure. If he wished for nothing more than my presence while he dined, then fine, that was all he would receive.

I kept my eyes upon the fire, longing for such a blaze in the room I shared with Mr. Darcy, when at last my dinner companion spoke. "Would you care for more wine?"

"I thank you, no, but I would welcome the opportunity to fetch a glass for my husband."

"Ah, that blasted Darcy. Must his name intrude upon our meal?"

"I cannot see how his name will make much intrusion when his person is confined to that small room. I do not understand why he is not allowed to join us."

"Because I've no desire to look upon his face... while I'm delighted by yours."

I hated myself for blushing, but I could feel the heat rise in my cheeks. I turned away and surveyed the room. It was rudely furnished and in great need of a thorough cleaning. The prominent adornment, other than dust, consisted of rifles and various other weapons stacked against the walls. These men possessed a veritable arsenal.

He rose and stood before me. "And does it give you such displeasure to gaze upon my face? Perchance my scar offends your delicate sensibilities. Is that it?"

He leaned against the table and inclined his face so close that I could have reached up and touched his cheek.

"Who did that to you?"

"The first man I ever killed." He chuckled lightly.

I drew back and turned my face away, unable to keep from recoiling at the thought. Reaching out, he took my chin in his hand, forcing me to face him.

"'Tis an ugly sight, I'm sure, but it could be worse. He could have cut off me pretty curls!" He winked and laughed.

"What would you say to that, Mrs. Darcy? Would I not have lost me true beauty then? Is that not what drives the ladies wild? I've had many a lass wish to twirl her fingers through such richness. Would you be one of them?"

Again I made no answer, for I refused to even acknowledge his taking such liberties with his improper suggestions.

"Mrs. Darcy? Shall you not respond to my question?"

"I do not appreciate your impertinence. If you wish to speak of more suitable topics, I shall do so, but I refuse to engage in flirtatious banter."

He puffed on his pipe for several minutes and steadily surveyed my person. Oh, how I hated being regarded in such a manner, as though I were nothing more than his entertainment!

"So you will not flirt." His tone was mocking. "Then what shall you do to amuse me? Do you sing perchance?"

What? I remained silent, staring at him as though he had lost his mind.

"Mrs. Darcy, I asked you a question. Do you sing?"

"A little... a very little."

He clapped his hands together. "Then let us have a song!"

"You have no instrument, sir. How can I sing?"

"Without one!" he announced. "And sing something lively, for I feel like dancing."

My eyes widened in unbelief. "You jest, sir, at my expense."

"Indeed, I do not. You shall sing, and we shall dance."

To my amazement, he tossed his pipe aside, and taking my hand, he bade me rise and follow him to the middle of the room.

"Now sing!" he commanded.

I could not believe he would humiliate me in this manner, but when he bowed before me as though we were beginning the dance, I knew that he was serious. Frantically, I cast about in my memory for any melody I might recall to which one could dance.

Hesitantly, I began to sing:

"Did... did you not hear my lady
Go down the garden singing
Blackbird and thrush were silent
To hear the alleys ringing."

Back and forth we moved to the music, touching hands at times, turning, swaying, and skipping to the notes. Suddenly, while continuing to dance, he joined me in song, his voice a rich, deep baritone.

"Though I am nothing to her
Though she must rarely look at me
And though I could never woo her
I'll love her 'til I die.

"Surely you heard my lady
Go down the garden singing
Silencing all the songbirds
And setting the alleys ringing."

All of a sudden, he stopped the dance, although he continued to sing. I stood there silent, while he finished the song still holding my hands in his.

"But surely you see my lady
Out in the garden there
Rivalling the wondrous moonlight
With the glory of raven hair."[1]

Wait! Why had he changed the last lines from "glittering sunshine" to "wondrous moonlight," and "golden hair" to "raven?" Perhaps it was done unconsciously; perchance he had forgotten the words. Yes, it comforted me to consider that as the sole reason.

With the final notes, he bowed before me and laughed aloud. "Well done, Mrs. Darcy. You're quite the songbird."

"And you as well," I admitted, grudgingly.

Retaining my hand in his, he escorted me back to the table, but before I could sit down, he pressed my fingers to his lips and peered up at me with a knowing look in his eyes, an expression that unsettled me even further. I attempted to withdraw my hand, but he held onto it. At last I could bear it no longer.

"Mr. Morgan, I acknowledge that I am your prisoner, but I appeal to your higher nature to treat me like a lady... a married lady."

"My higher nature? As opposed to what? The base criminal you and your kind consider me?"

---

1 *Silent Worship* from *Ptolemy* by G. F. Handel, arrangement and words by Arthur Somervell

"You *are* a criminal. You have robbed my husband and me. You have abducted us and now demand extortion from our kinsman. How can you deny the charge of criminal?"

He shrugged. "I have no wish to deny it. I am what I am. You, madam, accuse me of possessing a higher nature."

"It is not an accusation but rather a hope based on my observations."

"Indeed? And just what observation might give rise to this hope? Is it me fine dancing or perhaps you fancy me lovely baritone." He smiled as he lapsed back into the dialect of his fellow highwaymen.

I wondered why he did not speak like Sneyd and the others all the time. What kind of life had he lived before taking to the roads to rob and kill?

Dropping my hand, he walked to the fireplace before I answered his question.

"You have come to my defence more than once," I said softly, "and you have shown kindness in providing necessities for my husband and me."

He turned and walked back to the table, placed both hands thereon and leaned toward me. "Any kindness I've shown was for you alone, Elizabeth. I'd just as soon shoot your husband."

I drew in my breath at his cruelty, the hair rising on the back of my neck. I clasped my hands together below the table to keep them from trembling and prayed that he could not see the fear reflected in my eyes.

"If you have any regard for me, I pray you will not harm Mr. Darcy. And—and besides, would that not defeat your plan? My lord, the earl, will surely refuse any ransom if we are not both returned to him in good health."

When he made no reply other than to hold my gaze with an unblinking stare, I continued, hoping that I made sense, fearful that my speech came forth as senseless babble.

"Will you not tell me? How will you cause the transaction to come about? Has my husband's note been delivered to his uncle?"

"Ah, you'd like to have your questions answered, wouldn't you?"

He quickly rounded the table to stand by me. Before I knew what happened, he took my hands in his once again and pulled me to my feet, placing both of us much too close to each other.

"And what'll you give me in return if I tell you what you wish to know? A kiss, perhaps?"

He leaned his face close to mine, and I was conscious of his golden curls falling over his forehead.

"Mr. Morgan, you forget yourself. I am married!"

"But are you happily married? I think not."

"Why ever would you say such a thing?"

"Your marriage is no love match, Elizabeth. Anyone can see that."

I wrenched my hands loose and turned away, afraid to face him, fearful that my expression might confirm his statement. He would not have it, though, and, grabbing my shoulders, he turned me around and clasped me tightly. Tangling his fingers in my long hair, he pulled my head back and stared into my eyes.

"I speak the truth, don't I? The gentleman may love you . . . but you don't return his affection."

"Release me!" I hissed, my mouth so close to his that I could feel his warm breath.

I willed myself not to tremble, and in truth, I was so angry at his manhandling my person that I became emboldened with unusual courage. He hesitated long enough that I could feel his heart beat furiously against my breast. I realized then that the man was truly attracted to me, perhaps even enamoured.

Slowly and deliberately, he removed his hands from my arms, flexing his fingers wide. When he spoke again, his voice emerged deep and hoarse.

"What I wouldn't give to have met you a'fore Darcy did. If I'd wooed you, not even his riches would've proved tempting, for you would've known what 'tis to be truly loved."

I could make no answer. It took all of my effort to quell my gasping for breath. I had never seen such intensity in a man's eyes, such passion, and never had I been the object of so ardent a declaration. Oh, when Mr. Collins had proposed, he had used some silly, meaningless phrases, but I was convinced he knew as much of love as he did of laying eggs! The man was incapable of that depth of feeling, but Morgan—I believed what he said.

He gave every appearance of a man in love, but how could he? We barely knew each other, and what we did know hardly lent itself to love. Well, certainly not on my part. I could never care for a highwayman, a thief, and a kidnapper. And I felt certain it was only desire that stirred his heart, no matter the strength of his avowal.

Slowly I began to back away from him until I had reached the end of the table. When he advanced toward me and reached my side, I put up my hands as though to shield myself.

"I pray you sir, return me to Mr. Darcy."

"Come on," he growled, "I won't hurt you." Taking my arm, he pulled me down the hallway, unlocked the door, and pushed me into the room into the arms of my supposed husband.

"I hope you know, Darcy, what a lucky bugger you are... and Elizabeth, just so you understand, the man who gave me this scar was the *last* man I killed."

With one lingering, final look into my eyes, Morgan slammed the door and locked it.

Chapter Five

Completely unbidden, I began to weep uncontrollably. I buried my face in my hands while my shoulders shook with relief. It was some moments before I ceased long enough to realize that I now stood within Mr. Darcy's arms, and it was *his* voice I heard whispering comforting words in my ear. I realized that his hand was upon my head, and I did not struggle when he gently pressed my cheek against his chest. There he stroked my hair over and over, and once my sobbing lessened slightly, I was surprised to hear the ferocity with which *his* heart now beat in my ear.

"Elizabeth," he whispered, slipping his handkerchief into my hand, "Elizabeth, do not cry so. I cannot bear it."

I became aware of what felt like a kiss upon my hair, and then his lips touched my forehead in the softest of caresses. Was it my imagination?

Slowly, I raised my face to his and watched his darkened eyes travel down to my mouth and then back to meet my gaze. Our lips were so close that the slightest movement would have caused them to meet. We stood frozen, our breath quickening in unison, and my heart beating faster and faster until... I stepped back.

What sort of fanciful spell had been cast upon us?

I could not take it in and began to turn away, but Mr. Darcy would not release my hand. Instead, he led me to the table and pulled out a chair, indicating I should sit. He nudged his chair close to mine and sat before me, continuing to hold my hand while he poured a glass of water.

"Here," he said, entreating me to take it.

I took a sip and at last allowed my eyes to rise from my lap and meet his. We gazed at each other as though there was nowhere else to look. Was he as conscious as I of the gravity of what had just occurred? Surely I had not imagined the tenderness with which he had held me, the touch of his lips upon my head, and the unspoken strength of emotion manifest between us.

Whatever it was remained unsaid. Mr. Darcy's next words had nothing to do with our feelings for each other.

"What did Morgan do, Elizabeth? Why did that scoundrel cause you such distress? Tell me so that I may make it right."

I shook my head. "There is nothing for you to do, sir. I pray you will not make my foolish display of emotion into more than it is."

"I cannot believe that, for you do not give into sentiment easily. Morgan's actions created anguish in you, and you must tell me what happened."

Once again, I shook my head. "Truly, it is as I said. This entire ordeal has simply overwhelmed me, and I gave in to the relief of tears."

He narrowed his eyes, and I could see that he did not believe me. "What did the rogue mean when he said I was lucky?"

I knew very well to what he referred, but I could not—would not—tell him of the highwayman's words of love or the manner in which he had held me.

I looked away and shrugged. "I suppose he referred to your status and wealth. The man has been dispossessed of his inheritance, and he resents those who have taken it from him."

"It was not I who dispossessed him."

"No, but he relates those who have with your class, sir. He is truly an angry man who feels that he has been robbed."

Mr. Darcy released my hand then and stood up, pushing away from the table with what appeared to be an air of impatience.

"I hope I do not detect a note of sympathy in your voice for the villain."

"Not for his actions, of course, but one cannot help feeling some concern that his family has lost their land due to inequities in society. Morgan said his grandfather owned the land on which this cabin is built and that it was stolen from him."

"Stolen! I doubt that, and if so, it takes a thief to know one."

"Mr. Darcy, have you no compassion for those less fortunate than yourself? Those who were not born to wealth and inheritance?"

"You know nothing of my compassion, Miss Bennet."

"I beg to differ with you, for I have received your compassion, and I can testify that you possess the ability to bestow such on a woman in need. Why can you not acknowledge that there are men who are in like need of your forbearance?"

"I judge fairly those who deserve compassion—whether man or woman—and Nathanael Morgan does not."

Now my ire arose once again, and I could not keep from throwing wood on the fire. "I see. In much the same manner you deemed Mr. Wickham undeserving of your father's bequest?"

"I fail to see how with incivility you can accuse me of such misrepresentation. I am baffled as to why you persist with this irrational degree of interest in the concerns of men who are blatantly beneath you."

"Who that knows the sufferings of both Wickham and Morgan can help feeling an interest in them?"

"Their sufferings! I neither know nor care to know of any supposed sufferings of the highwayman who holds us prisoners, but I am well acquainted with Mr. Wickham and with his so-called misfortunes."

"And at your hand," I cried with great energy. "You have reduced him to his present state of poverty. You have withheld the advantages which you must know to have been designed for him. You have deprived the best years of his life of that independence which was no less than his due. You have done all this, and yet you can treat the mention of Mr. Wickham's misfortune with contempt and ridicule."

"Ah! I thank you for explaining it so fully. My faults, according to this calculation, are heavy indeed!"

He began to walk with quick steps across the room. "But perhaps these bitter accusations might have been suppressed had I lied and flattered you into the belief that I, too, had been ill-used and cheated as these men have obviously done. If I had begged your confidence with sad tales of how others had reduced me to a helpless victim, and how I had no other resort but to steal and cheat my way through life, perhaps then I, too, might enjoy the pleasure of your ignorant sympathy."

Halting suddenly, he drew near and turned his piercing gaze upon me. "But I abhor such disguise, and I refuse to play upon your emotions to warrant your good opinion."

"You are mistaken, Mr. Darcy, if you suppose that you might employ any such action to affect me in any other way, for from the very beginning—from the first moment, I may almost say—of my acquaintance with you, your manners, your arrogance, your conceit, and your selfish disdain for the feelings of others were such as to form that groundwork of disapprobation on which succeeding events have built so immovable a dislike."

I had also risen by that time, and we faced each other, declaring our righteously fervent viewpoints like two puffed up peacocks.

"You have said quite enough, madam. I perfectly comprehend your feelings and have now only to be ashamed of what my own have been earlier this evening. I propose that we say as little as possible to each other from this moment forward."

"On that we are at last in perfect agreement!"

If it were possible for fire actually to proceed from one's eyes, a conflagration would have erupted from Mr. Darcy's at that moment. I turned my back on him and made a great show of dragging my chair to the opposite side of the room. I sat down facing the wall, which proved to be a futile gesture on my part, for there is nothing quite so boring as staring at a dark, blank wall.

How had this evening descended into such a downward spiral? And what had caused me to turn on Mr. Darcy and engage in an argument? What was it about the man that could set me off like a harridan at the slightest provocation?

An hour later, I broke my self-imposed exile, picked up the blanket, and lay down upon the floor. I had sat in the corner and fumed excessively, making a great show of my exasperation with frequent sighs and clearings of my throat. They had no effect upon Mr. Darcy as far as I could determine.

At length, my fit of pique lessened, and I began to study the reasoning behind our altercation. For his part, I had little idea, but as for myself, I suspected it pertained to the feelings Mr. Darcy's embrace had evoked within me.

It would not do for me to experience any sort of attraction for the man. I had just voiced a litany of reasons—perfectly valid reasons—why he would be the last man I could ever care for, and yet my heart seemed determined to strike out on a path all its own, oblivious to my own good sense.

I feared that our imposed constant companionship had deluded me into thinking I might care for him, and that would not do. It would not do at all. It was far better to maintain our mutual dislike of each other. Far better and much safer, for I knew without a doubt that Mr. Darcy would never entertain the idea of marriage with a member of the Bennet family.

Marriage! From where had that word appeared? Impossible!

I shook my head slightly to clear away the unwelcome thought. He had made his disdain for my family's society evident from the outset, and any fanciful ideas on my part could only end in heartbreak. Of that, I was certain. My practical nature assured me that the distance caused by our mutual anger proved the wiser choice for both of us.

Still, I had great difficulty erasing the memory of standing within his arms, the comfort I felt as my head lay cradled against his chest, and the surprising tenderness of his touch. It had stirred strange, unfamiliar sensations within me, yet I found them oddly enticing.

Something about his embrace made me feel safe, as though I had finally found my way home, and yet something about it alarmed me—an unspoken warning that I could easily be swept up in a whirlpool of emotion that might prove my undoing.

After I lay down, Mr. Darcy sat at the table a bit longer. After a while, I heard the scrape of his chair, and by the light of the moon, I watched him approach. Without a word, he lay down beside me, and I moved over, shifting the blanket so that he could share it. I was thankful for the darkness, for I feared that if our eyes should meet, he might read my thoughts.

"Elizabeth…you must allow me to apologize for my behaviour. It was unforgivable."

Oh, no, do not apologize, I pleaded silently. How could I remain angry if he was kind?

"No more so than mine, sir. I should not have accused you in such a harsh tone. I fear that my sense of injustice sometimes overtakes my good sense."

"We both may have spoken hastily."

"True."

"And it will not do for us to be enemies, for we are in great need of comradeship."

"Indeed."

"Then shall we make a truce? I shall not accuse you of defending those whom you know little about, if you will not blame me for their circumstances."

But I did know the harm he had done to Mr. Wickham!

When I did not respond, he said, "Elizabeth, shall we not put off further discussion of this disagreement until we are in less precarious surroundings?"

I could agree to that. "Very well, sir."

"Good night."

"Good night, Mr. Darcy." I rolled over on my side and faced the wall.

"But I would talk with you about Mr. Wickham at a later time."

I sighed. What possible good would that do? Provoke another argument? "Good night, sir."

Sometime later that same night, I awakened to what sounded like gunshots!

Within moments, I heard horses snort and neigh, men shout, and doors slam. At first, I thought I was dreaming, but once I opened my eyes, I saw shadowy movements through the window.

"Mr. Dar—"

"S-h-h!" He placed his hand over my mouth.

Quietly we both sat up, and he then rose to a standing position. Staying well within the shadows, he advanced across the room to the window and peered out, only the barest outline of his profile visible. When further movement flashed across the window, he quickly stepped back, pressing himself flat against the wall.

We heard more raised voices, and I was certain one of them belonged to the woman, Gert. Then a clattering of horses' hooves could be heard gathering speed as though several people were riding around the house, and subsequently, into the distance. Moments later, we heard nothing at all.

Mr. Darcy chanced another look outside while I hastily stood up, smoothed my gown beneath my pelisse, and gathered up his greatcoat from the floor where he had left it.

Had someone come to rescue us?

My heart raced as I skirted the room, quickly reaching Mr. Darcy's side. He held his finger to his lips, cautioning me to silence. There was little need, for by that time my heart was in my throat, and I could not have found breath to speak. We stood thus, listening for the slightest sound, but silence endured. Whatever had happened outside was now ended, or so it seemed.

When he nodded his head to indicate that I might look out the window with him, I crept up from my crouching position and gazed out into the night. I could see but two or three stars barely illuminate the heavily clouded, ink-coloured sky.

And then we heard footsteps outside the door! That distinct click of the key roared in my ear as it turned in the lock. I held my breath, waiting to see who would spring through the doorway! The knob on the door did not turn.

After standing motionless and waiting for some time, Mr. Darcy walked softly across the room, and I followed close behind. He placed his ear against the thick door, but we heard no footstep, voice, or movement.

"Remain behind me," he whispered.

I nodded and watched his hand reach out to the doorknob. I thought my heart would surely leap from my chest when he slowly opened the door! The hallway appeared empty and dark, but in the distance at the end of the hall, a faint light shone, and a fire crackled and spit.

Mr. Darcy looked in both directions, and seeing the side door, he pushed against it with all his might. Alas, it was locked and would not give. There was no other way out of the cottage but through the room where Morgan and I had dined together.

Tightly clasping my hand behind him, he crept toward the light. We had just reached the doorway, when a voice called out. "Ain't nobody here but me."

Mr. Darcy and I slowly advanced around the corner. Gert sat on a stool by the fire, stirring the logs.

"They're gone. You can leave."

Mr. Darcy walked to the window and peered out, then moved back to the hall and explored it in the opposite direction.

"Where have they gone?" I asked, incredulous.

"Don't know. Don't care. But if you're leavin', now's the time."

Mr. Darcy returned to the room. "How long do we have before they return?"

"Like I said, don't know, don't care."

"Why?" I asked. "Why are you letting us go? Will they not harm you when they come back?"

"Nate don't touch me, and he keeps the others' hands off me. Besides, he's the one who give me the key."

What did that mean? Was Morgan allowing us to leave, or could this be a trap? The questions were surely reflected in my expression.

Mr. Darcy's eyes met mine, but there seemed to be little question in his. Quickly, he returned to the door and looked out into the night. "In what direction is the closest town, and how far away is it?"

"Jonah's Village lie twelve mile east of here."

"Is that the only one?"

"You asked what's the closest. Hazleden's nigh on to eighteen mile south-east, but you have to follow the creek and wind 'round through the wood a'fore you find the road. The clear path leads to Jonah."

"Come on," Mr. Darcy motioned toward the door with his head, "and button your coat. It has rained earlier, and 'twill be bitter weather until the sun rises."

After handing him his greatcoat, I turned to Gert, hesitating for a moment. "Thank you."

Spitting a stream of tobacco into the fire, she picked up a small sack and handed it to me. "Some bread and taties."

I took the bag gratefully and ran out the door behind Mr. Darcy. It was quite dark, the new moon reflecting barely a sliver of light before it ducked behind the clouds. He reached for my hand, and I had not the slightest hesitation in allowing him to hold it.

"Which way shall we go?" I whispered.

"To Hazleden."

"Why not take the path to Jonah's Village? It is closer."

"Too easy to find us that way. Come along and walk softly. I do not trust that woman. We may be headed straight into a snare."

"I trust her," I whispered.

"Why?"

"A feeling."

"Then let us hope your perception is correct, Miss Bennet."

We ran across the open space between the cabin and the river and soon disappeared into the tall brush lining the bank. The noise of water rushing over the dam ahead grew louder as we neared it. Earlier, I had told Mr. Darcy about hearing a waterfall, and now it appeared to be even closer than I thought.

The reeds and grasses thickened the farther we walked, and I wondered how he could see ahead. In less than a half-hour, we reached the dam.

"Stay," he whispered. "I shall return."

A sense of panic swept over me when he released my hand, and I peered after him, desperate to keep him within sight as he vanished into the darkness. Rustling in the trees caused me to turn quickly, but nothing appeared. Surely, there must be wild animals in these woods—or wild men.

My teeth began to chatter, and I clasped hold of my arms, willing myself to remain still. Yet, the combined noise of my teeth and rapid heartbeat seemed monstrously loud to my ear, surely alerting anyone within miles that I was there alone. I turned round again and again, thinking I heard something or someone.

And then I truly did hear a crackling step and another. I placed my hands over my mouth to keep from screaming, when a figure suddenly appeared before me!

"Elizabeth," he whispered, and I almost bit my lip in two before I recognized that Mr. Darcy had returned. With a great sigh of relief, I let out the breath I had been holding.

"I climbed down to the dam, hoping there was a bridge built across it. It is a makeshift structure at best, now covered not only with running water, but broken down in the middle, impossible to cross. We shall be forced to keep to this side of the river."

"How can we continue without light? We could fall in the water."

"True, but we must chance it. We are not yet removed far enough from the cabin to bide our time. We must advance. Follow closely, and do not let go of my hand."

He need not worry. I had no intention of letting him out of my sight again.

We travelled on through the night, how far I had not the slightest idea. More than once, we slipped into a bog of mud, and Mr. Darcy even stepped off the bank momentarily. Fortunately, the water was shallow at that point, and he quickly pushed me away and managed to free himself before we both fell in. My feet were growing heavier with each step, my shoes thoroughly clogged with thick layers of mud.

At last, Mr. Darcy halted and turned to look over his shoulder. My spirits rose when I saw the faint beginnings of morning light in the east.

He turned back to face me. "Can you go any farther?"

I nodded.

"Come on, then. The concealment provided by darkness will soon be lifted."

We ploughed on through the reeds. The sharp stalks scraped my hands and cheeks. Oh, how I wished for the protection of a bonnet!

And I was so thirsty, my throat hurt. All that water lay just a few feet away, and yet we could not refresh ourselves, for it remained far too dark to draw any closer. But soon—soon, I knew we could drink our fill. That thought made my feet move, that and Mr. Darcy's warm hand covering mine.

Eventually, a greater light appeared through the trees, illuminating the full expanse of the river. It was much wider than the creek by the cabin, perhaps at least three times its size in width, and I wondered at its depth.

Mr. Darcy kept an ever more constant eye on our surroundings. He turned his head from side to side and often looked over his shoulder. At last, he stopped abruptly, so much so that I walked straight into him.

"Forgive me."

I attempted to step back, and in so doing, lost my footing. He immediately reached out and caught me, saving me from falling into the mud. I was grateful, for the hem of my petticoat was covered in muck. I hoped to prevent my dress from a similar fate.

"No," he said, frowning, "it is I who should be forgiven. I have pushed you too far. I can see that you are spent."

He could not have spoken truer words, and I felt certain that my appearance portrayed it. I did not even wish to think how bedraggled I must look, my hair streaming down my back, my gown three inches thick in dirt. But what did it matter? We were free from our captors and out in God's good earth.

"I am well, sir. All I desire is water to drink."

"Of course. I shall help you down the bank, but take care, for it is slippery."

Cautiously, we climbed down to the water's edge. Both of us fell to our knees, cupped the water into our hands, and lapped it up like dogs. I had never tasted wine more refreshing than that cold, clear river water.

When my thirst was slaked at last, I washed my face, wincing as the water stung the cuts in my cheeks and forehead. My expression of pain did not go unnoticed, for the next thing I knew, Mr. Darcy turned my face to meet his. Gently, he ran his thumb across the scratches.

"Those blasted reeds! I never should have pulled you through them."

"No," I said softly, taking his hand in mine. "You did what you had to do. Do not fear. I heal quickly."

I heard his quick intake of breath—or was it mine—as I saw the tenderness in his eyes. He wore the same expression that had graced his face earlier in the night when he had held me within his arms. Slowly, we both stood up, and this time he was the one to break our gaze, turning his face away.

"We can no longer travel in the open. We must make our way into the woods." He led me back up the embankment.

An hour later, it was full daylight, and we were enmeshed within the deep wood. I hoped that Mr. Darcy had some idea of our whereabouts, for I was hopelessly lost. I could no longer hear even faint sounds of the river, and I worried that we had wandered far too great a distance from its boundary. The soles of my feet burned, and I suspected that blisters had formed beneath the first and second toes of my left foot.

"Mr. Darcy, I can go no farther." I reached out to brace myself against the trunk of a beech tree.

He turned and frowned. "Of course. Over here is a clear spot. Come and seat yourself against this sturdy oak."

He took my hand and led me a few feet more, where I scraped my shoes against the tree's bark, shedding most of the mud before I gladly sank to the ground. Covered in fallen leaves and bits of dried grasses, the hard ground felt as comforting to me as a corn-husked mattress.

"Shall you eat a bite of something?" he asked, kneeling beside me and taking Gert's small bag from my hand.

He broke off part of the bread, and I took it from him, but I refused the cold potatoes. While we ate, we discussed the possibilities of what might have transpired at the cabin. Mr. Darcy suggested that the highwaymen could have fought off another band of ruffians who had descended upon them, or in an even more likely scene, they may have turned on each other.

I recalled that this very morning was the deadline Morgan had dictated in the ransom note. Could they have gone to meet the Earl of Matlock and retrieve the gold? If so, why would he not have left someone to guard us? Why would Gert have released us?

"Many questions," Mr. Darcy said, "and few answers. What I should most like to know is who fired the weapons and the present whereabouts of those criminals?"

"I do wish you could have alerted your uncle to our location, but of course you could not with Morgan reading your message."

"Whether he read it or not, that information would have been impossible to relate, because I simply do not know where we are."

I sighed in agreement, and after a bit, I methodically began to massage the sides of my sore feet through my shoes.

"Why not remove them for a brief time?" he asked.

I shook my head. "I fear my feet are far too swollen. I might never be able to pull the shoes on again. I must persevere. I know it is imperative that we push on with great haste."

"Yes, haste is important, but in doing so, you must not be harmed. Your face and hands are scratched, and now your feet are injured. Of what could I have been thinking?"

I was surprised to hear his expression of remorse. "Do not distress yourself, sir. Our escape has been uppermost in your mind throughout this ordeal, and I am grateful."

My voice had unexpectedly softened with that last statement, and I felt a slight catch in my throat. His eyes met mine, diffused with that familiar tender light once again.

I forced myself to look away and break the spell.

We were now delivered from our imprisonment, and God willing, we would safely rejoin civilized society in the near future, a society that would prohibit any furtherance of the feelings recently awakened in my heart. Once we returned, all this would be as nothing more than a dream. He would once again be proud, wealthy Mr. Darcy of Pemberley, and I would be Elizabeth Bennet, daughter of a country gentleman, far below the echelon of society in which Mr. Darcy dwelt.

It was past time to put an end to this attraction taking root within my heart and which I dared suspect he might possibly return in kind. It was time to place some distance between us, to return to my saucy speech and manner. It had served me well in the past and would again, I felt certain.

And so, with a gleam in my eye, I spoke. "After all, I know what a tiresome creature I can be, and that I have tried your patience more than once. I did think I was up to this trek, though, since I bear the noted reputation of being an excellent walker."

I lifted my chin, giving him a somewhat cheeky smile. He coloured immediately, and I knew that he remembered hearing me so described by Mrs. Hurst and Miss Bingley in the dining hall at Netherfield. Until then, however, he did not know that, having stood without in the hallway, I had chanced to overhear the remark.

"Miss Bennet, I..." he faltered, casting his eyes about the glen as though searching for an appropriate response.

I could not refrain from sympathizing somewhat with his predicament. "It is of little consequence, sir. I have long been acquainted with Miss Bingley's disapprobation of me. I fear that I measure up neither to her standards of an accomplished woman nor those of her sister. In truth, I would guess that I have fretted away at least three-quarters of a moment because of the distinct certainty that I never shall."

He smiled slightly, relief evident in his eyes that I found the remembrance somewhat humorous.

"I hope that you do not count me a conspirator in their accounts. Although their brother and I are good friends, I do not share a similarity of opinions with Miss Bingley or Mrs. Hurst."

"Is that so? I must have been mistaken in my first impressions then, for you appeared nigh to identical in manners at the Meryton assembly, again at the party at Lucas Lodge, and at the Netherfield ball. In your censure of Hertfordshire society, I would have judged you and Mr. Bingley's sisters in perfect agreement. Have no fear, however, that I hold you responsible for their remarks. No, no, I should never accuse you of that—for you bear the onerous task of answering for your own."

"Oh?" He settled himself against the nearby beech, leaning back against its trunk. "Any in particular?"

I pursed my lips as though combing my memory, searching for the exact statement with which I might confront him. "As I recall, there exists an ample reckoning upon which I might rely."

"Such as?"

"Well, let me think on the matter." I pretended to continue my search, tapping my fingers against my chin. "Hmm, this will do, as I consider it a fundamental example."

I lowered my voice and put on my best rendition of his haughty tone. "Mr. Bingley, I am in no humour at present to give consequence to young ladies who are slighted by other men. That particular declaration certainly signifies.

"And then, of course, I often amuse myself with the recollection of your companion statement—she is tolerable, but not handsome enough to tempt me. Oh, yes, Mr. Darcy, you need not rely on either Miss Bingley or Mrs. Hurst for assistance in notable opinions or conversation. You are quite the master of your own."

He now frowned in earnest, any semblance of a smile quite vanished, as he raked his fingers through his hair. "I regret those statements. They were beneath me, as well as uncalled for and untrue."

Untrue? This would not do. Surely, he did not intend to compliment me. I would not allow him to persist in that line of speech.

"I see that your memory fails you, sir. Let me refresh it. As I recall, you appeared to be in ill humour the night of the Meryton assembly ball, disdainful of all you surveyed. In truth and in line with your nature, I believe your first account is accurate after all, and I shall not listen to you disavow it at this late date."

His response was silence and a long, steady gaze placed squarely upon me, a gaze that flustered me somewhat, one from which I eventually turned away.

"It is in the past now, Mr. Darcy. Please do not suffer yourself to think upon it. In truth, I grow weary of thinking, and if you consider it safe to do so, I would benefit from a short nap."

"Very well," he replied. "Do not worry for your safety. I shall remain awake and keep watch. I only regret that you must sleep on the ground."

"Ah," I said, using my hands to rake up a mound of leaves and then laying my head upon it, "but I have grown accustomed to the absence of a pillow."

Within moments of closing my eyes, I felt his hand gently lift my head, as he slipped his folded coat beneath it. "Allow me at least this trivial attempt at atonement for my previous blunders."

I opened my mouth to protest, but he silenced me by lightly placing his finger against my lips. "Just this once, Miss Bennet, I pray you will favour me with a *scarcity* of your sharp tongue."

Chapter Six

Mr. Darcy allowed me to nap for some time before I felt his hand on my shoulder. I sat up immediately for fear that we were in danger, but when he assured me that all was well, I felt relief that my only threat was a growling stomach. Gert's meagre rations had not satisfied my hunger.

He bade me rise and follow him, explaining that while I slept, he had explored a short distance from our retreat, and to our great, good fortune, he had discovered a narrow country lane that might possibly lead to Hazleden.

He guided me through a brief tangle of trees, and it did not take long before we reached the edge of the forest. From there, a rough roadway lay before us, its worn ruts indicating it was travelled, although how often, of course, neither of us knew.

"We should continue our journey well back from the road within the cover of these trees, lest our captors also use this path," Mr. Darcy said. "From here I can observe anyone coming from afar, and if it appears a harmless soul, I shall step forth and secure our passage. To be safe, you should remain out of sight, Miss Bennet, until I have found a ride for us."

I looked him up and down and wondered if he had any idea of his appearance. The once perfectly dressed gentleman who had begun this journey some days previous now appeared bedraggled, unkempt, and highly suspect. His beard and hair were untidy, the bottom of his long coat possessed a good six inches of soil and stain from his misstep into the river, and his once polished boots were scuffed and laden with layers of dirt and mud. I entertained serious misgivings that anyone would wish to give him a ride.

"Do you not think it more prudent that we ask together, sir?"

"I do not," he said hastily. "I do not need your assistance. It will be a simple task. Now keep behind the trees, and I shall walk nearest the open."

I did as he said, but beneath my breath, I muttered, "Stubborn man!"

We walked for some time. The sun had climbed high in the heavens before we heard the distant clatter of a horse and cart. Mr. Darcy darted back into the edge of the forest, and we remained concealed until the transport could be viewed clearly. Seeing that it contained only an old man driving what appeared to be an empty cart, Mr. Darcy strode forth from the woods, raising his hand to hail the driver.

The poor, frightened man took one look and immediately grabbed a whip and urged the horse into a faster clip! Although Mr. Darcy ran after the driver, entreating him to stop, the man's fear of the wild-looking stranger rushing from the wood prevailed. He and his horse and cart soon disappeared from sight.

"Stupid fellow! Why would he not stop?" Mr. Darcy was extremely vexed.

We continued plodding on through the perimeter of the woods. The day had turned muggy, unseasonably warm, and yet full of clouds threatening rain.

Eventually I removed my coat, growing uncomfortable from the steady pace at which we hiked. Mr. Darcy, likewise, stopped to take off his, and in so doing, caught it in a vicious snarl of thorns and briers neither of us had noticed. He laboured to dislodge it, accompanied by various exclamations, but the greater his attempt, the more entangled it became. I had just offered assistance when we heard the distinct sound of another rider or riders approaching.

Mr. Darcy warned me to remain hidden, and we both strained to see, hoping that the forthcoming traveller did not belong to the gang of highwaymen who had abducted us.

"It is but a single young man driving a cart," I said softly.

"Blast! I must get this coat loose before he passes by."

"Allow me to approach him, sir. Perchance I shall have greater success than you did, and he will offer a ride."

"You? Absolutely not!"

I, however, had already walked hurriedly through the trees toward the road.

"Elizabeth!"

"Free your coat, sir. I shall secure our passage."

I proceeded closer to the path, stepped out into the open, smiled and waved at the driver. Immediately he pulled on the reins and halted the horse. I could see a large pen in the cart, and noises indicated it contained some type of animal.

"Blazes, Miss, you gave me a fright," he called.

"Good day, sir," I answered, walking nearer. "You have come just in time."

I went on to tell him that my horse had suffered a mishap some ways back, and that I was in need of a ride. When he looked askance at my appearance, I explained that the accident had occurred the day before, and that I had wandered through the woods all night searching for the road.

"Could you tell me to where it leads?"

"To Hazleden, Miss."

"And how far might that be?"

"Another twelve mile or so."

"And might you offer me a ride? I would be most grateful."

"I go only as far as the cut-off to Mr. Martin's place, but I'll be pleased to take you that far."

I thanked him with another big smile and then added, "Just let me fetch my brother from the woods."

"Your brother, Miss?"

"Yes, he's had a slight mishap with his coat. It will take but a moment." I ran a few steps back and called, "William, this kind fellow has offered us a ride. Can you not hurry?"

The young driver looked somewhat apprehensive when Mr. Darcy emerged from the trees. "What's wrong with him? He don't look a fellow what had no accident. He look like he fell in with hard times."

"Oh, it is of little consequence," I said quickly, for I could see that Mr. Darcy had abandoned his greatcoat to the briar patch. Either because of losing that fight or because I had been successful in securing a ride when he had not, he appeared quite angry. Flushed and scowling, he barely nodded at the driver as I made the introductions.

"My name is—Mary, uh, Smith, and this is my brother, William Smith."

"Jack Burnaby," the young man said, doffing his hat and exposing a shock of red hair. He appeared to be a callow youth, about the age of my sister, Kitty. He hopped off the cart on the opposite side and made his way around back, where he loosened the slats across the rear and shoved the heavy pen aside.

"We are brother and sister now?" Mr. Darcy hissed. "What next? Shall you be my daughter?"

"Shush," I cautioned, "he will hear you." I then walked to the back of the cart, whereupon I was shocked to see a huge black and white sow inside a rude sort of pen. "Is it... quite safe to ride back here with your pig?"

"Yes, Miss. Sadie won't hurt your brother none. And you can ride up front with me."

"What?" Mr. Darcy exclaimed.

"Come along, William," I said quickly. "We must not delay this good man. He *is* offering kindness to strangers."

I refused to meet Mr. Darcy's eyes, keeping my head down as I hurried past him to the front of the cart, but I could feel the fierceness of his glare. I stopped short, however, upon finding the young man directly in front of me.

"Need a hand up, Miss?" A huge grin covered his face.

Mr. Darcy immediately stepped between us. "Never mind. I will assist my... sister."

Before I knew it, he placed his hands around my waist and lifted me up to the driver's seat. I murmured my thanks and closed my eyes at sight of the grimace on his countenance. Glancing over my shoulder, I watched him walk to the back of the cart and climb aboard, knowing with certainty that he possessed little appreciation for the seating arrangements.

All of a sudden, the pig began to squeal like a wild woman! She snorted and snuffed and tried her best to push her snout between the bars of the cage.

"Hush up there, Sadie," Jack yelled, then smiled and winked at me. "Don't mind her, Miss. I'm taking her over to Mister Martin's prize boar. 'Tis breeding time."

"Ah."

The young man and I conversed for much of the short journey. He was friendly and seemed harmless, and I attempted to discern as much as possible of what he might know about our whereabouts.

He told me that he lived with his parents on a farm about three miles back, that if he did his work well, his father had promised him a trip to

Hazleden on market day. When I asked if he ever travelled to Jonah's Village, he frowned, saying that his parents would not allow him to set foot in it because everyone knew that town had gone bad. Far too much riffraff lived there, and his father thought it a dangerous place for his wife and children.

He went on to say the locals claimed Nate Morgan and his men stayed around there from time to time. He had never actually seen Morgan, but he knew all about him since he was an infamous highwayman.

"Did you come through that way, Miss, when you met with misfortune?"

"No—we were on our way to Town when it happened."

"To London, Miss? Then you were travellin' the main road on the other side of the river?"

"Yes," I said, hesitating somewhat. I knew that I had never been on that road, but I was afraid to tell him the truth, that we had been kidnapped far from this part of the country.

When he looked puzzled, I said that we had wandered around during the night and found ourselves completely lost by morning. Quickly, I reiterated how grateful I was that he had come along, hoping that he would not ask me *how* we had crossed the river. He did, however. I was forced to prevaricate again, weaving a tale about how my horse stepped in a hole and broke its leg. I then doubled up with my brother until his horse fell as we crossed the river.

"You crossed the river?" Jack's eyes bulged out in surprise. "It's mighty treacherous in spots."

I agreed. "That's when we lost our other horse, along with my brother's money pouch."

"All your money's gone?"

"Utterly—at the bottom of the deep—lost forever."

I gave a great sigh and attempted the saddest expression I could conjure. Silently, I amused myself with the idea that if I did manage to survive this adventure and my reputation did not, I could always go on the stage, for I had acted more parts than I cared to during the last four days. I stole a sideways glance at the youth and felt satisfied that he believed my cock-and-bull tale.

"That is enough of my sad story. You say that you are on your way to Mr. Martin's? Is it far off this path?"

"About three mile west once I leave the road. I'd take you and your brother with me, Miss, but Mr. Martin's not much for callers. He don't even allow me in his house. I'll sleep in the barn near Sadie tonight."

"Does reason exist for his unfriendly demeanour?"

"Folk say he turned sour when his only boy run off and joined Nate Morgan's bunch."

I felt a chill run down my backbone. "And does he keep in touch with this son? Is it possible that he sometimes shelters the highwaymen?"

"Don't know, Miss, but I don't much think so, else me father wouldn't send me over there alone. He says that boy turnin' wild broke the old man's spirit, and that's why he keeps to himself."

"You say he is an excellent breeder of pigs, though?"

"That he is, Miss. Ain't a sow around here what can keep away from his boar! You ought to see that animal—he's the grandest in the county!"

Just then, Sadie erupted in another long round of excited squeals and snorts.

"She certainly seems delighted."

"She is, Miss. Wound up like a top, she is! I hope that old boar's had a good, long rest a'fore we get there."

I turned slightly to see that the sow finally had worked her way through the bars of the cage enough to nudge Mr. Darcy's back with the tip of her snout. I could imagine the anger and frustration he must be suffering. Goodness! I had managed to place him in a situation even more difficult to bear than my sister Mary's performance at the Netherfield ball.

Eventually, we reached the turn to Mr. Martin's pig farm. Jack offered his regret at not taking us all the way to the next village. I thanked him, however, and assured him that his aid had been of great assistance to us. Mr. Darcy said little, merely nodding curtly before we resumed our journey toward Hazleden on foot.

We walked in silence, staring straight ahead until the horse and cart could no longer be heard. Only then did I chance a quick peek at Mr. Darcy's countenance. I expected darkness and did not meet with disappointment.

His brows pulled together in a deep frown, his lips tightly pressed together. He plodded forward, each step angrily resolute. The muscle in his jaw even seemed to twitch in time with his tread. I, who cannot abide indefinite silences, finally broke the wordless tension.

"If you are angry with me, would it not hasten the resolution of our conflict if I were informed of your reasoning, for I cannot determine the cause if you will not speak."

He took a deep breath. "Do allow me the courtesy of time sufficient to recover from this recent experience before imposing upon me for conversation."

"Forgive me, sir, I did not mean to impose." We continued on a short way, but I could not let it rest. "I fail to see why the benevolence of a stranger should result in your resentful manner, unless this is further manifestation of your general nature which you warned me about earlier in our acquaintance and of which I am now more than well aware."

He stopped abruptly and turned to face me. I had already walked a few steps ahead before I noticed and turned back.

"Madam, if you had been forced to spend the last hour in far too close company with a pig the size of a small cow and endure its wild antics, not to mention its odour, your own amiable disposition might possibly be termed resentful!"

I struggled not to laugh or even smile, but his fit of pique was so petty and beneath him that I had to press my lips together to control my expression.

"You made a great sacrifice, sir. I am sure the pig will recall that leg of the journey with pleasure."

No longer could I maintain my composure, and as my shoulders began to shake, mirth bubbled up from within, and despite all my efforts, I burst forth in laughter. Mr. Darcy turned aside, but when I did not cease after a few moments, he faced me anew.

"I rejoice that I provide you with such merriment. Are you quite finished?"

I nodded, and in truth, I endeavoured mightily to quell my laughter, but as ofttimes happens when one attempts to stifle amusement, it only added fuel to the emotion, and so I continued in helpless, embarrassing abandonment. By that time, tears streamed from my eyes, and I doubled over with the pain caused by such wild hilarity.

Mr. Darcy turned to glare at me. If I had thought earlier that fire shone forth from his eyes, it was nothing compared to now, but I simply could not stop.

I shall be eternally thankful that laughter is contagious, for it eventually cracked even Mr. Darcy's stiff armour and he, too, began to smile and then softly laugh. Encouraged by my continuous inability to smother my response, he soon laughed aloud with me. Thus we stood beside the path, helplessly out of control for some time until slowly, sanity returned. Wiping my eyes with my hands, I marvelled at how handsome he was with his face lit up by laughter.

"Not only do I smell like the river and dirt, but now I reek of pig," he said, which started both of us again on another riotous uproar.

"Can you not see the look of horror on Miss Bingley's face if she were to meet up with us now?" I cried.

"At last I might be freed of her attentions, for I can hardly see her drawing near to one who looks and smells as I do."

"Nor I, sir."

I took a deep breath, and at length, I was able to gain control of my amusement. Yet, what relief swept over me with that spontaneous release provided by the sharing of hearty, abundant laughter! I felt at ease, as though I had slept ten hours on a fine feather bed. The old proverb flashed across my memory: *A merry heart doeth good like a medicine.*

And then as quickly as amusement overtook us, self-consciousness returned. We resumed our trek, and I did my utmost to turn my attention to the surroundings, acutely aware that once again Mr. Darcy and I had shared an intimate moment. Laughter and tears were closely tied, and it seemed that either one or the other had torn down the boundaries between us. I determined to restore those barriers as much as possible, beginning with a return to the danger of our surroundings.

"Could you overhear my conversation with young Jack, sir?"

"In between squeals."

I smiled again, but did not give way to laughter. "So you heard what he said about this Mr. Martin, that the boy could not take us to his house, and why I would not have accepted had he offered."

"Yes, because of his association with Morgan's gang. To refuse would have been prudent. Even though the boy thinks the farmer has broken relations with his son, it may be unlikely. He and his cohorts could take refuge there at any time. Yes, Miss Bennet, you did well to glean that much information."

I was pleased that he approved. "In truth, I was called upon to make up tales with such haste that I wonder at their believability."

"Well, no one but a besotted youth would have deemed your story true.

Your horse falls in a hole? And then mine falls into the river? My word, Elizabeth, we must have been riding two decrepit old nags."

I rolled my eyes. "I am well aware that it was an insupportable story, but we have been hard pressed to come up with numerous accounts these past days. I confess that my imagination has quite run its course."

"What I consider most bizarre and fail to comprehend is why you said we were brother and sister. Of all things—brother and sister! No one would believe that. Why not leave it as we were—husband and wife? We now have some experience enacting those roles."

"I feared the boy might mention to acquaintances that he had picked up a husband and wife. They, in turn, might know Morgan and pass the information on to him or one of his men. I changed our names for that reason. Mary Smith, I know, is unoriginal, but as I said, my creativity has vanished."

"I disagree. Your creative impulse is highly charged to paint *us* as brother and sister."

"But why, sir? Our appearance is somewhat similar. We are both dark-haired and possess brown eyes. I fail to see the incomprehensibility you claim."

Again he stopped walking and turned to me, his expression troubled. "It is just impossible! No one but that besotted youth would ever think we are in the same family. Married, yes, but never brother and sister."

Aha, now I saw his reasoning! I turned on my heel and began to pick up the pace, outdistancing him in an instant. "I understand your meaning, sir. You need not insult me further."

He hastened to catch up with me, which did not take long, as his long stride could make two of mine at any given moment. "Insult you? In what manner?"

"Evidently, you consider it degrading for anyone to think we are part of the same family! Do not worry, sir. No one would ever call you a Bennet!"

"You mistake my meaning! I meant no disparagement toward your family. If I had, do you think I would have earlier represented us as married?"

"One sometimes marries beneath oneself. That is more excusable than being born into such a family. I do not wish to discuss it further."

"I do. I shall not have you think ill of me."

"What I think of you is of little consequence. As long as that *besotted* youth believed me, we are secure. And on that subject, why ever should you describe him in that manner not once, but twice?"

"Because any fool could see that he could not tear himself from your fine eyes."

"My fine eyes!"

"Yes," Mr. Darcy said quietly, looking away. "I have described them thus myself in times past."

I was shocked at his disclosure. When and to whom could he have spoken of my eyes?

We did not return to the subject, however, for at that moment, we heard movement behind us. In the far distance, a rider-less horse approached, obviously lame, for its limp was pronounced.

United in thought, we hastened back to the perimeter of the wood, seeking its concealment. The poor horse continued on until it stood directly in our line of vision. Still saddled and bridled, a huge, red gash tore across its left foreleg.

"Wait here," Mr. Darcy cautioned before gingerly approaching the animal. I kept a watchful eye up and down the path but saw no one following the horse. Nervous and scared, the creature would not allow Mr. Darcy too near, and after several unsuccessful attempts, he gave up and returned.

"She's been shot," he said, shaking his head. "There is nothing I can do for her without a weapon."

"Shot! But who would—where is her owner?"

He shrugged his shoulders. "'Tis a dark portion of the country in which we are stranded, Elizabeth. Who knows what happened to the horse or its rider?"

I watched the wretched animal limp a few more steps, saddened that we did not have the means to end its suffering. Suddenly, something appeared familiar. I peered more closely, and my heart turned over.

"Mr. Darcy, does not that horse look like the one Morgan rode?"

He narrowed his eyes, following my gaze. "Morgan! Why do you say that?"

"Look below the saddle. A black feather like the one he wore in his hat is caught beneath the strap."

He cautioned me to wait and once again walked toward the animal. Although unable to draw close enough to grab the feather, when he returned, he confirmed that my suspicions were correct.

"That means Morgan may be shot as well if the horse is his. It also means there is a high possibility that he and his men are in this vicinity. We must return deeper into the wood."

Catching my hand, he pushed his way into the labyrinth of undergrowth, and we disappeared into the depth of the timber. How long we scrambled through the woodland, I know not. At length, my legs began to ache, and my blistered feet burned. For some reason, I began to sense a slight shortness of breath.

"Mr. Darcy, can we be climbing a hill?"

He nodded. "A marginal one, it seems. Unusual, for most of this land has been flat except for that small knoll near the highwaymen's cabin."

"May we rest a moment, sir?"

He stopped and looked around before answering. When still, I was struck by the silence. Not a leaf fluttered, bird chirped, nor creature scurried through the grass.

"We must proceed," he whispered. "It is too quiet. We must find a place to hide."

We struggled on through the wildwood, our breathing growing more laboured with each step. Not a doubt remained by then that we were ascending an incline. When I feared that I could not take another step, Mr. Darcy finally stopped short.

"Remain here," he said. "Let me scout out what lies ahead within that clearing."

We had come upon a break in the vegetation. There the land was rockier, filled with large stones and slight open spaces. I watched him advance into the glen and then climb up a slight cliff, disappearing around its curved precipice.

I recall how dry my throat felt—whether because I had nothing to drink for hours or because of the trepidation I felt at no longer having Mr. Darcy within sight, I know not—but I cannot think of that time without remembering the ache in my throat. What would I have done if he did not return, if he fell off that cliff, if he met with one of Morgan's highwaymen on the other side?

As I have always preferred to dwell on the positive, I willed myself to find suitable distractions. Surveying the surrounding coppice, I determined to count the variety of flora in which I stood. Beech and chestnut trees intermingled between the oaks with a plentiful supply of hawthorn interspersed here and there, as well. Examining the branches a bit closer, I spied a tangle of vines wound around the limbs of several shrubs. I stepped closer and was thrilled to spy remnants of once thick clusters of berries hanging therein.

Blackberries! My mouth watered, and hunger awakened at thought of the succulent, juicy fruit. Carefully, I reached into the maze of vines and began to pick the few berries overlooked by birds and creatures of the forest.

I had rarely tasted anything that gave me greater pleasure. I ate until my hunger was somewhat assuaged and then plunged deeper into the shrubs to collect fruit for Mr. Darcy. Without pail or basket, I was compelled to lift my skirt to hold the precious treasure. So entrenched was I in pursuit of the delicious food, that he returned unbeknownst to me.

"What a lovely sight," he said.

I looked up immediately and found myself overjoyed to see his face. "I did not hear you. Yes, look at the riches I have discovered! Lovely is the perfect adjective."

He looked quizzical. "Riches?"

"Blackberries!" I held my skirt forward to display the bounty.

"Ah, I did not see them. Excellent, Miss Bennet. I do believe you have happened upon the final portion of this season's fruit." He took a handful from my skirt and popped a good portion into his mouth. "But let us proceed. I have discovered a rough haven for the night."

"A haven? In this wild country?"

"Come with me."

He pushed the thick tree limbs aside, holding them until I had passed through the barricading growth. I scrambled to keep up with him and retain our supper while doing so. Eventually, I was forced to hold my skirt with one hand and cling to Mr. Darcy's hand with the other in order to climb the steep rocks. In doing so, I noticed that I could not do it without exposing a good portion of my petticoat. Somehow, it seemed unimportant. He and I had shared far too many familiarities during the last few days to bother about a petticoat that was four inches deep in dirt at least.

We rounded the cliff on which I had watched him disappear earlier, walked several yards more, and then stopped.

"Look here, Miss Bennet—it is a cave, high and dry, secluded from the wind, and hidden away in this wood. Is not this a perfect shelter for the night?"

"A cave! But is it safe, Mr. Darcy? Are there not wild animals within or bats or some such things?"

"None that I found. I've already explored as far as I could, and I discovered nothing other than some ancient, broken crockery, which indicates that others have previously made use of its remoteness."

We advanced up the stone formation and entered the shallow hole cut in the side of the cliff. Once inside, I could see that it was actually smaller than it had appeared from a distance. Mr. Darcy explained that he had walked back as far as light permitted until the cave ended in a hole. It was possibly large enough for a person to slip through and might lead to an underground cavern. He had earlier made a loud commotion and tossed rocks down the hole, but received no response from below. Neither animal nor man emerged, and he deemed it safe enough for us to stay the night.

I was conscious that the light was already beginning to fade, and darkness could not be more than an hour away.

"I know that you are suffering from fatigue," he said. "Why not sit here against the cave wall and rest? Perhaps you might remove your shoes. You said that your feet hurt."

I sat down with relief, acknowledging that he spoke the truth. He picked up a portion of an old stone bowl and after wiping it out with his handkerchief, I emptied the berries into it. We then both ate our fill of the fruit.

"But for scones and sweet cream, we have dined sufficiently," I said with a smile. It amazed me how easily my outlook had improved with our recent discoveries.

"And a decanter of wine would not be unwelcome," he added.

"I would not refuse a tall beaker of water."

"Nor I." He stood up and walked to the mouth of the cave. "Listen! Do you hear that? Does it not sound like the faint whisper of the river?"

"I cannot hear it from here, sir. Wait a moment, and I will join you."

"No, no, do not rise. Remain there and rest. But I do believe we are not that far from the stream."

"Can you see it?"

"No, but if I climb down that slope and follow the noise, I could be there within a short while."

He looked around quickly, and spying an old chipped pitcher, he grabbed it up with a pleased exclamation. Determined to bring back enough water for the night, he promised to return before dark. Once again, he urged me to take off my shoes and rest.

"I shall not be long, less than an hour."

I hated to see him leave. "How will you find your way back? What if we are lost from each other?"

He knelt before me and took my hand in his. "That will not happen, Elizabeth, I promise you. I would never leave you."

With a brief squeeze of my hand, he rose once more and departed down the cliff and through the trees. In spite of what he said, I rose and walked to the cave's entrance, watching until I could no longer see any trace of him.

A shiver ran down my spine as I thought of how alone I was, at the mercy of whatever lurked without. Just then, however, an unexpected stream of late afternoon sunlight burst through the canopy of clouds above, illuminating my face. I smiled at its warmth, suddenly filled with thanksgiving. In this heavily overcast day, I counted one more treasure.

I turned back inside, sat down, and unlaced my boots. Pulling off my stockings, I noted light stains of blood. As feared, raw blisters had formed beneath two toes on my left foot. It felt good to expose them to air, even though it was cool within the cave. I massaged the other parts of my feet that were sore but not blistered.

Gradually, my body succumbed to the weariness accosting it, and before I knew it, I drifted into slumber. How long I slept, I know not, but I awoke to the sound of footsteps crackling the twigs strewn along the ground outside the cave.

I sat up quickly, unconsciously smoothing my hair with one hand and drawing my bare feet beneath my gown, in anticipation of Mr. Darcy's return. The steps grew closer and closer, and I could hear strong breathing. He must have run back, and now the climb through the rocks caused his laboured breath. I opened my mouth to call out his name in greeting, when I spied the faintest glimpse of his head moving through the leaves of the trees just outside the opening to the cave.

I did not cry out—my greeting caught in my throat. I began to tremble, my heart raced, and my hands turned to ice, for with dismay I saw that the approaching person's curls were not dark... but golden!

Chapter Seven

To say I was frightened would not do justice to the feeling that descended upon me at the sight of the person making his way straight toward the cave. I was terrified! I knew that it could be none other than Morgan.

With great haste, I arose, not even wincing when my swollen, blistered, bare feet touched the cave floor. Frantically, I looked around, my eyes darting here and there. I grabbed a large, jagged piece of broken pottery. I clasped it behind my back and edged toward the rear of the cave, hoping that simple crockery would somehow protect me from the gun I knew the highwayman bore.

Where could I hide? The only option lay behind me, and I could not force myself to crawl into that deep, dark hole. I had to take my chances above ground where I could at least see my adversary.

Two more steps and he appeared, breaking through the leafy cordon into the open. A look of utter astonishment spread over his face. "Mrs. Darcy!"

My eyes narrowed at his appearance. Dishevelled, hatless, and muddy, Morgan appeared nothing like the handsome, rakish man with whom I had danced the night before. He wore his coat on one arm, but casually slung over the opposite shoulder hung a black cape tied loosely around his neck. I watched him reel toward me as though he were heavily intoxicated.

"Begging your pardon, Missus, but I can no longer stand."

With that, he fell to the floor of the cave with a moan, his eyes rolling back in his head! I ran to the mouth of the cave and looked out. Seeing that no one followed behind, I threw the shard aside and knelt beside him.

"Mr. Morgan, what—what is wrong?"

His only answer was another moan and a plea for water.

"I have none," I answered, "but would it help to eat? I have berries."

He shook his head and turned over slightly, crying out as he did. And that is when I saw it—blood, a great amount of blood coursing down his right side. I must have inhaled audibly at the shock of it, for he opened his eyes then.

"Mmm, my apologies, Missus. Know I am a sorry sight, especially for one in your condition."

"What has happened to you?"

"Shot in the shoulder by me own men. Ain't that a pretty turn of the screw? And here I thought they were loyal boys."

"We must stop the bleeding."

"'Twill be hard to do. The hole's deep."

"Wait here, I'll be right back."

I ran outside the cave, and after quickly looking around to make certain I was alone, I slipped off my petticoat. Picking up a stick, I rammed it through the material until I got a good tear started, whereupon I ripped off the lower muddy hem and threw it aside. I then tore the remainder into strips, knotting them together until I had a fairly long piece of muslin. Returning to Morgan, I again knelt beside him and gently prodded him until he opened his eyes.

"What?" he cried, reaching for his pistol.

"It is I, Mr. Morgan, you need not fear."

"Mrs. Darcy...Elizabeth." He groaned again and attempted to raise himself.

"Let me bind your shoulder, sir."

Clumsily, I assisted him to a seated position and removed the part of his coat caked in blood. I bit my tongue to keep from crying out at the ugliness of the wound. If only I possessed water, at least I might have cleansed it, but the best I could do was to wrap the muslin around it tightly, attempting a poor, awkward excuse for a tourniquet. It was evident he had lost an inordinate amount of blood and was in dire need of medical attention.

"Mr. Morgan, where are we? How far is it to the nearest doctor?"

"Too far for me. I fear there's little assistance any surgeon can render at this stage."

"You do not know that for certain. If you direct me, I shall fetch help while you rest here in the cave."

"You'd do that for me?" He smiled slightly and raised his good arm, touching my face with his finger and running it down the curve of my cheek.

"I would do it for any man."

Well, perhaps not *any* man, I thought. It would take a bit more Christian grace than I possessed to tramp through the woods in the dark, especially if it were Sneyd touching my cheek in place of Morgan.

"Where's Darcy?" he asked suddenly. "Did he forsake you? Leave you stranded in this place?"

"He has gone to the river to fetch water. I could not—that is, my feet hurt, and he wanted me to rest."

"How gallant! Always the gentleman." His voice was mocking.

"He is," I retorted. "And a kind one at that."

"Ah, do I detect a change in your feelings for the man?"

"I fail to comprehend your meaning. Mr. Darcy is a generous, compassionate... husband."

He laughed softly. "But not *your* husband, Elizabeth, is he?"

His eyes held mine in the steadiest of gazes, and without a doubt, I knew that I could no longer keep up the pretence.

"He was never your husband, and you're not with child, correct?"

I looked away, refusing to confirm his suspicions, but convinced that nothing I said would persuade him otherwise.

"It no longer matters, Elizabeth. You can speak the truth now."

"What do you mean? Will you no longer harm Mr. Darcy or me?"

"I never would have harmed *you*. Darcy, well—" He shrugged and then winced in pain caused by the movement.

"What about the ransom? Have you received your money? Is that why you were shot? Did your men argue over the division of spoils?"

"You might say that. Truth is, that scum, Sneyd, convinced them to turn against me a'fore we even left to fetch it. Last night after you and I parted, I spent far too long with that bottle of wine and more tankards of ale than I remember."

He drew in a deep breath. "When I stepped out of the cabin, Sneyd and Rufus waylaid me, demanding to know where Darcy's uncle was to meet me with the ransom. Naturally, I refused to tell them, and that's when

Sneyd accused me of plotting to run off with it all. Said I was besotted with you and planned to take you with me. Well, he was half right—I am besotted, but my life's not one for a lady like you."

I was aghast at his statements! I felt little shock at Sneyd's mutiny, but to hear Morgan actually declare his feelings filled me with dismay.

I could not return his affection, and yet for some unknown reason, my heart overflowed with sorrow for him, for whatever misfortune had rendered him such an angry man, for the ill-fated choices that had brought him to this moment, and for his wasted life. In another time, another circumstance, who knows what he could have achieved?

He went on to relate how his encounter with Sneyd resulted in a brawl, and how it had ended with a pistol pointed at him until he revealed the planned destination for receipt of the ransom. Sneyd and Morgan both ran to mount their horses, and they exchanged gunshots, the results of which Morgan and his horse both suffered.

Then Sneyd and the others rode away, the other men casting their lot with him. Gert had run out to help Morgan, but he took off in pursuit of the gang, unaware that his horse had been shot.

"But not before you gave her the key to our room and told her to release us," I said.

With a great sigh, he closed his eyes and leaned his head back against the wall of the cave. His face contorted in pain, and I was at a loss at how to alleviate it.

I rose and walked to the entrance, scanning the woods for any sign of Mr. Darcy. Oh, why could he not appear? He would know what to do. My search proved fruitless. All I could see was an absence of that brief, earlier sunlight, and all that approached were dark clouds and the beginning of a light rain. I walked back to the wounded man and knelt at his side.

"Mr. Morgan, would you not be more comfortable lying down?"

He roused slightly, his eyes clouded with pain.

"Here," I said, dropping to my knees and sitting beside him, "rest your head in my lap."

"Your lap?" He looked confused. "I'll stain your frock."

"It is of little matter. Come, I shall help you." Gently, I aided him in turning to shelter his injured shoulder and place his head in my lap.

"Are you an angel, Elizabeth?" He attempted to smile. "My mother… she was an angel. I remember her touch—the softest ever—even though her hands were rough as bark from scrubbing and cleaning all day long. She deserved better..."

His voice trailed off, and once again, he closed his eyes. I felt the heat from his head and recognized that fever consumed him. If he fell asleep, I feared he might not awaken.

"Tell me about your mother, Mr. Morgan."

"Wha—" He attempted to open his eyes again.

"Your mother—you were speaking of her—does she live near here?"

He frowned. "She lives among the angels now. The hardness of her life with that lot that fathered me took her far too soon."

"I am sorry," I murmured.

"She was a maid in my father's house. A maid when she spoke like a lady."

He uttered the words with a bitterness the likes of which I had rarely heard. I urged him to continue, and so he told me that his mother had been born the seventh child of a poor country curate. The family had once been gentry, but the parish his grandfather served consisted of a majority of houses that had fallen into difficult times, resulting in a genteel type of poverty.

"Reared in a God-fearing house, she was, though. That's why she gave me a name from the Bible. From the time I could talk, she'd tell me I was called Nathanael, after the apostle. Do you know the story, Elizabeth?"

I shook my head.

"'Nathanael was a man without guile,' she'd say. 'See that you grow into your name, Son.' Yes, a man without guile," he said, closing his eyes. "No matter. She died a'fore I turned bad. At least she was spared that sorry truth."

When he did not speak further, I prodded him to return to the story, hoping to keep him awake as long as possible. At first, he refused, attempting to slip away into the insensible world, but when I would not relent, he resumed his tale.

As a young girl, his mother had been sent from home to board with and work for an innkeeper. His wife was an invalid who had been confined to her bed five years. Although a pretty girl, his mother was timid and helpless against her master's advances and subsequently gave birth to Morgan when she was but fifteen years old.

The innkeeper had a daughter only a few years younger than Morgan's mother. Surprisingly, the girl accepted her father's dalliance and helped care for the baby. A bond grew between them.

When the innkeeper's wife died a year later, he did the right thing and married Morgan's mother. For a while, the highwayman enjoyed a somewhat normal childhood although they never had much and life was difficult. From the time he was a small boy, he was forced to work hard alongside his mother and sister, and often he went to bed hungry. There was no time for schooling, but his mother insisted that he learn to speak correctly.

Then when he was not yet nine years old, his mother took sick and died. His father lost the inn because of unpaid taxes and a love for the bottle, and the orphaned children were sent to live with their paternal grandfather in the country.

I recalled his earlier anger at how his grandparents had lost the land on which the cabin sat. When I asked if it was the same, he nodded, confirming my suspicion. Morgan was a lad of fourteen when that happened. He and his grandparents attempted to live by odd jobs, but eventually, they were consigned to the workhouse where his grandmother soon died, and his grandfather followed not long afterwards.

His sister had gone to work as a scullery maid for a squire two years earlier, much as his own mother had. Morgan eventually escaped the poorhouse and struck out on his own, angry and bitter at how life had cheated his family.

"And the girl, your sister—what happened to her?"

His face darkened in a frown, and he closed his eyes tightly. "No more. Too tired."

Although I persisted with questions, he either fell asleep or refused to answer. I thought of the sad tale he had told and wondered whether it was true. But why should he lie? One rarely lies about one's mother.

When he began to groan and turn his head from side to side, I instinctively touched his forehead, smoothing his curls back and whispering soothing sounds, much as one would do for a child. Briefly, his eyes flickered open.

"Sing," he whispered.

I leaned my ear toward him, unable to believe what I had heard.

"Sing that song from last night, Elizabeth. My mother taught me that tune."

A spasm of pain gripped him, and he began to twist back and forth once again. Neither my touch nor consoling words relieved him, and so I began softly singing the ballad to which we had danced.

"Did you not hear my lady

Go down the garden singing"

As though given a calming tonic, he grew still and quiet and I continued.

"Blackbird and thrush were silent

To hear the alleys— "

"Do not let me interrupt you," said a voice laden with sarcasm.

I startled, ending the song in mid-sentence. "Mr. Darcy!"

So intent was I in observation of Morgan's feverish face, I had failed to hear his return.

Pulling Morgan's coat back, Mr. Darcy quickly removed the gun from his waistband. One glance at his face told me that he was furious to return to such a scene. With a single movement, he grasped Morgan by the throat and thrust him from my lap! The highwayman cried out with pain when Mr. Darcy attempted to pull him to his feet.

"How dare you touch her!" he said, his tone deadly. "I shall make you regret you ever laid a hand on her!"

"No!" I cried. "Mr. Darcy, I pray you, release him, he is badly hurt."

By that time, Morgan was fully conscious, and his coat fell open, revealing the bloody wound concealed beneath. Mr. Darcy's eyes widened in shock, and he pushed him away, allowing the highwayman to fall back against the side of the cave and slide down to a sitting position.

"Ah, Darcy," he muttered. "So we *must* meet again. Pity. I much prefer Elizabeth's company." He then fell over, slipping back into unconsciousness.

I immediately hastened to explain what had happened, relating Morgan's account of his men's treachery. "Will you not help me see to him? If I can use your handkerchief, perhaps I can wash away some of the blood."

"Do not waste the water I brought for that task when it is raining. Far better to give him a drink."

"Yes, of course," I said, reaching for the pitcher Mr. Darcy had set down at the entrance to the cave.

He took it from my hands. "But not before you have drunk your fill."

"Sir, he is injured."

"And he is a murdering thief. You are thirsty, Miss Bennet, and you shall drink first."

We stared at each other. How hard he could be! I took the pitcher from him and drank. The water did taste good. I had forgotten how thirsty I was, but when finished I wiped my mouth with my hand and said, "Is that enough, sir, or shall you insist upon a particular amount?"

Ignoring my sharp remark, he picked up an old chipped cup and filled it half-full with water. Kneeling, he raised Morgan's head and placed the cup against his lips.

"Come, man, drink." He shook him, and none too gently, until he roused somewhat and did as he was told. When finished, he let him lie back, closing his eyes.

"We must get help," I whispered. "He will die if we do not."

"And how do you suggest we accomplish that? Night has arrived and brought the beginnings of a storm, along with a strong north wind."

I glanced outside and saw that he spoke the truth. It was now pouring, and lightning flashed in the distance.

"Yes, conditions are not favourable, but you *could* go on to Hazleden, find a doctor, and return with him."

"And leave you here alone with Morgan?"

I nodded. "It would be impossible for us to carry him without some type of litter, and someone must stay to give him aid."

"Are your senses addled, Elizabeth? In the first place, it is highly unlikely that I could find my way out of this wood in the dark and rain. Even more important, I shall not leave you in this godforsaken place at the mercy of a highwayman!"

"Look at him! He cannot harm me now."

"But his men can. If Morgan knows the whereabouts of this cave, do you not think it likely that Sneyd and the rest of those ruffians do, as well?"

"He's right," Morgan said, attempting to rise to a sitting position. I was surprised that he had overheard us, for I supposed him to be asleep. "This cave's a favourite of many a highwayman. They say even the famous Dick Turpin used it. Of course, that was far before my time, but I believe 'tis true because I found his initials carved on the wall back yonder." He motioned with his head toward the rear of the enclosure.

"And how would *you* recognize his initials?" Mr. Darcy asked, a sardonic expression on his face. "You cannot read."

What? How did Mr. Darcy know that?

Morgan smiled slightly. "You're brighter than I figured. Tell me, just what did you write in that note to your uncle?"

"Enough so that you and your men would be met with sufficient force."

The outlaw smiled again. "Did you at least tell them to meet us at the place I named?"

"I did."

Morgan chuckled. "Sneyd may get his due then."

Mr. Darcy asked him how far away the appointed place lay. Morgan replied that it was thirty miles from the cabin, about fifteen miles the other side of Hazleden. The time for the meeting had been set for that morning, so most likely by now either Sneyd and the men had picked up the ransom or they had been apprehended. They never intended to return Mr. Darcy and me to the earl. Instead, they planned to send him on a fruitless chase in the opposite direction.

"And what were your plans for us?" I asked Morgan.

Mr. Darcy looked at me as though I were dim-witted. "What do you think? Tea and crumpets?"

My eyes widened, and I caught my breath at the thought! I turned back to Morgan. "Does Mr. Darcy speak the truth?"

"Do not waste your breath asking for a straight answer from him. He would just as soon shoot us as look at us." He strode across the floor of the cave and peered out into the night.

I, however, kept my eyes fixed on Morgan. "Tell me, would you have killed us?" He looked away and closed his eyes. "I do not believe it. You could not have—you would not have shot us!"

"Why do you find it so hard to comprehend?" Mr. Darcy asked. "Was he not bragging just last night about the last man he killed?"

I whirled around and faced him. "That was the *only* man he ever killed."

"Do you expect me to believe that?"

"Yes, I do. He killed a man in self-defence, the same man who scarred his face."

"Ah, Elizabeth," Morgan said, groaning as he attempted to raise his head. "Must you ruin my good name? People 'round here think I'm the worst of the lot. If you go spreading that tale, no one will be afraid of me."

"Then why did you tell me?" I asked softly.

"Yes," Mr. Darcy said. "Why did you? What happened between the two of you last night?"

Morgan did not answer. Instead, he fell over in a slump, this time truly slipping into an unreachable state. I dropped to my knees and attempted to rouse him. When he did not respond, I spread his cloak over him, hoping to provide as much protection from the elements as possible.

By then, it had grown exceedingly colder. The wind rustled through the branches outside. The rain whipped the remaining autumn leaves against the sides of the cave. I shivered even though I wore a pelisse made of wool. Glancing at Mr. Darcy, I realized that his clothes were damp, and he anticipated a long night without his greatcoat.

"I should have gathered wood while you were gone, sir. What could I have been thinking?"

"What, indeed," he muttered, stomping around the cave, obviously searching for anything we might use to build a fire. Two or three small tree branches had blown into the cave before we arrived. He began to strip them of leaves, snapping them into twigs with more force than necessary.

I ventured farther into the darker rear portion of the shelter. Finding a generous amount of dead leaves and debris blown up against the wall, I used my shoe as a broom, sweeping up the refuse into a pile. Kneeling, I gathered up the shavings into my skirt and carried them to the middle of the cave where Mr. Darcy had placed the broken twigs.

He had turned Morgan over and now untied the small flask of gunpowder attached to his belt. My pulse quickened when I saw him also retrieve a sizeable dagger encased in a sheath attached nearby. And then I gasped—a large amount of blood had escaped the wound and lay pooled beneath his body.

"Look, Mr. Darcy! He will bleed to death!"

"He will," he said in the most matter-of-fact voice, "unless we get a fire started."

"A fire? That will help keep him warm, but how can that save his life?"

He set to work as he talked, measuring and sprinkling gunpowder over the mound of dried leaves, grasses, and twigs. He then took Morgan's flintlock pistol and struck it against a sharp rock.

"If I can heat that knife blade, I can sear the wound. Do you think you can hold his hands still?"

"Of course," I said quickly.

He struck the rock again and a faint wisp of smoke appeared. "Even though he is ill," he cautioned, "he is much stronger than you."

With another strike the smoke increased. He lowered it to the powdered litter, blew gently, and the requisite flame ignited.

"Now, let us turn him again and remove the bandage."

I pulled Morgan's cape aside as Mr. Darcy leaned over his injured shoulder. A quizzical expression flickered across his face when he took off the makeshift tourniquet.

"What in blazes did he use for a binding?"

He held the bloodied muslin out and then a shock of recognition passed over his eyes, as a long strip of lace slipped through his fingers.

"Is this—does this garment belong to you?"

I attempted the haughtiest expression I could muster. "Desperation calls for unusual measures. Let us not haggle about my petticoat but apply immediate haste in tending this wound."

His look was unreadable, seemingly a combination of disapproval and grudging admiration. Shaking his head slightly, he turned back to the task at hand.

"Morgan!" he called. "Wake up, man! Can you hear me? Wake up!"

"Must we awaken him?"

"He needs to prepare himself for what is to come. The cauterisation will most likely make him pass out, so do not be alarmed when it happens. Morgan! I say, Morgan! Wake up." He shook him again and again. Finally, the man opened his eyes, but it was obvious that he could barely see us through the haze of pain.

"I am going to sear the wound, man. Mrs. Darcy shall grip your hands. You must allow her to do so and not interfere. It will hurt like the devil, but it has to be accomplished." Mr. Darcy knelt beside the highwayman, looked directly into his eyes, and spoke slowly and distinctively, as though to a child.

"Don't—don't take too great a pleasure in it, Darcy," Morgan managed to say. I then took his hands in mine, and Mr. Darcy plunged the knife blade into the fire.

"Do not watch, Mr. Morgan," I said. "Keep your eyes on me."

"Much rather do that anyways, Miss."

With one swift, deft movement, Mr. Darcy pulled the blade from the fire and placed it against Morgan's shoulder. The man jerked and screamed aloud—a terrifying cry that reverberated around the cave—and then, mercifully, he fainted. Even unconscious, though, his grip on my hands did not lessen.

Mr. Darcy continued to hold the knife on the wound for what seemed like forever, but could not have been more than a few seconds. Then, laying it aside, he untied his neckcloth, took it, along with his handkerchief, to the entrance of the cave and washed them in the rainfall without. He used them to cleanse blood from around the wound, rinsing out the cloths again and again. At last, he seemed satisfied and covered the seared flesh with the re-washed wet material.

Only then did he turn his gaze upon me. "Are you ill?"

I shook my head, conscious only of the way Morgan still clutched my hands. Gently, Mr. Darcy loosened his fingers and released me from the highwayman's hold.

"You have gone quite pale. Are you certain you are well?" He helped me up and moved me closer to the small fire. "Sit here and drink some water."

While I sipped from the pitcher, Mr. Darcy covered Morgan with the cape and made further attempts to make him as comfortable as one could be, lying on a stone floor.

As I watched him, my senses slowly returned. Sick to my stomach, I now wished I had not eaten the berries earlier. I raised my hand to brush a strand of hair from my face and was surprised to find it wet, not with rain, but tears. Unbidden, I had silently joined Morgan when he cried aloud.

At last, seemingly content that he had done what he could for the man, Mr. Darcy returned to the cave opening and washed his hands anew in the rainfall.

I marvelled with what skill he had cared for him, how he had taken command of the situation and done what was best. With mortification I thought of how unreasonable my idea had been. It would have been foolish, indeed, to send him off in the storm searching for a way out of that forest in the dark. My emotions had caused me to demand the impossible while his calm, rational manner had provided the best solution.

"Are you feeling better?" he asked, as he sat down beside me, and stretched his hands out to the warmth of the fire.

"Yes," I murmured.

"Good. 'Twill not do to have two patients on my hands."

I looked up to see a friendlier manner about his eyes.

"Mr. Darcy, I must ask you to forgive me. I fear that my alarm caused me to make foolish requests. I defer to your better judgment, and I am grateful for what you have done. If Morgan lives through the night, it will be due to your skill and wisdom."

"You must prepare yourself, Elizabeth, for the eventuality that he may not live."

I nodded.

"Will your heart survive if he does not?"

My heart! "I . . . I do not understand what you mean, sir."

He averted his face and stared into the fire. "I sensed . . . an attraction between you and Morgan. Am I correct?"

"You are incorrect! I am in no danger of a broken heart, whatever his outcome. I do feel for him — one could hardly refrain from doing so — but it is nothing more than pity. I cannot help but sympathize with the injury he has suffered. That does not mean that I condone the unwise choices he has made. No, Mr. Darcy, you are mistaken as to any attraction between us."

"Partly, perhaps."

"Do you not believe me? Would you accuse me of dishonesty?"

"I believe you are as truthful as you can be. You, however, may not know the true depth of your feelings. As for Morgan, I know he is enamoured."

My face began to burn and not from the heat of the diminishing fire.

"You say that you do not return such feelings," he said, "but then why in blazes, may I ask, did I arrive to find you singing to him while his head rested in your lap?"

It was his countenance that burned now, aflame with anger and — could it be jealousy? Had Mr. Darcy play-acted the role of husband so long that he now believed he had that right?

"I tried to soothe him. He was feverish and restless, out of his head for the most part, and I sang simply to ease him somewhat."

"That tune sounded oddly familiar. It seems that I recall hearing the faintest snatches of it last evening when I listened at the door while you had dinner with Morgan. You then returned in tears and refused to tell me what had transpired. What is it you are hiding? Did the man make advances toward you?"

I closed my eyes in regret and resignation. He insisted on hearing the story, and eventually I gave in, telling him how Morgan had demanded that I sing and dance with him. He was angry that I suffered such humiliation, but he continued to probe, asking leading questions until he asked the one query I hated to answer.

"Did Morgan make love to you?"

When I told Mr. Darcy that the highwayman tried but that I rebuffed him, he rose and began to pace the short circumference of the cave.

At long last, he stilled and stood peering out into the rain. Almost at that very moment, the small fire consumed the final twig, flaring up for a moment only to vanish, plunging our shelter into darkness. A strong gust of wind blew in, and I shivered, pulling my coat closer.

"Well, that is the end of our fire," he said, turning back to face me. "The night is growing colder quickly. Should you not replace your shoes?"

I agreed if he would grant me privacy. While he turned his back, I scrambled to pull on my stockings and shoes. Although my feet still hurt, I was glad to see that the brief absence of wearing boots had allowed the swelling to subside somewhat.

We discussed the best place for me to sleep, agreeing that the back of the cave would be most protected from the elements. He then checked on our patient once again, felt his forehead, and placed his ear upon his chest to make sure he breathed.

"He is still feverish but, fortunately for him, in a deep sleep."

Mr. Darcy then announced that he would remain near Morgan in case he grew restless during the night. I wondered how he would face the cold with his greatcoat lost in the briar patch.

"Sir, how shall you stay warm? You have nothing with which to cover yourself."

He rubbed his hands together. "I fear it will be a long night."

For some reason I could not bear the thought of Mr. Darcy shivering through the night, cold and wet while I wore a warm coat. All through this ordeal, he had done much for me. Why, a lesser man might have abandoned me to the highwaymen while Mr. Darcy went out of his way to protect me. What could I do to help him keep warm?

Of a sudden, a shocking thought crossed my mind! Did I dare give voice to it?

I swallowed twice before speaking. "You must—well, that is—why not allow me to share my coat with you tonight, for you could grow ill with the mere protection of a redingote?"

He immediately refused, protesting that my pelisse was much too small for the two of us.

"But your clothing is quite damp from your walk through the rain," I replied, "making you easily susceptible to a dangerous chill. I insist that you be sensible, for I cannot care for two patients either!"

"I am only a bit damp, not wet through. I reached the cave before the rain descended in earnest. I shall be well."

I knew that was not true, that once again he was putting my interests before his own. "I cannot rest unless you agree to share my coat."

He looked at me in amazement. "Elizabeth, it simply will not do. We...well, we would be forced to lie—that is, to be exceedingly close together in order to share such a narrow little coat, for your figure is light and pleas—" He cleared his throat. "I could not impose upon you."

I sighed deeply. "Have we not shared a blanket three nights, sir? I believe I know you well enough to be assured you are not a man who takes advantage of a woman. It is not an imposition. I insist. I do not need to lie down. Can we not sleep sitting up?" I motioned toward an area in the rear of the enclosure. "Why not over here with our backs against the cave wall."

In the dim light, I could just make out the sceptical look in his eyes and the way his chest heaved as he sighed. "Very well, but I suggest we sit nearer Morgan. If he becomes restless or worsens during the night, one of us will awaken."

And so it came about that, somewhat awkwardly, we sat down, Mr. Darcy placing himself on the side closest to Morgan. I had unbuttoned my coat, removed it, and now opened it up to spread over the two of us. I quickly felt the lack of my petticoat, for the cold penetrated my muslin gown and undergarments. I shivered and drew up my knees so that they might benefit from the wrap.

Mr. Darcy was right, however, about the insufficiency of the garment. It covered neither of us. No matter how we turned it about, the wool pelisse was simply too small.

He pressed his lips together, looked around, and then once more cleared his throat.

"I trust you understand, Miss Bennet, that I am not attempting liberties, but if you would turn a bit more toward me and, uh, allow me to place my arm... here behind your head—" He gently slipped his arm around my shoulders, also turning toward me and drawing me into an embrace. "There. Now, rest your knees against my leg. Is that—is that too distressing?"

"No." For some reason, I was unable to manage more than a whisper.

"And if you—well, if you care to—you might lay your head on my shoulder." He slipped his other arm around my waist and pulled me even closer. "Now, are you warmer?"

"Yes," I whispered again. I wondered if anyone's skin had ever literally caught fire from the heat of a man's arm. If not, mine might be the first.

"And your coat now covers more of both of us. That is much better, so let us try to sleep. Good night, Elizabeth."

I could not answer. Every part of my body felt as though it were aflame! Never had I felt this way before—not when any young man had held my hand or briefly touched my waist when dancing, certainly not when Sneyd had clasped me to him in that vile, repulsive way, and not even when Morgan had held me against his wildly beating heart.

It was a familiar feeling, akin to the sensation I had experienced when Mr. Darcy held me last night, but now magnified a thousand times. This embrace was all encompassing, for I very nearly sat in his lap.

Not only could I feel the taut strength of his body, but the smooth power of his shoulder on which I lay, and the hypnotic rhythm beating in his strong chest beneath my cheek. My forehead nestled into his neck now exposed by his open shirt and the earthy, heady scent of his skin pervaded my senses. How could I find it pleasing when he had not washed in days?

What was happening to me?

"And Elizabeth?"

"Yes," I said, breathlessly.

"Do not fear the arrival of Morgan's men tonight. I have his gun and knife within reach."

"Thank you, sir. That is most reassuring."

How I lied! Reassurance was not what I felt at all!

If truth were told, I did not fear what lay without that cave. I feared what lay within... and most of all, what had taken hold of my heart.

Chapter Eight

If I live to be a woman of great age, so old that the majority of my memory fades, I shall never forget that night I spent in the cave with Mr. Darcy—or the morning after.

More than once during those dark, bitter hours, Mr. Darcy arose to tend Morgan. Bathing the highwayman's face anew each time did little to lessen his fever, but it seemed to comfort him and ease his restless thrashing about. Upon each occurrence, I scarcely awakened—I admit this to my shame—but dozed against the cave wall, missing the comfort of Mr. Darcy's warmth. With his every return, I gladly opened my coat, hurriedly cuddled close to him, and welcomed his strong, consoling embrace.

Evidently, some hours before daylight, the rain ceased, leaving a raw dampness in the air that seemed to permeate my bones. That time before dawn has always proved to be my deepest sleep, and fortunately, it did the same for our patient, for he did not awaken us for some time. The dimmest glimmer of sunrise filtered into my sleep-addled senses before I struggled toward wakefulness.

When I did open my eyes, I was amazed to discover that I lay across Mr. Darcy's chest, my mouth against his face, his arms clasped tightly around my back and waist! I thought it was but a dream—that I could not possibly have slipped into that position. The last I remembered, we had been sitting up, and now it seemed we had slid down upon the floor of the cave.

As I attempted to lift my head, my lips brushed against his cheek. Instinctively, he turned toward me, his eyes still closed. Before I knew what had happened, I found his mouth upon mine, his lips searching, pressing more and more until... my own lips parted. Deliciously, he began to kiss me with an increasing, intoxicating fervour. I felt helpless and could do nothing other than respond in kind. Still drugged in the early haze of sleep and drowning in this unexpected, pervasive passion, I felt my mouth go soft and slack, surrendering to his provocative exploration.

His arms tightened around me, and he began stroking my back, one hand finding its way to the back of my neck. I became conscious that my own fingers now tangled among his curls, caressing the silky strands again and again.

"Well, seems I was mistaken."

The sound of that statement jarred my senses as though a wild animal screamed in my ear. Immediately I awakened fully, as did Mr. Darcy! Opening his eyes, he gazed at me, as shocked as if he saw a spirit. Quickly we released each other, turning toward the voice. We sat up to see that Morgan was conscious—all too conscious it would appear.

"And here I thought you didn't care for him, Elizabeth. Won't be the first time a pretty face fooled me. Hate to interrupt, but I'm bedevilled with a powerful thirst." He still remained on the floor where he had lain all night, although he had now turned his face toward us.

Mr. Darcy jumped up, raked a hand through his hair, and straightened his waistcoat. He picked up the pitcher of water and took it to Morgan. Although the man could talk, he was still too weak to lift his head and had to rely upon Mr. Darcy for aid.

I, too, quickly rose and self-consciously attempted to smooth my skirt and hair. It was a hopeless task, however, and I donned my pelisse to cover my wrinkled clothing.

Unable to face either man, I walked to the mouth of the cave and stepped outside. The ground was soaked, the leaves on the trees laden with remnants of last night's raindrops. The approaching sunrise made them twinkle and sparkle like fairy lights. The wind had ceased, and although it was cold, the world seemed suddenly brand new.

Or was it my life that was brand new?

My lips still throbbed with the memory of his kiss, and surely I glowed from head to toe. How had such a thing happened? Why had he kissed me? And even more important, why had I kissed him back? Could I be in love with Mr. Darcy? Did that explain this tempest running amok within my heart?

Before I could think clearly, he stood beside me. I turned expectantly, but I did not know whether to smile or speak. What anticipation did he hold? He met my eyes briefly, and I was stunned to see the tortured expression therein before he turned away.

"Miss Bennet—Elizabeth, I…I hardly know what to say. I do not know what possessed me to forget myself in that manner. I can only ask you to forgive me. I never should have—if I had been more awake—" He sighed deeply. "I am floundering. I pray you understand it was all a mistake."

Mistake! He thought our kiss a mistake?

His words could not have stung more if he had struck me. My heart fell to my feet, and I forced myself not to sway visibly. Tears misted my vision, and all I desired was to escape his presence. Where could I flee?

I heard him say my name once more, but I lowered my head to the ground, unwilling to allow him witness to my emotion. Swallowing, I steeled myself to quell my shaking voice.

"Then let us not speak of it again," I said softly.

"But do you not want to—that is, should we not discuss—"

I shook my head. "I pray you will excuse me, Mr. Darcy. I need some time alone." Quickly, I stepped away from the cave and hurried into the sanctity of the woods.

"Of course," he called after me, "but take care that you do not stray farther than privacy demands."

My body's needs did demand compliance, but I wandered much farther than necessary. Over and over his words echoed in my head—*a mistake!* I was *a mistake.* Kissing me was *a mistake.*

Of course, it was. How could I dare to imagine he might love me? I was a fool, an utter fool. Again and again I berated myself with such thoughts. What must he think of me? Did he consider me wanton, a girl who shamelessly allowed such licence? Why had I lost control so easily and given in to him?

I had felt as powerless as a tiny leaf blown about in a great wind, unable or unwilling to resist the strength of his passion. I trembled, thinking how natural and easy it had been to allow him command over both my body and my heart.

And now, what would I do? How could I face him? Once again, all my old fears of what lay before me if and when we reached safety surfaced anew. Not only had I portrayed the role of Mr. Darcy's wife, I had shared a room and blanket with him night after night. Although we knew that we were innocent, what would society think when our story was revealed?

Perhaps it would not have to be known. I could not imagine that Mr. Darcy would reveal it willingly, but then I thought of the witnesses to his declaration that we were married—not just the highwaymen if they were apprehended, but Miss Bingley, Mrs. Hurst, and the servants attending the carriage. There would be many questions, and I had little hope that my honour could survive unscathed.

After this morning, I did not even feel I should escape censure, for surely my behaviour demanded such. I began to question myself anew—my motives, my foolishness, and my helplessness in the grip of Mr. Darcy's affections. Did I love him, and if so, how could I? Much of the time, I did not even like the man!

No, that last thought was false. I did like him. I admired him. I respected his strength, his intelligence, his courage and compassion. Heaven knows I did not always agree with him, but I knew him better than I had when we began this journey, and yet, I felt as though I barely knew him at all.

He was a reserved man, a quiet man, a man who rarely revealed his emotions, but still, had I not witnessed a greater range this week than he had exposed during his entire visit to Hertfordshire? Had I not seen him angry, arrogant, foolishly brave, and yet kind, tender and wise? And had I not caught but a glimpse of the raw passion he kept hidden from the world? I closed my eyes, remembering the unleashed force of his affection and wondering what greater depths lay just below the surface.

I shook my head, trying to erase the longing now awakened in my heart. Surely, the last four days and everything we had endured together had created a false intimacy, causing me to believe I cared more deeply for him than I truly did. After all, we had been deprived of restful sleep, catching what we could here and there. Our senses had been on constant heightened alert, and we had been thrust into each other's sole company with little escape both day and night. Surely, that could be the cause for my lapse in judgment, could it not?

With sudden swiftness, Mr. Wickham's accusations echoed about me. I recalled the harshness with which Mr. Darcy had treated him and Morgan, as well. Then I thought of his solicitous care of the highwayman through the night. I felt utterly bewildered.

Who was the man?

I cried for some time, but at last my tears subsided and sanity returned. Leaning against a tree, I had not noticed that its rain-soaked bark dampened my pelisse until I attempted to wipe my eyes and found my hands already wet from pressing against the tree trunk. At that point I was past concern for my appearance. What difference would it make to wear a wet coat?

I pushed my hair back, using my fingers to search for possible hairpins. I was relieved to discover the last two I owned and had just begun to pin a few strands back when I heard a horse whinny and crash through the underbrush!

"Who goes there?" a man's voice shouted.

I darted behind the tree and cowered low, hoping he could not see me. I heard him alight from the horse. I held my breath as his steps drew nearer, thinking surely my heart would jump from my chest.

Dear God, I prayed, *please do not let it be Sneyd!*

I heard the click of a cocked gun and screwed my eyes shut. If I were to be shot, I did not want to see it coming.

"Well, now!" the man said in wonder. I opened my eyes to see a gun pointed straight at me, but to my amazement, I found that it was not Sneyd who held it, but a handsome soldier, instead. He smiled and lowered the weapon.

"And who might you be?" When I did not answer, he asked, "Do you live around here? Have you seen a man and a woman travelling the roads?"

I shook my head, the only response I could manage.

"His name is Darcy, and she is Miss Bennet. Are you certain you have not seen them?"

My eyes now widened in wonder. "I—I am Elizabeth Bennet, sir."

"Capital! I cannot believe my good fortune! My men and I have been searching for you and for my cousin, Darcy. Is he with you?"

"Your cousin?"

"I am Colonel Richard Fitzwilliam."

I let out my breath with a great sigh. "Oh Colonel, I—I cannot tell you how glad I am that you are here!"

After I told him that Darcy and the highwayman were at the cave, he fired three shots in the air as a signal to his men. He then offered me his arm, and I led him up the path to the shelter.

On the way, I attempted to relate the major events that had transpired since Mr. Darcy and I had been released from the cabin and found the cave. He had questions as to Morgan's condition, which I answered to the best of my ability.

"Mr. Darcy seared the wound last night, and it is because of his good care that the highwayman awakened this morning."

"Well, I shall recommend my cousin's nursing skills to my physician," he said, laughing. "Perhaps he can find employment there if he should ever lose his fortune."

I liked the colonel. He was pleasant and agreeable, easy to converse with, and by the time we reached the cave, I felt comfortable in his company.

Mr. Darcy, however, met us with Morgan's pistol drawn and ready!

He, too, was much relieved upon recognition of his relative, and soon eight or nine more uniformed men had ascended to the cave. All of the soldiers were on foot, other than the colonel, having left their horses at the road in order to comb the woods more thoroughly.

They made short work of preparing a litter on which to carry the injured man, cutting down small saplings and using ropes from someone's pack to attach a blanket. Four of them held the litter while two more picked up Morgan and deposited him thereon. They did not take pains to lift him gently, but instead almost tossed him onto the makeshift device.

He cried out in pain, and I immediately stepped forward to assist him, but Mr. Darcy caught my arm, restraining me.

"Let him be," he said quietly. "'Twill not do to make a fuss over an outlaw."

"But he is seriously injured!"

"They are aware of the fact. You must not make a scene."

He held my arm none too lightly, and I was forced to acquiesce to his command. My better sense told me he was right, that I must remember to caution my responses, for the time of censure had arrived. My heart, however, yearned to give the poor man some measure of comfort.

Colonel Fitzwilliam approached us then and offered me his horse for the journey into Hazleden. "You look fairly haggard yourself, Darce. Perhaps you should ride as well, if Miss Bennet does not object."

I shrugged slightly, but Mr. Darcy declined, stating that he could easily walk the distance. However, when he walked somewhat unsteadily as we left the cave and had to reach out and grab a branch to gain his balance, the colonel insisted. "Here man, when is the last time either of you has eaten?"

I told him of the blackberries I had discovered last evening, but he brushed aside such simple fare, declaring that Mr. Darcy and I were probably both faint from hunger.

"Come on, Darce, swallow your pride and take the horse. I shall not have my men in need of constructing another litter. It is a good seven miles to the village."

With reluctance, Mr. Darcy mounted the great, black mare. He then reached down to lift me up as Colonel Fitzwilliam assisted me.

I caught my breath when Mr. Darcy's hands encircled my waist, and my pulse quickened as he settled me on the horse directly in front of him. It seemed that once more we were forced to endure each other's close company. I held myself rigid, leaning forward, striving not to nestle against his chest, but it was impossible. The horse took a single step, and I bounced backward. His arms closed around me as he held the reins, and I did my best not to tremble in his embrace.

The colonel walked beside us, and he and Mr. Darcy conversed for much of the first hour. They had caught Sneyd and the rest of the highwaymen the day before when they arrived to retrieve the ransom. Evidently, they were unskilled in the finer points of such treachery, and their innate ignorance contributed to their fairly easy apprehension.

Colonel Fitzwilliam stated that from what he had learned, they were a second-rate bunch of ruffians, lacking experience in the crime of kidnapping. They preferred local petty thievery and only recently had progressed into highway robbery.

"Highwaymen are, for the most part, a scourge of the past," the colonel said. "Unfortunately, this bunch strayed from their usual haunts and happened upon your carriage. A singular matter of bad luck, one might say."

"Indeed," was Mr. Darcy's only reply.

"I found it surprising that they should hold you for ransom. In truth, I doubted those chaps had the intelligence to think of such a scheme."

"They did not," Mr. Darcy said. "I fear that it was my idea."

"Yours? But why?"

"Because of me, sir," I said, joining the conversation for the first time. "They threatened to abscond with me, and Mr. Darcy spoke up for my protection."

"I see. Well, we shall return to civilization within the hour, and I trust neither of you is the worse for wear. Miss Bennet, I do hope that you, in particular, may quickly put this dreadful experience behind you."

I nodded but knew within my heart that it would be an exceedingly long time before I forgot one moment of this journey.

Shortly thereafter, the colonel left us, walking back to check on the prisoner in answer to a request from his aide. I felt the loss of his presence. Now even more than before, I was aware of how Mr. Darcy's arms encircled me, and how the canter of the horse caused us to sway back and forth against each other. And even more alarming, I was intensely aware of how silent Mr. Darcy remained now that we were alone.

I felt certain this would be the last time in my life that I would ever feel his arms about me.

THAT EVENING I WAS TO join Colonel Fitzwilliam and Mr. Darcy for dinner. Hazleden was not a large town, similar in size to Meryton, but it possessed more than one inn, and the colonel had made arrangements for us to spend the night at the finest the community had to offer. He had carried from Town a change of clothes for Mr. Darcy and one for me that my aunt had prepared.

I was most interested in his recital of how things had transpired in our absence, especially as to my family. Mrs. Hurst and Caroline Bingley had been forced to endure captivity in the carriage with the menservants for several hours before the men eventually succeeded in kicking the carriage door open. The highwayman had not only securely closed the door, but tied it shut as well.

I could imagine their suffering! Two gentlewomen bound and gagged with three menservants similarly constrained, all stuffed into the inside of Mr. Bingley's carriage, which was crowded when transporting only four passengers, and the servants attempting to kick open a securely-tied door when they, themselves, had their feet bound? Abominable, I am sure, but I was forced to chew my lip to refrain from smiling at the thought.

During the colonel's recital of these facts on our journey into Hazleden, I wondered if Mr. Darcy shared my amusement at such a vision. He did not indicate thus, and I quickly subdued such ill-timed thoughts. Was it only the day before that we had given ourselves up to the shared joy of uncontrollable laughter?

After being rescued by a mail coach, the sisters had reached London that first night, while we were held in captivity at the highwayman's cabin. They had immediately dispatched a messenger to the Earl of Matlock, who arrived upon their doorstep well past midnight. He had then sent express posts to Hertfordshire early that very morning, one to Mr. Bingley and Mr. Hurst and another to my father.

The gentlemen, along with my father and Jane, had arrived in London the next afternoon, and Colonel Fitzwilliam and his father had spent hours with the men discussing possible rescue attempts.

When I asked as to my father's health, the colonel assured me that although worried, he remained well. Mr. Bingley had retrieved my trunk, and he and the colonel had escorted my father and Jane to the home of the Gardiners that evening. The colonel remarked how pleased he was to meet them. I wondered at Mr. Darcy's reaction to such approval by his cousin of my Cheapside connections, but he remained silent the entire time.

At the inn, I endured curious stares while making my way upstairs to my quarters. Mr. Darcy and I were a surprising pair I am sure—dirty, unkempt and shockingly road worn.

Never had I enjoyed a bath more than the one I took in that small room above stairs. After washing my hair and scrubbing the journey's filth from my body, I asked the maid to refill the tub with clean, steaming water. I then dismissed her for a half-hour's time and simply soaked, revelling in the comfort derived from such luxury.

When the clock struck eight times, I knew that I must make my way to the dining room to join the gentlemen's table. The maid had assisted me in dressing, and I was pleased that my aunt had sent one of my favourite gowns, a pale green frock. I surmised that Jane had suggested it, for she knew my preferences as well as I did.

With a final peek in the mirror, I was about ready to leave the room. The girl had done well with my coiffure, but I peered closer in the glass. Circles lay beneath my eyes, and my face had grown thin.

What did it matter? I asked myself. There was no one below who would notice my looks.

Upon descending the stairs, I saw both gentlemen in earnest conversation at the table. As I made my way into the room, Mr. Darcy saw me first. They both stood and bowed while I curtseyed. How strange that we so quickly reverted back to society's formality, I thought, when only hours earlier, Mr. Darcy and I had undergone days of familiarity with each other.

I could not fail but admire Mr. Darcy's appearance. It was amazing what a bath, shave, and a change in clothes could do for that gentleman's image. He was remarkably handsome, and although he did not smile, I thought I detected a light in his eyes when he said my name.

"Miss Bennet, I see you have benefited from a return to civilization."

"She certainly has!" Colonel Fitzwilliam declared. "You look utterly charming."

I smiled and assured them that I was more than pleased to reacquaint myself with the niceties of life. I had rested over an hour on a soft feather bed.

"Is it not pleasant to have a pillow once more?" Mr. Darcy asked.

"Indeed it is, sir."

"Do you mean to say that while held at that cabin you did not even have a pillow, Miss Bennet?" the colonel asked.

"Nor a bed, sir." I laughed lightly, but then caught Mr. Darcy's eye and saw him frown with the barest shake of his head as though he were warning me not to speak further of our sleeping arrangements.

"That is insufferable! Where did those barbarians make you sleep?"

"The floor was our only option," Mr. Darcy interjected. "Shall we not speak of more pleasant subjects?"

"Of course," his cousin replied, as he filled our glasses from the carafe of wine placed on the table. He could not conceal the curious expression about his face, however, or the way he looked from Mr. Darcy to me and back again.

Fortunately, the serving girl appeared then, and we gave ourselves up to partake of the steaming plates put before us.

The colonel did attempt to speak of more mundane matters—discussion of the recent rains, the approaching Christmas season, and he questioned Mr. Darcy as to the abundance of sport in Hertfordshire—but by the close of the meal, our conversation inevitably returned to the harrowing experience we had just undergone. He informed us that he had dispersed a contingency of his men to the cabin to apprehend the woman.

"Gert? But why?" I asked. "She did not harm us. In truth, she is the one who released us."

"Yes, but she is a material witness, and it is up to Darcy as to whether he wishes to press charges against her for aiding and abetting in the crime."

When I turned to him, his expression was non-committal. "I think it best that she at least be questioned," he said.

"I fail to see any reasoning behind that statement," I said emphatically.

The colonel smiled. "Best to let us sort it out, would you not agree, Miss Bennet?"

No, I did not agree, but I bit my tongue and purposefully tried to modulate my tone. "What about the highwayman? Has he received medical attention?"

Instantly Mr. Darcy's eyes met mine, but it was the colonel who answered. "Yes, he has, and Mr. Jones removed the bullet about an hour ago. It seems you were correct. My cousin's amateur doctoring proved to stem the loss of blood, and if all goes as planned, the rogue should be healthy enough to join his mates in Newgate and heal in time for trial."

"Shall Morgan be imprisoned with the men who shot him? Surely, that would prove dangerous, would it not, Colonel?"

"Well, they will be bereft of weapons, so I see little to fear."

"Yes, but— "

"You must not worry about the highwayman's benefit. After all, he had little concern for yours," the colonel answered.

"I beg to differ, sir. Although Morgan did take us hostage, I believe ultimately it was he who was responsible for our freedom."

"What? I thought you said the woman released you."

"She did," Mr. Darcy said, "but she told us Morgan gave her the key."

"And while imprisoned, it was Morgan who allowed us certain necessities that added to our comfort," I added.

"Well, you owe him little gratitude for that. I would not describe sleeping on the floor as a comfort," Colonel Fitzwilliam replied.

"No, but— "

"What Miss Bennet means," Mr. Darcy interrupted, "is that in the long run, Morgan proved less menacing than his men, although that hardly proves him guiltless." He turned a piercing gaze upon me. "Would you not agree?"

I nodded and said nothing more. What could I say? Morgan *was* guilty of kidnapping, robbery, and extortion. The fact that he had saved me from Sneyd's attack or that he had spared us by allowing our release did not absolve him of those crimes. And yet, I longed for the colonel or whatever authorities who held him at least to know of his background and all that had happened to him. How could I speak of it, however, without appearing to favour the man?

I sipped from the glass of wine, my mind miles from the scene before me.

"Is that not true, Miss Bennet?" Colonel Fitzwilliam broke my musing, and I was ashamed to know nothing of what he asked. I begged his pardon, and he repeated the question, something about the beauties of the Hertfordshire countryside. I murmured my concurrence, and he continued.

"I recall visiting a portion of that county a few years back, and I enjoyed it immensely."

"Oh? I wonder that we did not meet," I said.

"My visit was constrained to the southern portion. Is not Netherfield somewhat north, Darce, near Meryton, I believe you said?"

Mr. Darcy nodded.

"I have never travelled through there. But since meeting you, Miss Bennet, I shall look forward to exploring that part of the country. Now, if you had proved to be part of the family that Darcy wrote and warned me about, it would be another story, would it not, Cousin?" He laughed and raised his eyebrows at Mr. Darcy, which pricked my interest.

"And what family might that be?" I asked.

"I do not know their name, but Darce here was all up in arms over some frantic husband-hunting mother with a houseful of unmarried daughters. Seems she handpicked his young friend, Bingley, for one of them, and it was all that Darcy could do to talk the man out of declaring himself."

My pulse began to race. I felt as though the blood had drained from my face. "Indeed? How interesting! Mr. Darcy is uncommonly kind to Mr. Bingley and takes prodigious care of him."

"Care of him! Yes, I believe Darcy does take care of him in those points where he most wants care. I would think Bingley very much indebted to him."

Mr. Darcy had begun to squirm in his chair. He sat up straighter, coughed lightly, and placed his hand at his throat as though his neckcloth might be in danger of strangling him.

"What is it you mean?" I asked. "Did Mr. Darcy give you his reasons for this interference?"

"I understood that there were some very strong objections against the lady, is that not correct, Darce?"

"Well, uh— " Mr. Darcy said.

"Is that true, sir? Do tell us." I demanded. "And why were you to be the judge? Why should you determine and direct in what manner your friend is to be happy?"

He stared at me, looked away, opened his mouth, and then closed it.

Colonel Fitzwilliam evidently was not even slightly aware of his cousin's discomfiture, for he simply laughed. "Believe me, Darcy rarely interferes unless it is warranted. All I can say is he is exceedingly fortunate that you, Miss Bennet, were the one to accompany him on this journey and not a daughter of that fortune-hunting mother. Would you not agree, Cousin?"

Mr. Darcy picked up his glass and took a long drink from it. I took the opportunity to rise from the table, which, naturally, caused both men to stand, also.

"Miss Bennet?" the colonel asked. "Are you unwell?"

"A sudden headache," I replied. "Perhaps I have tarried over the wine too long. If you will excuse me, gentlemen." I smiled at the colonel and turned aside.

Mr. Darcy pulled back my chair. "I shall see you to your room."

I turned and stared at him with an expression I made certain he could not mistake.

"Do not trouble yourself, sir. Stay and enjoy your wine *and* your talk. Perhaps you can further enlighten the colonel on the savagery of Hertfordshire society. I am perfectly capable of finding my own way. Good night."

Before he could make any response, I fled the table, but not before I heard Mr. Darcy admonish the colonel. "Fitzwilliam, have you taken leave of your senses? Must you repeat everything I tell you?"

I hurried up the staircase into the sanctuary provided by my room. Dropping my shawl upon the bed, I walked to the fireplace, grabbed the poker and jabbed viciously at the burning log. I was breathing heavily, my anger blazing as much as the fire before me. I began to pace back and forth, chewed my lip, and clenched my fists.

Very strong objections to the lady! How those words echoed round and round in my mind. Oh yes, and I knew exactly what those strong objections were—she had one uncle who was a country attorney and another who was in business in London.

"To Jane herself," I exclaimed aloud, "there could be no possibility of objection, all loveliness and goodness as she is! Her understanding excellent, her mind improved, and her manners captivating. Neither can anything be urged against my father who, though with some peculiarities, has abilities which Mr. Darcy himself need not disdain and respectability which he will probably never reach!"

When I thought of my mother, however, my confidence gave way, and I could not deny the imprudent behaviour of my younger sisters. Those objections, though, would have little material weight, were it not for Mr. Darcy's pride. Their want of sense would warrant a wound, but not as deeply as that of our connections. Yes, it was that worst kind of pride that had produced such venomous interference on Mr. Darcy's part.

How had I ever thought he might love me, I wondered, and even more, why had I ever entertained the idea that I loved him? It cried against my every belief. I had hoped to be swept up by love and that I would not have to marry without it. I knew for certain that I could not possibly love a man whose character I found sorely lacking.

I threw myself across the bed, pounded the pillow until feathers began to fly, and then I buried my face in my hands and began to weep.

What a fool I had been! How had I allowed myself to indulge in such fantasy?

And what was I to do with this aching need deep within me—this horrid betrayal of all I espoused—this painful, physical yearning to be held in his arms in spite of everything?

Chapter Nine

I did not speak to Mr. Darcy again until the time came to board the carriage and return to London the next day. Sometime during the evening before, a maid had entered my room with a message that the gentleman wished to see me, but I refused, instructing her to tell him that I had retired for the night. I was far too angry to trust myself to speak with him in a civil manner.

I still could not believe he had actively interfered between Mr. Bingley and Jane and then bragged about it in a letter to Colonel Fitzwilliam. I certainly was not interested in hearing any trumped-up excuses he might attempt to render.

Even though it was the first night I slept in a real bed in five days, my sleep was disturbed, and I spent far too many restless hours. The next morning the circles under my eyes appeared even more prominent, but with a maid to dress my hair and proper clean clothing, I at least felt presentable.

At my request, I breakfasted alone in my room on sausages, muffins, and steaming hot tea. I had just risen from the small table when the maid reappeared, stating that I was wanted below stairs.

"I told you to extend my regrets for breakfast," I said. "Did you not tell Mr. Darcy and Colonel Fitzwilliam?"

"Beggin' your pardon, Miss, it is not those gentlemen who ask for you."

"Then who?"

"It's an older gentleman, Miss, and a young lady," the maid replied. "They didn't give me their names, but they're ever so eager to meet with you."

I was dumbfounded as to their identity, for I knew no one who lived in

Hazleden. With a quick pat of my hair and a glance in the mirror, I left the room and made my way downstairs. The maid led me into the public room, and in a far corner, I saw the two souls I desired to see most in this world!

"Papá! Jane!" I cried, almost running into their outstretched arms. We kissed each other and embraced, my father clutching me closely in spite of the arena in which we met.

"Lizzy," he said softly, his eyes misting. "I feared I might never see you again."

"Oh, Father, I am well. Do not distress yourself."

"You look so tired," Jane said, openly crying. "You have deep circles under your eyes and scratches on your face and hands. Was it so very horrid?"

"Not so very." I smiled, attempting to make light of all that had happened, hoping to put them at ease. We sat down at the table, and the servant brought another cup and saucer for me. "The cuts shall heal. In truth, I have emerged without scars and nothing worse than these dark circles, which will soon vanish when I have slept in my own bed once more. You may depend upon it."

"Oh, Lizzy," Jane said, squeezing my hand. "We were all so worried about you."

"And I for you! I knew you would be concerned, fretting on my behalf. Tell me, how is Mamá? Has she left her bed these five days?"

Jane shook her head, but my father added, "Her appetite, I am happy to report, has not suffered during the ordeal. For that we can give thanks." We laughed, and I was thrilled that we were able to do so.

"But how—why are you here, and how did you know where to come?" I asked.

"Colonel Fitzwilliam was good enough to send one of his men with a message as soon as you were recovered," my father answered. "He arrived at Gracechurch Street last evening, and I made plans to depart before first light and see for myself that you were truly well. Jane would not allow me to leave the house without her. Your uncle wished also to come, and indeed, he is outside seeing to the arrangements for our return to Town."

"What a tiring trip for all of you. Here you have travelled since early morning, and you shall have to turn around and make the journey all over again."

"It will not tire us, dear Lizzy," Jane said, "if we have the joy of your safe company."

She caught my hand anew. In truth, I did not want her ever to let go. A few moments later, my uncle joined us, and I basked in the glow of my family's affection.

Both Mr. Gardiner and my father lauded Colonel Fitzwilliam with praise. They also spoke highly of the Earl of Matlock, telling how both men had gone out of their way to put their minds at ease, and how capable and efficient the colonel was in his detective work. More and more, I liked what I heard of Mr. Darcy's cousin and his family.

"'Tis a pity that Jane's affections are already attached to another," my father said with a twinkle in his eye, "or her mother would recover from her malaise quickly enough and have her set her cap for the colonel."

I turned to Jane, raising my eyebrows in expectation.

"My affections are not attached, Father," she said demurely, blushing like a pink rose.

"Then I must write to your mother straightaway. The impending thrill of securing an earl's son will surely cause her to spring forth from her bed!"

Jane and I both protested, laughing at his fanciful speculation. Mr. Gardiner, however, put the truth of the matter to utterance. "I am sorry, Jane, but I have it on the best authority that the colonel is a younger brother, and thus, must marry a woman of means. Otherwise, I am sure you would be first on his list."

We continued to talk happily, as though they needed to keep up my spirits. I wondered, though, in all their jesting why they did not include me as a possible match for the colonel. It was most unlike either my uncle or my father to leave me out of their teasing refrain. Perchance, they were treating me gently because of what I had gone through.

Not long past mid-day, our carriage was ready for the trip to Town, and so were we. I had little to carry with me—only the small valise my aunt had sent, which now held my soiled garments. There had not been time for the servant to launder them, and I elected to take them back wrapped in newspaper.

While overseeing the maid's packing, I received an unforeseen jolt! As she spread out the paper on the bed before placing my clothes on it, I happened to see a headline.

EARL OF MATLOCK'S NEPHEW STILL MISSING

The words amazed me! I had somehow never thought our kidnapping would make the newspapers—how naïve of me. I grabbed up the paper and directed the servant to secure another. Carrying it to the fireplace, I sank down on the settee facing it and began to read.

> *Mr. Fitzwilliam Darcy of Pemberley in Derbyshire has now been missing four days, along with Miss Elizabeth Bennet of Longbourn from the county of Hertfordshire. Highwaymen abducted the couple on Thursday from the London Road. When last seen, they were carried off through the woods in an eastern direction.*
>
> *Also robbed, bound, and left for dead on the road were Mrs. Ambrose Hurst and Miss Caroline Bingley. The ladies and their servants have now been rescued and returned to Town. The gentlewomen are in seclusion, still suffering from nervous conditions and the loss of their jewels and funds.*
>
> *The constable refuses comment as to any possible ransom sought for Mr. Darcy. Requests for information from his uncle, the Earl of Matlock, also remain unanswered. One of the recovered servants, however, reports that before they were kidnapped,* Mr. Darcy announced that Miss Bennet was his wife—*an acknowledged surprise to all of London.*

I stopped in shock and re-read that last line before continuing with the article. I could not believe it had been written in the papers for all to see!

> *Lady Catherine de Bourgh of Rosings Park in Kent, aunt of Mr. Darcy, has offered a reward of five thousand pounds for his safe return. Anyone with information concerning the case should report to the constable's office immediately.*

Although I scanned the remainder of the article, it mentioned neither Mr. Darcy nor myself again, but continued on lamenting the fact that the plague of highwaymen preying on innocent travellers was not a thing of the past as had been recently announced. Even though such instances were uncommon, the writer called for immediate means to rid the country of said curse.

Much of the article blurred in my thoughts because of that singular sentence that resonated in my mind: London society now thought Mr. Darcy and I were married!

Surely it could not be. It was impossible! Did not Miss Bingley and Mrs. Hurst explain that Mr. Darcy had made that statement solely for my protection? I wondered if he had seen the paper. Most likely he had. Perhaps, that was what he wished to speak to me about last evening, to warn me of what was to come.

I had thought he might wish to apologize or make some excuse in defence of the colonel's revelation. How foolish! He did not regret warning his friend against marrying into my family. I knew with what little esteem he held my connections. And now he was in a pickle, for he must explain to society in some way that he had not made a similar blunder. Oh yes, I could certainly see his need to speak to me and secure my cooperation in explaining the matter.

He had little to fear. I could hardly wait to make it known that Mr. Darcy was the last man I should ever marry!

Outside the sun shone brightly, providing welcome warmth against the recent cold wet weather we had experienced. My uncle and father awaited us at the carriage, and Jane and I hastened to join them. As one footman lifted up my valise, another opened the door for us to enter.

Jane had just placed her foot on the first step when we heard Colonel Fitzwilliam call my name. We turned to see the colonel and Mr. Darcy approaching from across the drive.

"Miss Elizabeth, I trust you have everything packed," the colonel said.

"Yes. I have little to carry, so it did not take long."

"Let me add one more item." He reached inside his breast pocket and, taking my hand, placed an object in it. When he drew back, I was amazed to see my garnet cross.

"My necklace! Colonel Fitzwilliam, where did you find this?"

"The highwayman had it."

"The highwayman?" my uncle asked. "Which one? Were there not three or four of them?"

"Four," the colonel answered. "Unfortunately, they had sold all the other stolen jewels, but Morgan, the ringleader, had this on his person. He offered it freely and asked me to return it to you, an action I, frankly, found surprising."

I had lowered my face to my hand, examining the chain, pleased to see it was not broken. When I raised my eyes at the colonel's words, I met Mr. Darcy's piercing stare instead. He held my gaze with such unspoken command that I found myself unable to look away.

"I, too, have no idea why, Colonel, but I am grateful for its return," I murmured.

"Well, shall we board?" my father suggested.

Jane climbed into the carriage, and I turned to follow, but for some reason when I placed my foot upon the first step, I drew back, suddenly overcome with revulsion and fear. My hands grew cold and yet clammy at the same time, and my head began to throb. I must have gone quite pale, for my uncle took my arm.

"Are you unwell? What is it, my dear?"

"I—I do not know. A sudden feeling of illness." I fumbled around, attempting to calm the uneasiness that had overtaken me.

"Shall you return indoors?" my father asked. "Perhaps a glass of water would help."

"Yes, a glass of water for Miss Elizabeth!" Colonel Fitzwilliam ordered a passing servant.

"No, no, I do not want to delay the trip. It is just—I cannot explain it." I turned to look at the carriage and felt the sickness wash over me anew. What was wrong with me? If I climbed aboard, I thought I might surely faint.

Suddenly, I felt Mr. Darcy's presence at my side. He took my arm and gently led me to a nearby bench. The others remained behind, an action I failed to question at the time. I sank down upon the seat while he stood before me.

"Elizabeth, are you afraid? Is it the thought of riding in a carriage that fills you with alarm?"

I looked up at him and nodded, unexpectedly aware that he was correct, and grateful that he put into words what I could not. He sat down beside me and covered my hand with both of his. To this day, I remember how warm his clasp felt, as though I had returned to that safe harbour I trusted and to which I might cling.

"Forgive me," I murmured. "I cannot account for my behaviour."

"No, no, it is to be expected. You are reliving the terrible event that happened the last time you rode in a carriage. 'Tis perfectly natural."

"But how shall I ever leave this place? I do not wish to walk to Town." I smiled slightly, and he did in return.

"No, we both have had enough of walking for awhile. Sit here for a moment until the feeling passes."

How long we sat, I know not, but I made not the slightest attempt to withdraw my hand nor did he remove his from holding mine. At last, he asked if I felt better, and when I replied in the affirmative, he nodded.

"Come, I shall help you board the carriage, but before you do, I want you to look around. Not only shall Fitzwilliam and I ride our mounts beside you as escort, but you will be surrounded by armed redcoats for guards, as well. On this trip you will not be harmed, I promise you."

He rose and led me back to the vehicle, assisting me up the steps and inside. There, he sat beside me for a moment, still holding my hand. "How do you feel now? Has the anguish lessened?"

"Yes, thank you, sir."

"Remember, I shall ride outside your window." He pressed my fingers briefly to his lips and then departed.

Jane, who had left the carriage when I became ill, quickly bounded up the steps and sat beside me, her blue eyes averted. My father and uncle followed thereafter, and it was but a matter of moments before we were off.

No one asked what Mr. Darcy had said—another strange occurrence—and I offered no explanations. I took several deep breaths, and each time I felt the panic begin to rise, I turned to the window where I could see Mr. Darcy riding on his great black horse.

We arrived in Gracechurch Street by late evening, and I hurried inside into the welcoming arms of my aunt.

"Lizzy, is it really you? Are you returned to us safely at last?" she cried.

I could only smile and nod and embrace her once again. There was much confusion greeting my young cousins, and Jane came to my assistance by answering their questions and shielding me from their unrelenting curiosity.

We had been ushered into the small parlour and urged to partake of a cup of tea. Both Colonel Fitzwilliam and Mr. Darcy declined, stating that they must depart and meet with their own anxiously awaiting family. I, too, refused the tea and asked my aunt if I might be excused.

"Of course! You must be exhausted. Jane, go with her, dear, and I shall send up a tray," Mrs. Gardiner exclaimed.

All of us convened in the foyer as the gentlemen were leaving. I had just climbed the first two stairs behind Jane, when I heard my father speak to Mr. Darcy.

"I understand. You must hurry home tonight to your sister, and you will want to see your uncle and aunt. Tomorrow will be soon enough for our talk."

"Thank you, sir," Mr. Darcy replied. "I shall meet with you shortly after mid-day, if that is convenient."

"Perfect," my father answered.

Mr. Darcy and Colonel Fitzwilliam then walked toward the stairs, and both of them bowed. The colonel expressed his wishes that I should recover quickly from the trip.

"Thank you, sir," I said, "and allow me once again to express my deep appreciation for all you have done to rescue us."

He smiled and turned his attention back to my aunt and uncle. Mr. Darcy, however, spoke directly to Jane. "Good night, Miss Bennet."

He then turned back to me and locked his gaze upon mine.

"Good night, Mr. Darcy," I murmured.

"May you rest easy tonight, Elizabeth," he said softly.

Gooseflesh crept up my arms. Why had he addressed me in that familiar way within earshot of others? Had it become such habit that it slipped out, or did it mean something much more important? Did it have anything to do with meeting my father on the morrow? Before I could even begin to consider the enormity of the possibility, he and the colonel walked out the door.

After I had changed into my nightgown, Jane offered to brush out my hair, a practice we had performed for each other since childhood. I gladly accepted, and throwing a shawl around my shoulders, sat at her feet on the rug before the fireplace. As she ran the brush from my scalp down the length of my curls, I revelled in the feelings of comfort and security derived from such a simple action. I was safe.

I closed my eyes and gave myself up to the rhythm, longing to be back at Longbourn, wishing it were a week earlier and I had never begun that journey to Town. Our greatest concern then had been how soon Mr. Bingley would call after the Netherfield ball.

"Jane, did Mr. Bingley travel from Hertfordshire to Town in the carriage with you and Father?"

"Yes, along with Mr. Hurst."

I rolled my eyes. "What stimulating conversation did *that* gentleman offer?"

She laughed lightly. "Very little that I can recall. We had gone but five miles before he began to snore."

"Excellent! Now tell me that Father also fell asleep, and Mr. Bingley took advantage of the situation to propose."

"Lizzy! Do be serious."

"But you were thrown together oft times throughout this nightmare, were you not?"

"At first."

"What do you mean?"

Jane sighed. "When we received that horrible post informing us of what had happened, Mr. Bingley called that morning. He was most kind and tried to be as reassuring as possible."

"As well he should have."

"He also offered his second carriage for our trip to London, and he suggested that we all travel together that evening."

"Well and good," I said, rising to stir the fire.

"But since we arrived in Town, I have not seen him."

"What? He has not called on you in three days?"

She shook her head, casting her eyes down to her lap. "I am sure he has had many things to occupy his time, what with his sisters' distress."

"But what was he like before that when you were together?"

"What do you mean?"

"Was he himself? Was he pleasant and amiable, and did he appear to be as much in love with you as ever?" I took the brush from her and began to apply generous strokes to her long, blonde hair.

"Oh, Lizzy, I do not know that Mr. Bingley is in love with me."

"How can you doubt it? I have never seen a man so attentive, so doting." She did not make any reply, and so I ventured further. "Has his manner changed since the Netherfield Ball?"

"No," she replied somewhat wistfully, "I cannot say that it changed. Of course, he did not call at Longbourn even once during the week after the ball, which seemed somewhat unusual, but you are aware of that. And then I received the note from Caroline saying the entire party was removing to Town, and shortly after that, Father came in and announced that you were to travel with them. Lizzy, I have the strangest feeling that Mr. Bingley might never have called again except for your misfortune."

And I knew the reason why! Mr. Darcy had already cautioned him against Jane. How could he! My blood ran hot just thinking about such a blatant injustice committed against my dear, sweet sister, but I bit my tongue and did not tell her. I could not bring myself to squash her hopes and dreams.

I laid the brush aside and crawled up on the four-poster bed, kicking off my slippers and hugging my knees to my chest while staring at the dying fire.

Jane rose and gathered her things. "You must sleep, Lizzy. I have kept you long enough." She walked over to kiss my forehead, and I caught her hand.

"Jane, stay with me tonight."

"But dearest, will you not rest better alone?"

I shook my head. "I do not want to be alone."

She sat down beside me and patted my hand. "Are you still afraid?" I nodded. "Then, of course, I will. Would it help to talk about it?"

I sighed. "Oh, I hardly know where to begin."

"At the beginning," she said.

And so I told her the story from the way Caroline Bingley had flirted with Mr. Darcy in the carriage to the moment Colonel Fitzwilliam surprised me in the woods.

She was horrified at my description of Sneyd and his vulgar remarks and vile threats, and her eyes grew wide when I described Gert, the other two men and the cabin where we all stayed. My picture of Morgan, however, caused her to gasp aloud, especially when I told her of his scar and how he had rescued me from Sneyd's ugly advances. She could not believe I had actually sung for him and that we had danced together, and when I related the story of his childhood, I saw the sympathy that I expected reflected in her eyes.

"Perchance, he is not as bad as he wishes people to think he is," she said softly.

"That is exactly what I think, Jane. He pretends to be a dastardly, infamous character, but in fact, he seems more like a poor, unfortunate youth who never really had a chance."

"You said he did kill someone, though."

"He did, and I do not know how it came about, but I believe it was to save his own life. The man evidently came at him with a knife or sword to inflict the wound that scarred his face."

Jane leaned forward and peered into my eyes. "Lizzy, do you care for this Morgan?"

I glanced away and rose from the bed to stir the fire yet again. "In another time, another place, I might have. As it is, I can only feel pity for him. And fear."

"Fear?"

"They may hang him."

"Is that not the punishment for theft and kidnapping?"

"Possibly transportation, but if he is wanted for killing that man, then murder will be added to his charges, and he has not a chance."

She lowered her eyes and made no reply. What could she say? I could see no way out for Morgan.

Silently, we pulled back the blankets and plumped our pillows. Jane was just about to blow out the candle when my aunt tapped lightly at the door and then opened it.

"I have brought you one of my sleeping draughts, Lizzy. I thought you might need it, for your father and I agree that a night of good, sound sleep will benefit you more than anything. Shall I mix it up for you?"

"Yes, please," I said.

She busied herself stirring the medicine into a glass of water.

"Has my father retired yet?"

"I believe he has. He has been under a great strain the last few days, my dear, but, of course, you realize that. Did you wish to see him tonight? I am sure he would not mind rising for you."

"No, no, it can wait until morning. It is just that—well, I wanted to ask him about the meeting he has arranged with Mr. Darcy. Do you know anything about that?"

My aunt and Jane exchanged glances.

"Come and sit here by the fire, Lizzy." I did as I was told, while Jane pulled up a chair, and Mrs. Gardiner sat across from me. "My dearest girl, there has been a great deal of talk. The gossip has even been spread in the newspapers. They say that you and Mr. Darcy represented yourselves as married when accosted by those highwaymen."

"We did, but only to save me."

"They threatened her with terrible things," Jane added.

"I can well imagine, and Mr. Darcy is to be commended for his actions, but you must see what this has done to you. When those men go to trial, the story will be broadcast far and wide."

"Everyone will know that we only pretended to be married, and they will know the reason why. I should think it a good thing!"

Mrs. Gardiner pressed her lips together and twisted her hands. "Lizzy, what kind of arrangements—how were you and Mr. Darcy—that is, where did you stay? Were you placed in the same room all those days… and nights?"

It felt like a great stone had fallen on my chest, pulling me down into a whirling vortex of dread. I hung my head and could not face her. "Yes," I said softly.

"Then you see what I mean."

"But nothing happened, Aunt. Mr. Darcy did nothing untoward. We did nothing wrong."

Was I lying? I had omitted what happened at the cave. I had not even shared that with Jane. At times, I fancied that perhaps I had somehow imagined it.

"Must all that be told?" Jane asked. "Why should anyone at the trial have to know where Lizzy and Mr. Darcy slept? It has nothing to do with the crimes those men committed."

"You are correct, Jane," my aunt said, "but I doubt there is any way it will not be revealed. As I said before, this has been in the newspapers. Reporters will be present, and questions will be asked. You can hardly expect criminals to protect Lizzy's reputation."

She rose to leave. "And even if by some miracle the particulars were not told, just the fact that Mr. Darcy declared you as his wife and you spent four days and nights in captivity together—well, people will assume the worst. Oh, it will not harm Mr. Darcy's good name, but Lizzy, unless he offers marriage—"

Marriage! There, the word had actually been spoken aloud.

"Well, it will do none of us any good to dwell on it tonight. Drink the potion, dear, and let it work its magic. And let us pray that Mr. Darcy will do the right thing or, if he is not willing, that your father and uncle can persuade him otherwise." My aunt patted my shoulder and kissed my forehead. "Good night, my dear."

She must have left the room, but I do not remember it. I sat there stunned, unable to move. Why had I been unable to face this inevitability? Why had I allowed my sanguine nature to believe that everything would somehow sort itself out once we were freed? Why was I such a fool?

"Lizzy?" I became conscious that Jane stood before me. "Shall you not do as Aunt instructed and take the medicine?"

Woodenly, I put the glass to my lips and swallowed its contents. I allowed my sister to lead me to the bed and tuck me in. After blowing out the candle, she crawled under the covers on the other side.

"Dearest, try not to worry," she said. "I have always thought Mr. Darcy a better man than you do. I think all shall work out well."

"He will not marry me, Jane," I said, my voice coming out utterly defeated.

"How can you say that? You do not know for sure."

"I know."

"But how?"

"Oh, do not ask me," I cried. I would not begin to tell her how he had ruined her chances with Mr. Bingley, how he considered any alliance with our family with abhorrence. I could not break her heart. "And besides, I do not wish to marry him."

"But Lizzy, consider that he is rich and handsome and has a great estate in Derbyshire."

"There is more to a man than wealth and looks and great estates. I should never marry a man whose character I could not admire. Remember how he disregarded his father's wishes and cheated Mr. Wickham of his inheritance."

Jane sighed. "No one is perfect, and you must remember, there are two sides to every story. Have you ever asked him about Mr. Wickham?"

"I have and he has not denied it. Oh, what does it matter? Believe me when I tell you, he will not ask me to marry him."

"But how do you know?"

"I just do." I turned over then, welcoming the drowsiness caused by the sleeping draught as it released me from a world I could no longer face.

Chapter Ten

The next morning I slept quite late. The sleeping potion had provided the first truly refreshing rest I had experienced in days. Glancing out the window, I could see that the sun had climbed high in the sky, and the morning fog was completely burned off.

Suddenly, I recalled that my father's meeting with Mr. Darcy was set for a little past mid-day, and I hurried to get dressed. Not bothering to call the maid, I washed, fastened my dress, pinned up my hair, and put on my shoes. I was pleased to see that the dark circles had now vanished from beneath my eyes, and I almost looked myself again.

I found the breakfast room empty, but the teapot was still warm, and I poured myself a cup. A maid soon appeared, asking if I desired breakfast, which I refused.

"Where is everyone?" I asked.

"Miss Jane took the children to the park across the way," she answered, "but not until that Mr. Darcy shooed them reporters away from the front stoop."

"Reporters? Here?"

"Yes, Miss, four or five of them. They been camped out there since early mornin', pesterin' me when I went out to pick up the milk and Firkin when he went for the paper."

"What do they want?"

She looked down, appearing hesitant. "Don't rightly know, Miss. Just askin' lots of questions about you and the gentleman."

"Oh," I said, sinking down upon a nearby chair.

"We didn't tell them nothin', Miss, I promise. Neither Firkin nor me said a word."

"Thank you," I murmured. "You say Mr. Darcy is here?"

"Yes, Miss. He's with Mr. Bennet and the master and mistress in the parlour."

"I see. Thank you; that will be all."

She left the room, and I placed the cup of tea on the table, having swallowed just a sip. I closed my eyes and sighed deeply. An uncomfortable knot burned in my stomach at the thought of what was being discussed in the parlour.

Well, I thought, I may as well face it. I would not have my father and uncle beg the man to marry me.

In the hallway, I observed that the door to the room where they gathered was closed, but just outside, I stopped, for I could hear conversation within.

"Naturally, I am aware of the inferiority of our alliance, of my family's objections, indeed, of its being a degradation in their eyes," Mr. Darcy said, "but that is a consequence I shall have to bear. There is nothing else to be done. We must marry and the sooner the better."

"Yes," my uncle agreed. "The sooner the better for all concerned in view of the widespread publicity."

My pulse quickened, and I felt the blood rush to my face. *How dare he!* I thrust open the door and walked in without knocking.

"Lizzy," my aunt said, immediately crossing the room to take my hand. "Did you sleep well?"

The others greeted me, and I somehow murmured my replies. All the while, I kept my eyes upon Mr. Darcy. He had bowed somewhat stiffly, but his colour was not heightened, nor did he appear ill at ease, but rather quite sure of himself.

"My dear," my father said, "come in and be seated. We discuss your and Mr. Darcy's future, so naturally you should participate."

"Thank you, Father. I confess I am at a loss as to why he is here as I do not see our futures corresponding in any way."

"Well," my uncle said, "you must realize the severity of the circumstances. Mr. Darcy has come this morning, perfectly willing and accommodating. He agrees with your father and me that you be married as quickly as possible."

"Married? I fail to understand your meaning, Uncle. Mr. Darcy has not asked me to marry him, and I certainly have not agreed to any such union."

"But it is all arranged," he said. "Things cannot be made right soon enough. I am sure you would agree."

"I do not agree." My tone sounded harsh even to my ears, and I did not mean to insult my uncle. "Begging your pardon, Uncle, but I do not see the need to make anything *right*. Mr. Darcy and I went through a terrible experience, but we are now rescued unharmed. We can both go about our lives from now on as though it never happened. I certainly do not see any reason for marriage."

My father took my hand. "You must face facts. The whole city is talking about this. You and Mr. Darcy said you were married. Witnesses have attested to the fact. You were then held in the same room for several days and nights. Mr. Darcy said you even told the highwayman you carried his child!"

I glared at Mr. Darcy. What had possessed him to reveal that?

"Papá, that was only one of many ruses we used to protect ourselves. You know it is untrue."

"Of course I do, my dear, but it will come out at the trial. Your name will be blackened."

"Why? Why should it be told? I do not understand why this should be!"

Mr. Darcy spoke then for the first time. "Might I speak with Elizabeth alone?"

"If she agrees," my father answered, turning to me.

I shrugged, and he and the Gardiners departed the room, closing the door behind them. Mr. Darcy walked to the fireplace and then to the window. He clenched his hands and placed his fist at his mouth more than once. I felt a nervous fluttering in my stomach as my eyes followed him about the room. At last, he pulled a chair out and sat before me, leaning forward.

"Elizabeth, the time has come to be sensible. There is no other way. We must marry."

"No," I said.

He flinched, recoiling as though I had struck him. "No? Just the singular word — no? This is all the reply that I am to have the honour of expecting? I might, perhaps, wish to be informed why, with so little endeavour at civility, I am thus rejected."

"I might as well inquire why with so evident a design of offending and insulting me, you chose to offer marriage? Was not this some excuse for incivility, if I was uncivil?"

"What do you mean? When have I been uncivil?"

"Outside the room I overheard your manner of conversation—how an alliance with me would be inferior, even a *degradation* in the eyes of your family! If you think *that* sufficient inducement to matrimony, then you, sir, have little experience in proposals."

I looked away, aware that my breathing grew laboured because of my anger. Although I willed myself to become calm, it was a futile endeavour, for memories of his unjust behaviour began to bubble up like a stew pot boiling over on the fire.

"But I have other provocations. You know I have. Do you think that any consideration would tempt me to accept the man who has been the means of ruining the happiness of a most beloved sister? I have every reason in the world to think ill of you. To think that you not only acted the unjust and ungenerous part there, but you bragged about it in correspondence with your cousin! No motive can excuse such behaviour."

He rose, and I did also, continuing to upbraid him. "You dare not, you cannot deny that you have been the principal, if not the *only* means of dividing them from each other—exposing one to the censure of the world for caprice and instability, the other to its derision for disappointed hopes—and involving them both in misery of the acutest kind."

I paused and saw with no little indignation that he listened with an air that proved him wholly unmoved by any feeling of remorse.

"Can you deny that you have done it?" I repeated.

"I have no wish to deny that I did everything in my power to separate my friend from your sister. Towards him I have been kinder than towards myself!"

He turned away and strode to the window, whereupon he must have observed the return of reporters, for I heard him utter an oath under his breath and cross the room briskly, placing one foot upon the hearth and his hand against the mantel before turning to face me again.

"You must understand that I did not entertain any suspicions of your sister's attachment to Bingley until the evening of the ball at Netherfield. Never had I observed on her part any greater preference for his company than for my own. If she had feelings for him, they were little displayed. There was a constant complacency in her air and manner not often united with great sensibility.

"Were it not for the remarks bandied about at the ball, I would not have felt the need to caution him. You must admit that your family's public assumption of their attachment was improper when my friend had not yet declared himself. I cannot excuse their impropriety of conduct, and I believed my warning to Bingley necessary. I know him better than most. He has a habit of easily thinking himself in love and just as easily falling out of love."

I was mortified at his description of my family's behaviour, perhaps because I knew it merited reproach. I would not suffer his depiction of Jane, though. It was false and unfair.

"You may know Mr. Bingley well, but do allow me to understand my own sister better than you do! Jane is everything good and kind and honest. If she does not flaunt her feelings enough to warrant your good opinion, that does not mean she does not possess them. She truly cares for Mr. Bingley, as she has never cared for any other. She—she loves him."

Mr. Darcy blinked several times and turned from my angry stare. He said nothing, as though he could not believe he had possibly been in error. He picked up the poker and jabbed at the logs.

"Whatever the case," he said briskly, "it has nothing to do with our present situation. If *we* do not marry, your sister nor any of your younger sisters, for that matter, will have the slightest chance of marrying well. Your entire family will participate in the shame and ruin of your good name. Elizabeth, you must see this."

"From your account, they have little chance of marrying well in either case. No, I do not see this."

"Then open your eyes! Reporters still remain outside Mr. Gardiner's door. They spent last night in front of my own house. If it is made known that we are not to marry, your reputation will be shattered."

"Perhaps here in Town, sir, but you forget that I do not live in London. What do I care of this society? I shall return to Longbourn where I am known and loved, and no one shall ever hear of this."

"Elizabeth, you are not unintelligent. The *London Gazette* and other newspapers are read in Hertfordshire, indeed, all over England. Your parents' friend, Sir William Lucas, boasts of his frequent trips to Town and his high connections. You cannot escape this, and neither shall your family."

I began to find it hard to breathe, as though a thick tourniquet had been wrapped around my neck. I strode to a small table where a tray had been placed containing a teapot, cups and saucers. I poured myself a cup and made a great show of stirring it, although I had placed neither cream nor sugar therein. I did not drink it. If I had, I felt certain I would have choked.

"Mr. Darcy, I refuse to enter into a marriage contracted upon obligation. Nor will I marry a man whose character I cannot admire." I placed the untouched cup of tea on the table and raised my chin in defiance.

"It is not merely this affair with my sister on which my dislike is founded. Long before it had taken place, my opinion of you was decided. Your character was unfolded in the recital that I received many months ago from Mr. Wickham. On this subject you have never explained your motives or actions. Indeed, what can you have to say? In what imaginary act of friendship can you defend yourself?"

He now began to pace back and forth, running his hand through his hair, obviously agitated. "Wickham again! Shall I never be free of that rake?"

"How can you accuse him so unjustly?" I cried.

"Because I know him!" he thundered.

He spoke with such authority and power that I found myself sinking down upon the sofa beside the table. I had heard that tone of voice before when he confronted Morgan or Sneyd as to my safety. "Will you at least do me the courtesy of hearing me out on the matter?" he asked.

I nodded. In truth, I could do little else, for when he spoke with such force, it filled me with alarm.

Once again, he moved a chair where he could sit before me. He frowned and sighed, a look of anguish suffusing his countenance, as he began to relate the story of his relationship with George Wickham.

He told of how Wickham's father had served as steward to his own father and that he and the son had played together as boys, that when old Mr. Wickham had died, his father had supported him at school and afterwards at Cambridge. Old Mr. Darcy had been fond of the young man, whose manners were always engaging, and he had hoped the church would be his profession, intending to provide a living in it for him.

Mr. Wickham, however, had been unable to prevent the son from opportunities of seeing him in unguarded moments, moments that revealed Mr. Wickham's true nature and behaviour.

"I knew that Mr. Wickham ought not to be a clergyman," Mr. Darcy said.

When the elder Mr. Darcy died some five years previous, Wickham resolved against taking orders and announced his intention to study the law. Mr. Darcy wished, rather than believed him to be sincere and agreed to give him three thousand pounds in place of the living.

All connection between them now seemed dissolved. How he lived, Mr. Darcy did not know, but last summer Wickham was again most painfully brought to his notice.

He leaned back in the chair, a tortured look of deep sorrow darkening his eyes. I had never seen that expression upon his face before, and it filled me with dread.

"I must now mention a circumstance that I would wish to forget, and that no obligation less than the present should induce me to unfold to any human being. Having said thus, I feel no doubt of your secrecy."

I nodded and murmured, "Of course."

He continued, laying before me a tale most shocking! Mr. Darcy's sister, Georgiana, who was more than ten years his junior, was taken to Ramsgate last summer with a lady, Mrs. Younge, about whose character Mr. Darcy and Colonel Fitzwilliam had been most unhappily deceived. By her connivance and aid, Mr. Wickham joined them in Ramsgate and recommended himself to Georgiana to such a degree that she was made to think herself in love with him. She was persuaded to consent to an elopement.

"She was then but fifteen years of age," he said, his tone utterly defeated. "Unexpectedly, a day or two before the intended elopement, I arrived at the coastal town, and Georgiana, unable to support the idea of grieving and offending a brother whom she looks up to almost as a father, acknowledged the whole to me. You may imagine what I felt and how I acted."

Regard for his sister's credit and feelings prevented any public exposure, but he denounced Wickham, who left the place immediately, and Mrs. Younge, of course, was removed from her charge. Wickham's chief object was unquestionably the young girl's fortune of thirty thousand pounds.

"I cannot help supposing," he added, "that the hope of revenging himself on me was a strong inducement. His revenge would have been complete indeed." His voice broke with emotion, and it was several moments before he could continue.

"I hope you acquit me henceforth of cruelty towards Mr. Wickham. You may appeal to the testimony of Colonel Fitzwilliam for the truth of everything here related, as he was one of the executors of my father's will and is acquainted with every particular of these transactions."

I was struck dumb, any idea of speech utterly unthinkable. I could not take it all in, could not fathom how deceived I had been. To think that I had admired Mr. Wickham, a man whose character was reprehensible, a seducer of young girls, who had not the slightest qualm at betraying the trust of a gentleman who had provided for his education and future. It was insufferable!

I did not wish to believe that Mr. Wickham had fooled me, but at the same time, I could not believe Mr. Darcy would invent such a tale. No, it had to be true. I sat staring at the fire. Astonishment and horror rendered me helpless.

How long I sat thus, I do not know. At length, I became conscious that Mr. Darcy now stood before me, hat in hand.

"I have given you much to think on," he said. "I shall leave you now. You must have time to yourself. Your aunt has invited my sister and me for dinner tonight. I shall expect your answer then."

"I have already given you my answer," was all that I could think to say.

"Do not say that is your final word until you have given consideration to this new information. Remember, Elizabeth, the decision you make will affect a great many people."

He bowed briefly and walked out the door.

The remainder of the day I spent in my room except for a brief sojourn about my aunt's garden. I was able to slip out the back door and escape the reporters' eyes, thankful for the fence surrounding the enclosure.

My family, naturally, had besieged me with questions upon Mr. Darcy's removal. I had asked for time alone, however, and they granted my request.

I observed the looks passed between them, the smile on my aunt's face, and the relief evident upon that of my father. They assumed that I was willing to consider this arranged marriage and merely needed time to become accustomed to the idea. That premise bore not the slightest ounce of truth.

I now knew for certain that I could never marry Mr. Darcy.

I had gone over and over the tale he had told, ashamed anew that I had ever believed Mr. Wickham's falsehoods. I, so vigilant to judge a person's character, had been completely taken in by his smooth words and agreeable manner. When I re-examined his actions, I had to admit he had seduced me by his attentions in much the same way he had poor Georgiana. But for the fact that I had no fortune, it could have been me enticed into an elopement.

I was utterly ashamed and stricken with remorse. How quickly had I believed him, and how easily I had denounced Mr. Darcy! Until that moment, I never knew myself.

My mind wandered back and forth over the past months since I had met the gentleman. Never had I actually seen him do anything that bespoke immorality, anything that betrayed him as unprincipled.

No, the more I thought upon it, the more I could see he was exactly the opposite—a man of integrity, almost to a fault. When he saw a wrong, he attempted to right it. He honestly believed, although greatly mistaken, that his friend loved a woman who did not return his affection and sought to rescue him from the clutches of a fortune hunter.

When I was in danger of God knows what evil, he immediately stepped forth and offered himself for ransom, attempting to protect me. Again and again, I thought of instances in which he had put himself in peril for my sake. And now, he was willing to throw away his chance for happiness—to forsake any opportunity of a suitable marriage so that my name would not be tarnished.

How could I allow him to make such a sacrifice? "Impossible," I said aloud.

I knew he did not love me. His words rang in my memory—*a mistake*! He kissed me but once and pronounced it a mistake. How could we live together the remainder of our lives when I knew that he would regret it every hour of every day?

No, I would not marry Mr. Darcy. No matter how I loved him, perhaps *because* I loved him, I would not permit him to make another mistake.

Dinner that evening was a strained affair, to say the least. My aunt had failed to tell me that she had also invited Mr. Bingley and Caroline to dine with us. Or perchance she had told me, and it flew right out of my head, for my brain was spinning wildly from all that had happened.

In any event, when dressing for dinner, I was surprised to see Jane take special pains with her appearance, and when I asked the reason why, I realized for the first time that we would have additional guests joining us. Of course, I was delighted for Jane to be with Mr. Bingley, but my heart filled with foreboding knowing I would be forced to face Mr. Darcy so quickly.

"Lizzy," Jane asked as she adjusted the combs in her hair, "you have made it plain that you do not wish to be questioned, but surely you can tell me. Shall you accept Mr. Darcy?"

"I feel such pressure. Will you think badly of me if I do not?"

"Of course not, but I am confused. Last night you were certain he would not ask for your hand. Now that he has proved you wrong, you are the one who appears to be against the marriage."

I made no answer, but lowered my head to adjust my stockings and wondered how much I should reveal to my sister. I had not told her of the intimacies between Mr. Darcy and myself, of his kiss, or even that we had shared a blanket at the cabin and huddled together under my coat during that long night in the cave. She knew only that we had been forced to stay in the same room both day and night.

"You talked in your sleep last night," she said. "Did you know that?"

Grateful for the change in conversation, I looked up immediately and smiled, moving to stand behind her at the dressing table and smooth the back of her coiffure.

"Did I? One never remembers what one says while sleeping. What did I do? Scream at one of those highwaymen?"

"No, I must have pulled at the quilt, for you said something like, 'Sorry, Mr. Darcy,' muttered words I couldn't understand, and then said 'You take the blanket.' After that, you turned over and rolled so close to the edge that I feared you might fall out of bed. I cannot believe you dreamed of Mr. Darcy, for surely you did not imagine sharing a blanket with him!"

She looked up to meet my eyes in the reflection in the glass. "Why, Lizzy, what is wrong? You have quite lost your colour. Are you faint?"

She jumped up and bade me sit in her chair. I made little of her fears but accepted the glass of water she fetched, glad that my pallor provided a diversion and that I was not required to answer her questions about my nocturnal ramblings.

Eventually we were forced to quit primping and make our way to the drawing room. Mrs. Gardiner gave her approval to our dress, stating we did not need to pinch our cheeks for our natural colour was heightened.

I was surprised at how quickly my countenance had recovered and hoped the arrival of our guests did not cause another drastic change in my appearance. I was filled with disquiet at seeing Mr. Darcy so soon, knowing he was coming in anticipation of an answer. I wished with all my heart that he would send his regrets. It was not to be, however, for within the hour, they arrived, and the small drawing room became filled with guests and conversation.

I watched Miss Bingley's eyes roam about the furnishings. A pinched look pursed her lips, and she lifted her nose higher as though she smelled something distasteful.

Mr. Bingley joined Jane almost immediately, and I was gratified to see that his attentions had not lessened since I had last seen them together. No matter Mr. Darcy's warning, it appeared that Mr. Bingley still found my sister enchanting.

I avoided facing Mr. Darcy, fearing the tension between us might be as apparent as if a trumpet announced it, blaring forth for all to hear. My aunt and uncle, however, made every attempt to keep things light, the conversation stimulating, and the situation pleasant.

My father was in good humour. He offered titbits from the latest book he had read for everyone's enjoyment. Mr. Darcy seemed surprised at his quotes. He was well acquainted with the author and joined in the conversation.

His sister, I am pleased to say, seemed a pleasant girl, somewhat shy but pretty. Her blonde hair and blue eyes contrasted against her brother's dark colouring, but I could see that they both possessed the same cleft chin, and when she smiled, I recalled that similar expression upon his face.

Caroline fawned over Mr. Darcy and Georgiana, ignoring me for the most part, which suited us both. Jane drew Miss Darcy into the conversation often, soon putting her at ease in her gentle way. Mr. Darcy appeared pleased that she was getting along so well, and I looked up more than once to find him smiling at me. I should have found pleasure in such rarity, but it felt more like a dagger piercing my heart.

When seated in the dining room, I looked around the table and felt sick to my stomach. The smells of the food, which I knew was delicious, now nauseated me. Except for Miss Bingley, they all thought I would be his wife, and perchance even she accepted it. There could be little doubt, for I had always been sensible. Only I knew the truth.

After dinner while the men enjoyed their brandy and cigars, Jane and

I discussed Georgiana's interests with her, discovering that music was her great passion. My aunt led her to the pianoforte, and she and Jane scanned the stack of music, selecting particular favourites.

I wandered to the window and pulled back the lace curtains to see that it had begun to rain once more. I thought of the night in the cave, the storm outside, and Mr. Darcy's comforting embrace. My mind, naturally, wandered to the firestorm that had erupted between us the morning after. I could feel his arms around me, his lips upon mine, how hungrily he had sought possession of my mouth.

Of whom could he have been thinking? I knew for certain it was not me. Did he not confess that very fact when he termed our kiss a mistake? Surely, there were some other lips he longed to kiss, some other woman he wished to hold in his arms. I shuddered at the thought.

"Miss Eliza," Miss Bingley said, appearing beside me and jarring me back to the present. "You do not appear any the worse for wear from your little excursion."

"Excursion?" I could not believe she would dismiss our abduction to that degree.

"Yes, you must have found it quite fortuitous to be thrown into Mr. Darcy's daily company. I know I would have found it exhilarating."

"No doubt," I said, "but then I was too busy keeping myself alive. I fear I missed the exhilarating part altogether. What a pity!"

She looked down her nose at me in that particular way she had and was just about to say something when the men returned to the room, and her attention was diverted.

Georgiana was prevailed upon to play for us. She was nervous, and I offered to turn the pages of the music for her. Quite accomplished at the instrument, she had no reason to fear playing for an audience other than her natural timidity. Everyone was appreciative of her performance.

"Now, Lizzy, it is your turn," my uncle said.

"Oh no, please, I— "

Mr. Bingley and Jane joined his pleas. Reluctantly, I took my place at the piano, opened a piece of music, and began to play poorly. With the exception of Caroline, however, the audience was kind in its judgment and urged me to render another. I wished nothing more than to leave the instrument when I looked up to see Mr. Darcy standing before me.

"I would greatly enjoy hearing you sing," he said, "for I have rarely heard anything that gave me greater pleasure."

Was that sarcasm I heard in his voice, or did I imagine it? Could he deliberately wish to humiliate me? Did this request relate to my singing for Morgan, for I knew that he resented my having done so?

"I am sorry, sir, but I am not in the mood to sing." I met his gaze and held it, refusing to back down or be bullied.

"My misfortune," he said. "Perhaps another time."

He turned away, and I rose quickly, seeing that Caroline hurried toward the instrument. Jane urged her to play, and she was more than willing to astound us with her expertise, causing her fingers to fly in a rousing sonatina.

Afterwards, my aunt suggested tables be set up for those who wished to play card games. My father declined, preferring to return to his favourite author, and Mr. Darcy asked if I would join him in my uncle's library in search of a certain book. I knew that most in the room were aware he did not seek a book, but they allowed us this subterfuge in order to be alone. I could not miss their knowing glances.

Mr. Darcy opened the door, and squaring my shoulders, I lifted my chin, prepared for what I must do and say as I walked before him.

Inside the study, he poured us both a glass of sherry and said nothing until we had taken a sip. We stood before the fireplace facing each other. Our eyes met as we lifted the tiny glasses to our mouths.

"The time has come," he said. "Unless you need longer to consider my question, I must ask for your answer. Do say if you require more time, as I am not in the habit of proposing, much less asking the question twice. Will you consent to be my wife?"

My heart was in my throat, and I had to swallow twice before speaking. "I do not need longer to consider it. I thank you for the honour, sir, but my decision remains the same. I cannot...I will not marry you."

His colour rose, and his eyes darkened. Otherwise, he did not portray any outward indication of emotion. "Elizabeth, be very certain of what you are saying, for I shall not renew my addresses again."

He held my eyes as though they were physically joined to his. I could not look away. "I am certain," I said, my voice barely more than a whisper.

He blinked more than once, his eyes as black as midnight. "Forgive me for having taken up so much of your time, and accept my best wishes for your health and happiness."

Placing the glass on a nearby table, he turned to depart the room, but I stopped him.

"Mr. Darcy, allow me to thank you for all that you did to protect me during the trial we were forced to endure. I shall never forget your kindness and—and your sacrifice."

His eyes had been downcast as I spoke, and when he lifted them to meet mine, I began to tremble at the intensity of his gaze.

"Elizabeth, I shall never forget what happened between us in the cave. I cannot rid myself of the guilt I feel for taking advantage of you."

I felt myself blush, remembering the intensity of his kiss and the shameless way I had responded. My voice shook as I attempted to make light of it.

"It is in the past and shall be forgotten if neither of us speaks of it again."

"We are not the only ones who must remain silent."

"What do you mean?"

"Have you forgotten that the highwayman witnessed my transgression, and in his evil mind it appeared that we were both willing participants? He may well testify to the same in a public trial."

My eyes widened at the thought, but I dismissed it. "That will not happen. Morgan would never betray—that is, I feel certain he will not speak of it."

Mr. Darcy's eyes narrowed at my words, and he held my gaze for the longest time.

"I see," he finally said. "Then I shall leave. May God help you, Elizabeth."

His voice broke and, turning quickly, he left the room.

What happened thereafter I did not witness, for I fled above stairs to my chamber and locked the door behind me. Throwing myself upon the bed, I gave way to the tears that had threatened to erupt all day.

I knew that I had just refused the only man I had ever loved and possibly could ever love. And why? Because I believed he did not love me. But what was that look about? That final shocking expression I had seen upon his face?

It was not long before my aunt and sister knocked at the door, as well as my father.

"Please go away," I cried. "I cannot speak to anyone right now."

They continued to ask admittance, but I refused. Never had I behaved so rudely in my aunt's house or to my father. I simply could not face them, not when I felt as though my insides had been ripped from my body.

I cried until I made myself ill, having to grab the chamber pot and lose the little bit of dinner I had managed to eat earlier. Fortunately, by that time, my family had given up and left me to my misery. I washed my face and pulled off my clothes. I did not bother to find a nightgown, but crawled into bed in my chemise.

A half-hour or so later I heard a light tap at the door once again, and Jane's gentle voice entreated me to grant her entrance. Sighing deeply, I rose and unlocked the door.

"Are you alone?" I asked before opening it.

When she replied in the affirmative, I turned the knob, and she gathered me into her arms.

"Oh, Lizzy, what have you done?"

"Destroyed all my chances of happiness." I gave myself up to a good cry on her shoulder.

At length, she drew me to the bed, where she bade me lie down and then gently washed my face. I asked her what Mr. Darcy had said to them, and she told me that he had met privately with our father for a few moments, and then he and his sister left the house. Caroline insisted that she and Mr. Bingley do the same shortly thereafter.

After the guests had departed, my father had said only that there would not be a wedding because I had refused Mr. Darcy.

"Papá is very upset, Lizzy. You must talk to him."

"I know, and I shall tomorrow. I just cannot face anyone tonight but you."

She hugged me again and crawled into the bed with me. "Talk to me. Make me understand why you will not marry Mr. Darcy."

"He does not love me," I said, my tone hopeless and defeated.

"He must care for you somewhat, else he would not have offered."

"Oh, but he would. Can you not see that? He is a good man and willing to do the right thing. He is even willing to sacrifice his happiness to save my reputation. How can I allow him to do that?"

"Your opinion of Mr. Darcy is greatly altered. A week ago you would not have described him as either a good man or one capable of sacrifice."

"True. But I am changed from the girl I was a week ago. The journey we were forced to endure has shown me the man's true character, and I discovered the flaw in my own. I was deceived by my own prejudice, Jane."

I then told her all that Mr. Darcy had related about Mr. Wickham and cautioned her that we must not reveal his despicable actions toward Miss Darcy. She was shocked and horrified, naturally, and could hardly believe it.

"Wickham so very bad! It is almost past belief. And poor Mr. Darcy! Dear Lizzy, only consider what he must have suffered. Having to relate such a thing of his sister — it is really too distressing. And poor Wickham! There is such an expression of goodness in his countenance, such an openness and gentleness in his manner. Perchance it is all a mistake. Perhaps he is not quite so bad."

"No, Jane," I replied, shaking my head. "You cannot have it both ways. One man has all the goodness and the other all the appearance of it."

She flopped down upon the pillow next to me, and we remained silent for awhile.

"Shall I blow out the candle?" I asked.

"If you wish, but I cannot make out one thing. Why do you insist that Mr. Darcy does not love you?"

I extinguished the candle before answering her. I lay down in the dark room and felt my loss anew.

"Never once did he mention the word, Jane. All of his reasons for marriage were practical and for my well-being. He never said he loved me. He did not even pretend to do so."

"Many people marry without love. Do you not think it might naturally come about if you consented to be his wife? He does not appear to dislike you."

"I cannot enter into such an unequal union."

"Are not all marriages unequal? The husband is always the head over the wife, you know that."

"I am aware of the law, but I refer to something entirely different."

"What is it?"

"I shall not marry a man who does not love me when I know that I have fallen desperately in love with him."

"Oh, dearest!" Jane pulled me close and allowed me to weep upon her shoulder once again.

"I want to go home — home to Longbourn where I am safe."

"Yes," she said softly. "Surely Father will take us tomorrow if we but ask."

He did not, however. We were to remain in London for some time to come.

Chapter Eleven

The next day was Sunday, and as was the custom in my uncle's house, the entire household, including the servants, met for morning prayers. My uncle chose a passage from Proverbs for his reading. I sat next to Jane on the sofa, still sleepy from the night before, my eyes swollen from weeping. I confess I had a difficult time concentrating on the text, and my mind strayed until I heard the following words:

> *"There be three things which are too wonderful for me, yea, four which I know not: the way of an eagle in the air; the way of a serpent upon a rock; the way of a ship in the midst of the sea; and the way of a man with a maid."*

The way of a man with a maid. Instantly I felt Mr. Darcy's arms around me. I remembered his mouth caressing mine and how easily he had taken command of my senses. Yes, the writer spoke the truth. It was too wonderful to comprehend. And then I felt abashed that my mind had wandered so far from the scripture and to a scene that should have caused me shame. I willed myself to return to the present and heed my uncle's reading.

> *"For three things the earth is disquieted, and for four it cannot bear: a servant when he reigneth; a fool when he is filled with meat; an unloved woman when she is married; and a handmaid that is heir to her mistress."*

An unloved woman when she is married. Once again, I was struck with the revelation of wisdom and the way my uncle's choice in scripture applied to my life. I knew with certainty that neither the earth nor I could bear marriage to Mr. Darcy, knowing I was unloved.

Tears began to well up within me, and I kept my gaze lowered, thankful that we were now praying. I blinked several times, and with the final amen, I was able to restrain the signs of emotion stirred up by my thoughts.

Mr. and Mrs. Gardiner, along with Jane and the children, left for church services shortly thereafter. My father had already said he and I would not attend because, in my present state, he felt I did not need the added burden of prying eyes.

As soon as they walked out the door, he asked me to accompany him into my uncle's study. He sat down upon the tapestry-covered divan and patted the place next to him, indicating that I should join him.

"Now, Lizzy," he said, taking my hand, "I am not about to scold you or even admonish you for your decision, although heaven help us when your mother hears that I have permitted you to refuse another proposal. You and I may have to take up residence in the stable when we return to Longbourn."

"Oh, Father, I do not care. Let us return home this very day, and I shall gladly move into the barn."

"Yes, well, let us hope it does not come to that. But I must ask why, Lizzy? Tell me the reason you have refused to marry Mr. Darcy. I know he is a proud, disagreeable man and has never paid proper attentions to you, but you are a sensible girl, able to overlook such slights and make the practical decision when called upon. I am afraid you will suffer for this, my dear, much more than you can imagine."

I lowered my head and chewed my lip. "Perhaps, but I cannot marry him."

"So he is a man of low character after all. Wickham's wild tales have merit?"

"Oh no, Papá. Mr. Wickham's inventions were just that—pure invention. Mr. Darcy possesses sterling character traits. He is generous, courageous, compassionate, and honest. He is not guilty of Mr. Wickham's accusations."

I had looked about the room as I talked, but when my eyes settled upon those of my father's, I saw the furrow in his brow deepen.

"From this account, I would believe you think highly of the man. What on earth would make you refuse him?"

"I pray you do not demand an answer." My eyes filled with tears in spite of my best efforts as I gazed upon his anxious countenance. I hated to cause him worry. "Trust me when I say I have made the right decision."

He studied my expression for some time, but at last he patted my hand again, leaned over, and kissed my forehead.

"Very well, have it your way. I could never refuse you anything, and I will not cause you more distress."

"And shall we go home today?"

"Not today, dear. You forget it is Sunday, and the coaches will not be available until the morrow, but first thing in the morning, I shall secure our tickets, and you and Jane and I shall leave on the mid-day excursion."

"Thank you, Papá." I kissed his cheek and, rising, selected a book from my uncle's shelves before leaving the room.

"Lizzy," he said before I reached the door, "I think you should know. Mr. Darcy said he would not make any announcement to the press and advised that we refrain from doing so, as well. The more time that elapses before it is made known that there will not be a wedding, the better it will be for you."

I nodded. That was kind of Mr. Darcy. He could have published it in the papers first thing—I knew that well—but once again, he attempted to protect me. Ah, well, I would leave London tomorrow and put all of it behind me.

We spent the remainder of the day quietly. My aunt and uncle returned from church with Jane and the children, and we sat down to a pork roast with all the trimmings. Jane had evidently told my relations enough that they did not question me as to my decision. I was grateful for their acceptance and understanding.

Indeed, I had a new appreciation for my family. I had always loved them dearly, but since returning, I felt their worth even more. I could hardly wait to see Mamá and my younger sisters, even though I had oft times done whatever I could to escape their presence. How easily we took each other for granted.

Jane and I took turns reading to the children that afternoon so that my aunt might take a nap. No matter how we tried, we could not persuade the two older children to lie down and rest. Both of them proclaimed they were too big for such babyish habits. The little ones, however, soon fell asleep, and Jane took our older cousins for a walk in the park. I would have gone with them but for the ever-present reporters still lurking outside the front door.

I meandered about the house, picked up several books and attempted to read, but could find nothing that held my interest. More than once, I wandered to the window, pulling the curtains back to peer outside.

What was I looking for? Did I expect to see Mr. Darcy come driving up, now ready to declare his undying love? Of course not. I knew without a doubt I should most likely never see him again, and the very thought made my heart ache.

Returning to my bedchamber, I lay down, vowing that I would take a long afternoon nap, but sleep would not come. Each time I closed my eyes I saw him standing there, that haunting expression about his eyes just before he walked out the door last night. What had it meant? Why could he not express his feelings? Why had I fallen in love with such a mysterious man, one of whose emotions I could never be sure?

You must listen to his words. The thought went around and around my mind. *He kissed you and termed it a mistake.* There was no getting past that.

The remainder of the day crawled by. Jane and I packed our belongings that evening, and I could hardly wait for the morning to dawn. The sooner I left London, the sooner I could begin my life anew. Once I left Town, I could forget all that had happened. How I longed to see Hertfordshire again!

The next day, however, I learned that my desires were in vain.

Shortly after breakfast, Firkin announced that there were visitors from the constable's office in the parlour awaiting the presence of my father and me. Papá had already left the house to secure our tickets for the post, and so my uncle took his place. He did not want the callers to have to wait for my father's return. He declared it would not signify if he arrived late at his own office.

Two middle-aged men greeted us, one dressed in uniform, the other in civilian clothing, holding his hat in his hands. My uncle introduced me and asked their business, whereupon they informed us that they were to hold an enquiry for the magistrate's office, and they desired to question me as to what had occurred during the entirety of the kidnapping and robbery. They also said my presence would be required in London until after the trial of Morgan and his gang.

"Certainly," my uncle answered after first glancing at me, "my niece will give you whatever information is necessary, but I do not understand why after doing so, she must stay in Town."

"The court," the man in civilian clothes explained, "must have the right to question you, Miss Bennet, during the actual trial proceedings. We are here today to gain whatever testimony you wish to give regarding the crimes before the case is heard."

My uncle immediately asked if I would have to testify publicly, and we were assured that would be unlikely, that Mr. Darcy's presence would be sufficient, along with that of the menservants from Mr. Bingley's carriage and any other witnesses the gentleman wished to call. If at all possible, none of the ladies—Miss Bingley, Mrs. Hurst, nor I—would be forced to submit to the indignities of a public trial. They, however, would not rule out the remote prospect.

I must have appeared stricken at the thought, for the man hastened to assure me that such occasion rarely came about. He then began to question me in detail about the entire situation, scribbling my answers upon an untidy wad of papers he had pulled from a faded brown satchel.

I told him everything I knew. In truth, I was glad to have the opportunity to relate what background I knew about Morgan. I hoped it would make things go easier for him. I took special pains to make certain they learned that he had provided for Mr. Darcy's and my comfort and arranged for our release.

"Exactly how did this Morgan fellow make things comfortable for you?" the man asked. "According to Mr. Darcy, you were held in primitive conditions."

"We were, but when I asked for water and a blanket, Morgan saw that we received it."

"Water and bedding could hardly be termed luxuries."

"No, but the others—Sneyd, in particular—would have denied us even those necessities. And did Mr. Darcy tell you how Morgan protected me from Sneyd's advances?"

The man glanced at his uniformed companion and shook his head.

I briefly described the incident wherein Sneyd had attempted to force himself upon me and then told of Morgan's rescue. I omitted the fact that Sneyd had touched me, and I did not feel it necessary to include the way Morgan had carried me back to the cabin. After all, I was not under oath, and neither fact was pertinent. When he asked if that was all, I nodded.

Much more had happened. Morgan had given me wine and a place at his table. He had danced with me and attempted to kiss me, but I would not reveal any of that. The man was in enough trouble. I did not wish to add to his woes.

At length, the official folded his papers and stuffed them inside the satchel. The men rose and thanked us for our time and cooperation. As they reached the door about to depart, the man in uniform turned back with one final question.

"Miss Bennet, might you know the date Mr. Darcy plans to return?"

"Return?" I could not make out what he meant.

"Yes, return to London."

"No, I cannot tell you. I did not know he had left Town."

"Is that so? I would have thought he would have told you, of all people. Yes, he left yesterday without telling his sister when he would return. She was quite vague about it all. 'Tis strange that no one can give us an answer. If he does call upon you before we see him, make certain he knows he is bound under the law just as you are. He must remain in Town until after the trial.

"And when might that proceeding occur?" my uncle asked.

"It is set for shortly after the beginning of the new year," the man replied.

After the New Year! I could not believe it would take so long. That was weeks away. I did not recall the men taking their leave or walking out the door. My mind was far too occupied with the dismal thought that I could not go home to Longbourn for a good three weeks or longer!

My father returned to the house shortly thereafter and found me with Jane and my aunt and uncle in the parlour discussing the change in events. He, naturally, was surprised and somewhat dismayed that I could not accompany him that day.

"I shall have to return this ticket for a refund," he said slowly.

"Papá, will you not return two tickets?" Jane asked. "I pray you will allow me to stay with Lizzy—that is, if you do not mind, Aunt.

"Of course you may stay," my aunt said. "Both of you girls are welcome to visit with us as long as needs be, for you are a joy to our house. I have just had another idea, however. Thomas, why not go to Longbourn, fetch Fanny and the younger girls, and bring them all here for the holiday? Would it not make our hearts merrier to be all together?"

"Oh, Aunt," Jane said, "how kind of you!"

"But will you have room?" I asked, aware that the Gardiner's house was not at all large, and she was inviting five more people.

"Of course, we will," my uncle answered, and my aunt agreed, saying my parents could have the room my father had used, Jane and I could share a room, and Mary, Kitty and Lydia could take Jane's bedchamber, as it was the largest. Within moments, she had worked out the sleeping arrangements and immediately turned her thoughts to menus.

"Come with me, Jane," she said. "We shall meet with Cook right now and make our plans for Christmas dinner!"

My uncle kissed her cheek and announced that he had to leave for the office. That left me alone with my father once more.

"Are you sure you can bear your mother's affliction, once she knows all the particulars of what has happened, Lizzy?"

"Of course," I said, smiling. "And who knows—by this time, she may have already secured another man for me to charm."

"There has been a rather steady stream lately," he agreed.

And so that night Jane and I unpacked our trunks and settled in once again at Gracechurch Street. She remained in her room since our family was not to arrive until a day or two before the holiday, and thus, I had the entire bed to myself. I stretched out fully but found that greater room in the bed did not cause sleep to come any easier.

Each time I closed my eyes, I would see Mr. Darcy, his dark brooding stare, the way his curls persisted in falling across his forehead, and the dimples I had glimpsed when favoured with one of his smiles. I could see him striding across the countryside, his greatcoat flying about as his long legs made quick work of any distance. I knew his familiar walk by heart.

I sighed and rubbed my eyes, attempting to erase the visions that tormented me. But like a persistent melody, I could not rid myself of thoughts of him. My arms ached to hold him just once more, to feel his own embrace tighten around me and his warm hand gently place my head upon his chest. Then, once again I could taste his lips upon mine, feel that urgent, persistent kiss force me to open myself to him. I grew warm all over at the memory of my response.

I trembled, amazed at how little I had understood about a man and a woman prior to this journey I had taken with Mr. Darcy. How little I had known of love, both its joys and its heartbreak.

On Thursday Jane and I attended my aunt on a shopping excursion. By that time, the reporters had given up trying to obtain any news from us and had forsaken, at last, their vigil outside my uncle's house.

Several acquaintances had made calls upon my aunt during the week. They all seemed unduly curious about my future plans, but they were dissuaded from pursuing such questions by my aunt's innocuous, gentle manner. Although I appreciated the diversion presented by such guests, I was in great need of escaping the house, of venturing somewhere other than into my aunt's garden out back.

It was thus with a measure of anticipation that I tied my bonnet and joined Mrs. Gardiner and Jane for an afternoon of meandering about the fashionable shops of London. Both Jane and I wished to select small gifts for our families for the coming holiday, and my aunt was in search of just the right lace to redo a collar on her oldest daughter's dress.

We milled about several stores and added our opinions to our aunt's choice of patterns. We stopped for tea in a lovely little place, and I was much amused to sit at the window and watch the assortment of townspeople come and go with such haste.

"Well, girls, I am almost finished," my aunt announced. "One more stop at Mrs. Bellamy's, and I shall have completed my list of tasks for today. What about you? Is there anywhere else you wish to visit?"

We both replied in the negative, content simply to accompany her. Mrs. Bellamy's turned out to be a dressmaker's establishment, one that my aunt frequented often enough that the owner knew her by name.

As they busied themselves choosing silk for a new gown, Jane and I wandered about. We fingered the ribbons and marvelled at the array of fabrics lined up for purchase. One could go blind from the choices.

"A very good selection," Mrs. Bellamy pronounced upon my aunt's final preference. "That shade of lavender is perfect for your complexion, madam." She wrote out the ticket, tallied up the amount to be charged, and watched as my aunt signed for the purchase. "The gown should be ready ten days from the morrow."

"Thank you," my aunt replied.

"And," the lady added in a conspiratorial tone, "might I remind you how skilled my girls are at making wedding clothes."

Jane and I glanced over our shoulders to see her lean toward our aunt's ear and give a definite nod in my direction.

"We should be honoured to make the future Mrs. Darcy's gown."

My brows shot up in horror, but my aunt simply smiled and turned to bid us depart the shop together.

"Aunt," I said on the street, "why did you not refute the dressmaker's error?"

"Hush," she replied, "let us not speak of it until we reach home."

I did as I was told, but the moment we entered the foyer of the house on Gracechurch Street, I once again asked for an explanation.

"Lizzy," she said, handing her coat and bonnet to the maid, "I did not see the need to give my dressmaker the details of your private life, just as I did not make the other shopkeepers privy to your future."

"Do you mean to say Mrs. Bellamy was not the only person who asked such impertinent questions?" Jane asked.

"Indeed not," my aunt replied. "I cannot recall one establishment where I was not questioned about Lizzy."

My mouth hung agape. "Oh, I did not realize! I never would have placed you in that position, had I known."

"Of course, my dear, but it is to be expected. Just because the journalists have left our stoop does not mean that London has quit talking. You and Mr. Darcy are still much discussed."

I met Jane's gaze, aghast at how naïve both of us had been. Only the night before, we had noted that people would probably soon forget all about me, if they had not already done so. Blithely I had gone about Town all day long, oblivious to the gossip following in my wake.

"I shall not leave this house again," I announced, "until my father comes to fetch me home."

"Oh, Lizzy, that is unheard of," my aunt said.

"Indeed," a male voice chimed in as we entered the small drawing room. "I do hope I can persuade you otherwise, Miss Elizabeth."

We looked up to see Mr. Bingley standing beside our uncle at the fireplace, a welcoming smile upon his lips and a light in his eyes when they rested upon Jane. After greeting him, my aunt bade us all sit down.

"This is an unexpected pleasure, Mr. Bingley," she said. "I hope your sisters are well."

"They are," he replied. "Caroline would have joined me but for a previous engagement. I have come with a purpose, however."

He looked at me and then at Jane, keeping his gaze upon her. "I hope Mr. and Mrs. Gardiner, you, and Miss Elizabeth will join Mr. and Mrs. Hurst, Caroline and me at the opera a week from tonight."

"The opera!" my aunt exclaimed. "How lovely! 'Tis a pity Mr. Gardiner and I already have plans for that evening."

"Ah," Mr. Bingley said, "that is unfortunate. It is a performance of *Don Giovanni*."

"Although we cannot attend, neither Jane nor Elizabeth is engaged for that evening as far as I know. Am I right, my dears?" my aunt asked.

"I understand the tenor is exceptional," Mr. Bingley added, beaming at my sister. "Say you will come." He continued to keep his eyes upon Jane until she smiled and glanced in my direction. "And you, also, of course, Miss Elizabeth."

"If Jane is willing, I shall accept gladly, sir," I said.

"I am willing," Jane murmured.

"Splendid! I shall call for you at eight o'clock. And, oh yes, Caroline and Louisa ask that you call upon them in the meantime, Mrs. Gardiner, and both of you, as well, Miss Bennet and Miss Elizabeth."

We smiled in agreement, although I could not imagine his sisters having issued such an invitation. Mrs. Gardiner asked him to stay for dinner, which he agreed to, and I was delighted at how the day ended.

Our guest was, as usual, pleasant and charming, and I could see how happy both he and Jane were to spend the evening together. I could not help but wonder whether Mr. Darcy had spoken of Jane to Mr. Bingley. Had he rectified the injustice he had rendered my sister? If so, I should be greatly pleased.

At the end of the evening as we bade him good night, my uncle asked Mr. Bingley if Mr. Darcy had yet returned to Town, and he replied in the negative, stating that he did not know when to expect him.

"Naturally, you know more about that than I, Miss Elizabeth," he said, smiling at me. "I do hope he returns in time for the opera, for I am certain he will wish to join us."

I simply smiled. He appeared to assume there was some connection between his friend and me. Had Mr. Darcy failed to tell him that we were not to be married? I went to bed that night, my mind in a muddle. How long must we keep up this pretence?

As far as I knew, Mr. Darcy had not returned to London by the day of the opera. In the intervening days, Jane and I had called upon Miss Bingley and Mrs. Hurst—an uncomfortable visit I have no wish to recall—and Mr. Bingley had called upon us twice more. Each time he wondered aloud when his friend would return, and of course, we were also at a loss for an answer.

I was thrilled that Mr. Bingley now openly courted my sister. With every visit, he appeared more and more in love with her. Surely, he would declare his intentions any day. For that reason alone, I hoped Mr. Darcy stayed away from Town. I suspected that he might have spoken to Mr. Bingley about Jane in a positive manner, but I could not be sure, so I wished for nothing that might spoil their progress toward happiness.

As time drew near for our special night, Jane and I tried on various gowns and practised several hairstyles. Neither of us had ever attended a gala at Covent Garden, and the thought filled us with excitement.

My naturally optimistic outlook had pushed my disappointment with Mr. Darcy far below the surface of my emotions into the deepest recesses of my heart—or so I thought—and I did my best to face each day with hope for Jane, filling my mind with the distraction of a possible spring wedding. Goodness, I was beginning to sound like my mother!

The sole drawback to my happier outlook occurred when I chanced to find my uncle's discarded newspaper. It appeared that most days he took particular pains to carry it off to his office, but twice during that week, I discovered it left behind in its usual place beside his plate at the breakfast table. As soon as permissible, I stole upstairs to my room and pored over the issues searching for any news of the highwaymen.

What I found alarmed me!

The fate of the accused had evidently taken on less importance than reports of newer crimes, for other than a reminder of the trial date, there was nothing written about them. However, in a gossipy column on the society page, I saw the following references that filled me with dismay:

London hostesses are abuzz with talk of feting upcoming brides, not the least of which is when to hold congratulatory teas for the future Mrs. Fitzwilliam Darcy. As the groom has been mysteriously absent from Town and the bride a resident of Hertfordshire, it is anyone's guess as to when the nuptials will take place.

And a second notice three or four days later:

Has Mr. Darcy left his bride at the altar? The gentleman departed London with Colonel Richard Fitzwilliam, son of the Earl of Matlock, early last week, and neither of them has been seen for more than ten days. Speculation rises as to when and if the marriage will take place.

Both items filled me with anxiety, and when I complained to my aunt that I thought it dishonest to allow such rumours to continue, she had a difficult time persuading me otherwise.

"Your father and Mr. Darcy agreed that nothing should be said publicly until after the trial is over. You must not stir up a hornet's nest by rushing to set things straight. Think of Jane. Mr. Bingley calls regularly. We would not want to do anything to set that amiss, Lizzy."

I was forced to agree with her and stifled my urge to march to the newspaper office and tell the unvarnished truth. It was after our talk that I noticed my uncle took more pains to carry the periodical out of the house before I came down for breakfast.

All continued on a somewhat even measure until two days before the opera. That morning Jane and I sat in the parlour with my aunt applying our attention to our needlework. I had little aptitude for sewing and had always wished my stitches as neat and tiny as Jane's. I had just stuck my finger for the fifth time and popped it in my mouth to ease the pain when we heard a loud commotion outside the door.

"If you will wait right here, my lady, I shall announce you," the maid said.

"I do not wait," an imperious voice boomed.

The servant opened the door, and in sailed an older woman dressed in silks and fur, a large feathered bonnet on her head, and a parasol in her hand, the point of which she used as a walking stick.

"Lady Catherine de Bourgh, ma'am," the maid said quickly.

My aunt, Jane and I all stood immediately and curtseyed.

Lady Catherine de Bourgh! It was Mr. Darcy's aunt of whom my cousin, Mr. Collins, was so enthralled. Her eyes swept the room, a disdainful expression about her countenance, before she narrowed her gaze upon Jane.

"You are Miss Elizabeth Bennet, I presume," she declared.

"No," I said, stepping forward. "I am Elizabeth Bennet. This is my sister."

"You?" she said, turning to look me up and down. "Your sister is much prettier. I would have thought my nephew had better taste." She nodded her head in my aunt's direction. "And this woman, I suppose, is your mother."

"No," I said again, "this is my aunt, Mrs. Gardiner." My aunt bowed again, a courtesy to which our guest was oblivious. She walked around the room, looking it up and down.

"You have chosen a most unfashionable part of Town in which to reside."

My aunt looked at me with a frantic expression and then answered as best she could that the house had belonged to her parents and held great sentiment. Before she could finish the sentence, however, Lady Catherine cut her off.

"This must be a most inconvenient sitting-room for the evening in summer. Why, the windows are far too near the street, allowing the noise and stench of London to invade your house."

Mrs. Gardiner did not attempt to answer that insult, but with great civility, begged her ladyship to take some refreshment. Lady Catherine resolutely declined and then turned her attention to me.

"Miss Elizabeth Bennet, there seemed to be a prettyish kind of small park across the street. I should be glad to take a turn in it, if you will favour me with your company."

My aunt urged me to go with her, and I hastened to retrieve my pelisse and bonnet from the maid.

I followed the lady out the door as she marched down the steps and into the oncoming traffic, looking neither to her right nor left. Miraculously, the carriages stopped short of running her down. I wondered if she had any idea how closely she courted disaster. She appeared oblivious to everything except the path ahead.

We walked a short distance before she entered an unoccupied copse, whereupon she turned and began her interrogation of me.

"You can be at no loss, Miss Bennet, to understand the reason of my journey hither. Your own heart, your own conscience, must tell you why I come."

I was astonished. "Indeed, you are mistaken, madam. I have not been at all able to account for the honour of meeting you."

"You ought to know that I am not to be trifled with. A report of a most alarming nature reached me this week. I was informed that you would, in all likelihood, soon be united to my nephew—my own nephew—Mr. Darcy. Though I know it must be a scandalous falsehood, I instantly resolved on setting off for this place so that I might make my sentiments known to you."

Now I understood. *The Gazette* had reached Kent.

"If you believed it impossible to be true, I wonder that you took the trouble of coming so far. What could your ladyship propose by it?"

"At once to insist upon having such a report universally contradicted!"

"Your coming to Gracechurch Street to see me and my family will be rather a confirmation of it, if, indeed, such a report is in existence."

"If!" She coloured with anger. "Do not feign ignorance! Has it not been circulated by yourself? Do you not know that such a report is spread throughout the newspapers for all to see? And can you likewise declare that there is no foundation for it? Has my nephew made you an offer of marriage?"

"Your ladyship has declared it to be impossible."

"It ought to be so. It must be so, while he retains the use of reason. But your arts and allurements may have made him forget what he owes to himself and to all his family. You may have used this kidnapping scheme to draw him in!"

I began to find it hard to catch my breath. How dare this woman accuse me so! "If I have, I shall be the last person to confess it."

"Miss Bennet, do you know who I am? I am almost the nearest relation he has in the world and am entitled to know all his dearest concerns."

"But you are not entitled to know mine, nor will such behaviour as this ever induce me to be explicit."

She began to stride back and forth, glaring at me each time she made the turn. After a few moments' parade, she stopped abruptly.

"Let me be rightly understood. This match to which you have the presumption to aspire, can never take place. No, never. Mr. Darcy is engaged to my daughter. Now, what have you to say?"

"Only this: That if he is so, you can have no reason to suppose he will make an offer to me."

Lady Catherine hesitated for a moment and then replied. "The engagement between them is of a peculiar kind. From their infancy they have been intended for each other. It was the favourite wish of his mother, as well as hers. While in their cradles, we planned the union."

"What is that to me?" I asked, shocked at her audacity. "If there is no other objection to my marrying your nephew, I shall certainly not be kept from it by knowing that his mother and aunt wished him to marry Miss de Bourgh. Why is he not allowed to make his own choice of bride?"

"Because honour, decorum, prudence—nay, interest, forbid it. Your alliance will be a disgrace. Your name will never even be mentioned by any of his family."

"These are heavy misfortunes," I replied, "but the wife of Mr. Darcy must have such extraordinary sources of happiness attached to her situation that she could, upon the whole, have no cause to repine."

"Obstinate, headstrong girl! I am ashamed of you! I am not used to submitting to any person's whims. I am not in the habit of brooking disappointment."

"That will make your ladyship's situation at present more pitiable, but it will have no effect on me."

She sank down upon a stone bench placed within the enclosure. "I will not be interrupted! If you were sensible of your own good, you would not wish to quit the sphere in which you have been brought up!"

"By marrying your nephew I should not consider myself as quitting that sphere. He is a gentleman. I am a gentleman's daughter. So far, we are equal."

"True," she said, rising and pointing the parasol at me. "But who was your mother? Who are your uncles and aunts? You cannot imagine me ignorant of their condition."

Aha! Now I saw the resemblance between nephew and aunt—that abominable pride. I was not to marry Mr. Darcy, but I could not resist baiting the hateful old woman. "Whatever my connections may be, if your nephew does not object to them, they can be nothing to you."

Her eyes widened as though she had been struck. "Tell me, once for all, are you engaged to him?"

How I hated to oblige Lady Catherine by admitting the truth. I hesitated a moment before answering, "I am not."

She closed her eyes, relief washing over her countenance. "And will you promise me never to enter into such an engagement?"

"I will make no promise of the kind. I shall not be intimidated into anything so wholly unreasonable. Your ladyship wants Mr. Darcy to marry your daughter, but would my making you a promise make *their* marriage more probable? Allow me to say, Lady Catherine, that the arguments with which you have supported this extraordinary application have been as frivolous as the application was ill-judged. You have widely mistaken my character if you think I can be worked on by such persuasions as these."

I took several steps away from her, but then turned back, my hands balled up in fists. "You have no right to concern yourself in my affairs. I must beg, therefore, to be importuned no further on the subject. You can have nothing more to say. You have insulted me in every possible method. I must beg to return to the house."

I whirled around and walked hurriedly up the path while she continued behind me, spewing forth further diatribes. I recall the words *unfeeling, selfish girl* and how I would *disgrace him in the eyes of everybody.* That time it was I who stormed across the street without a thought to passing carriages.

"I take no leave of you, Miss Bennet," she announced once inside her conveyance. "I send no compliments to your aunt. You deserve no such attention. I am seriously displeased."

I heard the wheels of the barouche turn as I opened the door and entered my aunt's house. Now why had I defended my right to marry Mr. Darcy with such vigour when I had not the slightest intention of doing so?

Chapter Twelve

The day of the opera arrived at last replete with a flurry of activities from morning to night. I was filled with excitement at the glamorous evening awaiting us and not a little apprehensive at the thought that Mr. Darcy would possibly attend. Mr. Bingley still had not seen him, so my fears were likely groundless. He might yet be away from London on whatever mysterious excursion he had taken.

I spent considerable amounts of time wondering about that trip. Had he returned to his home in Derbyshire? If he had, why did he not take his young sister with him? Of course, I knew nothing of his estate business, so perchance it was something of that nature that claimed his attention.

Or perhaps it was a lady in a distant county upon whom he called. I thought of how he had kissed me, seemingly unaware of whom he kissed. If he loved someone else, he would have been thinking of her, and if that thought were true, I could not bear to dwell upon it. I recalled the strength of his passion. I imagined the woman for whom that kiss was intended, and I wondered if she knew how fortunate she was.

Such worrisome thoughts prevented my attaining any true ease that afternoon, and I was relieved to have much to do to prepare for the evening ahead. A long perfumed bath followed by washing and drying my hair took up a good two hours.

Jane wished to style my coiffure, and I agreed, for she was far more talented than my aunt's maid. She took great pains to weave tiny pearl-coloured flowers through my curls that matched the shade of my gown perfectly.

"You shall wear my rose-coloured cloak," she announced, as she finished with my hair.

"But Jane, it complements your complexion more than mine."

"Not tonight when I shall be in blue. Aunt has offered her navy velvet wrap."

My eyes lit up at the thought of how lovely she would appear. Mr. Bingley would not be able to resist her.

We had just pulled on our long white gloves when my aunt tapped at the door to tell us he had arrived. I insisted upon going down first and cautioned Jane to wait a few moments so that she might descend the stairs alone.

"I do not want anything to distract Mr. Bingley from the heavenly vision he will have the pleasure to escort."

"Oh, Lizzy," Jane said, smiling shyly, but she agreed to do as I wished.

And my plan was not in vain, for Mr. Bingley could not tear his eyes from her, nor could he force the smile from his face, as she glided down the stairway. I did not miss how his hands lingered upon her shoulders as he assisted her with her wrap, or how long he held onto her hand when she stepped into his carriage. Oh yes, this would be a perfect evening, I was sure of it!

And the best news of all was that Caroline had decided to ride with Mr. Hurst so that her gown would not be crushed, or at least that was the excuse she gave her brother. We had only to tolerate Mrs. Hurst during the ride to our destination, and without Caroline, she was outnumbered and said little, if anything at all.

Arrays of lights and throngs of beautifully dressed people welcomed us to Covent Garden. I had never seen that many feathers in one place at one time!

Mr. Bingley led us up the great staircase to his private box, and I thrilled at the grandeur of the theatre and multitudes of gaily-dressed people seated below and in various boxes around the perimeter of the theatre. Below the stage, the orchestra tuned their instruments as we found our way to our seats.

I expected Caroline and Mr. and Mrs. Hurst to sit with us, but when we reached the apartment, Mrs. Hurst declared that room did not exist for three women in evening dress, although I thought the seating arrangements more than adequate. She and her sister seemed unduly concerned about crushed gowns that evening.

"I have it on good authority that Mr. Darcy shall be all alone tonight in his large, roomy box," she said. "I see Caroline has already been asked to join him. I shall send Mr. Hurst to join you, and I shall sit with my sister. Shall that not work out perfectly?" She bestowed upon us one of her famous smiles that reminded me of a Cheshire cat.

Mr. Bingley looked about the milling crowd and waved slightly in the direction of Mr. Darcy's box. Jane and I followed his gaze and saw Caroline firmly ensconced therein, sitting directly across from us. My heart beat a bit faster as I searched for Mr. Darcy's tall, familiar figure, but he did not appear.

"Darcy must have returned to London and met with Caroline as soon as she and Mr. Hurst arrived," Mr. Bingley said. "Perhaps he will come by and call upon us. It is of little consequence, of course, for we shall see all of them at intermission and at dinner afterwards. I know both my sisters are eager to spend time with you again, Miss Bennet, and you, too, Miss Elizabeth."

Oh yes, indeed, I thought, just as eager as I to be with them.

Mr. Hurst entered the box shortly thereafter and grunted his usual greeting. Jane and I removed our cloaks, and I tugged my gloves back into position before I sat down. I stepped in front of the plush gold velvet chairs and peered over the rail at the crowd below. I had never seen so much of London's high society in one place at one time. Fans, feathers and sparkling jewels intermingled with starched stiff collars and carefully groomed beards, all to the accompaniment of lilting laughter and rich, varied conversations.

Suddenly, somewhat of a hush seemed to settle over the theatre, and I turned toward the stage, expecting the program to begin. The musicians, however, continued to tune their instruments. No actors appeared on the stage.

Then I saw people turn their eyes upward in my direction and begin to whisper behind their fans. I glanced over my shoulder to see if someone else had entered our box, but no, there was only Mr. Hurst, Jane, and Mr. Bingley handing our wraps to an attendant behind them.

Could they be gossiping about my sister, speculating as to whether there was to be an announcement of their upcoming nuptials? But no, surely there would be smiles upon their faces at thoughts of a wedding. Instead, I saw disapproving frowns and harsh, disdainful expressions as they gazed at our box.

Then I stood amazed when some began to point with their fingers or fans, and I heard snatches of phrases: "*scandal... sham marriage... she and Mr. Darcy... who is she?... three days in the same room... will not marry... shocking!*"

I backed away from the railing and sank down upon the chair beside Jane. Surely my imagination ran amok. Surely people were not actually talking about *me* in such an insulting manner!

The servants began to turn the lights down low, and the conductor tapped his baton, signalling the audience that the opera was about to begin. It was not until after the conductor repeatedly tapped his baton on the music stand, however, that the talk died down.

I had glanced at Mr. Bingley when it began and saw the nervous, uncomfortable expression about his eyes and the strained manner in which he smiled. Jane reached over and held my hand, squeezing it until I almost cried aloud. Oh, what had I done?

Please, Lord, I prayed, do not let this gossip dissuade Mr. Bingley from his attentions toward Jane!

And then, thankfully, the great swell of music began, and all attention turned upon the stage and to the artistes providing the evening's entertainment. I tried with everything that was in me to concentrate on the story portrayed before us, but to this day I cannot tell you anything about *Don Giovanni.*

Mr. Bingley handed his opera glasses to Jane, and she shared them with me. I raised them to my eyes, but I do not remember any costume worn, aria sung, or scenery that decorated the stage below. All I could think of was the hateful way in which I had been treated.

What had caused this sudden outrage? Why did society now deem me an object of gossip and spite, when earlier this week shopkeepers had courted me in hopes of obtaining my business for the forthcoming wedding they assumed was to take place? These thoughts whirled round and round during the first scene, until at last an idea struck me.

Mr. Darcy must have returned and informed the newspapers that we would not marry!

Immediately, I turned my gaze from the stage to his box, and my breath caught in my throat to see him sitting beside Caroline Bingley, his face turned in my direction. I had not seen him enter, and my companions had not mentioned it. He must have slipped in under cover of darkness after the music commenced.

I glared at him but knew our seats were too far away in distance for my expression to have any effect. Nor could I see the tenor of his countenance, only his head inclined toward me. Quickly I returned my attention to the stage and applauded at the end of the second scene.

During the third scene, I believe some kind of wedding celebration occurred in the story, for I do remember a bride and dancing, but as for the gist of the story, I was lost. I was only aware of Mr. Darcy's gaze planted firmly upon my person. Each time I glanced his way out of the corner of my eye, I could see his posture turned toward Mr. Bingley's box.

I wondered if he was angry that Jane and I had accompanied his friend or if he had heard the gossip before the show began. Most of all, I wondered why his eyes never deviated, why he persisted in staring at me throughout the performance. Had the man not come to see and hear an opera?

At the end of the first act, I clapped almost too vigorously, so relieved I was to rise from view and exit for the intermission. Why I ever thought the situation would be more favourable without is beyond my comprehension.

Mr. Hurst left our presence immediately, rushing from the box in search of liquid refreshment. I followed Mr. Bingley and Jane down the staircase to the gallery below where London society now mingled, gaily greeting each other with bows and curtseys.

I soon found myself clearly and plainly snubbed. As the three of us made our way across the large lobby, the crowd cut a wide swath. People did bow to Mr. Bingley, but then looked down their noses at Jane and me and immediately turned away. Not one person spoke to my sister or me, and many a rude gesture was openly directed my way.

"I wonder where Caroline and Louisa are," Mr. Bingley said, his voice emerging somewhat higher than normal. "I know they wished to join us."

He looked about the throng, but they did not appear or seek us out. One glance at Jane's face told me how humiliated she was. This would not do! I felt impelled to free her from my constraint.

"Mr. Bingley, I pray you will excuse me," I murmured, slipping my hand from his arm. "Please do not be concerned—a sudden wave of fatigue. I shall return to my seat."

Before he or Jane could deter me, I hurried up the stairs, brushing past the couples who still descended. I walked down the red carpet as fast as decorum permitted. I kept my face averted as I searched for Mr. Bingley's box. At last I found it, pushed open the door, and rushed inside, while my breath came forth in great gasps.

I was dismayed to see patrons still remained below and in their boxes, and not wishing to be seen, I pulled a chair well back behind the long drapes hanging on the side. There, somewhat hidden from prying eyes, I sank down upon the seat and fanned myself. I sighed deeply, aghast at how the evening had turned out.

If only I could find a way out of the theatre and make my way back to Gracechurch Street! But how? I was trapped, and my presence assured Jane of sharing in my censure.

Had not Mr. Darcy warned me of this? Had not my aunt and uncle and my father done the same? But no, I had foolishly ignored their words, confident that I could handle any rebuke London society had to offer. What I had not realized was the vicious depth to which the *ton* would punish not only me but my innocent sister as well.

I leaned back in the chair and closed my eyes, hoping to restrain the tears about to betray my emotions, when I saw the door to the box open and Mr. Darcy enter. I immediately sat up straighter and lifted my chin. Whatever was he doing there? He looked about, an anxious frown upon his face, before he spied me.

"Miss Bennet! Are you ill? I saw you leave your party and hurry above stairs."

I glared at him and did not even stand in greeting.

"Elizabeth?" he said again, pulling a chair to the side so that he could sit beside me. "Tell me the cause of your distress."

"Those are fine words coming from you," I spat at him. "After what you have done, how can you pretend solicitude?"

"I have no idea to what you refer."

"Do not insult me further by asking me to believe you know nothing of what has taken place."

"I fear I do not have the pleasure of understanding you."

He reached for my hand, but I snatched it away and turned my face to the wall. "Do you mean to say you did not witness the cuts Jane and I endured before the opera began and in the lobby below?"

"No, I—I did not," he said, rising. "I just returned to Town this evening and was detained by several acquaintances without. I did not enter my box until after the performance began. Tell me what happened."

"Precisely what you predicted," I replied. "I was greeted with whispers, hisses, and pointed fingers before the performance, and *your* friends made certain that Jane and I knew we were not worthy of their acknowledgement during the intermission. That is why I ran up here to hide. I thought perhaps Jane might be spared if I removed myself from her presence."

His only response was to press his lips together, but I could see the vein stand out on his forehead, the one that indicated he was in high dudgeon.

"If only I could leave this place, could return to my uncle's house."

"Yes! That is what we must do—get you away from here immediately."

"We?" I was incredulous. "I have no intention of going anywhere with you, sir! That would only increase gossip."

He appeared to ignore my declaration and pulled out his watch. "There is still at least ten minutes left before the second act begins. Wait here. That will allow me time to have my carriage brought round. When your sister, Bingley, and Hurst return, make your excuses, and as soon as the lights are dimmed, go downstairs and out the front door. My driver will be waiting and will take you back to Mr. Gardiner's house."

I was amazed that he had devised a solution so quickly. He did not propose to inflict himself upon me but simply offered his carriage to spirit me away, which was exactly what I wished.

"Thank—thank you," I murmured, dumbfounded.

"Do not worry, Elizabeth," he said, "I shall make certain you get away safely."

My heart turned over at the kindness in his voice and the sympathy in his eyes. Surely, he must be the most handsome man ever created, I thought, especially in evening dress! With the slightest of bows, he turned and exited the box.

I remained behind the drapes out of sight of any returning audience members until the intermission ended, and Jane and Mr. Bingley returned, along with Mr. Hurst.

"Lizzy, are you unwell?" Jane cried. "Why did you desert us?"

"A sudden headache," I said.

"Shall I take you home?" Mr. Bingley asked.

"No, there is no need for you and Jane to miss the rest of the performance. Mr. Darcy has offered his carriage."

"Darcy? Is he here?" Mr. Bingley asked, looking toward his box.

I nodded and rose just as the lights dimmed

"Shall I not come with you?" Jane asked, concern evident in her eyes.

"No, all is well. Stay and enjoy the evening."

I bade them goodnight and slipped out the door. I passed not more than three or four couples hurrying to their seats as I ran down the great staircase. I did not even bother to notice if they directed disapproving frowns toward me. Crossing the wide lobby, my slippers lightly tapping on the polished floor, I willed myself to appear perfectly at ease as the doorman opened the doors for me.

How relieved I was to see a carriage waiting, a footman with his hand upon the door handle!

"Miss Bennet?" he inquired.

I nodded and he pulled down the steps. Once I was safely inside, he said, "Mr. Darcy suggests that you lower the shade, Miss."

"Yes, of course."

The opposite window was already covered, and I immediately applied myself to release the other. I heard the driver speak to the horses and felt the coach move. Only then did I breathe out a sigh of relief. At last, I was safe from public scrutiny. I could not wait to return to the security of my uncle's house.

We went only a short distance, however, when the carriage suddenly stopped, and before I could pull back the shade, the footman opened the door once again. I knew we could not have reached Gracechurch Street so soon. Did they propose to thrust me out in the middle of Town?

Then I heard Mr. Darcy's voice. "Thank you, Hudson."

He pushed the shade aside and climbed into the coach, seating himself across from me. "That worked out rather well, did it not?" he asked. "If anyone happened to see you leave, they thought you were alone. I arranged to be picked up two streets from the theatre."

I was surprised at his plan, but I said nothing.

"Are you warm enough?" he asked. "Shall I fetch a rug?"

I shook my head. It was so dark inside the cab that I could hardly make out his features.

"Now tell me, is tonight the first time you have been treated in this shabby manner?"

"Yes," I said brusquely.

I heard him utter an oath under his breath, but before he could address me further, I declared, "I find it quite odd that my public disfavour coincides with your return to London. I have not read the newspapers for the last two days, sir, but evidently you decided the time was right to publicize the fact that we are not to marry. I only wish my uncle had informed me. If I had known, I would not have ruined my sister's evening."

"You think I alerted the papers?" His tone of voice was shocked. "I just returned this evening. How could I have perpetrated the deed?"

"Well... if you did not do it, then who?"

"I do not know, but I shall find out."

Immediately, he tapped the roof of the carriage with his cane, and the driver slowed the coach and stopped. Mr. Darcy stepped out, and I pulled the shade aside to observe, having not the slightest idea what he was about. He asked if any of the servants had a newspaper.

A newspaper! Did he think they read in the dark? I rolled my eyes, but unfortunately, he did not witness my scorn. And then I was astounded to hear that the driver actually sat on a paper, saving it to amuse himself while waiting for the opera to conclude.

Mr. Darcy beckoned to the runners carrying the road torches, and one of them held his light close so that he might search the periodical. I heard him utter another oath, and within moments, he joined me inside the cab and instructed the driver to walk on.

"Well, there is the answer," he said with disgust.

"What do you mean? Is it in the *Gazette* as I feared? And does it reveal the source who told the reporters?"

"Did you happen to have a recent visit from my aunt, Lady Catherine de Bourgh?"

A feeling of doom descended over me. "I did, sir, two days ago."

"And did she demand an answer as to whether we would marry?"

"Yes, she did. I fear we did not part on the best of terms."

"No doubt," he said, sighing. "She has taken her revenge on you. The reporter quoted her."

"What does it say?"

"Nothing worth repeating. Suffice it to say the cat is out of the bag. All London knows there will not be a wedding as well as Lady Catherine's ill opinion of you. How I wish you had refused to speak with her!"

"She is hardly a personage one can easily refuse anything."

"True. I hate to even think of how she insulted you."

I said nothing. How could I repeat the dreadful things with which Mr. Darcy's aunt had threatened me?

"Do not bother to reply. I know her well enough. I can only apologize for any and everything she said."

"She was adamant that you are to marry her daughter," I said quietly.

"Ah yes, she persists in that delusion, although neither my cousin nor I have any desire to bring that occasion about. I am afraid my aunt lives in a realm of her own, wherein she thinks she can command obedience not only from servants but also from family members and everyone else within earshot. Believe me when I tell you that is one command that will not be heeded."

Why did I feel such relief when he said that? I had doubted that his cousin was the object of his affections ever since Mr. Wickham had told me she possessed a sickly constitution. I could see their marriage taking place out of duty to combine the family fortunes, but I could not imagine that Mr. Darcy loved a woman of that description. No, the woman he desired must be one of great passion who could respond to his own driving need.

I suddenly grew warm all over, aware that the cab was quite close, and we were alone in the dark. I pushed the hood of my cloak back, hoping it would lessen the heat causing me discomfort.

"I was surprised that you went away, Mr. Darcy," I said, attempting to change the subject. "The constable's office informed me that I must remain in London until after the highwaymen's trial. I fail to see why you were allowed to depart when I was not."

"You are correct. We are to stay here. I confess I did not bother to ask permission from the authorities before Fitzwilliam and I left. Did they question you about what happened during the abduction?"

"They did. I told them the necessary facts and attempted to explain Morgan's background, although I do not think it caused them to think any higher of him."

"No, I doubt that will happen, Elizabeth. You must come to terms with it."

I sighed and did not reply. We rode in silence for a while. "I hope you enjoyed your respite from London. Pleasure bent, I assume?"

"Hardly."

He did not elaborate, which vexed me, but I did not know how to question him as to his whereabouts without appearing unduly interested. I wracked my brain thinking of a subtle manner in which to accomplish my goal.

"I suppose you had business in Derbyshire," I said at last somewhat awkwardly.

"Does it matter where I have been?" I heard bemusement in his voice.

"Of course not," I snapped. "I was simply making conversation."

"I see."

I knew he was laughing at me, most probably flattered that I was curious as to where he had travelled. I resolved to say nothing more, even if my life depended upon it.

We rode in silence for several minutes before he said, "Fitzwilliam and I returned to Hazleden, Jonah's Village, and the country thereabout."

Nothing could have surprised me more! Why should he wish to revisit an area of such unpleasant memories?

"You may wonder at my choice," he said.

When I murmured my assent, he explained that they had spent two weeks searching out Morgan's former haunts, looking for clues as to his background and, in particular, who it was that he had slain.

"You do recall that the man has committed murder, do you not, Miss Bennet?"

"Of course, I do. He told me so himself."

"I am well aware of what he told you. I wished to ascertain if it was the truth or one of his tales. As it turns out, it happened years ago, but Morgan was never apprehended and brought to trial. The man he killed was a landowner, formerly of France, Monsieur Devereaux, who owned a large estate outside Jonah."

He stopped speaking and turned directly toward me. I could feel the force of his gaze even in the darkness. "And it seems you were right in your assessment, Elizabeth. Morgan took his life in self-defence—over a woman."

"A woman? But who?"

"You need not worry. 'Twas not one who had stolen his heart, but rather his half-sister."

"His sister? What happened?"

"She worked as scullery maid in Devereaux's kitchen, and Morgan, little more than a youth at the time, served as stable hand. One evening he heard screams coming from the stillroom and discovered the landowner assaulting the woman. When he interrupted the scoundrel, Devereaux sliced his face with a sword and then lunged for his heart. Morgan defended himself with the only weapon he carried, a pitchfork."

I gasped, cringing at the image, and I could not speak for several moments. Then a thought struck me. "It reminds one of his mother's plight."

"His mother?"

"Yes, do you not remember how I told you Morgan's father took advantage of his mother when she was but a maid in his house? There he was, witness to the same horrible deed repeated upon his sister."

"Perhaps that is how it played out in his mind. I cannot say. I do know that is when his life began as a fugitive. He and his sister fled before the authorities arrived, and from then on, he lived in the shadows as a petty criminal. 'Tis a shame he advanced into delusions of infamy, thinking he could act the highwayman."

"Now he faces kidnapping and extortion charges as well," I said softly.

"True. I cannot but feel somewhat responsible for that."

"Responsible! You? But why?" I asked, shocked at his statement.

"Because I suggested he hold me for ransom. As I told Fitzwilliam, I doubt any of those villains could have imagined such an idea if I had not planted it in their minds."

"Then I share in your guilt, Mr. Darcy, for if you had not sought to protect me, none of it would have transpired."

We were silent once more, the clip-clop of the horses' hooves the only sounds heard. Snatches of passing lights flickered through the sides of the shades.

"Why ever did you go in search of this information, sir? Why should *you* seek to aid Morgan?"

He did not answer for several moments, other than a deep sigh. "I know that you—well, that is, I have no wish to see the man hang. With the background we have uncovered, perhaps the murder charge can be dismissed. And besides, I wanted to do what I could for the woman Gert.

After all, she let us go."

"Gert? What has she to do with this?"

"She is Morgan's sister, Elizabeth. I thought you knew that by now."

"His sister!"

"Evidently, she led a rough life after leaving the Frenchman's house. Morgan retrieved her more than once until finally he installed her at that cabin in the woods. There he could afford her some measure of protection."

"Then there is some good in him, is there not?"

"There is, I believe, in every disposition a tendency to good and evil."

I grew quiet, recalling the scenes between Gert and Morgan. Those memories led to reliving the days Mr. Darcy and I had spent confined together in that small room... and the nights.

"Did you and Colonel Fitzwilliam revisit the highwayman's cabin?"

"Yes. It is all the same. Nothing has changed. Even the blanket still lies on the floor where—where we—" He broke off and pulled the shade aside as though he was distracted by a passing sight.

"At times it seems as though it all happened so long ago," I said, sighing.

"And sometimes as though it were only yesterday." His voice was so low I had to strain to make out his words.

I cleared my throat. "Mr. Darcy, do you ever—oh, this is insupportable! I know not why I even think about it."

"About what? Tell me."

"It is quite strange. At times I find myself almost wishing to return to that place. How can I?"

"To Morgan's cabin?" He sat up straighter, and I sensed an alteration in his demeanour, although I could not make it out inside the dark coach.

"No, sir, you mistake my meaning. I do not wish to return to the cabin, but to the wood after we were freed. I know we travelled in primitive conditions—afraid, hungry, without shelter—but at least we were at liberty. We knew the identity of the enemy and we stood... united." I pulled my cloak closer, suddenly chilled. "After tonight, in this society, I shall be as confined to my uncle's house as I was imprisoned in that cabin."

"Blast!" he said loudly. "It is utterly unfair that you should continue to suffer."

Neither of us said anything, riding in silence for some time before he spoke again. "I noticed a park across the way from Mr. Gardiner's house.

Might you not at least walk there with your sister? Perhaps Bingley and I could escort the two of you."

My heart leapt at the thought, not only of escaping the house but also at the chance to see him again. However, he dashed those hopes with his next statement.

"No, that would not do. If anyone saw us together, it would only cause more tongues to wag. People would say you were my—well, it simply would not do."

Just then, the driver pulled up on the horses, and I suspected we had reached my uncle's house. Within moments, the footman opened the door, and Mr. Darcy descended the steps from the carriage and then reached for my hand to help me out. I could feel the warmth and comfort of his touch through my glove. It seemed to travel up my arm and wrap itself around my heart. How I wished he would never let go!

We entered the small parlour, having been informed by the servant that my aunt and uncle had not yet returned from their evening out. I thought to ring for tea, but intuiting that both of us needed something a bit stronger, I suggested a glass of sherry, which Mr. Darcy did not refuse. We sat down and sipped our drinks in silence.

I was suddenly quite conscious that we were alone. It had seemed so natural at first that I thought nothing of it, for had we not spent days and nights in no one's company but each other's? We, however, were no longer hidden away in that cabin in the woods. We were inside a house in London, and servants did talk.

Almost as though we both became aware of the thought at the same time, Mr. Darcy rose to leave, stating that he should go.

As we approached the door to the foyer, I thanked him for escorting me home. "Once again, sir, you have come to my aid. I have taken advantage of your kindness far too often."

His eyes softened as they gazed into mine. I feared he could see the intensity of my emotions reflected on my countenance, might realize that I loved him, and so I averted my face.

"Mr. Darcy, I must ask you something."

"Yes?"

"Mr. Bingley has called often upon my sister since you have been away. Did you happen to speak to him about her before leaving Town?"

"How could I not attempt to right the wrong I did once you confided her true feelings to me?"

I caught my breath. "Thank you."

"I fear that I have been a selfish being all my life. As a child, I was given good principles, but left to follow them in pride and conceit. Unfortunately, I was spoiled by my parents, who, though good themselves, allowed, encouraged, almost taught me to be selfish and overbearing—to care for none beyond my own."

He let out his breath in a deep sigh. "Such I was, from eight to eight-and-twenty, and such I might still have been—but for you."

He looked down at me with such a strange expression that I felt as though I might drown in the depths of his dark eyes. "You taught me a lesson, hard indeed at first, but most advantageous. By you, Miss Bennet, I was properly humbled."

"I never meant to humble you, sir. How you must have hated me after what I said to you."

"Hated you! I was angry, perhaps at first, but my anger soon began to take a proper direction. I hope to show you by every civility in my power that I hope to obtain your forgiveness, to lessen your ill opinion by letting you see that your reproofs have been attended to."

I looked at the floor, not knowing how to respond. "You have done much to alter my opinion of you. I shall be eternally grateful if what you have done secures the happiness of my dear sister."

"Then let us hope Mr. Bingley's affections can weather society's onslaught."

"Yes, let us hope," I echoed.

"And if it does not come about, Elizabeth, do not blame yourself. It simply means he is not a good enough man to merit your sister's love."

Taking my hand, he kissed it and then walked out the door. Without thinking, I placed my hand still warm from his caress, against my cheek. If I never saw him again, I would rejoice that we parted on such magnanimous terms.

Mr. Darcy was the best man I had ever known or hoped to know, and I felt certain I should love him more than any other man for the rest of my life.

Chapter Thirteen

Christmas arrived a few days later and with it my parents and sisters, Mary and Kitty. Lydia, the youngest, had been invited to spend the holidays with Colonel and Mrs. Forster. He was in command of the militia quartered in Meryton and married to a much younger woman who, for some reason, had singled out my fifteen-year-old sister as her particular companion. Kitty's nose was out of joint at the lack of a similar invitation, but I felt uneasy that my parents had allowed Lydia to forsake our family's holiday for that of such a new acquaintance.

"Nonsense!" my mother declared when I voiced my concerns. "Your sister is much better off at Colonel Forster's where she may enjoy the company of the young officers than she would be here in Town where no eligible young men may call. And all because of you, Lizzy."

That began another round of complaints of how my senseless refusal of two proposals had thrown my sisters—my entire family—into the direst of straits. She went on and on and on, ending with the usual, "Oh, what is to become of us all?" refrain that my sisters and I could mimic in unison.

If not for my aunt's frequent interference and distraction of Mamá's interests, I feared that my ears might literally have fallen from my head, such was the intensity and duration of her objections.

Whenever spared, I hid either in my uncle's library curled up in a corner with a book, in my room where Jane sympathised with me, or in my aunt's garden at the back of the house. There I rambled through the miniature paths and lamented to the yellow tomcat that it was the time of year when little was in bloom except my mother's tongue.

I suppose we celebrated Christmas day and the ensuing festivities, but it all seems to blur when I think back on it. My pressing concern was the upcoming trial of Morgan and his gang and with its termination, how quickly I could return to Hertfordshire.

I had convinced my uncle to allow me access to the newspaper once he learned how hatefully Jane and I had been shamed at the opera. He regretted now that he had overlooked Lady Catherine's notice that Mr. Darcy and I were not to marry.

There was little published, however, about the trial beforehand, and I did not have any way of knowing whether Mr. Darcy's enquiry into Morgan's past would benefit the man. All I could do was trust that he would do what he could to keep the highwayman from hanging.

What I did find in the society portion of the newspaper were accounts of various parties and balls at Almack's and other establishments wherein Mr. Darcy's name was often linked with several young women.

He had been seen dancing the night away, one article claimed, with a Miss Templeton, Lady Jersey's niece visiting from Bath, and another time with the Countess Olenska's daughter from Vienna. I did not put absolute faith in the veracity of the reports, for I knew how little Mr. Darcy cared for dancing. I could not squelch the jealousy I felt, though, at the thought that one of them might be the woman he truly loved.

The one spot of joy in those days was the fact that Mr. Bingley continued to call upon Jane. Actually, he called upon all of us, but no one could mistake his partiality for my sister's company.

Neither of his sisters accompanied him on his visits, and he no longer even pretended to offer excuses for their absence. My mother, of course, continued to ask about them, believing his family supported his interests and that nothing could hamper the gentleman's quest for Jane's hand. How I hoped with all my heart that she might be correct. He, at least, was persistent in his courting although he had yet to ask that all-important question.

"Mary," Mamá demanded one morning before Mr. Bingley was to visit, "when you and Kitty walk in the park with Jane and Mr. Bingley this afternoon, make certain you lag behind them—well behind, mind you."

A light snow began to fall two hours before the visit that day, however, and my mother's plot fell by the wayside due to forces even she could not control.

"Is everything against us?" she wailed, casting her eyes to the ceiling of my aunt's parlour.

She made every attempt to leave the couple alone together in various public rooms of the house, but with so many inhabitants dwelling under the same roof, they were always interrupted. Each time he left without having declared himself, my mother threw up her hands, and her familiar refrain could be heard all over the house. "Oh, what is to become of us all?"

In bed at night, Jane and I would laugh about our mother's distress, but in reality I, too, wondered at Mr. Bingley's hesitation. Had Mr. Darcy been correct? Was he not man enough to bear the *ton's* disapproval and align himself with the now infamous Bennet family? Had I truly ruined my sister's chances of a successful marriage?

Jane would not allow me to voice these concerns aloud, and so I spent many restless nights wondering.

The week of the trial finally arrived, and my uncle planned to accompany my father to the proceedings. How I wished I could witness it, somehow unobserved by others!

The day before it began, I found myself quite nervous, unable to sit still for any length of time, my mind at sixes and sevens when attempting to concentrate on a book, music, or conversation. My mother's endless lamentations drove me to distraction. My father had escaped the house by hiding at my uncle's office, so I had not even his wit to entertain me.

At last, I slipped out the back door and through the garden gate. I had been warned to keep to the house or inside the back enclosure, but I simply could not restrain myself from leaving the premises.

I walked around the house, which covered most of the lane, and crossed the street to the park. A light wind whistled through the bare trees, tossing my curls about, even under cover of a bonnet. I did not care how cold it grew. I was relieved to be out of doors and able to walk.

I hiked down the path a good distance, passing the copse where Lady Catherine had threatened me, past the small pond, now too cold for even the ducks to emerge. A pair of nurses pushed their young charges in prams, bundled up against the weather. The women smiled and nodded, and I was grateful that someone other than my family greeted me with civility, aware that they knew neither my identity nor my notoriety. I was obliged for even the slightest bit of warmth in this bitter city I had grown to loathe.

How far I walked I know not, for my mind travelled even farther away from that peaceful park, across town to the Old Bailey where the trial would begin on the morrow. I could well imagine what would take place, although I had never set foot inside a courtroom.

I could see Sneyd's ugly countenance, how like a weasel he would seem, dirty in appearance and reprehensible in conduct. He would not hesitate to defame Mr. Darcy or me if it would add to his defence, nor would he help Morgan. After all, had he not attempted to kill Morgan? I could well imagine what lies he might heap onto the highwayman's list of offences.

As for Rufus and Merle, they had sided with Sneyd against Morgan. I doubted that they would hesitate to corroborate whatever untruths he told.

Mr. Darcy's word, of course, would be held in higher esteem by the court, and he would denounce the band of thieves, but what would he say in regard to Morgan? He said he did not wish him to hang for murder, but that did not relieve the highwayman from the charge of kidnapping and extortion, as well as robbery. I shook my head, all too aware that there seemed little chance he could escape harsh punishment.

By that time I had walked a great distance from Gracechurch Street. When my mind returned to the present, I saw that I had covered the circumference of the park and found myself emerging from the wood upon a city street with which I was not familiar. A row of houses similar to my aunt's lined up across the road.

Several carriages passed in front of me, and the sounds of the city now awakened my thoughts from those that had consumed me. I had just turned to retrace my steps through the park, for I had not the slightest intention of walking that public route, when a carriage pulled up and I heard a voice call to me.

"Miss Eliza? Is that you?"

I glanced over my shoulder, shocked to see Miss Bingley lean out the window of her carriage and address me. "Miss Bingley," I said, curtseying.

"What are you doing out here alone?" She beckoned for me to approach the coach.

"I—I went for a walk through the park and must have gone farther than I was aware. I actually do not know this street."

"You are some distance from Gracechurch Street," she announced. "You had better join my sister and me and let us take you to your aunt's house."

I thought that an extraordinary offer, coming from Caroline Bingley, but one I could hardly refuse. Climbing into the coach, I greeted Mrs. Hurst, who bestowed her usual brittle smile upon me.

"Miss Bennet," Mrs. Hurst said, "what a surprise! I had thought you in seclusion."

"Yes, Charles says you do not leave your uncle's house," Miss Bingley added.

"True," I answered. "I confess that today I simply could not stay housebound and allowed myself to steal away."

"Rather dangerous in this neighbourhood," Mrs. Hurst said, "would you not agree, Caroline?"

"Oh, yes. You really should not go out alone here so near Cheapside. Now, in our part of Town it would be perfectly acceptable, well not acceptable, but at least safe. Actually, one should never go out alone. It simply is not done. I know you are used to tramping the wood in Hertfordshire, but— "

"Yes, we acknowledge what an excellent walker you are," Mrs. Hurst agreed. "But Caroline is correct. You must not wander so far in Town, and especially not when you are under such scrutiny. Why, what if we had not been the ones who found you? What if it had been one of those horrid reporters?"

"Oh yes, Eliza. Charles says you are held a virtual prisoner in your uncle's house. What a terrible time of year for that to happen, with all the balls and parties! How you must suffer!" Miss Bingley actually pulled her face down as though she sympathized with me. I wondered if she knew how prune-like it made her appear.

"I am surprised to find you in this area," I said. "Are you calling on close friends?"

"Goodness, no! We took Charles to visit your poor family," Mrs. Hurst said. "He insists he must do what he can to keep up your spirits."

"That he surely does," I replied. "'Tis a pity you could not visit with him."

"We would, my dear," Mrs. Hurst said, "if not for a prior engagement claiming our allegiance. You understand."

"Of course. Mr. Bingley has given that same reason for your absence oft times recently."

"Oh, you know how busy one is during the holidays," Miss Bingley offered. "One's time is simply not one's own with so many calls to make. I confess the stack of invitations at our house grows higher each day. You understand, of course."

She paused then and gave a great sigh, and I felt certain it was done merely for dramatic effect. "Oh, but you do not, do you? There I go forgetting your plight once again. It breaks my heart to know you do not share in the season's festivities. It is such a happy time of year, and everyone is exceedingly cordial and merry."

She went on and on and on about *Lady this* and *Lady that* and the Countess's ball and being invited to the home of *Lord so-and-so* until I wished fervently that I had never accepted their offer of a ride.

"You must see a lot of Mr. Darcy then," I said, attempting to change the subject, "for I often see his name in the paper in attendance at those gala evenings. Did I not read that he danced the night away with Lady Jersey's niece? Are we to expect an announcement in that regard?"

"An announcement?" Miss Bingley repeated as though in a fog. "What kind of announcement?"

"Oh, no, no, no," Mrs. Hurst interjected. "You know the newspapers. You can never depend upon them for truth. As far as we know, Mr. Darcy has not made any declaration to anyone."

Except for me, I thought.

"We did, of course, read that there would be no alliance between you and Mr. Darcy," Miss Bingley said. "Naturally, that was no surprise to those of us who know him so well."

"And you chose to believe that, did you?" I asked. "When you just said the newspapers could not be relied upon for veracity?"

Miss Bingley's eyes immediately flew to those of Mrs. Hurst, both their faces appearing stricken!

"But—but the paper quoted Lady Catherine de Bourgh," Miss Bingley sputtered. "I do not believe for one moment a reporter would dare misquote a personage of her renown!"

"Miss Bennet," Mrs. Hurst added, "do you deny what was written in the newspaper?"

At that moment the driver pulled up outside my uncle's house, and the footman opened the door for me to alight.

"Ah, here we are," I said with a smile. "Allow me to thank you sincerely from the bottom of my heart for your assistance."

"But—but—" Miss Bingley stuttered. I did not answer and slipped out the door and down the carriage steps.

"Shall we come in as well?" Mrs. Hurst asked, responding to the frantic expression on her sister's face.

"And break your other engagement? Oh no, I would not dream of deterring you further. You have been more than generous with your time. Good day."

I ran up the steps and into the house. I could not keep the smile from my face as I made my way upstairs. That walk had done far more good for my outlook than I had hoped.

I covered only half the flight before Kitty called to me from below. "Lizzy, Mamá says you are to come into the drawing room."

"The drawing room? At this hour of the day? Whatever for?"

"Hurry!" she called, motioning with her hand. I pulled off my bonnet, as I retraced my steps and handed it to the servant along with my pelisse.

Inside the large room I found Mary reading a book, my Aunt Gardiner playing a game with her two older children, but not a sign of Jane or Mr. Bingley or Mamá, for that matter.

"Close the door, Kitty," my aunt said.

"What is it, Aunt? Why are we to assemble in the drawing room of all places?" I asked.

"Mr. Bingley and Jane are alone in the front parlour," Kitty said. "Mamá stands guard outside the door, and she has given strict orders that no one is to interrupt them."

My mouth gaped, astounded that even my mother would stoop to such tactics. "Oh, Aunt, I must go to Jane. Surely she is mortified! Mr. Bingley cannot mistake my mother's subterfuge."

"Sit down, Lizzy," my aunt answered. "Your mother has arranged it all, and there is nothing we can do about the matter now."

"You cannot approve! You would never stoop to such schemes."

"No, I would not have thought of doing so, but then my daughters are not yet of marriageable age, my dear."

I began to pace, unable to believe my own mother could employ such plotting. When I thought of how she had packed Jane off to Netherfield in the rain, though, causing her to become ill and forced to spend several days and nights at Mr. Bingley's house, I had to admit this latest plan seemed in character.

"How long have they been shut up in there alone?" I demanded.

"At least three-quarters of an hour," Mary said, peering closely through her glasses at the clock on the mantel.

"I must go to her." I headed for the door.

"Sit down, Lizzy," my aunt said. "Another five minutes should do the trick—as your mother puts it—if there is a trick to be done."

Sure enough, although I sat and fumed, chewed my lip and sighed often, within five minutes my mother opened the door, her face enveloped by one huge grin.

My younger sisters both questioned her at once while I rose to go to Jane. Mamá was so excited she could not get the words out. All she could do was nod her head, her face still frozen in that same jubilant expression.

"Fanny," my aunt said, "it is accomplished? Mr. Bingley has asked for Jane's hand?"

"I think so! I could only hear bits and pieces through the door, but I am certain I heard the words *marry* and *wife*."

"I am going to her," I cried, starting for the door.

"Yes, Lizzy, go!" Mamá cried. "And if Mr. Bingley wishes to speak to your father, I shall send a servant to fetch him from Mr. Gardiner's office post-haste!"

I walked down the hallway to the parlour as quickly as possible and pushed open the door without knocking. Jane and Mr. Bingley stood at the fireplace, her hands in his, their blonde heads close together. My heart leapt at the sight, shocked that for once my mother had been right!

"Oh, I am so sorry," I said, turning to leave, but Jane stopped me, and she and Mr. Bingley welcomed me into the room and revealed their good news. It was too wonderful to believe, and the entire house was soon so filled with joy I am surprised it did not visibly rock to and fro on its foundation.

Mr. Bingley stayed for tea and endured my mother's effusive admiration with valiant effort. I could not say which of the two—he or my mother—had the wider smile on their face. Jane blushed repeatedly at all that was said. I had never seen her so happy or so beautiful.

Mr. Bingley refused to have my father summoned back to the house. He informed us that Mr. Hurst was to call for him at half-past four, and he would have him transport him to Mr. Gardiner's place of business.

Before his expected leave-taking and after Mamá had been sated with food and joy and forced to lie down for a bit, I was able to speak with Jane and Mr. Bingley alone.

"You, sir, have turned this week that threatens great difficulty into one of great happiness," I said. "I trust you will not ever suffer because of the disgrace I have brought upon this family."

"You are not the cause of it, Miss Elizabeth," he said. "On the contrary, you have borne your plight with grace and continue to do so in the face of great adversity. I admire your courage, and I shall be proud to call you my sister."

"And I to call you brother."

Jane beamed as he kissed her hand and bade us farewell. "Oh, Lizzy, if only you could be as happy as I. If only—" She broke off then, both of us aware that my chance for joy was not to be.

I slipped my arm in hers. "Until I have your goodness, Jane, I could never attain your happiness. But this success will surely spur Mamá on until she finds an agreeable mate for me. And if I have very good luck, perchance he will not resemble Mr. Collins!"

At the close of the first day of the trial, the jury found the gang member, Rufus, guilty of highway robbery, kidnapping, and extortion. It was not until the second day, when I read the account in the newspaper and saw that his surname was Martin, that I discovered he was the pig farmer's son.

I thought of the young red-haired lad who had given Mr. Darcy and me a ride on the road to Hazleden, and his tale that Mr. Martin's son had fallen into bad company.

For a few moments, I allowed myself the luxury of amusement at recalling that entire incident and the events on the road afterwards. Had it only been a matter of weeks since we had laughed together with such unchecked mirth? Life now seemed quite altered and dark.

I had been surprised that a man's fate could be so easily and quickly decided. My uncle explained that it was actually somewhat unusual that each man was afforded a complete day of trial, that all of Morgan's men were not tried at once. And the jury's hasty decision was to be expected.

After all, once Mr. Darcy laid out the facts, and the footmen and driver of Mr. Bingley's carriage were called as witnesses, what defence could the accused offer? Rufus had mumbled answers to the judge's questions, but nothing he said could acquit him of the charges.

The highwayman called Merle suffered the identical fate the next day. In fact, the court let out early because the prosecution consisted of the same witnesses and statements. The accused did declare his innocence, but according to my father's account, the judge soon grew weary and dismissed any further outbursts. 'Twas a simple task for the jury to find him guilty.

I questioned my father and uncle extensively each evening, seeking details of the proceedings, but they were fairly reticent. I was thus forced to examine the newspaper's accounts. Thus far, nothing out of the ordinary had occurred.

By the third day, the date of Sneyd's trial, I grew concerned for Mr. Darcy. The burden of testimony had fallen on him throughout each trial, even though Mr. Hurst, Mr. Bingley, and my father were there to speak for the female victims.

Mr. Bingley called upon us each evening and spoke with admiration of the fine manner in which his friend executed his duty. He termed him a man of distinction and honour and said his reputation for integrity was well known in London circles. I could picture his upright demeanour, the tone of moral authority in his voice, and his clear recital of the facts of each case and even clearer denunciation of the criminals. Still, I worried at the constant strain he underwent.

In truth, I longed to comfort him at the end of each day, hold his hand, or smooth his brow. I had lost that privilege, I thought sadly, when I refused to become his wife.

On that Thursday set aside for Sneyd's trial, I was nervous as a cat. Jane attempted to comfort me, stating that things had gone well previously, and that it was almost over. My aunt, likewise, tried to pacify my uneasy manner, assuring me that Sneyd had not the slightest chance of being set free. That was not my concern.

I found myself anxious at what the hateful man might say about Mr. Darcy or me. In addition, of what might he accuse Morgan? There was no love lost between them—had he not shot him? He might try to place all responsibility for his crimes on Morgan, saying he had been unduly influenced, led astray, or forced to follow him. The more I brooded over the matter, the more imaginative I grew, envisioning impossibly dark outcomes.

Almost as soon as my father and uncle walked through the doorway that evening, I besieged them with questions, Jane following close behind.

Seeing the drawn look about my father's face, my aunt halted my onslaught. "Allow your father a few moments' peace. Thomas, Edward, come in and sit down. I shall ring for tea."

They followed her into the parlour, and I apologized. Still, I hovered close by, hoping for any word they wished to share concerning the day's events. Mamá had not yet returned from taking Mary and Kitty shopping, and so we were spared her demanding questions. I did not wish to appear as taxing as she often did, so I tried my best to employ patience.

After tasting the hot tea, my father laid his head against the high-backed chair and closed his eyes. My uncle, although normally quite jolly, appeared somewhat resigned. He took a biscuit from the plate Jane offered him, but seemed to forget he had it in his hand, making not the slightest attempt to pop it in his mouth as he had done the night before.

At length I could not bear the suspense any longer. "Uncle, I pray you tell us what happened today. I do not mean to press you, but— "

"Yes, Lizzy," he said, sighing. "I know all of you are curious. Well, the scoundrel called Sneyd was found guilty. For that we can be grateful."

"Of course, he was," my aunt said. "We did not expect otherwise."

"Then why do you and Papá appear so downhearted?" I asked.

He sighed again and glanced at my father, who had now raised his head, a deep frown wrinkling his brow. "Oh, just the strain of the day and... the length of the week are catching up with us. That is all, my dear."

I doubted that was all by any means. "Nothing was said out of the ordinary, then? That horrid Sneyd did not portray his true character by blackening Mr. Darcy's name or mine?"

"He revealed his true character," my father said. "Make no mistake about that. I shudder to think you were forced to endure his presence, much less his imprisonment."

"He was mean and crude and the worst of the lot, but he did not actually harm me, Father. Mr. Darcy and—in truth—the leader, Morgan, saw to that."

"Yes," my uncle said, "the two of them defended you today as well, Lizzy. I could not say which of them shouted the loudest, could you, Thomas?"

My father shook his head. "What is important is that the two together drowned out that villain's accusations."

My pulse began to race. What I greatly feared had come about. "What—what did he say?"

"No, Lizzy," my father said, rising from the chair. "Do not ask, for I shall not repeat it."

"But Papá," I cried.

My uncle rose at the same time. "Your father is right. Those words shall never be spoken under my roof. Let it be. It has all been denied and forcefully so."

I watched as they left the room, climbing the stairs together. My aunt rang the bell for the maid to clear away the tea service. Hearing the return of my mother and sisters in the hallway, she went to join them.

Only Jane stayed behind. She took my hand in hers. "Dearest, try not to think on it. What is done is done. Can you not put it behind you?"

"What was done? What was said? I must know!"

"But why? It will only distress you, and have not Father and our uncle said you were defended, that awful man's lies disputed? No one could believe him, Lizzy, no one!"

I hung my head, chewing my lip. *Ah, Jane, console yourself with such a delusion,* I thought but did not say aloud.

Even Mr. Bingley refused to tell me what had been said at the trial when I questioned him that evening. He appeared chastened and sober, his normally cheerful countenance subdued, his manner quieter than usual.

The only joyful moment during his visit was an invitation he extended from Mr. and Mrs. Hurst for all of us to dine at their townhouse on Thursday evening of next week. He said it was to celebrate the betrothal and that his sisters had delayed the event only because of the strain of the present week. I had my doubts about that, imagining the horror Mr. Bingley's announcement had caused among his relations. The difficult task of fitting into that family awaited my sister, but if anyone could win them over, it would be Jane.

After our guest departed, I hurried upstairs with my sister, doing my best to join in her excitement about next week's upcoming dinner. I listened patiently as she surveyed her wardrobe, already in quest of a suitable gown for the evening.

At last, I could bear it no longer and returned to the subject of that day's trial, questioning her as to anything Mr. Bingley might have said privately.

"He did not share any details of the trial," Jane said. "He simply said it was far better not to speak of it."

I knew then whatever had come forth from Sneyd's mouth had been vile indeed.

The following day I rose early, and as soon as my father and uncle left the house, I snatched the newspaper and locked myself away in my room. There I planned to pore over each page, searching for every word written covering the trial. I did not have to look far—it glared forth from the front page for all to see.

THIRD HIGHWAYMAN FOUND GUILTY

Mortimer Sneyd was found guilty last evening on all counts of kidnapping, highway robbery, extortion, and attempted murder of the ringleader of the scandalous gang, Nathanael Morgan.

A heated defence for Sneyd was attempted by calling each of the highwaymen as witnesses. His account was corroborated by the two men previously convicted, except when he asserted that he was the rightful leader of the highwaymen instead of Morgan. He sealed his fate with his conceit, for he insisted that it was his idea to kidnap passengers and hold them for ransom.

Morgan, the alleged ringleader, refused to answer any question or confirm any statement made by Sneyd. Neither would Morgan answer any of the prosecutor's questions, even when threatened by the judge with a stricter sentence for failure to cooperate. The only occasions upon which Morgan spoke were to shout down Sneyd's accusations against Miss Bennet, one of the kidnapped victims.

"That hussy lied to us!" Sneyd declared. "She and Darcy made out they was married. We'd never have forced them to sleep together if the truth be known! Besides that, she claimed she carried his child!"

He continued to accuse Miss Bennet of actions not befitting a lady. He said she used her "flirty ways" to lure him away from his loyalty to Morgan. He then declared that she had turned her wiles on Morgan when they dined alone.

Each time Sneyd invoked Miss Bennet's name in these scurrilous attacks, Morgan and Mr. Darcy both denounced him with loud and heated denials. Their outcry became so loud that the judge ordered a halt to the proceedings and demanded that the defendant desist such defamatory accusations. He also cautioned both Mr. Darcy and Morgan that they could not engage in shouting in his court, even if it was in defence of a lady's honour.

I lay back upon the pillows on my bed, my face flaming, my stomach burning from the emotions churned up by this public exposure. No wonder my father and uncle had refused to reveal the day's proceedings!

Although Sneyd had been convicted of his crimes, he had succeeded in blackening my reputation beyond my bleakest fears. Yes, his account had been denied by Mr. Darcy and Morgan, but I knew human nature—how once something was read in print, it remained in one's memory. Given time, rumours often blurred with facts until they were believed as truth, no matter how false.

I scanned the remainder of the article. It contained nothing more than notice of Morgan's trial to commence on the morrow.

Why I do not know, but I re-read the entire account once again, unable to tear myself from its ugly statements. Sneyd was defeated. Knowing he could not extricate himself from his crimes, he endeavoured to ruin all those he held responsible, blamed them for his own guilt, and yet convicted himself with his attempt to portray himself as ringleader.

What caused a person to be consumed by such hatred? I could not fathom it.

I looked over the report a third time. The only redeeming part of it was that Mr. Darcy and Morgan had at last agreed upon something—my defence. For that I was grateful. I thought of how often Mr. Darcy had protected me—how unselfishly he had acted on my behalf time and again.

Tears rolled down my cheeks as I thought of the expression upon his handsome face when he had offered himself for ransom to shield the ladies with whom he travelled. I recalled the kind manner in which he had held and comforted me in the cabin in the woods, how he rescued me from the opera, and of course, I could not erase from my memory how he had huddled with me that cold night in the cave and what transpired the following morn. If only he loved me! If only—

Much of the day, I remained in seclusion. I had lost my appetite and refused to join my aunt's table for tea. Jane looked in on me several times, and I implored her to make my excuses to my mother and aunt. She must have been successful, for they did not intrude upon my solitude. I was left to wallow in misery for several hours.

That evening I washed my face and put on a fresh gown. I wished to be waiting below stairs when my father and uncle returned from Morgan's trial. I had not the slightest hope that the outcome would prove any different from the previous days, but still I wished to hear the particulars. Sometimes I wondered whether I was developing an unnatural desire to be punished, so great was my curiosity about these trials.

My sisters, Mamá, and I joined my aunt in the drawing room to await the men's return. Mamá had grown weary of the week's distressful events, and she determined that we were to celebrate the end of the trials that night. No unhappy thoughts would be allowed. We would concentrate on Jane's fortunate alliance with Mr. Bingley instead.

"Leave it to Mamá to stick her head in the sand," I whispered to Jane.

"Lizzy, I am speaking to you in particular," Mamá declared. "You have moped about this house far too long." She walked over and pinched my cheeks. "Collect yourself! How do you ever expect to secure a husband when you appear on the verge of tears? Men do not like an unhopeful countenance, you know. Just look at Jane. Do you think she would have caught Mr. Bingley if she had gone about the house down in the mouth like you?"

"Yes, Mamá," I answered, but as soon as she turned her back, I closed my eyes in dismay.

A few moments later, Mr. Gardiner and Papá walked in. How surprised we all were to see Mr. Bingley and Mr. Darcy follow them!

My aunt and mother both exclaimed over their presence and welcomed them warmly. By that time, my mother had overcome her earlier disapproval of Mr. Darcy, especially since he had offered to marry me. She was still somewhat in awe of him, but she did her best to make him comfortable. Sometimes I wondered if she thought she might match him with Mary or Kitty.

"Jane, Lizzy, Kitty, Mary," she rattled off our names as though we were children, "greet the gentlemen."

We curtseyed and spoke to them. Mr. Bingley joined Jane, of course, while Mr. Darcy stood off to the side somewhat stiffly. One glance at his face showed me the strain he had endured that week. His eyes appeared tired, his usual, striking stare somewhat glazed, as though he had not slept adequately.

"Well, my dear," my uncle said, addressing me. "It is over. Morgan was found guilty of everything except attempted murder of Sneyd and, thanks to Mr. Darcy, he was also exonerated of the previous murder charge against him."

I sat down, unable to respond. Before looking up, I could feel Mr. Darcy's eyes upon me. When I raised my head, I was proven correct. His gaze did not waver.

"I am sure the newspapers will have a to-do over today's events, sir," my father said, looking in Mr. Darcy's direction. "The judge himself found it unusual for the prosecutor to produce witnesses in defence of the defendant."

"I do not understand," my aunt said.

"Colonel Fitzwilliam took the stand. He presented the court written, witnessed statements from servants at an estate near Jonah's Village, testifying that Morgan killed the owner, some Frenchman, in self-defence and to protect his sister from the man's attack. The sister herself testified to the same thing. She also witnessed the altercation between Sneyd and Morgan and swore that Sneyd fired the first shot. In addition, she told how Morgan had given her the keys to the room in which Mr. Darcy and Lizzy were held prisoners and instructed her to release them once the highwaymen had gone."

"Does that mean he may receive a more lenient sentence?" I asked.

My father and uncle shrugged, and Mr. Bingley looked in the direction of Mr. Darcy. "There is no guarantee," Mr. Darcy said. "The sentencing is set for Monday."

"Very well," my mother announced, rising and causing the gentlemen who were sitting to do so. "Let us have no more talk of trials or sentences or criminals this evening. Let us rejoice that it is over and turn our minds to happier times. Mr. Bingley, I found the loveliest piece of lace for Jane's wedding veil yesterday. I declare she shall be the most beautiful bride in the county."

"No doubt, ma'am," Mr. Bingley responded, and shortly thereafter, Firkin announced that dinner was served.

My aunt had placed Mr. Darcy beside me at the table. That night he was even quieter than usual, and I could think of little to speak of other than the trial, the topic forbidden by my mother. He did not encourage my attempts at dinner conversation, and at last I resigned myself to eating in silence.

As the final course was served, I was surprised when he spoke to me in a low voice, as though he did not wish others to hear.

"I hope you have not read the newspaper accounts of the trial. Reporters seek lurid details that provide sensational appeal. They care little whom they harm, nor whether accounts are truthful, as long as their readership is entertained."

"I confess I have seen them," I said, blushing at the remembrance of the terrible things that had been said about me.

He frowned and appeared quite distressed. Placing his knife and fork across his plate, he sat back in his chair and sighed.

"Then take relief on one account of which we have previously spoken. Sneyd testified that it was his idea to take hostages for ransom. Whether his statement is true or false, I care not. What is of importance is that I did not plant the idea in the minds of the highwaymen, and my need to protect you did not in any way cause an escalation of their crimes. They had planned a kidnapping before they chose us as their victims. You never should have felt responsibility for their misdeeds, and I am now absolved from any misguided guilt I took upon myself."

I had read that statement in the paper, but I was so caught up in Sneyd's evil statements about me I had overlooked its significance. I confessed that to Mr. Darcy, and he said much the same, that in the heat of the moment, during the horror of all that transpired when we were first held up, he had subsequently forgotten that Sneyd had raised the idea of ransom before he offered himself.

Our guests did not stay long after dinner. They both acknowledged that all of us needed to rest after such a troublesome week. Jane and I walked to the door with the gentlemen, and while Mr. Bingley bade Jane a somewhat prolonged farewell, I took the opportunity to speak to Mr. Darcy again.

"Thank you for your efforts this week, sir," I said. "I confess I was surprised to see you attend upon my family tonight, for I know you must be exhausted."

"I came for you," he said softly. "I wanted you to know that I did all I could for Morgan."

"That is considerate of you, but I fail to understand what you mean. I never doubted that you would do everything you could to see that justice was served."

"You do fail to understand. I did it for you."

"For me? I think your actions reflect that of an honourable man, and they have nothing to do with me. You would have worked to ensure the highwayman received a fair trial regardless of whether I was involved or not."

His eyes held mine so steadily it was almost as though he wished for me to look into his soul. "I hope I am that kind of man, that what you say is true, but I cannot be certain. I know only that Morgan's fate matters to you."

I blinked, unsure of how to respond. "I fail to comprehend why you think his outcome is of such importance to me."

"Have you not defended him time and again? Was it not your earnest desire that he be found innocent against the charge of murder?"

"Of course," I said. "I do not want him to hang. But your statement makes it appear that you still believe I have an undue interest in the highwayman."

He continued to stare into my eyes, pressed his lips together, and said nothing more.

"Mr. Darcy?"

"Good night, Miss Elizabeth," he said, his voice weary and defeated. He bowed and walked out the door, followed by Mr. Bingley shortly thereafter.

Chapter Fourteen

Throughout the weekend, I fretted and worried about Mr. Darcy's comments. Surely, he did not still believe I cared for Morgan!

Had I not assured him when questioned in the cave that I felt nothing more than sympathy for his injury and pity for his unfortunate upbringing? I recalled having said something akin to the fact that my heart would *not* suffer if he did not survive the gunshot wound. I could never care for a highwayman. What would make Mr. Darcy yet think I might harbour stronger feelings for Morgan?

It was most perplexing and occupied many of my waking thoughts. I even questioned Mr. Bingley during one of his daily calls as to whether he thought his friend might be suffering from fatigue after the exceedingly strenuous week he had undergone.

"Darcy did seem tired Friday evening when we left here, but I saw him at our club this morning, and he appeared himself—perhaps a bit quieter than usual, but my friend is never verbose."

"Shall we have the pleasure of his company today?" Jane asked, knowing I wished to have the answer.

"He mentioned something about an invitation to Lady Jersey's house tonight, although I do not know whether he has decided to attend. I believe Miss Templeton is leaving tomorrow, and there is to be a farewell dinner for her. I know Caroline and Louisa were thrilled to receive their invitations."

I rose from where I had been sitting on the divan beside Kitty. I could feel pinpricks of jealousy jab at my heart. Walking to the pianoforte, I ran my fingers down the keys.

"Shall you play for us, Miss Elizabeth?" Mr. Bingley asked.

"Oh, yes, do," my aunt responded.

"I am far too uneasy to apply myself," I answered. "I feel as though I am the pet in the proverb—*Care killed the cat.*"

Mary promptly offered to take my place at the instrument, and I moved aside.

"Lizzy, you have been forced to keep indoors far too long," my aunt responded. "I shall speak to Mr. Gardiner and see if there is not some way he can think of to grant you some relief."

I smiled slightly, assured her that it was not necessary, and then returned to Jane's side. "Mr. Bingley, shall you attend Miss Templeton's dinner tonight?"

"No, I have not the slightest desire to do so. I would much rather remain here—that is, if you do not object, Mrs. Gardiner."

My aunt shook her head, and Jane blushed. Kitty giggled and I nudged her with my elbow. Thank goodness Mamá was not in attendance, for she surely would have replied in a manner that would have embarrassed Jane even more. Mamá had gone with my father to call on a friend of Sir William Lucas, having promised him they would not forget to pay their respects while in Town.

I cleared my throat and addressed myself to Mr. Bingley once more. "I assume Miss Templeton's absence will be greatly missed in London society and especially by Mr. Darcy, if one can believe the newspapers."

He looked slightly confused. "I—I am afraid I do not understand your meaning. Yes, London will miss the lady, but Darcy has never mentioned any particular attachment to her."

"Ah, well, I should know by now how often the newspapers print false information."

I attempted to speak casually, as though it were mere gossip we discussed. In truth, I could have kissed Mr. Bingley for saying what he did!

On Monday afternoon, my uncle returned home early. The first words from his mouth were that the sentences for the highwaymen had been delivered. A special crier from the newspaper office had run through the streets announcing, "Public hanging! Public hanging! All four highwaymen will hang!"

I was shocked! It seemed beyond belief that someone would die for something they had done to me. True, I had been kidnapped, threatened, held against my will, and one of the men attempted to assault me, but still I could not fathom taking their lives in payment. I was now safe, in good health, perfectly well. Why should someone have to die?

My uncle attempted to explain that society could not tolerate criminals attacking citizens on the public roadways. People must be allowed to travel with peace of mind, unafraid of roving bands of lawless men. I understood and appreciated that truth. Still, I could not find Morgan's band of men guilty of crimes deserving death. I saw the need for them to be made examples to deter similar thieves from perpetrating like crimes, and yet, I wished with all my heart that none of them would die, not even Sneyd.

"Lizzy, you are too tender-hearted," my uncle said as he rose and patted my shoulder. "I leave her in your hands, Thomas. I do not know how else I may reassure her." He left his study, and my father took his place, seating himself beside me near the window.

"My dear," he said, "you must not take this to heart. You had nothing to do with the outcome. It is the law."

"But I did, Father," I cried. "How can I separate myself from what has happened? If not for me, they might not die."

"You forget you are not the only victim, Lizzy. Mr. Darcy was robbed and kidnapped, assaulted and threatened. Although they were not kidnapped, Mrs. Hurst and Miss Bingley received similar treatment and were held against their will, as well as Mr. Bingley's servants. Whether you were involved or not, Morgan and his cohorts would most likely receive the same harsh sentences."

He put his arm around me and patted my shoulder. "I pray you, dearest, do not suffer any more. What is done is done. Those men must pay for their crimes."

I nodded as though I agreed, but I quickly left the room and ran to the sanctuary of my chamber where I spent the remainder of the evening. I could not even join my family for dinner, such was my regret.

How I wished I might speak to Mr. Darcy! Surely, he could do something to change the outcome. But how could I ask him? I knew he had done more than called for to save Morgan from the gallows, and now it appeared even he had failed.

I recall little else of what happened between Monday and Thursday of that week. My thoughts were so cast down that I still cannot think of that time without distress. I am certain my family did what they could to attempt to lift my spirits, but all I can remember was a dark, dark place in which I dwelt and from which I longed to be freed.

If only there were not the dinner in Jane's honour at Mr. and Mrs. Hurst's on Thursday, we could have left London for home. I had begged my father until he agreed that we would depart first thing Saturday morning. Until that time, I kept to my uncle's house and mainly to my room.

On Thursday, my mother insisted that Jane, Mary, and Kitty accompany her on a shopping excursion. She had a great desire to visit one last warehouse to narrow her search for the perfect lace for Jane's bridal veil. Fifteen different swatches now resided in her collection, but she was adamant that one more—the perfect one—still awaited her, and nothing would do but that my sisters assist in its discovery.

My aunt had a number of calls she needed to make. My father had taken himself off to his favourite booksellers, and so that left me alone with nothing to do and no one to visit.

"Lizzy," my uncle called to me, as he picked up his hat and cane. "Shall you stay here all alone today?"

I sat at the window in the front parlour, watching the carriages pass without. "Yes, Uncle," I replied. "Just the children and me."

"The older ones are at their studies with the governess. And are not the little ones down for their morning naps? Then what shall you do by yourself all day?"

"I have nothing in particular planned," I answered, rising to see what he proposed.

"Why not come with me?"

"With you, Uncle? To your office?"

"I am not going to the office this morning, but to the warehouses at the docks. Would you not like an excursion down to the water's edge?"

"Yes, I would, but I thought it better for me to stay indoors."

"You have been inside far too long. Why, you have lost the very bloom from your cheeks. There is no one who will recognize you where I am going. Come along with me, and view a different prospect for a change. It will do you good, Lizzy."

I readily agreed and quickly put on my coat and bonnet. It was a rare beautiful day in January. The fog had lifted, and the sun now shone brightly, warming the chill blown in by a light wind. I could not believe how just leaving the house caused my spirits to rise. I watched the sights we passed as eagerly as a starving person gobbled up his only meal.

My uncle's carriage travelled a great distance from the house down through a part of Town I had never seen before. Soon we arrived within sight of the water, and I marvelled at the great number of ships waiting for the limited number of docks. An array of warehouses lined the street, and my uncle pointed out the particular one where his business awaited him.

He assisted me from the carriage and told me I might wander along the edge of the water and watch the workers load and unload the great ships. He warned me how far I might go and alerted his manservant to keep an eye on me. I agreed to his limitations and was perfectly content to remain on the walkway, pleased to watch the busy workers below.

I opened my parasol, as the sun was now directly overhead, and eventually I grew tired of standing in one place. I made my way down the incline a little closer to the water and watched with interest as one or two passengers carrying valises began to board a large ship out in the harbour. It seemed strange to me that people would attempt a sea journey at that time of year. I stood there but a short while when I was shocked to hear someone call my name.

"Miss Elizabeth?"

I turned to look straight into the sun's glare and had to shade my eyes. I could not make out who it was that had spoken to me. "Sir?" I asked.

"Do you not know me?"

The man took a few steps and walked into the shade where I could see his face. I could not believe my eyes, for it was Morgan!

Dressed in his customary black, his blonde curls blowing gently in the breeze, he appeared much the same as he ever did, but for the absence of the jaunty dark hat and feather in its band. That day he wore a simple black cap, much like those of the workers loading the ship. His hair had grown longer and now covered his collar. Perhaps a bit thinner, he appeared to have recovered from his wound.

He stood on the other side of a long rope stretched across the walk, separating those who boarded the ship from those on shore. I was astounded to see him and stood there, my mouth agape.

"It's me, Nate Morgan!"

"What—how—" I could not form a sentence.

"You look as though you've seen a ghost," he cried. "Take my hand. You'll see I'm real!" He reached for my hand, but I snatched it away.

"I—I do not understand. How do you come to be here, of all places?"

"I'm bound for America!" he cried. "With Gert—we're sailing for the colonies."

"America! But how? I thought you were to be—"

"Hanged? 'Twas 'til a day ago."

"But how did you—what happened?"

"Transported! My sentence is to be transported. Me and all the boys, that is."

"You are all going to the colonies?" I asked, unbelievingly.

"No, Sneyd, Merle, and Rufus are meant for Australia. They're forced to wallow in Newgate 'til the end of May, but when Darcy offered Gert and me the chance to board this ship to America leaving today, we jumped at it. Rough time of year to sail, but we'll take our chances. We've been gamblers all our lives. No need to change now."

I blinked several times and shook my head, unable to take it all in. "Mr. Darcy? What—what did he have to do with this?"

"He's the one that got our sentences commuted," he said with a smile. "'Tis hard for me to speak well about any gentleman, but I'm bound to give him his due. If he hadn't paid for our passage, we'd still be waiting 'til the end of spring, and we'd be sailing to Australia in the same ship with Sneyd. I suppose Darcy persuaded the judge that wouldn't make for smooth passage, having the two of us holed up in close quarters for that long a time."

A warm sensation began in my breast. Mr. Darcy had done this. Mr. Darcy had kept Morgan and his gang from hanging. He had paid for the highwayman and his sister to have a new life. If I had esteemed him before, it did not compare with the admiration and respect I felt for him now. He truly was the best man I had ever known!

"I am happy for you," I said. "You owe Mr. Darcy a great debt of gratitude."

Morgan smiled and looked down. "Don't remind me, Miss. Obligation doesn't set well with me. It takes some getting used to. But what about you, Miss Elizabeth? I heard you were not to marry. Can't be true, can it?

From what I saw, I thought you and he, well— "

"No," I said quickly, looking away. "We are not to marry. Please—I pray you do not speak of it again."

"Very well, Miss. Must say I'm surprised. Didn't think Darcy was a fool, not by a long shot, but any man who'd give you up must be, especially a man as much in love with you as Darcy."

I turned and stared at him. "Why do you persist in saying that? How do you know who Mr. Darcy cares for?"

"Don't, Miss, except even a blind man couldn't mistake the way he feels for you. The way he looks at you. The way he speaks about you. The way he'd give up his life for you. No way could he make it plainer except perhaps to shout it in the street for all to hear!"

Could that be true? Could I have been mistaken all along? Did Mr. Darcy truly care for me? I could not believe it and found I could not speak. After several moments' awkward silence, I finally said, "I wish you well in America. Will you be in confinement there?"

"Have to work seven years for a smithy. By the time I'm done, I should be a right good blacksmith."

"And Gert? What will she do during that time?"

"She's got a job in the smithy's house, and I'll be living there, too, so I can look after her."

"That sounds promising. I hope you will apply yourself. You now have the opportunity to make a new life for you and your sister."

"Aye, and I figure the years will go by fast. Who knows, perchance I can slip away before the sentence is up and make me fortune. I hear America's rich in land." He laughed and winked at me.

"Mr. Morgan! Do not jest in that manner. This is the chance you need, the opportunity to change, to make a new man of yourself."

"Leopards don't change their spots, Miss."

"Men change their ways, though. Remember your mother's admonition. This could be the occasion to prove her true—to grow into your name." I looked him directly in the eye, imploring him to be serious minded and heed my warning.

"Ah, yes, but you see, I go by Nate. Have for so many years I can't recall being called Nathanael since my mother died."

"Then why not alter things when you reach America? Why not tell people your name is Nathanael Morgan?" I leaned forward across the rope, hoping he would see how earnestly I felt.

"You know, if you came with me, Elizabeth, I just might do that," he said softly, taking my hand in his. For some reason, I did not snatch it away this time, perhaps hoping he could see that someone cared what became of him.

"You know full well I cannot."

He sighed and smiled, raising one eyebrow. "Aye, but a man can dream, can't he?"

He lifted my fingers to his lips and kissed them. Then, raising his azure eyes, he frowned at what he saw over my shoulder.

"Darcy again!" he muttered, and I whirled around to see the gentleman alight from his carriage. He stared at us, his mouth open, a deep frown across his brow.

"Guess he's come to make sure I get on the boat." Then, his voice louder, he called to him. "Don't worry, Darcy! I'm just saying me good-byes. Farewell, Elizabeth! Don't be forgetting me! May you dream of me every night 'til I see your bonny face once again."

I suppose Morgan boarded the ship then. I do not know, for I remained transfixed, my eyes on Mr. Darcy. I watched him quickly turn and open the door to his carriage, climb aboard, and signal the driver to depart. They made short shrift of the distance between the ship and the end of the street, disappearing from view while I stood watching.

When I came to myself and looked around, the highwayman had vanished onto the sailing vessel, and I never saw him again.

My uncle returned not long afterwards, and I joined him in his carriage. I listened patiently as he directed my attention to various points of interest, the different warehouses with which he conducted business, and two or three ships importing goods for his trade.

When at last we left the port, I told him of meeting Morgan, and how Mr. Darcy had caused the sentences of the highwaymen to be commuted to transportation. I questioned him as to how this had come about, and he assured me it was not unusual at all, that men of wealth and status were often able to influence the courts' decisions, especially when it provided labour for plantations in Australia and the West Indies.

He was somewhat surprised that Morgan was being sent to America, for since the war, England rarely transported convicts to the colonies. However, a man of Mr. Darcy's means could purchase passage and make it possible for Morgan and Gert to leave England for America.

"There is little a man as wealthy as Mr. Darcy cannot have if he truly wants it," my uncle said.

Once again, I was amazed at the ways of the world and with what ease the rich could have their way. I did not spend much time concerned with it, however, for a greater worry besieged me.

What had Mr. Darcy imagined when he saw me with Morgan at the shipyard? Surely, he did not think I had gone there to bid him farewell! Why, how was I even to know he was sailing? If he thought that I was in love with the highwayman, though, would I not have moved heaven and earth to find out where he was? Would I not have questioned my uncle until I learned that he was to be transported?

Oh, what must Mr. Darcy think of me? I could not bear to imagine him thinking so ill of me, believing I could possibly care for a man of Morgan's character!

All afternoon I stewed about it. When my mother and sisters returned from the warehouse, I questioned Jane as to whether Mrs. Hurst had invited Mr. Darcy and his sister to their house that evening for the betrothal dinner. She did not know but hoped that he had. She understood that the dinner party consisted of family, but since the Darcys were such close friends of Mr. Bingley, they might well be included.

That did not pacify me, for that meant there was just as much chance that Mr. Darcy would not attend. If only there were some way I could meet with him, could talk to him, could make him understand what had happened that morning, how it had all been nothing more than coincidence.

The afternoon wore on forever. After bathing, Jane and I styled each other's hair. Mamá insisted my sister try on four different gowns so she could select the most flattering for the evening. I reminded my mother that Jane was already betrothed. She did not have to appear perfect in order to secure Mr. Bingley—he was already hers—but it did little good. She still fussed and fretted over every detail of my sister's wardrobe.

How relieved we were when she, at last, retired to her own chamber to dress for the evening!

Sarah, the maid, had just fastened the back of my dress when we heard a knock at the bedroom door, and she answered it, retrieving an envelope addressed to me. Jane slipped her dress over her head and did not see me open it, for which I was grateful. Inside, a separate sheet of paper fluttered to the floor.

I dropped to my knees to discover a single ticket made out in my name for passage on the *Laconia*, sailing for Virginia on May 29th. There was no other message enclosed, not even a sentence of explanation, or a name indicating from whom it had been sent.

I knew immediately from whom it had come. *Mr. Darcy!* Who else would send such a thing? But why? Why on earth should he send me a ticket to America?

I sank down on the far side of the bed. My hands suddenly felt icy cold, although my face began to burn. He must assume I wished to go with Morgan, to join him in his new life, and he was providing my passage! There could be no other explanation.

I could not believe it. Could he insult me in any greater manner? I was shocked, horrified, and angry beyond belief! My hands began to shake as I crushed the ticket and envelope into a ball.

"Lizzy, are you ready?" Jane asked, peering into the mirror. "Do you have your gloves?"

"What?" I said, not comprehending. "Oh, yes, here they are."

"Then come along. I can hear Mamá calling to us from the hallway."

I rose and faced her, keeping my fist hidden in the folds of my skirt. "Jane," I began.

"Yes, what is it? Why, Lizzy, are you unwell? Your face is quite pink."

"I—I do not feel well. I believe I must beg to be excused and remain here."

I continued to offer explanations, pleading a sudden headache and sick stomach to my mother after Jane had hastened to find her. My aunt offered to stay with me, but I refused. I agreed with my mother that I would be fine by myself and would send one of the servants if I grew worse. I assured my family that it was nothing serious and was greatly relieved when, at last, they all trooped out the door and climbed into my father's and uncle's carriages.

From an upstairs window, I watched both vehicles turn onto the next street, then grabbed my cape, and flew down the stairs. Firkin stood at the front door. He asked if he could help and could not hide his shock when I told him I wished for him to call a hackney coach from the Spread Eagle stand on Gracechurch Street.

"But Miss Elizabeth, surely you do not plan on leaving the master's house alone tonight in public transportation!" he declared.

"I do and if you will not secure a coach, Firkin, I shall do it myself."

I refused to look away and stared him down. The poor man was in a terrible dilemma, and I should have felt sorry for him if I had been sensible, but I had only one destination on my mind, and nothing would keep me from it. The servant pleaded that he would lose his position once my uncle learned what he had done, especially if he allowed me to leave the house alone. After more argument, I at last struck a bargain with him. If he would call for the hackney, I would allow Sarah and him to accompany me.

Within moments, he had the maid fetched, dressed in her coat, and waiting at the front door. Shortly thereafter, she and I climbed into the hired coach while Firkin rode on top after giving the address to the driver.

I knew that what I was doing was wrong, unacceptable, and improper, but I no longer cared about what was right, acceptable, or within the rules of propriety. London society already shunned me. What was one more transgression?

I proposed to call on Mr. Darcy alone. Nothing would do but that I meet him face to face that very night!

It took some time to cross the city and reach the fashionable section of London in which he lived, time that might have caused me to reconsider and return to my uncle's house before I made a fool of myself, had I not been livid with anger and far too upset to think clearly. I wanted nothing except to meet with Mr. Darcy and to take him to task for shaming me in such a manner!

At his townhouse I announced that I was calling on *Miss* Darcy, of course, but that did little to erase the questions in the butler's eyes. He admitted us, explaining that Miss Darcy had gone out for the evening with Colonel Fitzwilliam. When I asked if her brother was in, his raised eyebrows provided the only clue as to his disapproval. He was well trained and made no verbal notice of my unusual request.

Firkin and Sarah stood behind me in the vestibule, and I knew they were mortified to have to attend a young lady asking to see a gentleman alone, much less calling at his house at night. I gave it little thought and no concern. I was long past caring about appearances. I wished only to confront Mr. Darcy.

I should have waited in the vestibule, but out of fear that Mr. Darcy might refuse to see me, I followed the butler down the great hall. I was properly impressed with the understated elegance of the house. If I had not been so caught up in resentment, I might have given it greater notice. For the moment, however, all I could take in was that it reflected his natural grace, just as I expected.

The servant opened double doors to a large library, entered before me and announced my name. Determined to gain admittance, I slipped in right behind him. The butler then withdrew and closed the doors, the muted noise resounding in my ears.

It was a vast room. Bookcases lined with volumes covered the walls from floor to ceiling. Across the room a huge fire roared. A solitary candle provided the only other light. In consequence, the room was dark. The fire caused shadows to dance about the walls and over the rows of books.

I blinked several times, adjusting my eyes to the dim light, unable to locate Mr. Darcy's presence anywhere in the room. I cleared my throat and advanced two steps before he spoke.

"Miss Bennet." He emerged from the shadows near the windows on the far wall, holding a brandy glass in one hand and a bottle in the other. His voice seemed slightly subdued. Walking slowly toward the light, he bowed somewhat unsteadily. "To what do I owe this unexpected pleasure?"

"I—I wish to speak to you," I said, taken aback. "Have you been drinking, sir?"

"I have."

"How much—that is, are you inebriated?"

"Not yet."

I turned around, heading for the door.

"Miss Be.ınet, will you leave so soon?"

"I shall not attempt to have an honest discussion if you are in your cups," I declared, not even stopping to turn around.

"I just told you I am not yet drunk. Sit down."

I stopped and turned, suddenly somewhat afraid of the tone of his voice. He had spoken the last words like a command, loud and hard.

"I shall stand," I said, willing my voice not to tremble.

"As you will. Now, will you tell me why you visit me all alone and risk further damage to your reputation?"

"I should think my reputation matters little to you. Not after you insulted me in the manner you employed today. At last I know exactly how little you think of me!"

"Insulted you? In what way?" He held out his hands, still clasping the bottle of brandy and nearly empty glass.

"With this!" I cried as I walked toward him, unfurled the wadded-up ticket and thrust it forward. "How dare you purchase this ticket to Virginia and have it delivered to me! Do you think to banish me from England? Is that how you rid yourself of the embarrassment my presence causes you?"

"Banish? You choose a harsh term in reference to a gift. After the tender scene I witnessed at the harbour today, I thought to afford you the means of joining the man with whom you are obviously in love." He spat the last words out as though they left a bitter taste on his tongue.

I could not believe what I heard! He did actually assume I loved Morgan. What I had feared was all too true.

"How can you accuse me so?" I cried. "How can you think I would give my heart to a highwayman?"

He walked to the fireplace and placed the glass on the mantel, the brandy on a table nearby, before turning to face me.

"I have tried, madam, with everything that is in me to deny it, but today you forced me to face the truth. When I saw you travelled to the port to bid Morgan farewell, I could no longer conjure up anything that would make me disbelieve it. There is no need for you to keep up the pretence. I saw you allow him to kiss your hand. One cannot help whom one loves. If your heart is his, then..." His voice died away, as though he had given up, that the attempt to speak was too much for him.

"You are mistaken, sir. I happened upon Morgan by accident today. That is all it was—an accident, coincidence, whatever you choose to call it. I do not love him!" I said with feeling, stepping closer so he could see my face in the firelight. "What must I do to convince you?"

"No need exists whereby you must deny it. I am resigned to it. You love the scoundrel, and there is nothing I can do to change it." He turned away and stared into the fire.

"Why do you persist in saying that? I know whom I love, and it is not Morgan! How can it be, when I love you?!"

Oh, what had I done? How had my tongue betrayed me?

Instantly he looked up, and although I attempted to turn away, I felt the force of his eyes upon me, willing me to meet his gaze when all I wished to do was hide my face. Before I knew it, he crossed the distance between us and stood so near I could smell his scent, feel the warmth of his body emanate toward me.

"What? What did you say?"

"I love you," I whispered, "and I wish to God I did not."

I said nothing more, simply stood there watching, waiting. I had lost all sense of honour, dignity, presence. I stood naked before him, my heart exposed and hurting, my shame lying open for his ridicule. Against every intelligent part of me that screamed I should be silent, I had blurted out the truth, the absolute, unalterable truth: I loved him. God help me, I loved him.

"Elizabeth," he breathed.

And then unbelievably, I felt his hands upon my arms, pulling me toward him, gathering me into his embrace. I felt as though I stood to the side watching it happen to some other girl, some incredibly fortunate woman whom this man wished to touch, to hold close.

I watched his face incline toward mine, his lips coming ever nearer. His breath warm on my cheek, I saw his eyes move from my eyes to my mouth and then, oh so gently, his lips touched mine, and I began to tremble.

With tender caresses, he kissed me not just once, but once more, and then again and again and again. A pervading pit of fire began far, far down within me, so deep I could not fathom its source, a sensation I recalled from the single time before when his lips had touched mine. I felt myself lean into him, my hands spread wide open upon his strong chest, mindlessly moving back and forth and then upward, until I reached the warmth of his neck and those enticing curls edging his collar.

By then his kiss had grown harder as he forced my lips apart, taking my mouth with a fierceness that cannot be described, until I surrendered and allowed him to do what he willed. I was lost, utterly and completely lost in him, and I wished never to be found.

When, at last, he released my lips and began to kiss my cheek, my ear, and the place right below, my mouth throbbed in rhythm with my heart, and I trembled anew in his arms, clinging to him for fear that I could no longer stand.

"Elizabeth," he whispered again and again as he led me to the sofa, never relinquishing his hold, nor lessening his embrace.

Once seated, he eased my head onto his chest, and I felt his hands smooth my curls back as though he would soothe and comfort me while his heart beat in my ear with a wild, furious rhythm. It was only then that I realized I was weeping.

"My dearest, loveliest Elizabeth, do not cry. I can bear anything but your tears." I felt his lips upon my eyelids. He gently kissed away my tears, his tenderness more than I could abide. "Why are you crying? Tell me."

"Because I have humiliated myself before you and because I am helpless to cease from doing so," I whispered.

He sat back and lifted my chin so that I was forced to face him. "Whatever do you mean? I do not understand."

I kept my eyes closed, turning my face aside. "Oh, why do you torment me so? I come here unescorted. I allow you to hold me and kiss me as though I were a woman of the night. I even confess that... I love you. How can I not find that humiliating?"

When he did not say anything, I lifted my eyes to find him smiling at me. "For one so intelligent, you are a silly little goose. What do you know of women of the night?"

"I know enough. Only that type of woman would approach you alone at night, would allow you to force her into making a declaration, and would allow you to kiss her in such a manner when you have made no similar avowal."

"No similar avowal? What are you saying? Did I not propose marriage to you, Miss Elizabeth Bennet?"

"Yes, but we both know why—to protect my good name, to rescue me from society's disapproval. I know that you do not love me."

He smiled that infuriating smile once again. "Oh, you do, do you? What is going on in that strange little mind of yours? How can you possibly think I do not love you?"

I blinked and swallowed. "In the cave—"

"Yes, I remember what happened in the cave only too well."

"You kissed me and then said it was a mistake. You did, sir. You said kissing me was a mistake."

He took my hands in his and brought them to his mouth. "I did, Elizabeth. I never should have taken advantage of you in that way. It was a mistake to do so, quite brazen and thoughtless of me. That was what I meant."

I could not believe what he was saying. "That is truly what you meant?"

He nodded.

"So... so you do love me?" I whispered.

He reached out and took my face in his hands. "Of course, I do. I cannot fix on the hour, or the spot, or the look, or the words that laid the foundation. It is too long ago. I was in the middle before I knew that I had begun."

I closed my eyes, knowing he was about to kiss me. Tenderly, his lips met mine, but I pulled away, a new thought having struck me. "Then why, sir, did you not declare yourself? Why did you not say you loved me? Why all that useless talk that we *had* to marry, that it was best for my family, best for my reputation? Never—never once did you profess your love! How dare you allow me to suffer all these weeks?"

"I am a fool," he said, "an utter fool. I thought everyone could see how I felt and you most of all. I feared that *you* did not love *me*. All this time I suffered from the delusion that Morgan had captured your heart. Can you now fathom how I have suffered? After all, you defended him time and again and exercised much effort pointing out my faults!"

"Oh, I did!" I cried, glimpsing for the first time the predicament Mr. Darcy had endured, the manner in which he had read my actions. "I am the fool, sir, not you."

"Let us not argue with the bard. We are mortal and therefore guilty. But no more, Elizabeth. From this day forward, we shall speak plainly. I love you with all that is within me, all that I am, all that I ever will be—all that I ever hope to be."

"And I love you," I said, growing weak, as he pulled me against him and once more began to ply me with kisses. I could not seem to control my hands. They roamed back and forth over his hard, powerful chest, while his strong but gentle hands caressed my back and shoulders. I matched his hungry fervour with that of my own, allowing him to recapture my mouth over and over.

At length, he sat back and held me at arm's length. Both of us struggled to catch our breath. With a groan, he released my hands and stood up, walked to the fireplace and rested his forehead against the mantel. When he turned his handsome face to look over his shoulder at me, I saw the hungry passion still alive in his eyes, and my heart turned over.

"Elizabeth," he said, still breathing deeply, "You must leave this house. I do not want you to—God knows I do not—but for your sake, I must get you out of here and a safe distance from me."

I nodded slightly and unknowingly began to chew my lip, keeping my eyes on him.

His eyes narrowed, and I saw his chest move heavily as he breathed. "Do not—" he faltered. "Do not do that, Elizabeth."

"Sir?"

"Do not chew your lip. If you knew how often I have watched you do that—and what it does to me." The expression on his face caused me to blush from head to toe. There was little need for him to say more.

I rose and gathered up my cloak. Instantly, he stood behind me and spread the garment around me, smoothing it over my shoulders, his hands lingering. I closed my eyes and sighed deeply. I could not keep from leaning back against him, and within moments, he turned me around and placed his forehead against mine as he fastened the garment at my neck.

"I fear that we have a problem, sir," I said softly, "of which you may not be aware."

"I have a problem of which I am acutely aware, but to what do you refer, my dearest?"

I smiled and then lowered my eyes. "When last we spoke of marriage, you vowed never to renew your addresses to me, and I know full well that you are a man of your word. Does that mean we are to remain unmarried for the remainder of our lives?"

"I did say that, did I not?" he mused, frowning slightly. "Another bit of foolishness."

"What shall we do? If you cannot propose again, it seems a hopeless case, does it not?" I raised my eyes and made them as wide and seemingly innocent as possible.

"It does," he agreed, a statement I had not expected. "However, you must not expect me to resign my life to this exquisite state of torture, Elizabeth."

"I must not?"

"No indeed, you must not!" He grabbed my hand and pulled me toward the door. "Come with me."

In the hallway, he instructed his butler to make haste and have his carriage brought to the front door. Firkin and Sarah stood where I had left them, expressionless but for their eyes wide with wonder. Mr. Darcy asked me who they were, and I explained that they were my uncle's servants who had accompanied me, to which he readily praised them for their care of my person and indicated they were to join us as we marched out the front door.

He placed Sarah and me inside the carriage while Firkin took the footman's position at the rear. Mr. Darcy announced that he would ride up front with the driver, commenting that he could do with a blast of cold night air.

As soon as the horses began to walk on, Sarah asked if I was well, and when I answered in the affirmative, she asked me our destination.

"I have not the slightest idea," I answered.

In truth, I did not care as long as Mr. Darcy led the way.

Chapter Fifteen

I truly did not know where Mr. Darcy intended us to go. I thought possibly he would return me to my uncle's house at Gracechurch Street, and quickly, before my family returned from dinner at the home of Mr. and Mrs. Hurst, so that no one but the servants would know of my daring, impetuous, and highly improper visit to his house. However, his carriage did not turn toward Cheapside, but remained in the fashionable portion of town. In fact, it travelled but a short distance before turning into Grosvenor Street and shortly thereafter pulled up in front of the residence of Mr. Hurst.

As we climbed the steps together, I gave him a quizzical look, but all he said was, "Will you trust me?"

"With my life, sir."

"Then follow my lead."

Once indoors, the butler said the family and guests were at table, whereupon Mr. Darcy asked him to allow us to join them. The servant hastened to oblige and snapped his fingers at a passing footman, barking orders for two additional places to be set.

"Mr. Darcy and Miss Bennet," the butler announced, as he opened the doors to the dining room and stepped back so that we might make our entrance.

"Darcy!" Mr. Bingley cried, rising from his seat, "and Miss Elizabeth, how delightful! Do come in and join us. We have just finished our soup."

There was a general uproar of surprise among our friends and family. Each of the gentlemen rose to acknowledge my presence, Mrs. Hurst urged us to sit down, and Caroline Bingley remained speechless.

"Thank you, Mrs. Hurst, Bingley," Mr. Darcy replied, although he made no effort to sit or to allow me to do so. Instead, we advanced into the room and stood near the end of the table. He had tucked my hand inside his arm before we entered the room, and he kept his hand placed over mine, making certain I did not leave his side.

"Lizzy," my mother said, "I thought you unwell. Why are you here and with Mr. Darcy?"

"If you will allow me to explain, ma'am," Mr. Darcy said. "I beg your leave for interrupting the meal, Mrs. Hurst, and I ask the gentlemen to be seated. I fear that what I am about to say may take some time. I must impose upon Mr. Bennet concerning a matter of grave importance."

"Importance?" Mamá cried. "More important than my daughter's betrothal dinner? I think not!"

"I pray you will forgive me, Mrs. Bennet," Mr. Darcy replied, "but when you hear my tale, I think you may find it takes precedence."

Colonel Fitzwilliam, who stood next to Georgiana's chair, began to frown. "Has something happened, Darcy? Do you require my services? Come man, out with it." Others at the table began to murmur similar remarks.

My father held up his hand. "Let us give the gentleman a chance to speak. Shall you and I excuse ourselves, Mr. Darcy?"

"If it is all the same, sir, I prefer to speak before all of you." Mr. Darcy turned and looked at me as though he were asking for my assent. I still did not know what he proposed to do, but I smiled up at him.

"Very well," my father said and motioned for the gentlemen to take their seats. Everyone had ceased eating, of course, but when they seated themselves, no one picked up their spoons again except for Mr. Hurst who continued on, seemingly unaware there was anyone or anything in the room more interesting than his soup.

"Mr. Bennet," Mr. Darcy said, "some weeks ago I asked for your daughter Elizabeth's hand in marriage, did I not?" My father answered in the affirmative, and I heard a faint groan emanate from that portion of the table where Miss Bingley sat.

"At the time, I related the fact that due to no fault of her own, she had been forced to spend three nights locked in the same room with me, an occurrence that mandated we marry. Alas, Elizabeth refused to accept my offer."

"She did," my mother cried, "oh, she did! The ungrateful, uncaring girl! I have chastised her daily since then, Mr. Darcy. Daily, I tell you!"

"Very wise, ma'am," he replied. I could sense his amusement. "Since her refusal, Elizabeth as well as your family, has endured scorn and public humiliation. Any sensible girl would retract her refusal, especially when I was obliging enough to offer her time to consider it, but the second time I asked for her hand, once again she told me no."

"Oh," my mother cried, "twice? You asked twice? Lizzy, how could you!"

"Mamá," I murmured, beseeching Jane with a frantic look so that she attempted to calm her.

"Shocking, I agree, ma'am," Mr. Darcy said, and I closed my eyes. *What was he doing?*

My uncle came to my rescue then. "Mr. Darcy, I fail to see what good it does to bring up all this?"

"If you will permit me, sir, I shall make it evident. The last time I asked for Elizabeth's hand in marriage, I confess I spoke rashly. I told her I would not renew my addresses again."

"Oh, thank God," Caroline said, reaching for her wine glass.

"Sir, is there a point to all of this?" my father asked.

"Indeed," Mr. Darcy said. "It is my painful duty to tell you that tonight Elizabeth arrived on my doorstep uninvited, having travelled in a hired cab, alone but for two of Mr. Gardiner's good servants."

A sudden collective intake of breath could be heard throughout the room. "I fear there is more. Your daughter and I spent a good three-quarters of an hour or longer alone behind closed doors in my library. For verification, you may consult Mr. Gardiner's servants, who presently wait in the hall."

My father rose once more, his brows knit together in a scowl. "Is this true, Lizzy?"

I looked away at first but then held my chin up and agreed. Mr. Darcy looked down at me, and I could see the satisfaction in his eyes. He seemed to be thoroughly enjoying his performance.

"But why?" my father asked. "What on earth would be of such importance that you would engage in such behaviour and put yourself at risk?"

I pressed my lips together, wondering how I might word my reason prudently. "Papá, a misunderstanding had arisen between the gentleman and me that warranted immediate attention."

"What type of misunderstanding?"

"One due entirely, I am afraid, to my ignorance," Mr. Darcy interjected. "I feared that because of her refusal of my offer, Elizabeth did not care for me, but I was mistaken, you see. Tonight, behind the closed doors of my library, she confessed that I am indeed the fortunate man she loves after all, in spite of my numerous faults."

He turned to face me, took both my hands in his, and slowly shook his head while gazing into my eyes. "Mr. Bennet, if Elizabeth were my daughter—and I am eternally grateful she is not—I would instruct my child that she may not call upon a gentleman alone at night, confess her love for him, and not expect to pay the consequences. I would then demand that the man in question agree to marriage, and I would insist that my daughter marry him! I think every honourable man in this room would stand behind you in that decision. Do you not agree, sir?"

I held my breath, shocked at his audacity, at how cleverly he had kept his word not to ask for my hand in marriage. The entire inhabitants of the room seemed to hold their breaths also, silent, save for the sounds of Mr. Hurst continuing to slurp the last remnants of his soup, his spoon scraping against the bottom of the bowl.

I glanced at the table. Jane appeared shocked, Mr. Bingley somewhat nervous, a faint smile played around my aunt's eyes, and my mother seemed dumbfounded, blinking as though she could not make sense of it until, all of a sudden, she recovered and cried aloud, "Yes! Yes, Mr. Bennet, that is exactly what you must do! You must *make* Lizzy marry Mr. Darcy!"

My uncle rose from his chair. "I agree, sir. As Elizabeth's kinsman, I assert my right to make certain you do the proper thing, Mr. Darcy."

"And," Mr. Bingley said, also standing, "as—as her future brother, I add my voice in support as well."

"Representing my father, the Earl of Matlock, and Darcy's family," Colonel Fitzwilliam said as he stood erect and did his utmost to keep a straight face, "I feel it my duty, Cousin, to demand that you act in an honourable manner."

Every man at the table had now pledged their agreement except one. Mrs. Hurst attempted to catch her husband's attention. "Psst, Ambrose! Ambrose!"

"What?" he asked, raising his head slightly from his bowl.

"Say something!" she hissed.

"Humph?" he grumbled and slapped his spoon down on the table. "Yes, right! Bring on the next course!"

By that time a droll expression covered my father's countenance. He cleared his throat and folded his hands together. "Well, Lizzy?" he said, raising his eyebrows as if to ask whether I agreed.

When I nodded vigorously, no longer able to restrain the smile breaking forth upon my face, he said, "Then you leave me little choice. I see before me an unhappy task. For once, I must be in perfect agreement with your mother. Daughter, I insist that you marry Mr. Darcy."

"Yes, Father," I said.

"No!" Caroline cried, but her sister must have kicked her under the table, for she said no more, and a joyous uproar commenced throughout the entire room that drowned out her dissent.

As each person rushed upon us and offered their best wishes, hugged me or kissed my cheek, and shook Mr. Darcy's hand, I stole a glance upwards at his handsome face. It was bathed in smiles, his dimples winking in abundance. He beamed down upon me in return, full of the best kind of pride and tender regard.

After much ado, we were led to the table and placed side by side. Fresh wine was poured, and numerous toasts were offered in our honour. At last we all applied ourselves to the remainder of the feast. Mr. Darcy and I skipped the soup, for Mr. Hurst had eaten our portions, and proceeded to the next course.

We both ate with unusual appetite. For some reason, we suddenly found ourselves beset with ferocious hunger.

After dinner the ladies and I heard a great deal of laughter filter down the hall from the library where the gentlemen enjoyed their brandy and cigars. Jane and I blushed at Mamá's pointed remarks that talk of our upcoming marriages would most likely prove to be the topic of the men's conversation.

Mrs. Hurst, surprisingly, put on her most agreeable expression and actually played the part of gracious hostess quite well. She congratulated me and said she looked forward to a long association between our families now that the Hursts and Darcys would be almost related. She spoke of Pemberley's charms with great enthusiasm, and I could see that she hoped to continue to be invited as a guest once I became mistress of the great estate.

Even the impetus of continued invitations, however, did not provoke a similar response from her sister. Miss Bingley remained sullen and uncommunicative, tucked away in a corner chair with a glass of sherry that I noticed she refilled often enough.

"Miss Bennet?" I heard a soft voice and turned to find Miss Darcy at my side. "I am very pleased that you have accepted my brother. I have never seen him so happy."

"Thank you."

"I hope you shall be content leaving your sisters and joining yourself to such a small family."

"But I look forward to our acquaintance as sisters. Pray, call me Elizabeth."

She smiled shyly. "And you must say Georgiana when speaking to me."

"I shall, I shall," I said with great enthusiasm.

Not long afterwards, the gentlemen joined us. Mr. Darcy strode to my side, a gleam in his eye. Mrs. Hurst prevailed upon Georgiana to play the pianoforte. She did her utmost to avoid Mary's attempts to gain her attention. I smiled across the room at Jane. If our sister did succeed in making her way to the instrument, I felt certain not even Mary's pitiful performance could ruin the evening.

At the end of the gathering, Mr. Darcy and Mr. Bingley escorted Jane and me to our father's carriage to join Mary and Kitty for the ride home. How thrilling it was to allow Mr. Darcy to kiss my hand before others who now acknowledged it as his right.

"I shall call first thing tomorrow if that is acceptable," he murmured.

"Of course." I smiled up at him.

"Until then," he whispered, turned my hand over and kissed my palm, which sent shivers of delight running up my spine.

Did he know how that simple action caused me to grow weak? From the rakish look in his eye, I suspected he knew exactly what he was doing. Two can play such games, I thought.

Purposefully, I parted my lips and ever so slowly began to bite my lower lip. I watched with satisfaction the effect it had on him. How skilfully he struggled to repress his emotions, the only clues being his sudden intake of air and consequent heaving chest.

"Goodnight, Fitzwilliam," I whispered and climbed into the cab.

OUR FAMILY'S RETURN TRIP TO Longbourn was once again postponed because of my engagement. Nothing would do but for us to stay until the next week so that Mamá could tote me to the warehouses to select silks and laces for my wedding gown and trousseau. She dared not leave such important decisions to me alone without her expert opinion. I protested that I still could not show my face in public without scorn, but Mr. Bingley and Mr. Darcy soon banished that excuse.

With much forethought and planning on the part of Mr. Darcy and much active cajoling on the part of Mr. Bingley, my mother was persuaded to consent to a double wedding for Jane and me and much earlier than my sister's previously planned ceremony. At first, Mamá had been adamant that she could not plan a wedding in less than three months' time, but after extensive praise of her abilities by both men and the added extravagance of their promises to secure special licences, Mamá agreed to a wedding ceremony to be held in the middle of February. She could not disregard the distinction of two daughters marrying by special licence.

As soon as my father approved the plans, which he was content to do, Mr. Darcy and Mr. Bingley contacted the offices of the *London Gazette* and published our announcements forthwith. At last, I could read my uncle's newspaper with alacrity and without misgiving.

The day the notices were printed, Jane and I walked in the park with our intendeds, accompanied by Kitty and Georgiana. A light snow had fallen that morning, just enough to coat the barren landscape, causing it to appear fresh and new.

My younger sister talked Georgiana into scraping enough snow together to fashion snowballs, and soon they began to pelt Mr. Bingley with them. He, in turn, retaliated in like manner while Jane stood by laughing.

Mr. Darcy took the opportunity to take my hand and steal away from our companions. He hurried us into a copse of shrubs and evergreens so that we might be somewhat hidden from public view, ostensibly to protect me from the snow being thrown—or so he would have said if questioned. There he pulled me close in a tender embrace. He lowered his head until his cheek met mine and I could inhale that delicious scent of his that filled me with such delight.

"How I have longed to hold you," he murmured. "It seems we are never alone, Elizabeth. How can you keep your wits in a house containing so many?"

I laughed lightly. "You forget that I have never known any other. I do feel sympathy for Mr. and Mrs. Gardiner. Their house has been filled to capacity far too long. Although they would never say it, I feel quite certain they will be relieved when we depart on the morrow."

"Shall you miss having such a big family around you after we marry and you have only Georgiana and me with whom to share a home?"

"At the moment, sir, I would be content to share a home with only one other person."

He placed his forehead against mine, his arms entwined around my waist, holding me snugly against his warm body. "And just who might that one person be?"

"Someone tall and handsome who thinks himself exceedingly clever."

"Clever?" He leaned his head back against the bark of the tree against which he stood. "In what way?"

"Do not play the innocent, sir. I yet marvel at how shrewdly you succeeded in arranging our marriage without going back on your word and offering another proposal. I shall take it as a warning that, from this point on, I must heed your conversation with great care and acknowledge that you mean what you say without exception."

"A prudent decision," he said, smiling slightly.

"I suppose that is why your ability to invent tales surprised me so. On that terrible day when we were accosted by the highwaymen, I was astounded at how quickly you delved into the imaginary."

"Yes, I did rather hastily declare you my wife, did I not?"

He took my hand and led me to a stone bench within the hidden enclosure of shrubs. "When I recall that day, I remember that I had not the slightest hesitation in doing so. The idea sprang to my mind immediately. It seemed no less natural than drawing breath. At times I wonder whether I did not already think of you as my wife, that uttering the statement only gave credence to the desire buried deep within my heart."

"I thought you said it only to protect me."

He nodded. "But I could have said you were my sister and afforded you the same measure of protection."

"Perhaps," I said, "and perhaps not. As I recall, in another conversation you declared with great emphasis that no one would ever believe us brother and sister. In any event and for whatever reason, it is done."

He looked down at the ground, but not before I glimpsed regret in his expression. "In truth, I am the one who could never think of you as my sister. The idea was completely unnatural to me. If I had, I might have spared you the pain and the suffering you have endured here in Town."

He stood up and clenched his fists. "What a selfish being I truly am, Elizabeth! If I had called you my sister, you might never have experienced this last hellish month."

I rose and caught hold of his arm. "Do not torment yourself. If you had done things differently, I might have been abused by Sneyd or even . . . Morgan. You did the right thing. All has turned out well."

He inclined his face toward me. "And can you honestly say you do not harbour any ill feelings toward me in regards to the past?"

I smiled. "The feelings I have are now so widely different from what they were then that every unpleasant circumstance attending it ought to be forgotten. You must learn some of my philosophy. Think only of the past as its remembrance gives you pleasure."

"With me, it is not so. Painful recollections will intrude which cannot, which ought not, be repelled. I can yet see the anguish upon your beautiful face the night of the opera."

I raised my hand to his forehead to smooth away the frown. "Fitzwilliam dearest, you think far too much."

I stood on tiptoes and kissed his cheek. He caught my hand and kissed the exposed skin at my wrist between my glove and sleeve. Then reaching for me with his other arm, he gathered me close and bent to kiss my lips.

Beginning slowly, he contented himself with soft, chaste kisses, until I slipped my arms around his neck and leaned against him. Within moments, his passion mounted, and with it, the fervour of his mouth upon mine. I felt that now familiar release of my will as his caresses easily forced me to surrender to him, caught up in the tide of emotion his slightest touch excited within me.

How long we stood enmeshed I do not know. We emerged from our bliss, however, with a jolt—a cold, wet jolt! An icy snowball cooled the ardour of passion, when it landed upon our cheeks and within seconds slid down our necks!

I screamed and he uttered an oath before we looked up to see our younger sisters race away, giggling with glee.

"Kitty!" I cried.

"Georgiana?" Mr. Darcy asked, wonder in his tone. "My timid, shy little Georgiana is a party to this evil?"

"Oh dear, I fear her association with my family may lead her down the path to corruption."

We both began to laugh, and scooping up hands full of snow, we formed our own weapons and soon embarked on a mission of our own. Once again, Fitzwilliam surprised me, acting the child as much as Mr. Bingley or Kitty or I. The haughty, arrogant, proper Mr. Darcy still harboured a bit of the boy within.

THE DAY ARRIVED AT LAST whereupon we were to leave London for Hertfordshire. Jane and I were thrilled at the news that both Mr. Bingley and Mr. Darcy decided to travel with us. Mr. Bingley determined to remain in the country until the wedding took place and make Netherfield his permanent residence thereafter. We were less than thrilled to discover that Mr. and Mrs. Hurst and Caroline Bingley were also to accompany us.

Thus, it came about that we made the trip in three carriages. Mamá, Mary and Kitty rode in my father's carriage so that Mamá might have a seat to herself for comfort, Papá and Jane joined Mr. Bingley and Mr. Hurst in Mr. Bingley's carriage, and Mrs. Hurst, Miss Bingley, Mr. Darcy, and I rode in his carriage.

How strange that I was to make the return trip with the same three companions with whom I had embarked on that momentous journey. Several things were different about this excursion, however. For one, Mr. Darcy's carriage was finer, larger, and more comfortable than that of Mr. Bingley. Still, two people seated together were forced to jostle against each other from time to time, occurrences Mr. Darcy and I endured with great tolerance, seeing that, on this trip, he and I sat together facing Mr. Bingley's sisters.

Miss Bingley had not yet reconciled herself to our forthcoming marriage. Oh, she knew well enough that it was to happen, but it was evident she still struggled to speak with civility in my presence, if she spoke at all. I bore up under that trial as best I could, but Mrs. Hurst seemed determined to cause the two of us to become friends. Once again, I wondered whether her concern stemmed from the goodness of her heart or whether she looked to her family's future interests in retaining a connection with the owner of Pemberley.

We had bid our farewells to my aunt and uncle early that morning. My aunt held me close and whispered, "Be happy, Lizzy," in my ear.

With earnest expressions of gratitude, I kissed both of them goodbye, and we all looked forward to our reunion at the wedding in little more than a fortnight.

Before we drove out of view, being the final carriage in the caravan of three, and while I still waved to our relations, Mrs. Hurst undertook her campaign to strike up a friendship between Caroline and me.

"Miss Bennet," she began, "since we are all to be family very soon, shall you not call my sister and me by our Christian names? And in turn, might we have the pleasure of addressing you by yours?"

"Of course, Mrs. Hurst," I replied.

"Then, Eliza, you must call me Louisa."

I murmured her name and wished I could instruct her not to shorten my name to Eliza, but I restrained myself and smiled.

"You and Caroline must be about the same age," she went on. "Now that we are all to be one family, you must explore your common interests. Were we not just speaking of this, Caroline?"

Her sister gave her a look that indicated the opposite, but she did make the effort and nodded in confirmation.

I pressed my lips together, wondering what Miss Bingley and I could possibly have in common and also what Mr. Darcy thought of this line of conversation. I chanced a glimpse at his countenance, but he stared out the window at the scenes of London passing by. I could see that it was left to me to supply possible suggestions.

"We both enjoy music," I began, "although Caroline is far more accomplished on the pianoforte than I."

She snorted and I saw Louisa nudge her with her elbow. "But you have such a lovely voice," Mrs. Hurst said. "Does she not, Caroline?"

"Yes," her sister said, refusing to add to the compliment.

I sighed and looked out the window. The conversation was insupportable. Caroline had not the slightest interest in being my friend, and we had nothing in common except that her brother was to marry my sister. Mrs. Hurst continued her endeavours to introduce various topics on which we might agree, but nothing would induce Caroline to put herself out to advance the exchange to any degree. I was relieved when Louisa, at last, gave up and resigned herself to riding in silence.

I let out my breath and settled into the swaying hypnotic rhythm of the coach, allowing myself to lean against Mr. Darcy's arm, our legs touching from time to time as well. He did not seem to mind. In truth, he appeared to take up much more room than necessary so that we might be forced to sit close together.

Within a half-hour's time, we had left Town, and I rejoiced to view the passing countryside. Even though winter was upon us, the landscape brown and barren, I still gloried in the open spaces uncluttered with crowded rows of houses and shops. I smiled to see flocks of sheep search about for sparse blades of grass in the meadows, and up above wisps of clouds strewn across the wide blue sky. Oh yes, at last I could breathe freely.

"Is it not lovely, Fitzwilliam?" I asked softly.

He smiled at me and nodded. "'Tis a peaceful, pastoral scene. Does it make your heart yearn for a long walk?"

"Aye! I can hardly wait to return to the country lanes around Longbourn."

Caroline snorted again. "Oh, please, Eliza. Do not tell us you plan to continue tramping through the woods like a gypsy now that you are to be mistress of Pemberley. You must think of your new position in society, or at least consider Mr. Darcy's reputation before you are seen running through the wilds."

I sensed the tension rising up in Mr. Darcy. Evidently, Mrs. Hurst could see it, as well, for she said quickly, "Caroline and I would be glad to advise you on these things, my dear. You can hardly be expected to know all the changes you must bring about before you move into that great estate. My sister and I have long moved in such exalted circles, and we would be more than happy to aid you in the necessary modifications."

I took a deep breath, willing myself not to react as I wished. "That is an exceedingly generous offer, Louisa."

"But unnecessary," Mr. Darcy interjected. "I am more than satisfied with Elizabeth exactly as she is. I would not have the slightest alteration made in either her behaviour or her character. As for walks in the woods, I have come to possess a distinct fondness for them myself."

Caroline frowned, Louisa sniffed, and nothing more was said for several miles.

I noticed that we had reached a wooded area by then, one in which Mr. Darcy appeared particularly interested. He leaned toward the window and surveyed the passing landscape as though in search of something. Within moments, he tapped the roof of the carriage with his cane, signalling the driver to stop.

"Is there an inn here?" Caroline asked. "I can see naught but trees."

The footman opened the door and lowered the steps, whereupon Mr. Darcy exited the carriage and stood looking about for a moment. "This area is where we were apprehended by the highwaymen. I desire to examine the scene if it will not cause any of you distress for me to do so."

We assured him that it would not, and I rose to leave the carriage and join him, causing Louisa and Caroline promptly to do the same. Papá's carriage and that of Mr. Bingley had already gone on ahead and did not make the stop with us.

Mr. Darcy stood and scanned the line of trees. He then walked back and forth where the highwaymen had stopped us the first time.

"Mrs. Hurst," he asked, "can you show me where Bingley's carriage was pulled off the road? I cannot place it." She welcomed his attentions and led him into the wooded area, stating she believed the site was nearby.

"Why ever does Mr. Darcy wish to explore this horrid scene?" Caroline complained. "I should prefer never to visit it again!"

"I tend to agree with you," I said. "It holds nothing but painful memories."

I shuddered slightly, having suddenly visualized images of Rufus sitting astride his horse holding a gun on us, Merle rummaging through our valises, and Sneyd demanding our jewels. I looked about and could almost picture the first time I caught sight of Morgan dressed all in black, that jaunty feather tucked in his hatband, waving about in contrast to his golden curls.

"Where have they gone?" Caroline whined. "I want to leave this place."

"It must have been terrible for you," I said. "Bound and gagged and hidden in the woods. However did you manage?"

"It was insufferable! I cannot begin to describe it. We were shoved and crammed into that coach with menservants! I doubt that I shall ever recover from such mistreatment. I still suffer from nightmares, and Louisa does, as well."

She sighed and tossed her head. "You have no idea how fortunate you were to be taken, Eliza. At least Mr. Darcy remained by your side to protect you, and you were never abandoned or left to defend yourself against those criminals. Oh yes, you are fortunate, indeed."

"That I am, Caroline," I said quietly, although images flashed through my memory of the times I was forced to fend for myself against Sneyd as well as Morgan.

How would it benefit either of us to tell her of my experience? Because of her jealousy, she had closed her mind against me, and the most I could hope for was civility between us. For Jane's sake, I would do what I could to promote such grace.

"I suggest we do all that we can to put the memory behind us," I offered. "We have both suffered in our own ways. We have shared and survived a common peril. Perchance, in some unforeseen manner, the experience will bind us for all time. I know I shall never think of the beginning of that journey without remembrance of you."

She turned to meet my gaze. "You may be correct. We are survivors, are we not? Our degree of suffering does not have to equal, I suppose, for us to extend a common understanding toward each other."

"Nor a common sympathy," I added, smiling. I was rewarded with the faintest hint of a similar expression crossing her face.

Mrs. Hurst returned about that time, emerging from the wood alone. Somewhat out of breath from her walk, she struggled to speak without panting. Eventually I understood that Mr. Darcy wished for me to join him, as she waved her handkerchief in that direction. I stepped quickly and hurried to find him, eager to depart Caroline's renewed whine to complete the journey.

It was not difficult to locate Mr. Darcy within the grove of trees and shrubs, for he knelt within a portion that had been flattened by Mr. Bingley's carriage months before.

"Elizabeth," he said, looking up, an air of excitement in his manner, "I have found it!"

"Found what, sir?" I replied.

"My father's money clip! I discovered it here, along with a woman's necklace. It must belong to Miss Bingley or Mrs. Hurst." He stood up and held out his hand, wherein I saw a thick gold money clip in the shape of the letter D.

"I thought Colonel Fitzwilliam said all that was stolen by the robbers had been sold, but for my cross. How did you know to search in this place?"

"When I met with Morgan, he confessed that he had dropped part of the loot sometime either during the robbery or on the ride to the cabin. I took a chance that the loss might have occurred before we left this site to embark upon that long ride through the woods."

"When you met with Morgan?" I echoed. "I do not understand. When did such a meeting occur?"

He took my arm as we began to exit the woods. "After he was sentenced and before I spoke to the judge about commuting his decision to transportation, I visited with Morgan at Newgate Prison. I offered him the opportunity to go to America in return for certain promises."

"What kind of promises?"

"The assurance that he would do all in his power to make a decent life for Gert in Virginia, meaning that he would forsake his old ways and dedicate himself to becoming a law-abiding citizen instead of a lawbreaker."

"Is that all?"

He took a deep breath and swallowed. "No. I also told him that if he ever did anything to harm you in any way, and I learned of it—I would kill him."

I swallowed as well. "Did you tell Morgan you planned to send me to Virginia?"

He shook his head. "When I met with him, I had not even thought of purchasing your passage. Yet, I still feared you and he might someday be united, and I wanted to put him on guard. I wished him to know that someone else cared what happened to you and would take every means to protect you."

"Oh, Fitzwilliam." I stopped and turned to him. Once again that tormented expression played about his eyes. "I cannot bear that I caused you such worry and fear."

He took both my hands in his and then looked around where we were standing. "This spot—this very spot is where Morgan sat on his horse, and Sneyd thrust you into his arms. I can still see the way his hands encircled your waist and how he pulled you close against his chest, his rough cheek brushing against yours. I wanted to kill him, Elizabeth! God help me, if I had possessed opportunity, I would have!"

I reached up and touched his cheek, turning his face to meet mine. "It is over, dearest. From this day forward, only your hands shall touch me, and I shall lean upon no one but you. I shall nestle safely in your arms. Let us leave the past here. It is dead and finished. We are alive and well and, God willing, have a lifetime in which to create memories that will fill our hearts and cancel out those that torment us."

He leaned toward me, and although he could not take me in his arms then and there, I rejoiced to see the light return to his beautiful dark eyes, the anguish vanish, replaced by love and joy and eager anticipation of days to come.

Chapter Sixteen

The day we returned to Hertfordshire, rain set in, and it continued for nigh onto three weeks but for the briefest of respites. The cold, raw temperatures of late January and early February only added to the general unpleasantness of the climate. Consequently, I was forced to stay indoors, and my longing for a good tramp through the woods remained unsatisfied.

The inclement weather, however, did not halt Mamá's frantic wedding preparations. My father's carriage was called for daily so that she might frequent the dressmaker's establishment in Meryton and meet more often than needed with the vicar of Longbourn church.

She raided her friends' stillrooms, begging gifts of their finest dried blooms with which to decorate the sanctuary. Urging the advice of Mrs. Philips and Mrs. Long and seeking their opinions of her proposed arrangements, she then promptly disregarded them. Thus, the muddy ruts along the road from Longbourn to Meryton grew ever deeper with each passing day.

Still, I was happy to be at home, away from the clamour of London and its noisy, crowded atmosphere. One would hardly deem our house quiet, but by comparison, its country setting filled me with a peace I had not experienced since leaving it over two months earlier.

My sister Lydia's return added to the degree of giggles and wails. If not regaling us with joyful accounts of her days spent with Mrs. Forster and her retinue of young officers, she mourned bitterly the loss of one young man in particular.

It seemed that Mr. Wickham had attached himself to Miss King, a relative newcomer to the area, but one of some importance. She had recently inherited a fortune of ten thousand pounds, and Lydia was inconsolable at the news. She declared that if she had a fortune, not only Mr. Wickham but several of the young officers would ask for her hand, a vision reinforced by my mother.

"Of course, I should choose Mr. Wickham," Lydia announced, "for if anyone could make me be true, it would be him. Is he not the handsomest man you have ever seen in his regimentals?"

Kitty agreed with her, but both Jane and I admonished her not to engage in such idle talk. Jane suggested that it was not proper to speak in that manner of a gentleman already attached to another while I lectured her on the importance of choosing a man of worth, not just looks.

"Oh, pooh!" Lydia declared. "Just because Mr. Wickham did not choose you, Lizzy, is no reason to denounce his merit."

"She can afford to now," Kitty said, "since a man ten times his worth has asked for her hand."

Lydia made a face and threw the bonnet she had been trimming onto the table. "Mr. Darcy may be rich enough, but I think him a bore. Can you imagine spending your life with such a strict, proper man? I much prefer a man of excitement. One could never grow restless married to Mr. Wickham. There is such an air of daring about him!"

Neither Mary's moral platitudes, nor anything Jane or I said could dissuade Lydia from her foolish ideas.

My elder sister and I had privately decided not to share with our family the information about Mr. Wickham's indiscretion with Georgiana because of the embarrassment it might cause Mr. Darcy and his sister. Thus, when warning Lydia, we were forced to speak in general terms of Mr. Wickham's lack of character. Since it had little visible effect on her inexperienced outlook, I took relief in the fact that Mr. Wickham had now removed himself from the marriage market in Hertfordshire.

"Besides," Jane later said in my bedchamber, "Mr. Wickham would never importune one of our sisters even if he were not attached to Miss King, for he must marry money."

"Now that you and I are moving up in the world, Jane," I said, "our sisters' circumstances are somewhat altered. A man with Mr. Wickham's outlook might see our connections as promising. Yes, it is a very good thing that he is safely settled on another."

I do not know whether it was the forced indoor confinement that caused those weeks before my wedding to crawl by at such an interminable pace or not, but rarely had I wished for anything to pass as greatly as I yearned for that time to elapse.

Mr. Darcy and Mr. Bingley called daily, but we were rarely granted more than a moment alone. My father's house seemed to grow smaller each week. I felt as though we were smothered in people and not only members of our household. Mrs. Long, Mrs. Philips, Lady Lucas, and other friends of my mother called regularly. Mrs. Forster, accompanied by several of the young officers of the militia, attended upon us as well. And then, the week before the wedding, Mr. and Mrs. Collins returned to Hertfordshire to stay at Lucas Lodge.

It seemed that Mr. Collins was now out of favour with Lady Catherine because he and I were cousins, and she had not yet reconciled herself that I was to marry her nephew. My father's bizarre sense of humour caused him to advise Mr. Collins that if he had a choice, he should stand by Mr. Darcy, as he had more to give. Thus, we were treated to frequent visits from Charlotte and her husband. Although I enjoyed time with my good friend, even a little of Mr. Collins's obsequious presence strained Mr. Darcy's patience to the breaking point.

Jane and I were often invited to visit Netherfield, but there Mr. and Mrs. Hurst and Caroline prevailed upon our attentions, and Mr. Darcy and I found ourselves alone only upon the odd occasion and then but for a moment or two.

I sensed that he was growing increasingly frustrated and watched him resort to his unsociable behaviours frequently. He spoke less and less, entering into conversation only when forced. He spent undue amounts of time gazing out the windows of both Netherfield Hall and Longbourn, and his impatience with my mother, Mr. Collins, Caroline Bingley, and my younger sisters grew ever more obvious.

At last, I suggested he refrain from calling for a day. The rain had let up that evening, and as he bade me goodnight, I said, "It appears we shall have a favourable break in the weather. Why not spend the entire day tomorrow out of doors in sport with Mr. Bingley and Mr. Hurst?"

I could see the relief in his eyes, although he expressed regret at not visiting me.

"Perchance a brief absence will do us both good. On the following day, you may find yourself racing back to see me." I gave him an arch smile as he kissed my hand. I should miss him, but I knew he needed time away from my family.

The next morning I rose early, buttoned my pelisse, and grabbed my bonnet, intent upon a long, solitary walk in the woods. If Mamá were awake, she would have warned me about soiling my petticoat on the muddy roads, but I cared not a whit. I longed for the freedom of no other company but my own.

Just as I reached the front door, however, the heavens greeted me with yet another round of raindrops. It was not a heavy storm, but a persistent drizzle, and cancelled any opportunity for a hike. With a great sigh, I picked up a book I had left in the parlour, grabbed an apple from the dining room table, and slipped out the door.

Making a hurried dash, I ran around the house, crossed the courtyard, and entered into the back part of the stable used primarily for storage. Bridles, saddles, blankets, and various grooming tools hung neatly from pegs on the walls, against which the winter's supply of hay bales was stacked.

None of the servants was about, and so I selected a blanket, threw it over my shoulder, and climbed the ladder to the hayloft where a mountain of loose hay awaited me. A favourite retreat since childhood, I thought it a perfect refuge in which to hide. I spread out the horse blanket and mounded up enough hay for a pillow before reclining with only an apple and a novel for company. It was not a walk, but at least I could be alone for a while.

Some time later, I heard the arrival of a carriage and peered through the space between the rough boards of the stable wall. My Aunt Philips had arrived, along with Mrs. Long. Once they entered the house, the servants drove the carriage into the main stable.

I knew I should go in and greet them, but the thought of giving up my solitude convinced me to remain exactly where I lay. Besides that, I had unpinned my hair so that the plump knot did not rub against my scalp as I reclined. I had little desire to redo my coiffure just to see my mother's visitors. I returned to the adventure I had been reading, content to conceal myself as long as possible.

I do not know when I fell asleep, but as is often the case when reading, my eyelids began to droop and eventually closed. How long I slept, I know not, but I do recall how I was awakened.

"Elizabeth," Mr. Darcy said softly, trailing a wisp of hay along my cheek. I remember slapping at it to remove the tickle when I heard him chuckle. Opening my eyes, I found his face just above my own, his lips so enticingly near I could have kissed him with the barest of efforts.

I laughed and attempted to raise my head but found his arms on both sides of me, providing a provocative restraint. "Why are you here? How did you find me?"

"The housekeeper told me of how you slipped out early this morning," he said. "As to why I am here, listen." Thunder boomed in the distance, and I could see flashes of lightning through the opening below. "One can hardly engage in any type of sport in this weather unless it is my favourite pursuit—ensnaring you in my trap!"

I could not keep from giggling again. "And now that I am caught, what shall you do with me?"

"Oh, perhaps this," he said, kissing my cheek, his breath warm, his lips gently caressing. "Or, I could do this," he added, nuzzling the other cheek. "And then there is always this." He moved his lips to my forehead. "And this, most definitely." He nibbled my left ear. "Or especially this." He proceeded to the spot below my right ear while I trembled with delight.

"One never knows. I might even do this," he said, his voice almost a growl. His lips touched mine with the lightest of kisses. I rose slightly, hoping to keep his mouth upon mine, but he pulled back just enough to thwart my desire and raised his eyebrows.

"What is this? Can my prey possibly wish to be ensnared?" His eyes widened in mock surprise.

I answered by taking his face in my hands. I pulled him down until my lips met his, my eyes closing with pleasure. Softly I stroked his mouth with my own, my caresses growing ever deeper and more urgent until I heard him groan and gather me up into his arms, whereupon he proceeded to match my desire, his own growing stronger moment by moment.

At last we drew apart, and he rolled over. He lay beside me on the blanket, nestling my head upon his chest as he stroked my hair. His heart beat in my ear with a turbulent rhythm, and I could feel him struggle to control his breathing.

"Elizabeth, you have bewitched me."

"How can I, when I reside within your trap?"

He laughed softly. "In truth, it is you who have trapped me, and I am caged within a pen from which I never desire release. Do you have any idea how you tempt me with your curls freed from restraint?"

At the moment, I had forgotten that I had unpinned my knot and raised my hand to pull my hair back. He snatched my hand away. "No, let it be. I love to see it down."

"How can you? It is all untidy and wild."

"I recall the first time I watched your curls fall. You rode in front of me on Morgan's horse. I saw your bonnet loosen and drop to the ground, and then one by one, your dark tendrils slipped from their pins and trailed down your neck."

"I was mortified to appear so dishevelled in your presence," I murmured, remembering how I had searched for a means to rectify my appearance.

He slowly shook his head. "Your description is untrue. I thought you captivating. Ever since we returned to civilization, I have longed to reach up and throw away those pins." I could feel him bury his face in my hair, as he kissed my forehead.

"Oh, I do love you so!" I cried as I raised my head from his chest, cupped his face with both hands, and began to kiss him once again. His response was equally urgent. He rolled me over onto my back and began the process of kissing me with such abandon that I feared my heart might burst. At last and only moments before I thought I could not bear the excitement building within me, he pulled away.

Quickly he sat up and put his hand to his mouth in that manner I had come to know so well. He did not look at me until he had regulated his breath. I knew that I should rise to a seated position myself, but in truth, I felt too weak to move.

After a time, he turned his head and looked over his shoulder. The desire in his eyes did little to aid my resolve. I knew full well that one of us had to be the stronger, and I prayed that it would be Fitzwilliam.

"Three more days, Elizabeth," he said. "Three more days, and I shall not stop."

I blushed, but could not keep from smiling.

"Until then we must stay out of haylofts," he said.

"Must we?" I said wistfully. "Why is that?"

The barest glimmer of amusement played about his eyes. "You know why. Have mercy and do not tease me."

I raised up on my elbows and lifted my chin. "I am innocent."

He nodded, saying nothing for a moment, and continued to stare at me. "Yes, I know. If you were not innocent, you would realize in what danger you now reside."

"Danger?"

"Yes, Miss Bennet, danger." He turned and reclined upon one arm.

I placed my hand upon his cheek and gazed into his eyes. He took my palm and kissed it, a practice he had already discovered filled me with delight.

"I am not afraid of you, Mr. Darcy," I tried to say bravely, although my voice trembled somewhat.

"But I am," he whispered, kissing my palm again. Then rising, he leaned down and pulled me to my feet. "Come, my love. Let us return to the lion's den and enter our true cage. For the present, I have enjoyed all the sport I am allowed."

Early on the day before the wedding, the Gardiners arrived from London, a welcome addition to our household. They left their children in Town with Mrs. Gardiner's sister, for they knew Longbourn would be brimming over with people.

My father and uncle quickly secluded themselves in Papá's study to escape the general mayhem caused by two brides at the mercy of a nervous mother. The only sounds we heard were strains of their laughter drifting through the door now and then.

Mamá claimed most of our aunt's attention, as she thought it imperative that Mrs. Gardiner know every detail of the wedding plans. She insisted that I model my wedding bonnet for my aunt's approval, but before I could even place it on my head, her interest had leapt from my bonnet to the handkerchief she had embroidered. She wished Jane to carry it with her bridal bouquet, and she waited impatiently to hear her sister's praise of her fine needlework.

In between attending to our mother's frequent need for reassurance that Jane and I had indeed placed sprigs of rosemary among our gowns already packed in our valises, Jane attempted to settle in her chair and apply herself to the novel she was reading. I could see the look she wore, however, and I doubted that she could concentrate on the book.

I did not even pretend to be at rest. Over and over, I walked to the window, pulled the curtain aside, and peered out. There was nothing to be seen but rain and more rain. Would it never cease?

The weather was so poor that the day dragged by with an unusual absence of expected callers. My mother suggested taking Aunt Gardiner into Meryton to call on Mrs. Philips, but neither of them was brave enough to face the weather.

"Perchance, she will visit us," Mamá declared, "as well she ought, for you have made the trip from Town in these inclement conditions, and she should be willing to exert some small effort."

"I would not insist that anyone go about in this rain, Fanny. I will see my sister on the morrow at the wedding."

"Oh, that reminds me—the wedding breakfast! I must talk to Cook and go over the menu once again. You must come with me, Madeline, for I wish for you to see the dishes I have selected."

Jane and I exchanged pointed glances, as we sympathized with poor Cook. Our mother had surely reviewed the menu at least a dozen times! I sighed as I watched Mary resume her place at the pianoforte while Kitty and Lydia whispered and giggled together in a corner.

All seemed as expected within Longbourn, and yet I could not remain still. I missed Fitzwilliam, and I willed the hands on the clock to move more quickly, for he and Mr. Bingley were invited to dine with us that evening.

At length, I relinquished the hope that standing at the window might make the rain stop falling and sat down beside Jane. She looked up, smiled, and returned to her book.

"You may as well put that aside, for I know you cannot keep your mind attuned to the plot."

"And how do you know that?"

"You have failed to turn a single page for the last hour."

Jane laughed lightly and placed her marker between the pages. Turning to me, she gave me her full attention. "Does this day seem as long to you as it does to me?"

"Utterly! I believe it is the longest day of the year!"

"We are silly, are we not? If Papá sees our behaviour, he will declare it to be so."

I nodded. "I find it silly and strange and yet somehow delightful that I can no longer be truly at ease when I am not in Mr. Darcy's presence. It is as though part of me—the essential part—is missing."

"May you always feel that way, Lizzy, and you as well, Jane." Aunt Gardiner placed her hands on our shoulders. Her presence surprised both of us, and Jane asked how she had escaped our mother.

"I convinced her to rest for awhile. I said, 'Fanny, you look a bit peaked.' She rushed above stairs to her bed to refresh her bloom in time to receive her dinner guests. And what of you girls? Should you not do the same?"

Jane and I complied with our aunt's suggestion and climbed the stairs, although we both knew that neither of us would sleep. In truth, I did not even make the attempt, but followed Jane into her chamber. There, we lay on the bed and opened our hearts to each other as we had done all our lives.

"Are you afraid, Lizzy?" Jane had turned on her side, her back to me, and I could not see her face.

"Of what?" I placed my hand on Jane's shoulder and gently tugged at her to turn back to me. When she did, I saw the blush covering her face.

"The wedding night, of course. Do you think it is as dreadful as Mamá has said?"

"No. If it were, why would so many women agree to marry?"

"What choice does our sex have? If a woman does not marry and she does not possess a vast fortune, she is doomed to be taken in by a brother or sister and to live out her days as a poor relation. She has neither home nor child of her own."

I sat up and looked directly into Jane's eyes. "And yet we do have a choice. If you are afraid of Mr. Bingley, you should not marry him."

"I do not fear Charles but the unknown. What if I do not know how to please him?"

"Dearest, every person in Hertfordshire knows that Mr. Bingley is besotted with you! You cannot help but please him."

"But the way Mamá described it—" Jane's eyes grew big and round.

"I think we should pay no more attention to what Mamá has told us of the wedding night than we do to any other subject of which she speaks." I smiled and shrugged, and I was gratified to see my sister's lips twitch slightly.

Rising from the bed, I walked to Jane's dresser and began to place her combs in my hair, peering in the mirror to determine which I liked best. "On my wedding night, I plan to follow Mr. Darcy's lead. He has never yet taken me down the wrong path."

Jane turned to lie on her stomach facing the foot of the bed. "I believe you learned a great deal about him on that journey you were forced to endure. I suspect that even now you have not told me everything the two of you experienced. "

I took great pains to remove the combs and smooth my hair back into place, thus avoiding her direct gaze. "On that journey, Mr. Darcy and I faced dangerous, unexpected hazards daily. We were forced to rely on each other. We lived by our wits and the grace of God."

Turning from the mirror, I wrapped my arms around the bedpost and leaned against it. "I learned what kind of man Mr. Darcy truly is, and I learned to trust him. The unknown does not frighten me, Jane. Does not scripture say that perfect love casts out fear?"

That evening my uncle renewed his acquaintance with Mr. Darcy and Mr. Bingley, and Jane and I were pleased to see their genuine appreciation of each other's company. We passed a pleasant evening together, even though Mamá lamented the weather frequently, afraid that the roads would be impassable.

"Do not fear the rain, Mrs. Bennet," Mr. Bingley said. "Darcy and I shall be in place at the appointed time."

"But what if the river rises?" Kitty asked.

"La, yes," Lydia added. "What will you do if you cannot cross the bridge?"

"We will swim," Mr. Bingley declared, causing my younger sisters and my mother to clap their hands in delight.

Mr. Darcy and I stood near the window, and I could not keep from watching the raindrops course down the pane.

He reached for my hand. "Do you share your mother's concerns about the weather?"

I shook my head, but I could see that he did not believe me. "Perhaps a little."

He turned to face me and raised my chin with the tip of his finger so that I was forced to meet his eyes. "I promise you nothing will keep me from your side on the morrow. I shall marry you, Elizabeth Bennet, no matter how high the water rises."

It was late that evening after Mr. Darcy and Mr. Bingley had left for Netherfield before Jane and I climbed the stairs together. We met Aunt Gardiner outside my chamber.

"So everything is in order?" she asked, smiling. "All prepared for the great day, and now to bed?"

We nodded. "In spite of Mamá's worries, I do think all will be well," I said.

"Your young gentlemen appear as much in love with the two of you as ever. It does my heart good to see you happy. Now that all the unpleasantness is over, you can look forward to the future with the greatest assurance of hope."

Jane and I kissed her and reminded her that we owed much of our present joy to her hospitality and gentle guidance. We retired that night filled with pleasure. While we slept, my mother's prayers were granted, and the rain ceased at last. In its place, a light snow began to fall. We awoke to find the countryside dusted white with a hint of sunshine winking through the clouds.

I could hear my mother's voice crying, "Hill! Hill!" and the scatter of footsteps, as my sisters and the servants scurried about.

I yawned and stretched, rolled over, and thought of Fitzwilliam.

"Good morning, almost husband," I whispered.

I rang the bell for the maid and proceeded with my scheduled ablutions. I was a bride that day, and I felt certain a happier bride had never existed.

My mother and my younger sisters ran back and forth between Jane's bedchamber and mine while we dressed, adding their suggestions—or orders, in Mamá's case—about our preparations.

At length, I had bathed, perfumed, and corseted my body. I sat patiently while the maid transformed my unruly hair into an array of curls. I stepped into the beautiful white gown, and my aunt placed the lace-trimmed bonnet and veil upon my head. Even I could not help but be pleased with my appearance in the floor-length mirror.

I turned around to see Jane enter the room, a vision too lovely to behold. It was all either of us could do to restrain our tears, but fortunately within moments, my uncle called from below stairs that it was time for us to depart. The tears would have to wait.

A collection of carriages were lined up outside Longbourn Church by the time we arrived. My younger sisters retrieved our bouquets from Aunt Philips in the foyer, and after handing them over, they scampered inside. Lydia and Kitty hoped to seat themselves by Lieutenant Denny and Captain Carter, while Mary frowned at them in disapproval. Mr. Gardiner escorted my mother and aunt into the sanctuary.

"Well, Jane, Lizzy," Papá said, holding out an arm for each of us to clasp, "you are both about to marry fine men."

"The very finest of men," I said, and Jane murmured her assent.

"I could not have parted with either of you to any less." He kissed Jane's cheek and then mine, and a lump rose in my throat at the sight of the mist about his eyes. He would not give us time for sentiment, however. Lifting his head, he led us through the great double doors.

Inside I sensed that the pews were filled with guests, but in truth, I could not tell you who was there. I had eyes for only one person standing at the end of the aisle. I suppose the vicar stood there, as well as Mr. Bingley. I, however, saw only Mr. Darcy—my Fitzwilliam—waiting for me.

The expression on his countenance was deadly serious, his eyes piercing mine. It was that same look I had seen him direct upon me so often, one I had in the past erroneously thought of as disapproval but now recognized as Fitzwilliam's intense struggle for self-control. He needed me, he wanted me, he loved me, but he would hold it all deep within. I could read it all over his face, and it made me smile.

It was not until after we had endured the wedding breakfast and raced through the bridal arches with Jane and Mr. Bingley that Fitzwilliam smiled. All through the meal and endless line of friends and family extending their best wishes, I never saw his countenance ease or felt a lessening of the tension that beset him. Therefore, when his face broke out in smiles as he led me to the carriage, it was as welcome as the sun pouring forth through the clouds in all its splendour.

Even before the carriage reached the end of the drive, we had turned to each other, love and desire culminating in a tender, tentative kiss. For some reason, I suddenly felt timid, knowing that now we were married, a kiss could mean much more than when we were betrothed. Once his lips met mine, however, my shyness evaporated as I tasted his sweet mouth and felt that exciting rush of anticipation envelop me.

"I love you, Mrs. Darcy," he murmured, drawing me into his arms.

"I love you more, Mr. Darcy," I replied.

"Impossible!" he declared, kissing away my protests.

Ah well, I thought, I shall let him have the last word this time, since he convinced me in such a beguiling manner.

JANE AND MR. BINGLEY TRAVELLED to London for their wedding trip, but Fitzwilliam wished to take me home to Pemberley, and I had not the slightest desire to go elsewhere. Since it was a great distance to Derbyshire, my husband's uncle had offered us the use of his country estate, Ardengate, in which to break the first day's journey.

We stopped to change horses on the way, but still the trip seemed long. I know not whether it was because of our anticipation of the evening to come, but Fitzwilliam, in particular, appeared more than eager to reach the grounds of the great house.

A great house it was, ancient yet well maintained. I was amazed at its size and grandeur. Inside all was prepared in expectation of our visit. I was shown to my spacious, elegant chamber, where a maid unpacked my bags and helped me dress for dinner. The meal was held in a great dining hall with a table fit for a banquet instead of merely two people. Upon entering the room, my husband shook his head.

"This will not do," he announced to the butler hovering nearby. "You have placed Mrs. Darcy and me at opposite ends of a table clearly intended for a large gathering. Kindly remove her plate, and set it next to mine on my right." The servant snapped his fingers, and two footmen immediately did as directed.

Over a sumptuous feast, we talked of the day, of our relations, and of the wedding itself. Eventually, we began to speak of the previous night, the last night we had remained in an unmarried state.

"Did you sleep well last evening," I asked.

"I cannot say that I did," he replied. "It must have been almost midnight before Fitzwilliam arrived with Georgiana. Even though he was not granted leave from his duties until the last moment, I am fortunate that he was able to escort my sister. I am glad my cousin and sister shall remain in the country for a few days as guests of Mr. Bingley's sisters. It will give her the opportunity to recover from the journey."

"I hope she may enjoy time spent with my younger sisters."

"I am certain that she will. She and Mary can play duets until they drive your father and uncle from the house!"

We laughed at the thought, and then he sobered. "And what of you? Did you sleep well the night before we wed?"

I looked at my lap before answering. "I confess I could not go to sleep," I said softly, "until I thought of you."

"And what did you think of me?" His tone was teasing.

"Oh, how handsome and charming you are." I gave him an arch smile. "I marvelled anew at the way you recommend yourself to strangers! And I dreamt of the balls we will hold at Pemberley, for I know how you love to dance."

"Are those traits you would have me develop?" I had thought we were teasing, but his tone grew quite serious.

"To be more handsome or charming is impossible. As for the remainder of my silly attempts to tease you, dismiss them with nary a thought. I would not alter you in any way."

He smiled and leaned back in his chair. "You must forgive me. I do not always understand when you speak in jest. I fear I shall be in need of daily exposure to your lively ways."

"You need have no fear on that account. That I can promise you."

"But now tell me true, once you thought of me, were you able to sleep?"

I nodded as we gazed into each other's eyes. "Somehow I felt your presence, and I slept quite well."

A light kindled in his eyes, and he reached for my hand. "I, too, have always slept better within your presence."

THE NEXT MORNING I AWAKENED entangled within Fitzwilliam's embrace, my head on his chest, my hair flowing over his shoulder. I felt him stir and tighten his arms around me before kissing my hair. I raised my face just enough to glimpse him through drowsy eyes, and it made me smile.

"Good morning, Husband," I whispered.

"Good morning, Mrs. Darcy," he replied, kissing my forehead again. "Mmm, this is the perfect way to awaken—holding you in my arms. I knew it for truth upon its first occurrence."

"What did you say?"

Now it was his turn to smile. "The first time I woke up with you in my arms, I knew that I wanted to awaken in that manner every day of my life."

I giggled and hugged him closer. "Ah, I know to what you refer—that morning in the cave."

"Y-e-s," he said, stretching out the word, "that was particularly enjoyable, but I had roused from slumber with your arms around me prior to that morning."

I raised up on one elbow. "But that is impossible. What can you mean?"

"You truly do not know? At the time, I did not think you were awake, but I suppose in my vanity, I had hopes."

I sat straight up and stared at him. "Of what are you speaking?"

He looked away, pressed his lips together, and then turned back to face me. "I am speaking of that room in the cabin in which we were locked for three days and nights. The first evening after your outburst summoned the highwaymen, and Morgan forced us to share the same blanket, you huddled against the wall, never turning even once. The second night was another matter."

My eyes widened, and I gasped. "What—what did I do?"

"Nothing so very bad, my love. Do not distress yourself. It is just that I awoke to find you cuddled up against me, your arm thrown across my chest."

"But I never knew it! How could I not know that happened?"

"Well, I took every precaution not to cause you embarrassment. I slipped out from under your embrace very carefully, even though I must tell you it was the last thing in this world I wished to do."

"Fitzwilliam!"

"My dear, do not look at me in that manner. I am just a man, after all. And you know you are a beautiful woman." He reached up and began to caress my bare shoulder, stroking my neck with a tender touch.

"Pray, do not distract me," I said, disturbed that my voice was a bit shaky. "Was that the only time I imposed upon you in that manner?"

He smiled that inviting smile of his that revealed the answer. I sighed and rolled my eyes. What else had I done to humiliate myself?

"Do you recall the gunshots that wakened us on that third night?" he asked.

I nodded. "I called out your name."

"And I put my hand against your mouth immediately to silence you, did I not? That was because you had slept on my shoulder for some time, your mouth buried against my neck. I had not far to reach to quiet you."

"Oh!" I cried with dismay. "What must you have thought of me?"

He lay back, raised his arms and placed them behind his head. "I thought you enchanting, and the greatest temptation I had encountered in my life. I knew without a doubt that as soon as we escaped or were rescued, I had to make you my wife."

"And you assumed I wished to marry you as well. Of course, you did. My behaviour led you to believe I loved you."

"Elizabeth, I think a part of you did love me a little even back then. You fought against it. That was evident. Perhaps, though, that secret, hidden part of your heart knew you loved me even when your speech and actions when awake indicated the opposite. I like to think when asleep, you revealed your true feelings. And then, of course, there was Morgan and my mistaken belief that you cared for him. That diminished my hopes exceedingly." His voice turned sour, as though he tasted something bitter.

I threw myself upon him, stretching out my arms to pull his from beneath his head so that they might encircle me.

"Is it possible that you know me better than I know myself, Fitzwilliam? It is for certain you know more about the ways of love. One thing, however, you do not know, and I shall tell you now so that you never forget it. You are the only man I *have* ever loved and the only man I *shall* ever love. And I intend to wake up beside you every morning of my life!"

From that time on, mornings proved to be the favourite part of our day.

Chapter Seventeen

I have now lived with Fitzwilliam Darcy more years than I have lived without him and yet, to this day, he still surprises me. The hour I think I might sketch the illustration of his thoughts or the moment I conclude that I can predict how he will react, he proves me false by acting the opposite. I sometimes accuse him of doing so just to keep me unbalanced. He feigns ignorance of what I speak, proclaiming that he is a typical man, easily read, as mundane as last night's soup. He is nothing of the sort.

Bits of grey now streak his dark curls, but they still entice me to tangle them in play as much as ever. A few lines have deepened in his forehead and between his brows, but they do not diminish his handsome face. Instead, he appears experienced, distinguished, and wise. I have learned with effort not to assume that, because I know him better than anyone, I perceive how his mind works. In expressions of either love or displeasure, he continues to leave me breathless.

I would not have you think ours has been a faultless union. I do not believe such a thing exists. How could two people of strong wills dwell together without some degree of friction? Our arguments have been forceful and vigorous—both of us at times refusing to bend—but our periods of atonement and reconciliation have proved equally spirited and fervent. We have separated twice in our marriage, and then not by choice, for only the deepest of concerns could keep us apart.

Unfortunately, the first such occurrence took place the summer after we were married. From our wedding on the seventeenth day of February through the first day of August, Fitzwilliam and I enjoyed an idyllic honeymoon. Caught up in the joy and novelty of our love and passion, we had little time or thought for anyone but each other.

By Easter, Georgiana joined us at Pemberley, but she was a welcome addition, of course. A gentle soul and easy companion, I grew to love her more and more each day.

None of us had the slightest desire to return to Town for the Season. I had endured enough of London to satisfy me for some time, and Fitzwilliam was content to remain in his beloved Derbyshire. He announced that we would wait until the following year to make our return in spite of numerous invitations we received from his friends wishing to entertain us and make my acquaintance. I took pleasure that he extended our regrets, more than willing to put off facing the renewed scrutiny of the *ton*.

I have said all this so that you will understand why the month of August descended upon us with shock and horror. We were forced to interrupt our tranquil country life when I received a letter from Jane informing us that Lydia had run off from her friends in Brighton with none other than Mr. Wickham!

She had travelled to the seaside as guest of Mrs. Forster when the militia removed from Meryton and transferred to a shire near Brighton. I had cautioned my father by letter not to allow her such licence, but by the time he received my missive, Lydia had already departed. I issued the warning because of Lydia's general unthinking, forward behaviour, never imagining that Mr. Wickham had any interest in her whatsoever, although I knew she had long looked upon him with a young girl's fancy.

Even though his engagement to Mary King had been broken not long after it began, I still assumed he would seek to marry a woman of means. The fact that he eloped with Lydia just did not make sense. They had been traced as far as London, and my father had travelled to Town, but so far, neither he nor my uncle had found a hint of their whereabouts.

I suffered deep shame at news of my sister's behaviour, not only because of how it affected Georgiana, but because I knew how unthinkable it was that Mr. Wickham should soon become my husband's brother. Fitzwilliam said little after reading Jane's letter.

A dark cloud of anger and resentment descended upon him and, consequently, upon the entire house. When called upon to enter the conversation at dinner, he answered with only the briefest responses and retired to his study afterwards, where he remained behind closed doors for hours. Georgiana and I endured an awkward evening. We spoke of everything but the huge, monstrous thing that dwelt between us.

At last my sister retired for the evening. Still, my husband did not join me in the parlour. I ventured into his study where I found him at his desk, deep in thought. He barely acknowledged my presence and bade me only the briefest good night before I walked upstairs. For the first time in our marriage, I fell asleep alone and not without tears.

I wondered whether he regretted having married me, whether all his earlier judgments about the unsuitability of my family had returned to haunt him and he found himself mired in a marriage he now faced with abhorrence. Without his warm, comforting presence lying beside me, I allowed my imagination to run wild.

He awoke me early the next morning, already dressed, having never inhabited my bed.

"Elizabeth, I have come to bid you a hasty good-bye. I leave for London with the morning light."

"London, but why?" was all that I could utter in an incredulous, stupefied manner.

"I go in search of Wickham and your sister."

I could not speak for the shock of his statement.

"I know his habits, the lower parts of Town where he may have hidden Lydia."

"But my father and Mr. Gardiner are there. Why should you have to subject yourself to this degradation?"

He raised his eyes to mine, and I saw the pain therein. "Do you not see that I am responsible? It is due to my reserve and want of proper consideration that Wickham's character has been misunderstood. Hertfordshire received the man in ignorance of his true nature. If I had but warned your father about Wickham, none of this ever would have happened."

I leaned forward and clasped his hand. "No! I will not permit you to say such a thing. None of us—you or I or my father—suspected that Wickham would prey upon a young girl without fortune. You are not responsible! Pray, do not heap such distress upon yourself."

"I must go. I cannot live with myself if I do not." He kissed me as though we might never meet again, and with one last tormented look, he strode out the door before I could rise or convince him otherwise.

I spent the next ten days equally as tormented, if not more so, for I did not hear a word from him and had not the slightest idea what was occurring. In the beginning, I was at a loss to explain her brother's actions to Georgiana, and she grew more and more reserved as I began to withdraw from her company. Eventually, I revealed what had transpired. She said little, and I wondered how she truly felt. By that time, not only did I worry over Lydia and my family, but I suffered the additional fear that my relationship with Georgiana might be damaged.

At length, I received a terse note from Fitzwilliam that said, *"My undertakings have met with little success. I shall be detained for some time."*

In the meantime, Jane and I exchanged several letters, none of them containing favourable news. Papá had returned to Longbourn, his efforts fruitless. I thought of how large and heavily populated London was, and decided that the couple could not select a better place to hide.

My father's outlook was bleak, and he kept to himself, while Mamá had taken to her bed, ill at the thought that the family had been ruined. Although Jane continued to hold out hope that Wickham and Lydia were married, my own thoughts grew less hopeful with each passing day.

Fitzwilliam spent the entire month of August in London, returning to Pemberley without notice on the third day of September. He walked into the house, weary and downcast, even though his efforts had been successful. My husband had discovered Wickham and Lydia's whereabouts and forced the man to marry my sister, an action the scoundrel never intended. Still, Fitzwilliam blamed himself that Lydia was married to such a man.

Much later, I learned in a letter from Aunt Gardiner that my husband had not only secured Wickham's agreement, he had purchased the man a commission in the regulars, paid off the majority of his debts, and obtained a special licence so that he and Lydia could be married within the month.

Mr. Darcy and Mr. Gardiner battled it together for a long time, which was more than either the gentleman or lady concerned in it deserved. But at last your uncle was forced to yield, and instead of being allowed to be of use to his niece, was forced to put up with only having the probable credit of it, which went sorely against the grain.

After reading my aunt's letter, I sought out my husband and found him in his study poring over accounts. I walked around the desk and stood over him before he had a chance to rise. When he pushed the chair back, I promptly sat down in his lap and wrapped my arms around his neck.

"I know it all," I whispered. "You truly are the best of men."

Taken aback, he questioned me, but I silenced him with my kisses. I felt as though I could never kiss him enough!

Lydia and Mr. Wickham moved far away from both Longbourn and Pemberley, and although Fitzwilliam could never receive *him* at Pemberley, yet for my sake, he assisted him further in his profession. Their manner of living was unsettled to be sure, moving from place to place in quest of a cheap situation and always spending more than they ought. Wickham's affection for her soon sank into indifference. Lydia's lasted a little longer, and in spite of her youth and her manners, she retained all the claims to reputation that her marriage had given her.

Kitty, being removed from Lydia's influence, greatly improved to her advantage by spending much time with us or under Jane's gentle guidance. Both she and Mary eventually made suitable marriages to men of honourable character, if not great fortune.

Within a year of their marriage, Mr. Bingley and Jane left Netherfield and purchased a house in a northern county within thirty miles of Pemberley. This move added greatly to the satisfaction of both my sister and me.

Georgiana never married and spent her days either at her establishment in Town or with us in Derbyshire. Her expertise on the pianoforte increased each year, and she acquired quite a name among those who appreciated her skill and artistry.

My family was saddened at the fact that within five years of my marriage, Mamá died of a trifling little cold that settled in her chest. My father, subsequently, spent much time in Derbyshire, perusing my husband's extensive collection of books or contenting himself watching his grandchildren grow at either our house or Jane's.

At the age of two and twenty, I gave birth to my first son, Thomas Fitzwilliam Darcy, whom we called Will. He was the image of his father, so much so that I sometimes wondered if I had any part in his creation other than giving birth. I adored him, though, and motherhood as well. Two more sons followed within the next four years: Charles Edward, who spent his childhood following in his older brother's footsteps, and James Henry, a boy destined to go his own way.

Fitzwilliam proved an indulgent but excellent father. He delighted in training the boys to ride from the time they could walk. Our oldest son shared my husband's temperament, and they enjoyed each other's company exceedingly.

From his youngest days, Edward became entranced with all things nautical, and we made many trips to Bath and Lyme Regis so that Fitzwilliam could further our second son's interests. He grew up to launch a distinguished career in the Navy.

Henry was born with a hint of my mother's auburn curls and a bit of recklessness and strong will to go with it. As he was my youngest, I could not help but spoil him, and he and his father often found themselves at loggerheads over whose will would prevail. Fitzwilliam accused me of coddling the boy, but I found him difficult to discipline. He could quickly sway me to his way of thinking when he threw his sweet arms around me and buried his face in my neck. I longed for another baby, and I confess I did my best to restrain Henry from growing up too quickly.

Fitzwilliam and I continued to share a bed every night, and our love grew stronger with each passing year, but by the age of six and twenty, I ceased to conceive. It caused me some concern, but my husband very little. He said he would be perfectly happy to welcome another child if we were granted one, but he took pleasure in our three sons and also in the fact that I was not consumed with all that takes over a woman's life when she is with child.

"Your waist is as tiny as when we married," he declared one evening in my bedchamber, spreading forth his warm hands to encircle it and draw me close.

I could have corrected him with the bitter truth that it was two inches larger, but I rather enjoyed his delusion and contented myself with untying his cravat. I unbuttoned his waistcoat and slipped it off his shoulders while he played with the buttons at the back of my dress.

He had never been a patient man with buttons and over the years had ruined many a gown of mine, so I drew away and undressed myself, all the while watching him do the same. That hungry look of desire that persistently lit up his eyes still filled me with delight. Delicious anticipation ignited that fire deep within that could only be quenched by my husband's strength and passion.

I RESIGNED MYSELF TO MOTHERING three sons while I watched Jane give birth every year or two to daughters. She had five by the time she was thirty and showed little signs of abatement. The year before I reached that same momentous age proved to be another difficult time in my marriage and the means of a second enforced separation.

Lady Catherine never fully reconciled to her nephew's marriage although she had learned to treat me with civility when we were forced to reside in each other's company. Still, she much preferred to visit Mr. Darcy alone.

In the beginning, he insisted that he would not call upon her if I did not attend, but eventually, I persuaded him that I much preferred to remain in Town while he made short trips to Kent. Lady Catherine would have liked to hold him captive for a fortnight, but she soon discovered that would not occur unless I was invited. And so we made our tentative peace and lived thus for the first nine years of our marriage.

And then Lady Catherine de Bourgh died.

Although she named her daughter, Anne, as heir, she had appointed my husband and Colonel Fitzwilliam co-executors of her will. Both men, of course, were called to Rosings at the news of her death, and because of the extensive property holdings and various sources of income that comprised his aunt's fortune, my husband was forced to remain there much longer than he had foreseen.

My dearest Elizabeth, he wrote, *I shall most likely remain in Kent for four to six weeks. Anne is quite helpless, and Richard and I are compelled to see that our cousin's interests are provided for and ensured.*

I greeted the news of my husband's absence from Pemberley with regret, but soon resolved to put our time apart to good use. Mr. Bingley had recently employed the services of an accomplished portrait artist, a Mr. Dupuis from Bath. He painted an enchanting portrayal of Jane, capturing her ethereal beauty with each talented brushstroke.

Since Fitzwilliam's birthday was but two months away, I determined to have Mr. Dupuis paint a grouping of my three sons and myself as a surprise for my husband upon his return from Rosings Park. Thus, I sat for the artist daily during the six weeks Fitzwilliam was away.

Mr. Dupuis suggested I wear a ball gown and I, naturally, selected my husband's favourite—a soft rose silk. The nanny, with the help of other servants, managed to dress my three wriggling boys in matching navy suits, which was no small feat in anyone's estimation.

The next difficulty arose in persuading three active young men to sit still for any length of time. Mr. Dupuis directed me to recline on a cream-coloured velvet chaise and then attempted to place the boys around me. Seven-year-old Will stood at my head, five-year-old Edward perched near my feet, and Henry, who was three, reclined upon my bosom.

Georgiana clapped her hands with delight when the artist completed placing the boys exactly as he desired. He then took three steps back, picked up his easel and brush, and the perfect pose fell apart. Edward pinched Henry, who put up a squall, causing Will to race to the opposite side of the chaise and thump Edward.

"Boys! Boys!" Georgiana cried to no avail.

It took their nanny, their aunt, and myself to restore a moment's peace, and then promises of iced raspberry sorbets before the children returned to their places and then for only the briefest of time. After three days of such insanity, I wondered why I had ever thought the idea feasible. Mr. Dupuis, however, assured me that by then he had outlines of each of the boys' positions, a favourable sign.

"From now on, I shall only require the presence of one child at a time," he said, "and, of course, you must sit for me each day, Mrs. Darcy. That should ensure a more peaceable hour, should it not?"

His solution pleased me, for I knew I could control one son at a time. Georgiana, of course, attended me each day, bringing her needlework or a favourite book belonging to the child required to pose. I was grateful that she was willing to read, sing or do whatever it took to help me keep the little one in the proper location.

Mr. Dupuis, himself, proved entertaining to the children. A striking man, he was tall and blonde with hair that hung below his shoulders. Most days he secured it at his neck in a *queue*, but at times he allowed it to hang loose, wild and unruly. It provided a constant source of curiosity to Edward, for he had never seen a man wear his hair in such a style.

"Mum, does Mr. D. not look like the bogey-man?" he asked one night.

"Why, Edward, what makes you say such a thing?" I replied.

"When his hair is all bushy, he scares me."

I hugged him before I sent him to bed, reassuring him that the artist was not a man to fear. In truth, I found Mr. Dupuis an attractive man in an uninhibited, artistic manner. I could picture him quite at home in bohemian circles within London, and Georgiana and I spent many an evening wondering at his background. Eventually, when the boys' pictures were completed and I was the only subject remaining, my sister and I ventured to question the artist.

He was open and forthcoming, and to our disappointment, sadly lacking in mystery. He had not lived a romantic, fanciful life as we had imagined, but had grown up outside Bath, the son of a seaman. His mother was terrified he might lose his life at sea, and thus, she had encouraged his artistic talent. She proved successful in persuading him not to follow his father's profession.

And so I passed the days, waiting for Fitzwilliam to come home. His most recent letter indicated he would return on Saturday next, and I entreated Mr. Dupuis to complete the portrait two days before.

"Yes, Mrs. Darcy," he assured me. "In truth, if I can capture but two or three final details, I shall finish today."

"Oh, that would be lovely," I replied, smiling.

He approached me and pulled a long tendril of my hair forward so that it trailed over my shoulder. "There, that is exactly as it was the previous day—perfect," he murmured, stepping backward.

Unbeknownst to either Georgiana or me and quite unexpectedly, at that very moment, Fitzwilliam walked into the room.

"You have described my wife correctly, sir," he said, his voice hard and angry, "but by what means do you presume you have the right to touch her?"

Before I could say anything, with one rough, swift move, Fitzwilliam grabbed Mr. Dupuis by the arm and pushed him away from me, causing him to fall over a table filled with various paints, thinners, brushes and scrapers. Georgiana and I both cried out, fearful that he would advance further and strike the young man.

It took some doing and much explanation before we successfully convinced my husband that the scene he had walked in upon was innocent and that Mr. Dupuis had done nothing improper. Naturally, Fitzwilliam's birthday surprise was spoiled, but that was of little consequence. I was simply relieved to see his good humour return and the artist accept his apologies.

That night in the seclusion of his bedchamber, I attempted to make up to my husband for his unfortunate homecoming. He made love to me, however, with a desperate need, as though he still could not erase the fear that had overtaken him upon finding me with another man.

Afterwards, I held him in my arms, his head upon my breast, until his breathing stilled, and he appeared at rest. I thought he had fallen asleep when his voice proved him awake.

"Elizabeth, have you forgiven me?"

"Of what should I forgive you?" I murmured, my body and mind consumed by a delicious lethargy.

"My behaviour earlier was that of a brute. I do not know why I reacted with such little control. I saw that blur of blonde hair, and when the man touched you, all I could think was—Morgan!"

I caught my breath. *The highwayman!* We had not spoken of him in over nine years. I could not recall when I had last thought of him. And still he haunted my husband? I could not believe it.

"Oh, my dearest, my darling," was all that I could say. Repeatedly, I murmured words of love and reassurance, kissing his hair and his forehead until he raised his head and his lips met mine. That night our last child was conceived.

She was born on the occasion of my thirtieth birthday. We named her Elizabeth Jane Anna, but she was Beth from the first time her father took her in his arms. He adored her, as did I, and she grew up the spoiled pet of the entire household. Even her brothers, who could find countless ways to disagree among themselves, doted on their little sister. In their eyes or in the eyes of her father, she could do no wrong.

Consequently, by the time Beth was sixteen, she was a handful. Fitzwilliam had taught her to ride when little more than a toddler. Unfortunately, she now terrorized him by racing about the grounds at a speed we both feared might easily break her neck.

By that time, Edward took his place in the Navy, and Will had completed his education at Cambridge. Our oldest son spent much of his time in Town, establishing his presence as the heir apparent to Pemberley. He was a fine young man, however, and did nothing to sully the Darcy name, or at least nothing of which his father and I learned. Henry was another matter.

At twenty, our youngest son, a desultory student at best, announced that he was leaving his studies and wished to travel. His father, naturally, disapproved and ordered him to return to Cambridge. He hoped Henry would make the church his profession, but I knew my son was not made for the clergy, not with the desire that bedevilled him to see more of the world.

Countless arguments ensued between father and son until the entire house was beset with gloom. Each time I took Henry's side, Fitzwilliam accused me of still coddling the boy. When he insisted his will be obeyed or the boy disinherited, I accused him of harshness and rigidity.

At length, when neither side would give in, Beth intervened with her father and convinced him to permit her brother two years' leave from school, wherein he might satisfy his longing if Henry promised to return at the end of that time and complete his education in a satisfactory manner. I was surprised at my daughter's sensible solution but not at her ability to convince her father. She could have made him think black was white if she so desired.

Thus, Henry set off for America in 1836. Even though I had argued his case with Fitzwilliam, still I dreaded to see him go. A heavy heart beat in my chest as we stood outside Pemberley, bidding him safe passage. Not even seeing Edward off to the Navy had filled me with as much foreboding as watching Henry leave for parts unknown.

I stood waving my handkerchief as long as I could see the barest outline of the carriage hurtling down the roadway. Suddenly, an image of my mother flashed across my vision. How many times had she stood outside Longbourn and waved farewell to one of her daughters? Until that moment, I never understood what she must have felt.

Those two years passed slowly for me. Henry was an infrequent correspondent. I could count on one hand the number of letters I received.

Whilst he was away, however, the time was not uneventful for us.

Will married a lovely young woman from a good family of whom his father and I approved. They took a house in Town but visited us often. Edward advanced in his career and sent colourful missives from various ports. Beth was presented at court, an exciting event for her, but one that filled her father with anxiety. From then on, he was forced to endure a houseful of young men far more frequently than he wished, for she not only was pretty but would enter marriage well dowered.

At last the day arrived when Henry returned to us unannounced.

I sat in the garden at Pemberley, watching Fitzwilliam and Beth train a young mare my husband had recently acquired. Although the riding grounds were some distance from where I sat, I could watch their progress with pleasure, safely ensconced among my roses and hydrangeas, marguerites and daisies. I had never come to share my husband's love of horses, just as he did not share my passion for gardening.

I heard footsteps approaching from behind my chair, but I assumed it to be a servant with the pot of tea I had ordered. How thrilled I was to find, instead, my youngest son kneeling beside my chair and whispering, "Mother?"

We embraced for a long time, and when he released me, my face was damp with tears of joy. I began to call for Fitzwilliam and Beth, but Henry restrained me.

"Pray, Mother, let it be just the two of us for a few moments. I have so much to tell you."

"Will you not have to repeat it for your father and sister?" I asked, but he just laughed and said he did not mind.

He began to tell me of his adventures in that strange, new land called America—how he had disembarked at Virginia and explored the towns and villages up and down the eastern seaboard for much of the first year. Within months, however, he grew restless and pushed on into what he called the wilderness, eventually making his way to the southern border and a city called New Orleans.

"You cannot envision the great spaces in that country, Mother. There is land enough for the entire world and much of it still inhabited by savages."

Naturally, that alarmed me, and he spent no little time assuring me he had not so much as glimpsed an unfriendly Indian.

He then began to describe the city where he spent the second year of his visit—New Orleans—a mixture of French, Spaniard, English, and Negro. He spoke of great houses called plantations and fields of white cotton maintained by slaves. I was glad to see the institution troubled him, but his eyes still filled with delight when he described the port city itself and its exciting manner of life.

As he took a moment to catch his breath, I asked if he had made friends. "I met a girl," he responded softly, looking away.

"Ah, and is she someone special?"

"She is beautiful. She has long dark curls and her eyes—Mother, I have never seen eyes like hers—they are the bluest blue one can imagine. Her name is Elizabeth." He looked up and smiled. "With that name, how could she not please me?"

I sighed and began to chew my lip before I asked if she came from a good family. His response was less than satisfactory, somewhat evasive. He said her mother had died in childbirth. Her father and an aunt, who was now well up in years, had raised her. When I questioned Henry as to her father's status, he grew somewhat defensive.

"America is different. People are not divided into classes as we are. A man does not have to be a gentleman to be a man of importance in New Orleans."

"You mistake my meaning, son," I replied. "I simply wish to know whether Elizabeth's father is a good man."

"He is certainly successful. He owns three of the busiest saloons in the city."

"Saloons! Henry, have you spent the last two years at gaming tables?"

"Of course not!" He rose, drawing away from me somewhat.

He walked about for a moment or two before settling upon the stone bench facing mine. "Mother, I am no longer a child. I am two and twenty years old now. You cannot expect me not to have—well, I am a man, after all."

I assured Henry that I did not live in a rose-coloured world and understood what he said. Still, I had no desire for my son to waste his life in riotous living.

"Maturity requires wisdom," I said softly, "a goal your father and I wish for each of our children."

"I know, and that is why I have returned. I am more than willing now to take up my studies and settle down as Father desires. However, I reserve the right to choose my own way in life. I may return to New Orleans someday. You must accept that."

His eyes wore that same pleading look he had used all his life when beseeching me to see his side. I knew that now was not the time to argue, and so I looked away.

I returned to the subject of Elizabeth, and he was more than willing to describe her anew. He could not get over her striking eyes and said he was even more surprised to see them duplicated in those of her father.

"He said he knew you, Mother."

A warning bell began to sound in my heart. *Eyes that were the bluest blue? A blue never seen before?* I steadied my voice to appear at ease as I asked the man's name, but I was not surprised when Henry replied, "Nate Morgan."

"I cannot imagine you and Father knowing someone like him. Indeed, I challenged his assertion," Henry said, "but Morgan was adamant. He described you—well, you as I have seen in your bridal portrait, more than twenty-five years ago."

When I questioned him as to how my name had come up in conversation, Henry told of how Morgan had immediately sought him out when his daughter told him of meeting a man from England named Darcy. His first enquiries had been to ascertain that Henry was the son of Fitzwilliam Darcy, and then he had asked for the name of his mother.

"When I said your name was Elizabeth, Morgan's only response was, 'You have her eyes.' He said he knew you before you were engaged to Father, but he was surprised to learn you had married."

Henry looked down at the ground for several moments before raising his eyes to mine. "Mother, I had the impression the man might have been in love with you at one time. Am I correct?"

I rose and gathered up my basket of cuttings, feigning great interest in straightening the stems. "That was a long time ago, Henry. Your father and I chanced to meet Mr. Morgan while travelling. We maintained only a brief acquaintance, and there was never any attachment between the man and myself."

I chanced a glimpse at my son's expression and could see a shadow about his eyes. "I stand corrected," he said at last. "Morgan gave me the impression he knew both you and Father more intimately. He spoke of

Father with respect although perhaps somewhat grudgingly. It bespoke envy more than anything else."

"Perchance because your father has lived a moral, upright life while Mr. Morgan traffics in saloons," I declared.

"Pray, do not be condescending. Have I not told you I am no longer a child? I can certainly see the difference between Father and Morgan. I know which man is considered the better in anyone's eyes. Yet, I cannot help but think that, while Father has been content to live his life safely hidden away here at Pemberley, Morgan has followed his dreams. Not only has he struck out on his own and made a fortune, but he longs for more."

When I made no response, Henry looked away as though he still yearned to be there, across the sea, and not here at his home.

"He offered to sell me his New Orleans establishments because he plans to head west to a place called San Francisco. It sits on a bay that leads out into the Pacific Ocean and promises to be a port of unimaginable riches."

"Surely he was not serious about your becoming the proprietor of saloons! Henry, you are far too young to even think of such a thing."

"I know. Do not distress yourself. Naturally, I refused, but I must admit the idea appealed to me."

When I rolled my eyes, he took my hand and entreated me to sit beside him. "Morgan told me he asked you to come with him when he sailed for America."

I was astounded! How could the man reveal such a thing to my son? Neither Fitzwilliam nor I had ever told our children of the highwaymen or the kidnapping that had transpired so long ago. I do not know why—it just never seemed appropriate in light of the life we had made together.

"Mum," Henry said, "do you ever have second thoughts? Have you ever longed, in the deepest part of your soul, for a more exciting life than Father has given you buried away here in Derbyshire?"

"Henry, listen to me. I have never considered myself *buried away* by any means. Your father and I have travelled to Paris, Vienna, Frankfurt, and to Florence several times. If I asked him today, he would take me anywhere I wish to go. I have no desire to leave this place. How can I make you understand? This is the life I chose, and it fills me with a joy that cannot be replaced by travel to faraway lands."

He smiled and raised my hand to his lips. "Have it your way. I will not trouble you further. Will you admit, however, that you did have a choice? You could have picked Morgan instead of Father?"

I shook my head. "No, my son, there was never any choice."

I looked up and watched Fitzwilliam lead our daughter around on the new chestnut mare, his curls still falling over his forehead in that same enchanting manner they had all those years before.

"Your father won my heart a long time ago. No other man ever had a chance."

Epilogue

And now, my children, with these final strokes of my pen, I conclude my story. I have written it down for each of you: Will, Edward, Henry and Beth.

I shall hide it away at the bottom of this deep old chest that contains memories I hold dear—letters from your father, brief though they may be, your baptismal certificates, the garnet cross my own father gave me when I was a girl, the first red rose I cut from Pemberley's garden, now faded and pressed, along with various mementos of your childhood and the years of my marriage.

Someday long after I am gone, it is my hope that one or more of you, or your children, or perchance even your grandchildren may happen upon this old trunk stored in the attic at Pemberley. I trust that someone will possess enough curiosity to dig deep enough to find this little book.

It tells of a journey that took place when I was young, a journey that changed my life and that of your father, a journey I began as a girl and ended as a woman.

CPSIA information can be obtained at www.ICGtesting.com
Printed in the USA
LVOW082140220712

291112LV00003B/68/P